Asoka: *A Love Story*

The King Who Brought us the Buddha.
And Championed Animal Rights, Religious Tolerance,
Vegetarianism, Healthcare, and Values of Democracy

A Novel

Harish Singhal

Dedication

To the present and future generations:

History has produced two kinds of leaders: the great ones who advanced the cause of humanity—equality, freedom and the happiness of all men; and others who mistook pomp, brutality, oppression, bluster, or avarice—for greatness, or religion.

Let us choose our heroes carefully.

Acclaim for Harish Singhal's Asoka

Published in May 2010 in India, the novel has received enthusiastic reviews.

National literary reviews

"Singhal sticks to realistic descriptions and relies on imagination. The result is admirable...(His) rendition of the intimate is bold and exquisite...the sheer expanse of the novel is exhilarating. Singhal churns together fact and fiction to produce a magical story of love...Anyone can make history, but it takes a genius to write it."– **The Asian Age** (published from Delhi, Mumbai, Calcutta, Chenai, and London)

"A rollicking roller-coaster of a book that thrills, touches our emotions... enchants with its descriptions... Singhal is at his best in his broad, colorful sketches of character and descriptions of nature, his grasp of emotion and easy depiction of grandeur and dream, love and loss... The Kalinga war is depicted with rare energy...A sweeping epic that reclaims the grandeur of story-telling.--**The Hindu** (a national newspaper)

The Readers

"Wonderful. I cried in the last seventy pages." –David Booth, published author of fiction in the *Washington Square, the Farallon Review* and others

"Very enjoyable, lively and vivid." – Richard Buxbaum, professor, UC Berkeley, USA

"This is a fascinating book." Rena Valeh, freelance editor, London, UK

"I enjoyed your writing, and the questioning of such matters as "God," "life and death," "religion," "emptiness," "happiness..." Rachel Neumann, editor, Parallax Press, USA

"A gem." Kennard Lawrence, lawyer, USA

"A creative masterpiece." –Prem Mittal, ex-govt. executive, India

"A fabulous book." –Sunita Baveja, businessperson, India

Disclaimer

This is a work of fiction. Names, characters, places, and incidents either are the product of the author's imagination or have been used fictitiously. Any resemblance to actual persons, living or dead, or events, is purely coincidental.

Copyright © 2011 Harish Singhal

ISBN-10: 0983690308
ISBN-13: 9780983690306
Library of Congress Control Number: 2011908981
Chris-Budd Press, San Carlos, CA

First published in U.S: 2011

Printed and Published in U.S.

by

CHRIS–BUDD PRESS

U.S.A

Contents

Acknowledgements

This time around, Asoka had a rather un-kingly beginning—he spent his time in my humble company. After over eight years of writing and research at the UC, Berkeley, the MS was read by my friend Richard Buxbaum, a Professor of Law at Berkeley, an avid fiction reader, and once a literature student of late Nabokov, the Nobel Laureate. Asoka was born when I got two thumbs up from him.

I am grateful to my development editor David Booth and my comprehensive editor Lissa McLaughlin—both published authors and creative writing professors at prestigious U.S universities who made substantive suggestions. Lissa McLaughlin's gift for editing, and her enthusiasm for Asoka both humbled and inspired me.

I wish to thank my friend J.P. Das, a published poet and novelist, for his insights and Vijay Krishn Lakhanpal and SN Chaturvedi for their lively discussions. And thanks to those who courageously read the early draft: Sailesh Lall, Pratibha Goel, Ken Lawrence, my daughter Amrita. I am indebted to Jane Wilkinson for many ideas. And last, but not the least, thanks are due to my wife who stolidly defended the fort while I wandered for years in the Amazonian jungle of a fiction writer.

Preface

The following discussion is for the curious reader.

I. Is Livia a Historical Figure? Historian Sylvain Levi writes: Seleucus... concluded a matrimonial alliance with [Chandragupta] which no doubt introduced a Greek princess into the Mauryan household. How did it happen? After Alexander's death in 323 BC, Seleucus, one of Alexander's generals, annexed Persia; Chandragupta Maurya, an ambitious young man then, drove the Greeks out of India, and established the first Indian empire sometime around 320 BC. Seleucus returned and attacked India in 305 BC to recapture the former Greek territories. Chandragupta rushed to the frontier and defeated Seleucus. A treaty was signed by which Seleucus ceded parts of Afghanistan (Kabul, Herat, Kandahar, Bactria) and also gave his daughter (name not known) to Chandragupta. Livia is that daughter in the novel. After his defeat, Seleucus sent his personal friend Megasthenes as ambassador to Chandragupta's splendid court. Magasthenes has written about the Indian emperor and his court. When Emperor Bindusar, Chandragupta's son, asked Seleucus's son, Antiochus, to send him "wine, dried figs, and a sophist." Antiochus, the Persian emperor, graciously replied, "We shall send you the figs and the wine but in Greece, the laws forbid a sophist to be sold." Regardless, Livia's presence in the Maurya palace may explain Asoka's total acceptance of other religions.

2. The Lost City of Pataliputra. It was a famous city in the ancient world known for its splendor and its magnificent palace. It was located close to the modern city of Patna. If you take the train from Delhi to Patna, you will be riding over a part of the lost great city, now buried under the railway track; the Maurya Palace lies under the nearby Kumrahar village. This walled city had a population of about 300,000. Fa Hian, a Chinese Buddhist monk, visited the city around 400 A.D and described the grandeur of the city and the Palace: halls full of elegant carvings and inlaid sculpture work, colossal edict-pillars–single shafts of stone, thirty to forty feet high monoliths—beautifully polished and sculptured. Awed by the exquisite workmanship of the palace, he wrote the work must have been performed by "spirits", since no human hands could achieve that kind of perfection. Sometimes after the visit of the Chinese traveler, the city fell on bad days. When Hiuen Tsiang, another Buddhist Chinese traveler, visited it around 635 A.D, he found the city "long deserted," hundreds of monasteries, temples and stupas lay in ruins. The Archaeological Survey of India's records show that part of the old city was perhaps lost to the waters of the Ganges. By the time of Moslem invasion in 12th century, the city had vanished, and was lost to history for over a thousand years. When the British began unearthing the lost city, even the natives had not heard of the city of Pataliputra. The British did locate couple of local priests who had heard the name by oral tradition. The Chinese traveler's narratives helped in fixing its location near modern Patna. The British excavated parts of it under Patna in middle 19th century. The pomp and the chivalry, the intrigues at the court and the battles fought around the strong fortifications of Pataliputra in early days are vividly depicted in the Indian drama, *Mudra Rakshasa*, which, although composed in the middle ages, seems to have been based on earlier books now lost to posterity.

3. Was Asoka a Romantic King? Asoka had published his edicts on rocks and pillars in Prakrit and Brahmi—the earliest Indian scripts after the ancient Sanskrit had become obsolete. By 3rd-4th century AD, Prakrit and Brahmi had become indecipherable, and the pillars had been ravaged by time. One Mogul emperor had two pillars dragged to Delhi to flaunt his glory. In the 19th century the edicts were deciphered, but then no one could figure out which king had issued them, since the edicts indicated they were the work of some king by the name of "Piyadassi." Who was King Piyadassi? The scholars were puzzled. Painstaking scholarship in 19th century revealed that Asoka consistently used that name in his inscriptions. Why did Asoka use a name that no other king had used before? Perhaps, it was the name by which his beloved addressed him. Was Asoka a great lover? Certainly, his actions, his conversion, his edicts show an extraordinary sensibility. Perhaps, Buddhism is his Taj Mahal.

4. Kalinga War. Kalinga is now the state of Orissa. Although, as usual, history is silent on this point, it is most likely that the war was fought over the statue of Jain god "Jina." In short, the war was over religion. The statue had been stolen a century earlier from Kalinga and was already installed in Pataliputra when Asoka came to power. When Kharavela, Kalinga's Jain King, came to power more than a century after Asoka, to avenge the centuries old injury, he attacked and conquered Asoka's kingdom, and took back the Jina. Even today, Kharavela is a legend in Orissa for restoring Kalinga's pride. The Kalinga war, perhaps, gave Asoka a naked view of the destructive power of religion and made him rethink his own religion which was intolerant, incited violence, and glorified wars. It made him a big proponent of religious tolerance, secular state, and a believer in peace and human happiness.

5. Cannibals. Kalinga (now Orissa) tribes are known to have practiced cannibalism until the end 19th century. Sporadic cannibal acts are still reported in the news media. In 19th century, the British tried to stop human sacrifices for worshipping a god.

6. Asoka's Empire. Except for four small states in South, the territory over which Asoka ruled would today include India, Nepal, Bangladesh, Pakistan, Kashmir region, and Afghanistan. His empire would not be equaled in size by any other Indian ruler for two thousand years—until the British. In his time, Asoka's empire was the largest and the mightiest in the world.

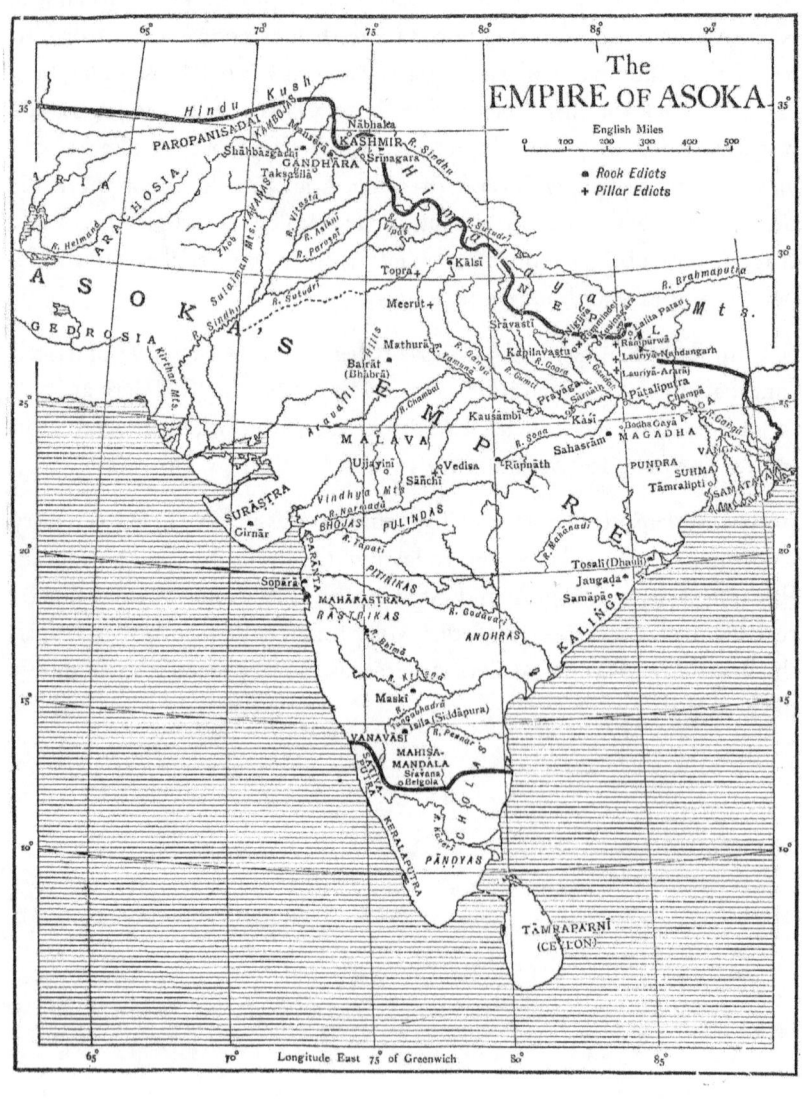

Introduction

Asoka was the third King of the Maurya dynasty (322-180 BC). After a bloody war, he conquered Kalinga, and a year later turned Buddhist. What happened? Thereafter, he went on to institute far reaching democratic reforms. Asoka has shaped today's India more than any other leader: vegetarianism, compassion for life, religious tolerance, and love for peace. H. G. Wells called him the greatest king in world history. Though the Lion Capital of his famous Sarnath stupa is now the national emblem of India and its wheel decorates India's flag, he is known as a "Buddhist" king in India, and in the West hardly anyone has heard about this great leader.

Because he gave up the Vedic religion (now Hinduism) and became a Buddhist, he was neglected by ancient Vedic scholars and disappeared from India's history for over fifteen hundred years. The adoring Buddhist scholars painted him as a demon who became a saint because of his conversion after the war. In the early 20th century, the Oxford and Cambridge historians included just one chapter on Asoka in their volumes on the history of India. He was not worthy of a full scale study. Influenced by the Buddhist literature, the British concluded that Asoka turned to Buddhism because of the bloodshed in war—a conclusion that is contradicted by a reading of his edicts; it also flies in the face of circumstantial evidence: his upbringing as a prince, his Vedic religion which glorified wars, the warrior tradition of Kshatriya caste, and the royal tradition of conquests. As regards his alleged squeamishness for bloodshed, it is conveniently forgotten that he killed his brothers for the throne and had put down an uprising in Taxila. Furthermore, neither history nor modern psychology supports the inference that bloodshed in war turns human beings to Buddhism. If it were so, Buddhist monasteries would have been flooded with rulers, generals and soldiers after every war.

So why did he give up his religion? Modern psychology suggests an event of intense emotional shock or pain—like the loss of a dearly loved one in or around the time of war—as the most likely reason. Personal loss, suffering, helplessness, or a close encounter with mortality has transformed many a men. Asoka himself was aware of it and talked about it in one of his edicts. As a result, he steered his country away from the glorification of war, the divisive caste system, the parade of meaningless rituals and the tribal practice of animal sacrifices—in short, away from his religion. He searched for spiritual and moral values and found them in Buddhism--he called those values the essence of all religions. But he was also an emperor and an ambitious one at that. He wanted to unite his people but could not do so as long as the society was based on caste divisions and social injustice. So he set out to govern by humanistic values: equality, social justice, religious tolerance and free medical care. All this in 3rd century BC! He revolted against violence and the oppression by the rulers; he forbade the use of coercion and tried to prevent miscarriage of justice and arbitrary imprisonment without a fair trial. He aimed to provide happiness to his people, and we now know that those are the prerequisites for human happiness. His reign was one of uninterrupted security and peace. He is relevant because the problems created by religion and the oppressive rulers are still very much with us. He is the Pole star. In 21st century, America does not yet have a universal health care system, and many countries are still governed by dictators and theocrats.

Perhaps, it is no exaggeration to say that two thousand years before America's Declaration of Independence, Asoka-- in his unique way— had ruled by values similar to those laid down in the Declaration. He kept religion separate from the State. He did not talk about Buddha or Buddhism because religion to him was a personal matter. If he wanted his people to convert to Buddhism, it was to free them from the caste system and the Vedic dogma and rituals. He allowed slaves to buy their freedom, and if a female slave had a child by her master, both mother and the child were set free. Lincoln would have applauded this practice. He made Buddhism a popular religion and sent Buddhist missionaries to several countries. That was his agenda of reform. By sheer energy and determination, he turned Buddhism, an obscure, regional sect then, into a world religion. He is the St. Paul of Buddhism. Furthermore, he greatly influenced Hinduism which is different today from the Vedic religion of Asoka's times largely because centuries after his death, Hinduism had to fold a persistent Buddhism into its own belief-system to survive.

For all his influence and his achievements, a biography of Asoka is not possible. In the 3rd century BC, no historical records were kept. Only the Brahmin caste had access to education—and this practice continued for centuries—but the Brahmins had no time for or interest in history. They spent their time in pursuit of wealth, flights of fancy, and in writing one religious treatise after another to keep their stranglehold on the society—a practice that led to India's decline later.

What we know about Asoka has come down to us from fragments of literature and his edicts. However, the following broad facts are undisputed: Asoka was born a prince; he put down an uprising in Taxila; his first wife was the daughter of a merchant; he was governor of Ujjain; he killed his brothers for the throne; his coronation came three years after the accession; he attacked Kalinga (Orissa) eight years after his coronation, the war was fought at Dhauli, he killed hundreds of thousands of men; he converted to Buddhism about a year after the conquest; he built pillars and stupas across India and published edicts on rocks and pillars, sent Buddhist missionaries throughout India and to several foreign countries including Ceylon and Burma; he helped in the codification of Buddhism; and his son converted the King of Ceylon to Buddhism.

The novel has been constructed from the edicts, historical fragments; the writings of Asoka's contemporary foreign historians like Megasthenes; and recent historical research. But also from Asoka's actions, decisions, words and expressions used in his edicts that show an extraordinary mind and a surprisingly nuanced sensibility. As a ruler, he seems to be even ahead of our times. The novel gives a glimpse of ancient India and the beginnings of modern India. But above all, the aim is to give the reader a feel for Asoka, the Man. Set in a period that historian A. L. Basham described as "The Wonder That Was India"— the novel takes the reader on an adventure to India's golden age where a city mysteriously lost to history, an old way of life, ancient epics, scriptures, culture and philosophy, all come alive and reveal a world long lost to time.

PART ONE

Awakening

I

Nine year old Tissa, Asoka's younger brother, had woken with a headache, so Asoka left him in camp and went to the river with two armed guards. Eight large brick terraced steps led pilgrims down to the ghat, the bank for bathing. The long sandy patch between the last step and the river allowed for the monsoon floods. In the middle of the top red brick step stood a fifteen hundred-year-old Pipal (Bo) tree, huge and wide-canopied. Lord Buddha had found enlightenment under a Pipal tree, so this tree had become very famous. A knee-high clay platform had been built around its trunk and on one side of it stood a two-foot high lingam stone, called the Brahmeshwara, the Lord of Creation. Women devotees loved this phallic symbol, and bathed it in holy water and pampered it with milk and flowers. A Naga shrine to the water snake deity stood on the other side of this platform, and was only worshipped in passing, with a nod.

The sight of the shimmering, open expanse of water sent Asoka running down the steps. Throwing off his clothes and sandals, he jumped into the river and swam as far as the dhobi ghat, the laundry man's bank, beyond which crocodiles lived. There he watched with fascination the chanting washer men scrubbing each garment with soap, lifting it overhead, pounding it on a large flat stone, rinsing it in the river with a flipping motion, then wringing the garment from each end, until the cloth looked like a twisted gooseneck.

Asoka, eleven, had come on a pilgrimage to river Vaitarni in Kalinga, with his mother Suba, and Dadi-ma- grandmother - Livia. He had accompanied his mother on several pilgrimages, but this was his first with Dadi-ma. This time he had his horse and he was excited. He hoped to gallop his Caspian horse but Dadi-ma reined him in when he once briefly disappeared. The road from Gaya narrowed as it passed through the woods and he'd had to ride with the party or sit in with his mother. *What an ordeal*, he thought. After weeks of travel and overnight camps, he finally reached the little town of Rajnagar in early summer. Early next morning, his mother, Suba, came looking for him. He was already up feeding his horse when he saw her staring at him. She told him to take Tissa, his younger brother, with him for a dip in the holy river. Then she left.

After lunch, Asoka and Tissa went out with the guards on an elephant to browse the town's little shops which were filled with trinkets for women and untailored pieces of clothes for men such as turbans, towels, and loose undergarments. Browsing at the only toys shop in town, he bought a dark wood sword to add to his collection. Returning to the camp, Asoka found his gatekeepers busy with visitors. Itching to gallop his horse with no one breathing down his neck, he winked at Tissa, and telling the guards they were taking the horses out for exercise, the boys trotted away.

On the forest trail, the air smelled deliciously moist. Asoka left Rajnagar behind and urged his horse into a gallop– the wind in his face, trees flying past, sunlight and shadow going round in a whirl, the deer frozen in its tracks, the gazelle sprinting ahead, the fox darting to the side to thump into the brush, the monkeys leaping from tree to tree, the birds screeching away. When he heard the rumble of elephants in the distance and saw the lengthening shadows, he stopped for Tissa.

At last Tissa showed up, scared. 'We didn't tell mother. This forest is so dense and dark. Let's go back.'

'Tissa, stop shaking in your pants,' said Asoka, irritated. 'In a few months you'll be ten. The sun hasn't even set. Look up there, there.' He pointed to a dimming sun behind the treetops. 'We'll be back before dusk.'

'I want to go back,' Tissa whined.

'Let's find a peacock for the evening meal,' Asoka said, and Tissa was distracted.

They rode out another mile or two. The forest grew less dense, with shafts of sunlight filtering through the leaves. Suddenly, Asoka's horse neighed and veered off the trail. He called out, 'Tissa, he's thirsty. Look for a stream.'

He heard a faint drumbeat.

'People! They'll have water!' Asoka spurred his horse forward.

Flames flickered between the trees in the distance. Drawn by the drumbeat, he closed in on the crowd, dismounted, and tethered his horse. From behind a tree, he stood watching bouncing bare breasts and swiveling round hips that seemed to swell in front of him. The people had dark skin, matted hair and flat noses, and leaf curtains hung over their hips. *Skulls!* Asoka forgot about his horse. All around him, women jiggled and served liquor in skull bowls,

'I am going back,' Tissa called out but Asoka paid no attention. Only when his horse whinnied did he remember and lay down his bow and quiver. With his little sword by his side, he took a few steps toward the crowd.

A naked youth of about his age was tied to a tree, with firewood stacked around him. Nearby three long-snout pigs lay on lighted logs, squirming and squealing.

Asoka stared at the youth's terror-stricken face. What had he done wrong, he wondered. He tiptoed behind the tree, touched the boy's arm to warn him, and started to slash the rope with his sword until the boy shook his hands free. Suddenly two men came running and retied the boy as Asoka hid behind a tree. When he saw a lighted torch approaching, he began to run.

'I am a prince!' he thundered behind him. 'Don't touch me!'

Jumping over the brush, zigzagging through the trees, Asoka clutched his sword and tried to find his horse. The torch was closing in. Suddenly he turned and thrust the sword into an oncoming body. The man howled as he fell on the blade, blood gushing, snuffing out his torch. Asoka tugged at the sword, and seeing another light, started to run again, wiping the blood from his hands onto his chest and sleeves.

The men grew invisible as night descended. Then Asoka saw two torches gliding in midair toward him. Soon others appeared, clapping drumsticks, beating tom-toms, brandishing lights. *I'll return with the guards,* Asoka thought as he saw flames flickering in the horse's eyes. He made a dash and tugged at the reins but missed the seat. His left hand fell on the crupper, his right on withers but then it slipped. He hung on by the fingers of his left hand and leaned against the horse's belly, trying to mount, when something struck his head. He dropped instantly, and a man jumped on him. Head reeling, Asoka struggled to push the smelly body away, but others arrived screaming, and grabbed his arms and ankles. Kicking and cussing, he was dragged on his stomach toward the crowd.

The flames turned the dark night a flickering brown, the trees flashed pink and purple, the pigs howled and the youth yelled and screamed. The drumbeat grew louder and the dancing got wilder. Asoka was dragged before a tall man with shoulder-length hair and jagged teeth. Around his neck hung skulls, like hollowed-out balls of onyx, that glowed in the flames. He looks like Lord Siva, thought Asoka, but Siva never looked so mean. The chief whistled, and the music stopped. Pointing to Asoka, he addressed the crowd, and men and women clapped and jumped.

His mouth stuffed with rags, Asoka was stripped and tied to a tree from chest to feet by a rope. People jumped and screamed as a thin, muscular man, his lips pushed out by his crooked teeth, walked Asoka's horse into the crowd, then tethered it to a tree. Now they began to dance round the burning youth.

The pigs' screams faded and died. Covered with red-brown clay, the youth baked in the eager flames. Asoka closed his eyes until the youth's howling ceased, then looked up. The boy's head was slumped on chest. Having never seen cannibals before, Asoka was filled with loathing.

The chief emptied skull after skull of liquor, then started to dance— hair swirling, hands spread wide, tongue hanging out. Nearby, children shrieked with joy and Asoka saw they were playing ball with skulls and leg bones.

'Barbarians!' he fumed in desperation and rage. 'I will kill you all when I am king!'

He started to sway to the beat, camouflaging his efforts to get free. Some in the crowd laughed to see him. *When they've pigged and fallen drunk, I'll escape,* he promised himself. *Baba,* grandfather, he prayed, *do not leave me to these animals.* He felt the rope loosening a little.

The flames flickered on the trees like ghosts, and Asoka prayed, trying to shut out the chatter, the clank, the drumbeat, the hissing flames. He closed his eyes, asked Baba for help, and imagined horses galloping over the flames, spearing the barbarians dead as they went. Armies clashed in the darkness, and thundering horse hooves split the earth, which swallowed the tribesmen whole like giant gobs of meat. *What if Tissa lost his way?* he thought with a shiver. When he opened his eyes and saw the charred youth, tears began streaming down his cheeks.

Riding over the youth, then a gust of warm air came and stroked his face. He shivered. The men were still drinking liquor but the dancing had slowed. Asoka felt he been tied to this tree all his life.

In the distance he heard the rumble of hooves but dismissed it as a figment of his mind. But the faint clacking and clatter kept coming from the bowels of the earth and would not be silenced.

Like the rumble of high sea waves lashing the shore, he heard hooves pounding the ground. A chill of joy ran down Asoka's spine.

In the distance he heard faint cries of "Asoka."

Tissa? It is Tissa! He tried to jump and shout, but the rope and the rags held down his excitement.

Later, Tissa would say that in the glow of flames, he recognized the shining white coat of Asoka's horse.

Suddenly, the music stopped and a commotion ensued as men and women—their sweating bodies glistening in the firelight – screamed and ran helter-skelter. Heads were rolling on ground. Asoka recognized Radhagupta's ringing voice. 'No arrows! Only the spear and the sword!'

Most of the tribesmen disappeared into the night but not before the pig bones had been stripped clean. Four had come running to untie him and whisk him away to a hiding place when the horsemen fell upon them with war cries. Once freed, Asoka fell to his knees, and noticed with surprise that the sacrificial body had not been touched.

'Tissa, it is too late, too late,' he sobbed on his brother's shoulders.

Back at the camp, his mother Suba held Asoka to her bosom. 'There was an evil eye on him,' she kept saying. 'Thank God it passed.' He heard her friend say to his mother, 'Those destined to be great have to walk through fire first.'

Nightmares woke Asoka for many days and each time, his mother ran to him and held him close.

Radhagupta comforted Asoka. 'Before devouring the flesh with salt, lemon and rice,' he explained, 'the cannibals make sacrifices to gods. To please his wives, the chief takes the virile parts to help him do a man's job. The ritual was just starting when we arrived and rescued the body. I had the boy cremated by our rites. He is now in heaven.'

His calm voice relieved Asoka's horror, but not his sadness.

2

Suba nearly fainted when Asoka returned from the cannibal camp. His hands, face, stomach and knees were bloody, the jute rope had scraped open his skin, and he was incoherent. She and Livia cleansed and nursed the wounds for hours. Unable to stop crying, Suba feared the ordeal could scar him for life. In her fretful sleep that night, she saw herself burning. The thought tortured her: *I have only myself to blame. My pride nearly killed my son!*

Married at sixteen, Suba was the youngest and prettiest queen of King Bindusar. She reveled in the privileges of youth, beauty, and royalty. Every day before her bath, she spent hours applying fresh cream to every part of her body to keep the skin soft. From the day Asoka was born, she had been obsessed with being Raj-Mata, the mother of the king. Not that she was overly ambitious. Like other queens, she simply could not bear the idea of another queen's child becoming king. Asoka was her eldest, so he had to shoulder the burden of her dreams. Awake and asleep, she prayed for him to be king, kept endless fasts, consulted astrologers, and had priests perform ritual killings, although she loved animals.

Suba had been brought up in an orthodox religious family. Her education consisted of reading stories from the epics *Mahabharata* and the *Ramayana*. Before her marriage, she had never travelled outside the town where she was born. Now she went on pilgrimages to the holy cities of Varanasi and Prayag by the Ganges. When a priest told her that only mother Vaitarni (the holy river where the Pandavas in *Mahabharata* went to perform religious rites) in Kalinga— a vassal state of the Maurya empire on its south-east border—could grant her that boon, Suba thought nothing could stop her, but the King wouldn't agree. One of his ministers told him the sad story of a relative who had lost two sons to cannibals, and warned, 'Anything is possible there!' Unfazed, Suba sought her friend Livia's help even though Livia was mourning her own son. Then one day, Livia invited her to discuss the pilgrimage.

Suba was fond of jewels and also of the gods who gave her the opportunity to travel and gossip freely outside the confines of the palace. Wearing a green dress and a midriff-baring saffron choli, blouse, she eagerly told Livia her reason for supplicating mother Vaitarni. Hiding the real reason from the king, she only told him she would pray for another son. 'But he said it makes no sense to risk two sons to get one,' she said to Livia.

'Don't worry. I'll approach him,' Livia promised.

A few days later when Livia told her she was successful, Suba threw her arms around her. 'Oh, I am so happy! I can tell Asoka will be king. Mother Vaitarni made you change the king's mind.'

'Choti-ma, she beamed, 'I can't do without you.'

Livia smiled broadly. 'Don't think about it, Suba. We need each other. Now let's tell Asoka about the cannibals.'

'I'd rather not. He's just eleven. It will give him nightmares,' Suba replied.

How well she remembered that first morning in Rajnagar, the day of Asoka's terrible ordeal. She had risen early and gone looking for her son, who was already up feeding his horse. With love and pride, she stood gazing at his big eyes, large forehead and glowing face. 'Take Tissa with you for a dip,' she'd told him, then left to find Livia.

At the ghat, the view from the top of the brick platform filled her with a sense of the divine. The sun was rising over the river, and the moist air was suffused with gold. On the opposite bank, rows of trees looked in the mist like a range of dark green mountains. She bowed to Lord Brahmeshwara, offered flowers and milk, then went down to the water. Many ascetics sat cross-legged along the bank, lost in meditation. The river was full of silvery Reba carp, a small fish about a foot long, with three thin yellow stripes. Out of piety, she tossed them little bites of dough. Eyes closed, a man stood on one leg in the waist-deep water facing the sun with folded hands, chanting 'Om Surya, Om Surya.'

Suba dipped her toes, then wading gingerly to her waist, lowered her head under water three times, each time asking mother Vaitarni to make Asoka king. He was fifth in the line of succession and she knew he had no chance. She did not dare ask for her own health, for fear of annoying the gods.

She got changed, and went out to distribute clothes and money to the ascetics, the poor and the children. She learned that a famous Mauni Rishi— an ascetic who observes silence - lived nearby. A great astrologer, he broke his silence for an hour every morning. Eager to find out if Asoka would be king, Suba hurried to see him. His aide told her the Rishi would see her next day and she said she would return.

But everything changed that afternoon. Suba regarded Asoka's ordeal as her punishment and she shuddered to think what might have happened to her son. She prayed she had not offended any god, yet she realized her ambition had jeopardized Asoka's life. She forgot about the Rishi. 'From now on,' she vowed, not without sadness, 'I'll let it be.'

3

Livia's perception of Asoka changed after his encounter with the cannibals.

At barely seventeen, she had arrived as a trophy wife at the grand palace because King Chandragupta Maurya had defeated her father, the Persian emperor, in war. Her exotic Greek looks and youth made her Chandragupta's favorite, but did not save her from being widowed at twenty-two, after the birth of their son. Nine years later when her son died, Livia went into deep depression. Her best friend in the palace, Suba, aged thirty two, was the youngest wife of the ruling emperor Bindusar. Suba was so moved that she promised Livia her son Asoka when Livia recovered from her disabling grief. Suba even gave Livia a gold ring from her middle finger to seal her intent.

Soon Livia realized that she had not only lost her son but her dignity as well. Women shunned her, afraid her bad luck was contagious. Livia's past glorious days haunted her. *Pataliputra was my city of sweet-scented flowers! My Babylon! When I went out in chariot on Royal Boulevard to watch the flowers in spring, people swarmed to see their beautiful young queen! I loved wrapping myself in the fragrance of power.'*

But now in a foreign land, she was powerless.

That spring morning in Pataliputra, with the breeze caressing her body, Livia restlessly paced the palace garden, thinking, *'This is no country for a widow to live in without a son!'* She went inside and took the ring from her ivory box, stood gazing at it as if it were the enchanted stone of destiny. Suddenly, hope burst forth. 'I laugh at the idea of fate,' Livia mocked. 'I am not the daughter of a chest-thumping, glitzy little Indian king with his big moustache jumping out like porcupine quills! If my womb won't, my mind will bring forth a son. I will adopt Asoka and rise from my grave.'

She had come to love Asoka. One afternoon as she sat by the pool watching him swim, her body convulsed with pain, as if the pool had become her womb. That evening she gave Asoka a high spirited, untamed, small white Caspian horse with large limpid eyes. Her father, Seleucus, had sent it to her to lift her spirits. After a few kicks and bruises, Asoka subdued the horse after feeding it oats from his hands for three weeks. He called it Agni after the Vedic Fire god.

He now adored Livia. King Bindusar, the son of Chandragupta, was a stern father who wanted his sons on a leash. He was impressed. To Livia, he said half-seriously, 'Choti-ma, younger mother, take Asoka off Suba's hands. It would be good for him and good for you. He is wild like the horse you gave him.'

But two years had passed since Suba made the offer. Doubts arose in Livia's mind and she began to look for ways to increase the pressure on Suba. Then she remembered that a few months back, Suba had told her how the King had forbidden her to go to Kalinga. Now Livia sent for her and promised to approach Bindusar. She sent the king a gift of Greek wine—his weakness—and followed it with a personal visit. 'Together Suba and I will take care of the boys,' she told him. The king relented. Suba was delighted and eagerly, Livia began to prepare for the trip, her eyes on the prize.

On the day of their departure, Livia woke early while it was still dark. The easterly morning breeze was sweeping the city. But she stayed in bed, fantasizing. When the bells started to toll at the crack of dawn, she imagined the scene: four brown— turbaned guards coming down the narrow stairs from the five storied watchtower, each with a lamp in hand, to open the heavy, embellished city gate; the doors creaking, opening slowly, unveiling the city; the waiting lines of men moving, the bullock carts squeaking and rolling, the lowing, bleating animals, shoving and pushing, spilling over some fruits and vegetables, bumping through the crowds. She lay listening to the clanging bells until they stopped, and the city awoke.

The King had appointed the thirty-five year old Radhagupta as leader of the pilgrimage party because Kalinga was a densely forested state and the local tribesmen often made lunch of travelers. He came from the city of Taxila, formerly under Greek rule, and would arrive at the palace at the appointed hour even though he knew that royalty followed its own clock. An hour later, Livia was still pottering around when curiosity impelled her to look out of her window. In a helmet and cavalry uniform, Radhagupta was standing by his brown horse. Crowds of animals, horsemen, foot soldiers, and hundreds of porters and cooks stood in several columns behind him. *Rain or sunshine, he is always on time,* she thought. Two hours later, she and Suba showed up on the palace terrace, beautiful and flustered, and followed by maids in loose colorful clothes. Livia turned as she heard a clang. A maid had dropped perfumes, cosmetics and mirrors onto the floor. *She must have been pulling up her skirt,* Livia thought. *Even if their hands are full, they are always pulling up their skirts.*

At last, the caravan started around noon and Livia and Suba fell asleep from the unceasing rocking motion of the carriage. An hour later, Livia woke up. Suba was tossing about on the opposite seat, stretching and yawning. Gazing at her, Livia smiled. 'Suba, do you know 500 animals and 600 men are accompanying us on this trip? We royalty carry so much baggage. Slow of body and mind, we are rather unaccomplished. Obsessed with our jewels and over-decorated palace rooms, we become our possessions. We are bloated with the gas of happiness. Living our lonely lives on stage, masquerading, gasconading filled with quiet despair and loud deodorant. But you, Suba, are different. You share, you are generous. You are alive!' Still sleepy, Suba turned her pretty head and looked at Livia with half-closed eyes, smiled broadly, and produced two perfect dimples. Then she fell back into a half-coma, hands dangling on the sides, mouth dribbling saliva. *How easily you fall asleep,* thought Livia. *Only because you have two sons!*

The whole trip, Asoka kept complaining that Dasrath, his cousin and closest friend, should have come with him. Once when he vanished for a while on his horse, Suba's heart sank, but Livia panicked. When he showed up, she warned him, 'Asoka, next time I will have you fenced in by twenty horsemen.' That did the job. Tissa, Asoka's younger brother, slept most of the way. So did his mother, except when she talked.

Perhaps the knocks and jolts on the road have lowered her guard, thought Livia, as Suba told her about her life with the King. After her wedding she said, the chief queen had conspired with Purohit, the chief priest, to keep Suba out of the palace—and away from the King—for three years. The queen came up with the ruse that Suba's stars were fatal to the King. Livia's eyebrows arched, 'Poor you! How diabolical!'

Suba paused then said, 'The chief queen detests me and my sons. She thinks they threaten Sasima.'

The fifteen year old Sasima was the crown prince.

'I think the chief queen detests you because the King prefers your bed,' Livia laughed. 'Why should the queen resent Asoka? Her son is the crown prince, not Asoka.'

'Nothing is etched in stone, Choti-ma! The King can always change his mind!' Suba winked. 'And I could become Raj-Mata.'

Big dreams! What chance do I have? thought Livia, suddenly overcome with nausea. She stuck her head out of the window.

'Stop! Stop!' Suba shouted, handing Livia a cup of water.

A faint smile appeared on Suba's pretty face. Moving closer, she whispered, 'I'm fed up with the queen. Last time, at my father's house, I started a havan — sacrificial ritual—to do her in.'

Livia's eyes widened. 'Can a havan do that?'

Suba said, a little sheepishly, 'A bull sacrifice is very powerful!'

Inside, Livia laughed at Suba's naivety. *A Greek princess,* she thought, *relies on her guts, not on mumbo-jumbo.*

The party rested after reaching Rajnagar at noon. Early the next morning, Suba and Livia went to the ghat, the bathing bank. Suba set off on her own to bathe and do worship in the river. Livia took a quick dip, changed and sat down to watch, chin on knees. Men and women were bathing in their clothes, standing and worshipping in the water or chatting and eating sweets. Children shrieked, trying to break loose from parents. A panicked couple ran around asking everyone about their missing young son. The Brahmins were turning god into gold with their ululating hymns—only the sound mattered, not the words. The air was filled with piety as if the gods themselves were hovering.

The cacophony, the smell of frying foods, the incense, and fresh flowers, all set Livia thinking. *The River is like life. It gives something to all. No one returns empty handed. It rewards those who come to bathe and worship, it rewards those who come to watch the spectacle or the changing colors of the water; it even rewards those who come to feast their eyes on eye-popping female flesh peeping through water soaked clothes. What color! What faith! What atmosphere!* To her surprise, she found herself asking the benevolent Vaitarni to give her Asoka.

After some worship, some charity, and an aborted attempt by Suba to see an astrologer, Suba and Livia went back to the camp. They had lunch and sat chatting under a shady tree. Asoka and Tissa went out with guards on an elephant to browse the town's little shops. In the afternoon, Radhagupta announced that the Kalinga crown prince and his wife had made a surprise appearance. They brought gifts of jewels and fruits. Livia stayed back to wait for the boys while Suba went to welcome the royal visitors. After a while she sent for her and Livia joined the guests, telling her guard to send in the boys when they returned. The meeting was still on when a frazzled guard broke in to say that Asoka and Tissa were missing. Everyone rushed out in panic. The visitors left and hell broke loose. A wailing Suba sent men out in all directions. An hour passed and Suba was near collapse when Tissa arrived without Asoka. Radhagupta rushed out with Tissa and his men. When he returned with a shaken Asoka, it was already night.

That he had killed a barbarian and come out more or less intact from the ordeal greatly impressed Livia. For the first time after the death of her son, her hopes of becoming 'Raj-Mata' revived with full force. Like fresh leaves on a bare tree in spring.

4

On the journey back, a pall hung over the women. Suba feared the King's wrath while Livia feared Suba would renege on her promise. A few weeks later, the party stopped by the Mohana River near Gaya to camp. The evening meal was served in the cool of night. Inside the tent, Asoka and Tissa played Chaturang, a dice game like an early version of chess, developed around the time of the *Mahabharata* to test war strategies. After the meal, the women went for a walk by the riverside under the stars. Turning to Suba, Livia said, 'Suba, I feel so close to you. I will tell you about my life when we reach Pataliputra.'

Suba yearned for adventures. In her head, Persia, Egypt and Greece stirred up visions of romance as does the sight of a new lover. She had been asking Livia about her love life prior to coming to India, but Livia resisted, not wanting to recall such painful memories. Now Livia saw a reason. *It will bring tears to her eyes,* she thought, *and then I'll strike!*

The starry night, the gurgling water, the cool breeze, and the prospect of unraveling Livia's past all made Suba effusive.

'Choti-ma,' she said, 'my sons are special. Tissa takes after his father and lives by rules; Asoka is willful and sensitive like me. Yesterday, for the first time, he admitted to me the cannibals captured him only because he tried to save the sacrificial boy. How stupid! Tissa saw the cannibals and turned back. But Asoka must stick his neck out for the riffraff. Same womb and yet so different!' Overflowing with motherly love, she sighed, 'Choti-ma, life is so beautiful!'

How her eyes shine when she talks of her sons, thought Livia. *As if she was holding the jewels of a diadem in her hand.*

Suba took Livia's hand. 'Choti-ma, my life does not matter. I only want the best for my sons.' Then without thinking, she said, 'If I die, will you take care of them?'

Turning her head away, Livia said, 'Don't be silly!' She lowered her voice to subdue her excitement. 'Just to reassure you, of course I will. Of course, Suba, I will!'

Back in Pataliputra, the King was incensed at Suba. He ordered Asoka not to ride a horse for three months, telling him, 'I am very disappointed in you.'

Livia saw her opportunity and invited Suba to join her. Suba appeared in a purple sari, red vermilion running through her parted hair, and a red mark on her forehead. Radiant with anticipation, Suba said, 'Choti-ma, the green chiton robe and the gold belt look so pretty against your olive skin.'

Her heart pounding, Livia told her the story, then gave back Suba's ring and asked for Asoka. Stunned, Suba turned pale. Having a highly exaggerated view of her own goodness, Suba freely indulged in verbal generosities and symbolic deeds. If asked to live up to her word however, she offered excuses and apologies. She stammered, 'Asoka is already like your son!'

Livia snapped, 'But not my son!' She frowned. 'Suba, I trust you to keep your promise.'

Wiping her brow, and without a word, Suba staggered out of the room.

Livia knew she had failed. That night she tossed sleeplessly, clutching her pillow and brooding over the horror of her existence. Feverish, deafened by the silence, she clasped her ears and let out a scream. Roxanne, her maid and friend, came running from the next room and gave her a cup of warm milk to calm her. 'Livia, go to sleep. I'm sure you'll come up with something new tomorrow.'

'I was diligent,' Livia said to herself, 'I went to Vaitarni. I told her my story. I had her word, her ring. I arranged for Kalinga. All to no avail! It cannot be! It cannot be!'

She got out of bed, changed into a chemise and looked out of the door. It was dark outside, and a pale sliver of moon hung in the sky. Shadows flitted, leaves hissed on trees, and a dog barked in long strains. Over and over, the bark started on a low note, rose gradually to a crescendo, stayed there, then descended into a whimper. It seemed the dog's grief was too deep to be barked away in a few short gasps. Like hers.

She found a book, and lit a lamp by the bedside, which threw her large shadow on the wall. 'That's who I have become. I should never have been sent here!'

She lay down again in bed, letting the memories take over.

Oh, Chandra, with you I left behind my virginity. Then you left me in a dark night, on a snowy peak, and I must find a rock, to warm my heart, if not my body. I had a son, an emperor who now rules Hades, a sunless country, cleft with chasms and sulphurous flames, where Ixion, Sisyphus and Tantalus writhe in pain. But he is king, and once he serves his time, will rise like Phoenix, an Antaeus! Find me that child, a ghost whose shadows I can fill with flesh. A body plumed in crimson and gold.

Head throbbing, she got up and began to pace. 'What do I do now? Sit on my haunches and sob away my life?'

In the days following, Livia's resentment grew. *What did Suba mean when she offered me Asoka? Was she drunk? Mad? She played with my grief!* Livia sat blowing her nose, crying, feeling sorry for herself, staring at the void before her. Then she decided, *I have come too far to turn back. I will be myself, I will be Greek. She asked for it.*

She invited Suba for a reconciliation meal. Suba looked ravishing in a saffron sari, and Livia's heart sank. *It would be so much easier if she looked just plain.* Hardening her heart, she served Suba the meat-mushroom curry with trembling hands. *Zeus!* she prayed, *Help me! I have no choice.*

Once Suba left, Roxanne, Livia's confidante, spy, and counselor, came running to her room and stood towering over her, her motherly breasts pressing Livia's nose and pale cheeks. 'Livia,' she said in her thick Prakrit accent, 'You will be Raj-Mata!'

Cheerlessly Livia replied, 'Tell me that on his coronation day.' She sent Roxanne away, thinking: *Why wouldn't Suba part with one son? She was too greedy. Now I end up with both. All my life will I grieve for her. How cruel that our happiness is never complete. A bit of this, a chunk of that is always missing.*

A few days later Suba became ill, and non-stop Vedic chants went up in the palace. Despite them, she died. A rumor spread in the palace that the chief queen had performed a bull-sacrifice for her demise when Suba was in Kalinga.

It was easy for Livia to get the King's permission for custody of Asoka and Tissa. A few months later— since she spoke Greek, Persian, Middle Egyptian, and Prakrit, the language of Pataliputra—Livia asked for and took over the Department of Foreign Visitors.

The game of "Who'll be the Next King" continued, the chief queen moving about with power and certainty, Livia circling with guile like a hyena. Though Suba was out of her way, the queen did not let her guard down. It was not in her nature; she still remembered that when Livia was Chandragupta's queen, she had tried to have her son declared successor. She watched her turf like a tigress.

Having got her first wish, Livia began to work on the next. Sitting in her garden, she spent the mornings gazing at the distant towers, thinking of Raj-Mata's golden-armed high chair. Day after day, she promised herself, *I will drip in Asoka's veins the wine of ambition, the same that flowed in my father and my Lord.* She visualized his life: *he will avoid poetry and philosophy, which cool down the lust for power; his friends will be army generals; he will win Sasima's trust to make it easier for him to take off his head at the right moment.* That she was endangering Asoka's life did not bother her.

Asoka had lost his mother. As if this was not devastating enough, he'd also lost his father's love. He had angered the King, whose affection was doled out for achievements and good behavior, not misadventures unworthy of a Maurya prince. Suba never got the chance to ask the King to forgive him. In his heart, Asoka blamed the queen for his loss. Lying awake at night, feeling like an orphan, he would bury his face in his pillow to hide his tears.

5

For thirty days people had been pouring into the city. Through the eleven miles of its length and two of width, the roads were filled with people. The inns, hostelries, eating places, drinking establishments, serais, lodges, and gaming houses were all packed, leaving the locals a little discombobulated. On the Necklace road that circled the city, Afghans, Persians and Greeks bumped and bumbled toward the Market grounds to smell fresh produce or just to watch the bustling scene. Nearby whirred the textile looms; the ironsmiths sat on their haunches pumping bellows at their fires. A beefy man on the threshold of a butchery coaxed a reluctant ox to step up inside; a few onlookers cheered the bull. Distaff in hand, a laundry man walked to the river. A woman with a large behind carried a small load, and a shriveled ass bore a large loose bundle. A distracted man fell over the ass, pulling down the clothes. Four men, naked to the waist, bore on their shoulders a red palanquin. In it sat a plump courtesan with small eyes and a large nose ring, smiling at strangers. A large water pot on her head, a dark woman in tatters, thin as a reed, zigzagged as she walked—eyes crossed, lips pursed, neck compressed. A pug-nosed chariot driver rushed through the crowd—overtaking a horseman, two bullock carts and three donkeys, and brushing a Brahmin's shoulder. 'You molt of a tarantula!' screamed the fat Brahmin, flailing his hands and running after the driver. In five strides, the Brahmin tottered to a standstill, yet kept his tongue running. A milkman walked two white milch cows but was stopped in his tracks by a herd of goats. One goat broke loose and began to frisk and squawk, like a man reeling under the revelations of a god. The traffic came to a halt, people fussed and fumed and did the turkey trot. A few righteous crusaders brought the goat in line after a sound thrashing. (If the goat were human, it would have become a prophet—the last. No questions asked). The milkman went his way, chanting obscenities in Sanskrit.

Asoka was now seventeen, a dangerous age for a young man in any country or clime. This is the time when body runs ahead of mind, when every young woman looks divine, when poetry sprouts and prose is pushed underground. This was Asoka: large eyes, high cheekbones, a few strands of hair flopping over a sloping forehead. Yearning for love, hoping to perform awesome deeds to win his father, dreaming of becoming crown prince.

Leaving the palace, Asoka and Bitan walked north to the Fairgrounds. Bitan, also seventeen, was thin and tall, with dark curls, and had just arrived from Taxila. He was studying religion and philosophy there—the "in thing" for bright, spirited young men of the time. The two had immediately struck up a friendship. Walking north on Royal Boulevard, Asoka recited a few lines from the poem he had read the previous evening, 'The Girl Wearing a Garland', his face flushed with youthful pleasure. Bitan told him about snow and the great mountains in Taxila, and about his loving grandfather. Asoka said he too adored his grandfather. At the intersection of Necklace road, Asoka turned west to the Fairgrounds; on the east side stood the Market grounds, the temples and the artisan guild buildings. Suddenly, Bitan stopped.

'Asoka, take a deep breath. Can you smell it all? Flowers, incense, ghee, melted butter, and above all, steaming cow dung. Keep your eyes on the ground!'

Inside the Fairgrounds, some young men had dyed their beards purple, red or green, to match their dress. Many had no beards—as a result of the Greek Alexander's influence. Some carried parrots or mynah birds on their shoulders —nature's original music equipment. The price was that wet-warm sticky feeling that suddenly came upon the young owner—fresh bird droppings.

The two friends jostled young females, stopped to watch musicians, dancers, brewers of love potions, mimes, drummers, wrestlers, acrobats, fire-eaters, minstrels, clowns, soothsayers.

'All kinds are here—the thin-nosed Persian, the hawk-nosed Afghan, the dark Egyptian, the olive-colored Greek. I have seen them all in Taxila, but they look different here. What a wonderful world it is!' Bitan gushed. They kept going, watching.

With a small braying donkey slung on his shoulder, a holy man told the crowd, 'Listen to what he is saying: "Pass me their sins! Pass me their sins!" I tell you, he is no ordinary donkey. An early incarnation of god Ganesha, he came to me one night in sleep.' People stared at the donkey. Two red vertical vermilion lines were painted between the eyes. Some laughed and walked away. Others looked for divine signs and found plenty. Bowing with folded hands, they threw change at its hooves. A few touched it gingerly and feeling inspired, dropped extra coins.

Then a little boy pushed a stick in an elephant's trunk, and the irked beast began to run and trumpet. Women shrieked, men scattered, and the frightened boy nimbly disappeared in the crowd. A quick-thinking Mahout pierced the elephant's neck with his iron goad, and it howled then quieted down. Panic gone, excitement returned to the crowd.

They walked to the tent theatre to see the play, 'The Ramlila,' God Rama's story, which was about to begin amidst drums, tambourines, lutes and flutes.

Suddenly Asoka said, 'Oh no! I'll have to skip it today! I just remembered the horse race!' It was scheduled for later that day, and Asoka had been preparing for the last four months in the hope of winning and gaining his father's admiration. In his mind, this was the path to becoming crown prince.

Bitan told him he had placed a wager on the race the previous day.

'Wagering on horses is not allowed!' Asoka exclaimed.

Bitan smiled impishly. 'I found a man—the manager of the White Flag lodging house. What's more, I bet on you! My wager was so much better.'

Asoka said, 'You bet on a dark horse!'

At a crowded eating establishment the hungry friends waited, and when a man got up to leave, flung their bodies on the bench. A bald fat cook stood behind hot fumes rising from a large wok—his round face glistening with grease and sweat. Asoka shouted the order to him.

Meat was served on a large leaf, rice wine in an earthen cup. Biting into a tough piece, Asoka said, 'I don't think you've met Sisupal yet. He's our age and very funny. He's the son of Kalinga's Prime Minister, and he's studying statecraft here...'

Then, he heard Sisupal's voice. 'Hello, Asoka.'

Asoka turned. Sisupal was standing in line for food.

The two friends made room for stout Sisupal, causing much resentment on the bench. Oblivious, Asoka said, 'Speak of the devil... Sisupal, Bitan is our Radhagupta's nephew from Taxila. If looks could kill, he would kill like Alexander. And he plays the flute too. You should see his fingers moving restlessly on it, as if the flute were a pretty woman.' A smile spread over Bitan's face.

Sisupal, broad-nosed, wore heavy talcum on his dark fleshy face to whiten his skin, and black powder round his small eyes to make them look bigger.

Looking at Bitan's hands, he said, 'Asoka! So Bitan has long arms, long hands and long fingers. So where is the connection to the flute?' His eyes inadvertently fell on his own stubby hands, his eyebrows twitched, and they all laughed.

His lunch arrived.

Chewing on buffalo's rump, Bitan asked, 'Sisupal, what brought you to Pataliputra?'

Sisupal smirked. 'A bull-sacrifice by my priest-father made the crown prince Kalinga's King. He in turn made my father his prime minister. So you can say I came riding on a bull.'

Asoka grinned, 'The power of Bull!'

Their stomachs stuffed with ox brains, buffalo rump and wine, they dragged their bodies away. A plump young woman smiled at Sisupal, beckoning him with her forefinger and he took off without a word.

'The face painting worked!' Asoka teased. Just then Asoka saw a girl in a green skirt and yellow choli. 'Varsha!,' he called out, waving and quickly walking over. A few days back, at a drinking establishment, he had bought flowers from her so that his eyes could fondle her bosom. Now he talked to her for a few minutes, looking at her round face, brown hair and large brown eyes, admiring her full hips and shapely body. Then Sasima, the crown prince, appeared, gave Asoka a dirty look, grasped her hand and walked off. After a few steps, she turned and stared at him for a long moment. What was she saying? Asoka wondered as he walked over to join Bitan.

'She's in demand. No wonder this city is called a pleasure garden.'

After an hour Sisupal returned, looking glum. 'How did it go?' asked Asoka.

Sisupal frowned, 'She bilked me of forty-five pana! Forty-five! I told her it was highway lechery!'

Asoka laughed, 'Did you get something back?'

'She said, "Come again!" and gave me this red jujube to suck on. I must look such a fool. You know, for that much money, I could have bought a whole cow!' Sisupal groaned.

On the way to the palace, Asoka smiled. 'Sisupal, much as you love cows, cows won't do! Keep pure the Aryan race. Anyway, she must have told you the price.'

Sisupal scratched his head. 'At the time, I was engrossed in a couple of things.'

Asoka comforted him. 'Naturally ! Don't fret. You paid for her establishment, dress, music lessons, erotic training, and income taxes.' He laughed, 'You did a good deed!'

'Now,' Bitan smiled at Asoka, 'don't worry where Sisupal sunk his money. Think of how you can salvage mine.'

Asoka nodded absent-mindedly. Worried he'd be bumped off by the loyal cronies of the crown prince, he was planning on taking the lead in the race from the start.

6

Wearing an orange cap, Livia was sitting on the verandah of her apartment reading a book, when a maid announced the chief queen wished to see her at noon.

Livia had not seen her in a long time and it pleased her to notice that the flesh on the queen's face was sagging and her waistline disappearing into her hips. *A good edifice once*, thought Livia. *Now in ruins!*

'Sit down, sit down,' the queen said, pointing to a plain chair kept for women fallen in her eyes.

'Sasima is so handsome! Like you.' Livia flattered her.

A broad smile spread over the queen's fleshy face. 'You remember!' she said, overcome with nostalgia.

Livia was in a hurry. Getting up, she said, 'Asoka will be home soon.'

'Sit down, sit down,' the queen said, opening her mouth wide and daintily inserting a rolled betel leaf. She kept chewing, spat some juice into a golden bowl and gulped down some, while Livia waited, cursing, watching the queen licking, lapping, nibbling her lips, as if she derived the pleasure of kissing from the bites, the gushing saliva. *When was she kissed last?* Wondered Livia. Once Suba had told her that in bed, the King was a meat and potatoes man.

At long last the queen spoke. 'This is about the race. You know Sasima will win. My son! He is just too good, bless his handsome face! Asoka knows it's not really a race; it's a ritual so the public can adore the crown prince. Their future king. Tell that to Asoka. You know the protocol.'

Protocol? Livia's insides fumed. She coughed out a laugh. 'I know, I know.'

She left dazed, thinking, *She's a Basilisk who kills by her breath!* For the first time she saw that the queen was as determined to protect the crown prince as Livia was to dislodge him.

Later, Livia drew Asoka's "tilak", the auspicious red vermilion mark, on his forehead, to send him off to the race. She told him what the queen had said. 'Don't just dismiss her words.'

Asoka glowered at her.

In the Vedic religion, the horse was a symbol of power and victory. The King loved the army's horse races. He had started one for princes only, to test the valor of his sons: Sasima, the eldest and crown prince, then Dasrath, next came Marut and Pavan (twins their mother had named Hot and Tot for easy identification when they started talking gibberish), and Asoka. Tissa was under sixteen, so not eligible for the race.

The King and the Queen came royally dressed. They sat on a platform in high chairs behind the finish line, with Livia behind them in a green chiton. Leaning forward, she said, 'The public will go wild when Sasima crosses the finish line!'

The queen, her mouth full of juice, turned back and said with a twang, 'Bless his handsome face! My son!' A few drops of noble sentiments soiled her white dress.

Each prince came to the race with a mission: Sasima to win, and Dasrath to boost Asoka's morale. Dasrath's mother was dead, and he was stoical. 'I am a dead horse,' he told Asoka, 'with no one to stand up for me before father.' Hot and Tot came to prove their loyalty to the crown prince. Motherless also, Asoka considered himself just as unprivileged as Dasrath. By winning the race, he longed to win back his father.

The horses were lined up, and there was the usual chanting of hymns and blowing of conches. Long-faced priests sprinkled rice and water on the horses' even longer faces. The King looked around and signaled: the "dundhabi" — the kettle-drum — blasted, and the horses were off. Located outside the city on army training grounds, the inverse U-shaped two mile race track had five lanes. The queen had carefully assigned a specific lane to each prince: Sasima on the extreme left, Dasrath, on the extreme right, Asoka between Hot and Tot with Tot to his right.

The King gazed at his sons with pride. *This race is like the race to the throne*, he thought. *All look good in the going. In the end, the nimble, the determined son will get my crown.* Caressing his salt and pepper beard, he settled down to watch.

The previous year's winner, Sasima went into a gallop from the start. Distracted by the scent of Sasima's filly, Hot's brown horse went chasing her tail. Dasrath's horse had an unusually long tail which caught Asoka's attention at the wrong moment: too quickly Asoka loosened the reins, startling his black-white horse—a philosopher type—into a sudden gallop. Almost thrown from his seat, Asoka recovered but trailed, passing the first flag.

Asoka overtook Dasrath at a gallop, his eyes on Sasima in the distance. Then Tot swerved into Asoka's lane, forcing him left, and Hot quickly cut right, slowing Asoka down. Hemmed in between them, Asoka looked for a chink. Sasima, meanwhile, was galloping away. 'Sasima, Sasima...' chanted the crowd.

Trailing in the outer lane, Dasrath saw Asoka's predicament. Chasing Tot, he affectionately clucked his horse, his bushy tail flying like the tresses of a maiden fleeing an undesired pursuer. The second flagpole passed.

Swiftly swerving left, an angry Tot abruptly cut to right to slam into Dasrath's horse. But Dasrath darted straight into his lane, leaving Tot off balance, which allowed Asoka to fly past both Hot and Tot.

Galloping at full speed, Asoka raised his head and saw Sasima sprinting away in the distance. Asoka's ears filled with, "Sasima... Sasima!" growing louder by the minute.

Asoka glued his eyes on his horse, crouched to its mane, and pressing his strong thighs around its white belly, clucked, and let go of the reins. The horse's nostrils flared, its chest swelled, its legs spread out in long strides, and it began flying on all fours with the rhythm of a wave. Quickly casting a glance back, Sasima panicked and went for the whip. His filly baulked. Coming up fast, Asoka swerved left to Hot's lane and flew past Sasima just beyond the third post. Sasima bent over his filly's mane, gently patting her, and she forgave her master and surged, soon running neck and neck with Asoka's black and white horse. It was now touch and go. All chanting ceased as every spectator held his breath. In the last few laps, the filly's surge began to fade, and Asoka touched the finish line by a length. The crowd went dizzy, jumping and waving. 'Asoka, Asoka!'

The queen's face turned ashen, as if she smelled rebellion in the air. Livia glowed but squirmed inside.

His heart beating like a drum, Asoka stood confused, gazing at a sea of waving hands. Only when King Bindusar stood up, garlanded Asoka, and warmly embraced him, did he know he had won. The warmth of embrace made Asoka's heart pound. *I did it! I did it!* he thought, astonished. Suddenly he felt on top of the world. He had regained his father's admiration.

The royal couple left soon after the race. Bitan went with Sisupal to collect his winnings, and Dasrath left to be with Bhairavi, his love. Asoka started toward Livia's carriage, waiting in the wings. Suddenly, Sasima appeared with Hot and Tot and said threateningly, 'You must want your teeth knocked out!' He disappeared just as fast.

Asoka's temples turned red with anger. 'Sasima,' he said, walking on, 'I feel good today, so you are forgiven! But don't count on it tomorrow.'

Surely he would replace Sasima as crown prince in the not too distant future, he thought. He had no idea that his life was about to take an abrupt turn.

7

Annoyed at his stubbornness, Livia told Asoka not to celebrate. Heedless, he invited his friends to his apartment in the Prince Palace where he had been living since the age of fourteen when every prince had to move away from his mother.

The evening started with liquor made from raw sugar, and Asava, a wood-apple wine. After a couple of drinks, running his fingers through his hair, his big eyes shining, Asoka began to brag.

'I love horses. They are like men—philosophers, thinkers, stubborn, lazy, timid and brave. Hauling a heavy, horizontal body on reed-like legs, they look ridiculous. But what speed and grace! I asked Dasrath if I could use the whip. And he said "Asoka, the Arabian horse sleeps in its master's tent. Treat it like the woman you love—feed it, caress it." Well, that's what I did. But now I need the real thing. I am going for Varsha.' He looked around, and not seeing Dasrath, said, 'Where is that great lover?'

A maid brought wine made with flour and mango juice. At last, Dasrath showed up. He looked pale. He had gone to apologize to Sasima for inadvertently helping Asoka. Sasima was his last hope for getting the queen's permission to marry Bhairavi. He had been in love with the fair complexioned eighteen-year-old slave girl for three years.

The King and the Queen knew about the affair. The King's Secret Service employed servants and courtesans to keep a watch on the princes. According to Rishi Bhardvaja, an ancient sage, "Princes, like crabs, eat their begetters. Princes lacking in fatherly affection should be quietly dispatched." Those were old times. Now the practice was to send such princes to the frontier where wine, women and tribes produced the same result without the guilt.

No one expected the princes to live a celibate life. Their teachers had instructed them: Never forget your family's honor. If you have to, do it with servant girls or courtesans, do it unseen, unheard, in dark and secluded places. Spend no more time than is necessary. Don't show tenderness or affection, which is unmanly, and more so in a prince. And always pay now: later you may be king.

But Dasrath had violated all the rules by falling in love with a slave girl. To the King, love was a fever cured by a traditional marriage, which may taste medicinal like an herbal broth, but provided relief. Dasrath had become a pariah. Having lost access to the King, he was clutching at straws.

Asoka exploded, 'Sasima's so arrogant and patronizing, he will never help you!'

Dasrath was taken aback. 'Asoka, I don't think so. He's promised to help.'

Asoka sneered, 'That coward. He only thinks of his own interest.'

'I don't know what you have against Sasima,' Dasrath retorted. 'He does drink, but so do we all. As for womanizing, we wish we had his winning ways. I think you hate him because you are so unlike him and he is the crown prince.' He got up to leave.

His face flushed, Asoka said haughtily, 'Yes, I am different. I am better. He may be more handsome but men are judged by deeds, not looks.'

Bitan tried to mediate, 'Dasrath, finish your drink. Asoka, let's get some fresh air.'

Soon, the men calmed down. A maid brought more wine, put the pitcher down and left. Bitan and Sisupal's eyes followed.

Bitan wowed, 'Two little boys fighting under the skirt!'

Others laughed. But Asoka sat brooding. After a few minutes, he said, 'So I don't like him because he is the crown prince! And he hates me because I beat him in language, then grammar, and now the horse race. I am no Hot and Tot. What do I care?'

Dasrath teased, 'If I were the crown prince, wouldn't you love me?'

Asoka burst into laughter and downed a cup of wine. 'That would be funny, very funny. You'd begin to think you could fly. A donkey doesn't become a horse if called "horse", nor a monkey "chimpanzee." Sasima thinks he came out of the mouth of Brahma, the creator, and not from his mother's womb.'

Dasrath was shaking his head in amazement when his sister Charu, who was fifteen, entered the room smiling self-consciously, in a flared green skirt and a skimpy red choli. In her haste to sit next to Bitan at the other end, she knocked down a floor oil lamp and a few drops leapt at Bitan's vest. As servants rushed to clean up the mess, Charu began to cry. Caressing her back, Bitan said, 'Don't cry Charu! It happens!'

Since Bitan had been staying with Asoka, Charu joined Dasrath every evening, and kept re-arranging her 'du-pata' – a piece of cloth to camouflage breasts– which somehow kept slipping off her half-baked breasts. She looked at Bitan adoringly, rushed to fill his cup, and if he played flute, went into a rapture even though he was no virtuoso, and it was an ordinary flute with three regular holes.

Dasrath asked Charu to get Bhairavi to join in the fun. When Bhairavi refused, Dasrath himself dragged her to the party. At Bitan's insistence, Charu took some wine, her face red. Caressing her cheeks, Bitan said, 'Charu, I am rubbing off the red wine!' Pressing his hand to her cheek and moon-gazing into his eyes, Charu stammered, 'I... your flute.'

Sisupal had grown up seeing gods in stone. Now bleary eyed and secretly in love with Charu, he could have sworn he saw her and Bitan rolling on the carpet, making love and soiling it. As the evening progressed, he became morose. When Bitan caressed Charu's cheeks, Sisupal left, thinking, *And I can't even touch her toes!*

Bhairavi was not enjoying the party and asked Dasrath to leave. He got up but Charu wouldn't move. With a stern look, Dasrath pulled Charu up by the arm and she reluctantly walked to the door, her eyes fixed on Bitan.

Walking her to the Princess Palace, Dasrath asked, 'Are you in love with Bitan?'

Turning red, Charu stammered a feeble, 'No,' and hung her head. Stroking her back, Dasrath warned her, 'Be careful, Charu. If the queen finds out, she'll wed you to an old man. Or worse!'

He didn't know his words would be prophetic.

8

To punish Dasrath for helping Asoka, the queen called Sisupal the next day, and offered him Charu's hand in marriage. Sisupal's tongue froze and blood flooded his head. Suddenly he became a caparisoned bull, his shiny turbaned red head charging at his bride's door, thirsting, thrusting, clutching her swollen knobs, her lovely tufted tail up in the air, cooing, mooing, wild sounds rising with waves of pleasure. The queen was shocked—no lightning rod was attached to her head—when she bent down and touched Sisupal on the elbow. At last he blinked, his jaw snapped closed, and she asked him to return to Kalinga to tell his father to consult an astrologer, and fix a marriage date. Sisupal apologized for his temporary loss of hearing. The queen assured him she'd noticed nothing but manly behavior.

Charu's crime was falling in love before marriage. From the king's viewpoint, every lover presented a grave security risk. A daughter could only marry the "boy" appointed by her parents after careful screening. Sometimes she was married to an invalid. It was not uncommon for a married princess to expend her passion on illicit love, or on frippery and gold that bankrupted her kingdom, or even on some erotic religion in vogue. Many fled into the waiting arms of strange god-practitioners. Perhaps natural passions turn crooked when denied proper vent.

His cheeks puffed up with pride, and his button-eyes shining, Sisupal ran to Bitan to convey the great news. Heartbroken, Bitan threw away his flute. Now he could not please his grandfather by marrying into royalty. Dasrath felt utterly worthless. The news stunned Asoka. Enraged, he smashed some precious pieces of Choti-ma's Persian pottery, then told her to go and ask the King to rectify the mistake.

But Livia always followed her own agenda. 'No,' she said. 'It would further antagonize the queen.'

'So keeping her on your side,' said Asoka, his anger rising, 'is more important to you than Charu's happiness?'

Livia calmly said, 'I am tired of thinking for you, Asoka! As for Charu, she is only finding out what every commoner knows: royalty has no right to happiness.'

'If you won't go, I will,' said Asoka. 'Charu will not spend her life in that tribal land!'

Livia remembered her own marriage. 'Are you telling me a father does not have an absolute right over his daughter?'

Asoka shrugged his shoulders. 'Choti-ma, only Charu owns her happiness.'

Confident, he went to the Council chamber next morning to see his father. The King's love of wine had given him a wine-belly. Often he fell asleep in the middle of a philosophic conversation, after a hearty evening meal.

The King sat in his jeweled high chair, looking out the window. Asoka's eyes fell on the crown and he stood admiring it.

'Are you keeping out of trouble, Asoka?'

'Father, I have a request.'

Bindusar's eyes narrowed.

'Father, Bitan wants to marry Charu. And she will be happy with him.'

Hearing a seventeen-year-old talk about happiness irritated the King. 'Asoka, you may know about horses but not about happiness. Charu's happiness is where I marry her. She will keep an eye on Kalinga.' The King motioned him to leave. 'I have more important matters on my mind.'

Suddenly his father's eyes seemed small and his nose looked flat. Asoka left wondering at his father's folly. *We need Charu in Kalinga? What's the Secret Service for?*

That evening Asoka went to console Charu who was disheveled from crying all day. Kissing her on her head, Asoka said tearfully, 'Charu, I failed!'

'Brother, it was in my stars!' Charu wiped a tear from his eye. 'I will marry him in my next birth.'

9

Bitan went back to Taxila, broken-hearted. Asoka's boyhood friend Visal left for Persia, Sisupal for Kalinga. Dasrath stayed rapt in Bhairavi. Now fifteen, Asoka's younger brother Tissa was discovering that a woman who was not his mother could be fun. Asoka asked Varsha out but she told him she was going away and would be back in spring.

Asoka began paying attention to women and even emulated Sasima. He would say, 'Levity come,' invoking an imaginary god of frivolity, 'enter my soul! Shine in my eyes and sit on my tongue! Blather! Open closed doors. Get results! Quick!'

He tried learning the ten-stringed Vina—the seven-note musical scale from which grew the "raga" and the "tala", with their rich rhythmic textures and endless improvisations—but soon tired of practice. His actor friend, Kausal, advised him to check out the army officers' wives. Fed up with the binge drinking and machismo of their men, these women kept themselves going with love—not war—strategies. Approaching a young wife with a good figure, Asoka showed her how, for a rendezvous with a lover, she could track time by sandbox. She said she tracked time by the level of alcohol in her husband, but that her hands were full. 'I'm not taking any new lovers. Check back in ten weeks,' she said, and mentioned a friend.

He asked the baby-faced friend in which of the six seasons did she yearn for a clandestine lover? Varsha, rains (July, August), Sharat, autumn (September, October), Hemanta, winter (November, December), Sisir, frost (January, February), Vasantha, spring (March and April), or Grisma, summer (May and June)?'

'In all seasons. But I'm pleasure-loving and avoid inexperienced lovers. They stick. They take work.' Showing Asoka the door, she said, 'Come back in a couple of years.'

Now he knew what he had suspected: *he was resistible to women.* It hurt. After a few hours in a drinking establishment, he returned home in low spirits. Frustrated, he blurted out, 'Buts on buts! Damn the women! Always, I have to wait. My friends have a blast while I sweat over language, grammar and all that crap. Last month that feminine looking Kausal had seven women! He'll have eighty four in a year at that rate. I don't think he cares about body or face or even age. And mind! What's that? The hind? Never mind! A happy man! But nothing I do works. My victory ruined Charu's life and hurt Dasrath and Bitan. I feel like a criminal for winning the race. Yet I'd be a total wreck if I lost. I don't know what to do. I am a fool to always want more. I could drag maids to my room, but they smell. Besides, force in pleasure is poison in food. Good God!' Asoka held his head, 'I could happily die tonight in my bed, happy to be unchained from this growling animal. Will God forgive me for returning my virginity untouched?'

He escaped into the moonless night for a jog. For an hour and half he pushed himself on the garden trail, streaming with sweat until he collapsed, breathless. Lately, he had discovered that stretching the body's limit of pain smothered smoldering desire—if only for a few days— and left him feeling exhilarated. To wash off, he dived into Nandi lake, howling with pleasure and electrified by its frigid waters. After swimming for an hour then limping over to the water's edge, he rolled onto the sandy shore and lay naked on his back, exhausted, losing himself in the silence of dark night—no leaves stirred, no birds fluttered—inhaling the scent of citrus trees, and gazing at the winking little stars, softly beckoning him above.

Numb, healed, he went back to his studies. Most evenings though, he spent at the lake, thinking of Varsha, of the expression in her eyes when she had turned back to look at him. *Was it defiance? An invitation? Or just a bold front?*

On the first day of spring, he went out looking for Varsha. There she was, draped in green and in the halo of his love. She saw him, smiled and hurried to close the shop. They walked hand in hand to the park near the temple, talking about the coming "Holi," the Bacchanal color festival. She told him red was her favorite color. He decided that very day to paint her breasts with his hands – one would be red and the other green. For the next two days, they hugged and kissed, and he walked her home, his arm round her waist.

Next day, he took Varsha to a grove in the park. Sitting on a stone bench screened by high shrubs, he lovingly fed her pink slices of guava, while thinking about the Caspian horse he had tamed in couple of weeks by feeding it oats. Then Varsha startled him. 'Let's go to the temple flower room. We can be alone there.' He thought, *And that horse was so stubborn!* On the way holding her hand, he kept staring at the lights going up in the street to hide his unbearable excitement.

The "Aarti"– prayers – had just started in the temple hall. Men and women were ringing hand bells and chanting songs, swaying before God. Varsha went straight to a dimly lit room in the back. Asoka quietly bolted the door after him. In one corner, yellow-orange marigold flowers were piled, in another a fat book lay on a table, and on a bench in the middle sat a fat oil pot. He lifted the heavy iron pot and dropped it on the pile of flowers, grumbling, 'The chanting is so loud!'

Her back to him, Varsha took off her du-pata and started filling it with orange marigolds. Leaning on her, he put his arms round her, his hands luxuriating in her bosom. She turned and gave him a lingering kiss. Blood rushed to his temples, suddenly all chanting ceased, and the room became a cave—well perfumed, quiet, with just a suggestion of light—fit for practicing meditation, or the art of love. Pulling up her skirt, lifting her up by the fleshy hips, he laid her on the bench, kissed and made love to her. Several marigolds lay crushed, scattered on the floor.

Her legs were shaking when Varsha came out of the room.

'I'll walk home by myself.'

Asoka kissed her and left the temple.

Outside, it had rained. On the deserted road, the cobblestones glistened, a yellow mist filled the air, and stars glittered in the freshly washed black sky. Asoka stood under a lighted lamp, watching raindrops clinging to the tiny buds on a bare tree, shining like crystals. He passed the drinking establishment where he had first met Varsha and fondly looked in—a man sat alone at the same table drinking wine.

He had a sudden urge to hold her. Running on the slippery road Asoka fell on his nose and wiping the blood on his sleeve, he gave up the idea, but that night he dreamt of her.

The dream turned into a nightmare.

10

Pundit Sidhnath was furious with his granddaughter for returning home late. A Brahmin, he helped people realize their dreams—a son, a job, a rich wife, a handsome husband, quick wealth, good health—by performing havans, rituals. Sadly, his own life kept falling apart. At forty-three, he had lost his wife, then, despite his havans for grandsons, two granddaughters arrived—calamities he called them. Then his son died and he had to support his large family. A few years later, the women started selling flowers to supplement income. When Varsha, the eldest, turned sixteen, he had no money for her marriage but plenty of worries.

He took Varsha to the courthouse to lodge a complaint against Asoka. Chandragupta Maurya's prime minister Chankya had made 'danda' (punishment) the basis of law. With help from spies, laws were strictly enforced. Private interviews were forbidden between litigants and judges. A man well-versed in the laws of God, Pundit Sidhnath was ignorant in the ways of law.

He asked the court clerk the procedure for filing a claim for rape. Seeing his worn out clothes, his slight build, and the scabs on his scalp, the clerk turned rude. He made him wait, accusing him with his glare of the temerity of being alive, then shoved a book in his face. Used to suffering the daily ignominies of the poor, Pundit Sidhnath quietly retired to a corner, sat down on a chair with a thumb-sized hole in the middle, put the book down on the dusty desk and started turning pages: marriage contracts, wives' property rights, the breakdown of marriage, adultery, labor law, partnership and so on. Frustrated, he went back to the clerk, who sat whistling, looking at the ceiling.

'Can't you see I'm busy?' the clerk bristled, resuming his rather musical whistling and looking up at the ceiling. Pundit Sidhnath beat a hasty retreat. As soon as the clerk took a break, he rushed up again with folded hands, and the clerk contemptuously snatched the book and dived right into sex offenses.

Giving the clerk a fawning smile, Varsha's grandfather returned to his chair, his finger clinging to the page. He glanced furtively around, then plunged into the forbidden world of fetishes and perversions. The law's explicit language shocked him. He had enjoyed some raunchy stuff in the holy Vedas in his days but nothing like this. His fancy titillated, he asked Varsha to get him a betel quid. *Why now when never before?* she wondered. The Criminal Code described acts Pundit Sidhnath had never even imagined existed: 'Punishment for sex between man and woman other than through the normal passage.' *What could that be?* he brooded, turning sad and pensive. *Did I miss out in my youth?*

He skipped the part on homosexuality—to him that was worse than bringing a dog to bed. In his mind, God frowned upon whatever he disapproved of in the least. Then he read: "He who forgets himself so much that he has sex with beasts shall be fined 12 pana." He kept turning pages, as goats and sheep marched on forelegs inside his head. "For sex with the image of a goddess, fine is 24 pana." 'Animals!' he blurted, startling the man standing next to him. 'What did you say?' the man growled. Flustered, Pundit Sidhnath, a gentle soul, bowed and profusely apologized.

He glanced outside. Varsha was still out. Relieved, he went back to his hurried titillation. A provision caught his eye: "Any man having sexual relations with the Queen shall be boiled alive in mustard oil." 'What?' he blurted horrified. The mustard oil's pungent smell rushed to his nostrils, pierced his head and tossed him back to his youth when he had performed a bull-sacrifice for a small-town old king. That night the young queen sent for him. On his way to the palace in the creaky royal chariot, rocking back and forth on the hole-filled dirt road, he fell into an orgy, roused by the affinity of motions. In a dimly lit palace room, with the queen's anticipation humming at high speed and higher altitude, the eagerly awaited moment arrived. Fee-faw-fum. The cuckoo failed to sing. Paradise lost. Mid-air burnout. High velocity descent. Combustion. In flames, the queen exploded. 'This time the bull shall do a priest sacrifice!' Thrown out on the street in the cold, Pundit Sidhnath kept running all night till he reached a new town. He had never forgiven God for denying him his one chance at greatness. Now years of anger dissolved into gratitude. He bowed to God for rescuing him from the greasy, fuming hell. When he opened his eyes, Varsha stood there with a puzzled look, a quid in her hand.

Wiping sweat from his head, Pundit Sidhnath got down at last to the task at hand. He found the punishment for deflowering a girl by force: cutting off the middle or forefinger, or a fine of 200 pana. He mused: *I am an old man. What will I do with a spare middle finger? Or even the forefinger?* Surprisingly, the fine for theft or burglary was a hefty one thousand. Well-versed in the riddles of the Vedas, he analogized the 'deflowering a girl by force' to burglary.

The clerk recorded Varsha's statement to the effect that her virginity had been burgled and that she had possessed it prior to the theft. The clerk asked for evidence, and she produced her skirt—blood and all. He raised the items to his nostrils and made sure the evidence was fresh. The clerk explained that witnesses would be helpful. If a witness had left town, a royal summons would be issued.

A copy of Complaint was served on defendant Asoka. He had three days to file a response. Since it involved a prince, a copy was served on the Chancellor—The Head of the Department of Law and Justice. He rushed to hand it over to the King. The King immediately summoned Asoka.

Bindusar loved five things: Persian and Greek wine, imported dry figs, philosophic discussions, and peace of mind. But above all he loved family honor. He was particularly sensitive to the reputation of the Mauryas. His father, the great Chandragupta Maurya, had been born in low caste. Once he became King of course, the Brahmins apologized and discovered that he actually belonged to the legendary warrior family of Sun.

When Asoka walked in, Bindusar was pacing the room. The King glared at him. 'The race has gone to your head!'

Asoka said firmly, 'Father, there was no rape.'

Bindusar was not only King, but the family patriarch. Under the Vedic law, family members had to obey the patriarch. No admonition by a senior male member could be contradicted or rebutted by the junior, while the mud flinging was in progress.

Red with anger at Asoka's audacity, Bindusar flung the Complaint in his face. 'Is this a hymn in your praise?' he thundered.

Wisdom flashed. Asoka lowered his head.

The King ranted on, his diamond and ruby rings flashing angrily at Asoka, along with his eyes. At long last, Asoka's silence and submission cooled his anger. The King said, 'I just don't understand! There are servant girls in the palace, and courtesans outside.'

'Father,' Asoka said feebly, 'the trial will show there was no rape.'

The King jabbed his finger at the Complaint on floor. 'It does not say you touched her with a feather! Such behavior will not be tolerated! Is that clear?'

'Yes, father.' Asoka's head was still down.

There was an awkward silence. 'If you think I will save you, you're dumb. I will tell the judges to do justice. It will be a lesson to you all.'

His legs shaking, Asoka emerged humiliated, longing for Varsha, certain that it was a mistake. She would stand by him in the trial, and exonerated, he would rise once again.

II

A crowd turned up to watch the trial. People stood outside the court denouncing Asoka's uncontrolled lust. Varsha, her mother, and her grandfather were already there when Asoka arrived with Tissa, and was ushered in by the royal guards. Asoka's faint, secret smile was meant only for Varsha. She ignored him.

Varsha whispered something to her mother, who turned and glared at Asoka. Asoka was convinced her grandfather had forced her to file the complaint and that Varsha would convey her helplessness through her glances, and would tell the truth on the witness stand. He looked at her several times, but she avoided him.

The judges arrived late looking pompous and grave, wearing loose dark grey robes with a narrow orange-yellow border stripe. Everybody stood up. Plaintiff was called in.

'Would you prefer to take the oath before Fire, Water, or a Brahmin?' the court clerk asked.

'Water', Varsha said.

After the oath, one of the judges warned her to tell the truth or face a fine for perjury.

At the clerk's direction, she began her statement. 'I went with Asoka to the temple to attend the evening worship. Instead, he took me to a chamber behind the prayer hall, locked the room and raped me.'

'Raped?' Asoka looked angrily at her, and she averted her eyes.

The judge asked her to elaborate. She recollected the incident, then produced the blood-and -semen soiled skirt. Gasps went up from the audience.

One of the judges asked her if she was willing to marry the defendant. 'No.' She didn't hesitate.

'She got that right!' Asoka fumed.

On the witness stand, Varsha's mother stated under oath, 'That evening my daughter came home limping, disoriented and bruised in the tender. I helped her walk to the room. If she were a willing partner, she would have been elated or at least under self-control.'

Sympathizing with the mother, the judges shook their heads.

Asoka was called in. His youthful looks immediately made him suspect.

One of the judges asked, 'What's your defense?'

Asoka stated, 'Honorable Judges, the act was by mutual consent. We met in the late afternoon, had a snack and spent some time in the park. She led me to the flower room in the temple. She did not resist. I saw no blood. If she says she bled, she may have been a virgin.'

One judge cross-examined him. 'What about the limping, the disorientation, the pain?'

'Perhaps she was afraid of her grandfather and made up a story.' His voice lacked conviction.

Judge: 'Do you have any witnesses?'

'Yes,' Asoka said.

Tissa walked to the stand.

'Your honor, I am Asoka's younger brother. Asoka is incapable of rape.' People exchanged glances.

The judges smirked. 'What do you mean? Are you saying he is incapable of sex?' Some in the audience sniggered and guffawed.

Tissa solemnly said, 'No, Judge. Asoka is incapable of force. He needs feelings to do the act.'

Puzzled, one of the judges asked, 'What do you mean?'

Embarrassed, Tissa said, 'Every prince takes servant girls by force to his room. Not Asoka. He would not touch them.'

'Hmm,' muttered the judge, shaking his head, uncomprehending. He looked at Tissa, 'Well, here we are talking about what he did, not how he felt. Anything else?'

'No.' Tissa got down from the stand.

'Any more witnesses?' asked the judge.

Just then Dasrath entered the room, panting. He was sworn in, then said, 'I was in the temple when Asoka came in with the girl. He did not see me. Just as the prayers started, I saw Asoka walk to the room behind the worship hall. Curious, I followed. The two were holding hands and laughing and I heard the door being bolted. There were no screams, no knocking for help. I heard some sounds but only the usual ones. After more than an hour, I saw them come out; she seemed shaken, but nothing to suggest rape. A rape does not take that long. After the two walked out, I went home. I heard of the charge only later.'

One of the judges confronted Varsha with Dasrath's statement.

'I sell flowers,' she said, 'and I went into the room to get some. Once in, his behavior changed. He began to pant, he had a sword on him and his hand kept moving towards it. I admit I did not shout or raise a cry, because I was afraid he would stab me.'

'Stab me?' Asoka's nostrils flared.

Asoka was called in again. 'Did you keep your hand on the sword before and during the act?' The judge asked.

Asoka said, 'I do remember putting my hand on the handle once or twice. But it was to get the sword out of my way.'

Then the clerk explained the punishment for rape: cutting off the middle or index finger, or a fine of 200 pana.

The judges went into deliberation. In his chamber the Presiding Judge Raghu, bald and stocky, twirled his moustache. 'This young man is a prince. What are the chances of his becoming king?'

Always serious, Judge Girinath, a huge man with an equally huge belly, drawled 'No chance. He is fifth in line, out of the King's favor, and he is a troublemaker. Still, I can't find him guilty.'

Judge V, middle aged and one-eyed, having lost it in a war, concurred.

Judge Raghu said, 'I concede he is not guilty. Even so, we have to find him guilty. The King asked me to "do justice." I have a hunch he does not want Asoka to go free. But if we punish him and he later becomes king, where would we be? I tell you, never write off a prince!' He told them of a prince in a southern state who had summarily hanged all judges after he seized power.

Judge Girinath, the large judge with an equally large conscience, said sardonically, 'Judges do that every day! For once, the prince turned the tables on them.' From the literature of the time, Judge Girinath knew about corruption among judges.

Judge Raghu ignored him and said, 'V, what do you think?'

Before V could answer, Judge Raghu saw a man's head moving up and down outside the window. He got up and closed the window.

Judge Girinath remarked, 'I'll light a lamp. This room is a little dark.' He picked up a flint.

Judge Raghu said, 'No, no, put down that flint, Girinath! Purveyors of justice like us don't need light. The less light the better. Even our robe is dark, with only a touch of light. Justice is a mystery. Even to us. We don't want anyone to know, hear or see what goes into our decisions. That will destroy us, Girinath! It is this mystery that allows us to walk holding our heads high, filled with God knows what.'

V needed a favorable recommendation from the Chief Judge for a better paying job. Now he laughed uproariously. 'Chief, you are a philosopher too! And always a strategist! You have my vote!'

Gratified, Judge Raghu said, 'To play it safe, we have to please the King.' He turned, 'Girinath, do you agree?'

Judge Girinath sat silent and grim, being a man of principle.

Stroking his bald pate, head on his chest, his eyes straying, Judge Raghu began to think of a way to win over Girinath. Then his eyes fixed on something that looked like a large pot. Slightly raising head, he looked up and down at the pot before him. O, a paunch! *Sure enough, this belongs to our own Girinath!* Judge Raghu said to himself with delight. Astonished that all these years it hid from his view.

He seized the moment. 'Let's have lunch. It'll be on me.'

Judge Girinath now smiled broadly.

Over a huge lunch, the judges chatted for two hours about everything except the case before them. Then Judge Raghu declared the unanimous guilty verdict: A fine of 200 pana, and compensation of 200 pana to the grandfather of the girl. The plaintiff's claim for burglary of virginity—the fine for burglary was 1000 pana—was dismissed.

Under the Mauryan judicial system, there was no appeal except to the king. An appeal to King Bindusar was ruled out—there was no point. The judicial system required the defendant to pay the penalty the same day, or be jailed.

Asoka was in a bind. Except for the crown prince, the princes received little allowance. What they got, they promptly spent on gambling, drinking and girls. Their mothers funded the rest of their needs. Livia had been forbidden by Bindusar to help. Asoka landed in jail.

The Warden was a barrel-chested, dark man with long hair and a narrow forehead. An affable man, he liked his inmates. He comforted Asoka, 'Don't worry!'

The jail had no lamp, no bed, and the clay floor was cold. Rats scampered about at night, and lizards kept falling from the ceiling. Asoka's head hurt from Varsha's betrayal. On the clay wall, he etched with his nails a serpent with two human female heads: he stood the serpent on trial, and declaring it guilty, sentenced it for life on the wall.

Chewing on brick-hard bread, Asoka brooded on his life aloud. 'I have been cast out into the cold night, fatherless! The royal air is foul.'

Hearing him, the Warden came running. He bent over, and touched his head. 'Prince Asoka, please get some sleep.'

Asoka said, 'Sleep? There is no sleep in hell!'

'Try!' said the Warden, and left.

Asoka murmured, 'I need fresh air!' He looked around, and realized the cell had no window. Suddenly, the memory of his mother, who had come every night to open his bedroom window, burst upon him, and he began shaking with sobs, as if she had just died. He sobbed till his eyes ached. Then he lay motionless, hands crossed on his forehead, grieving that she would never kiss him, hold him, or look at him again. He would never tell her how much he missed her. Intermittently he kept breaking into sobs.

He could get out of jail the next day on accepting one of three corporal punishments: nine strokes with a cane, twelve lashes with a whip or thirty-two slaps to his face, while hanging upside down from the ceiling.

He opted for the lashes. The low caste Warden believed that the Brahmin judges were arrogant and self-seeking, and that justice was the last thing on their minds. 'I correct injustice whenever I can,' he boasted to friends.

In his court, Asoka was not guilty. The Warden applied the lashes himself, barely touching Asoka's skin. Asoka burst into tears.

The Warden rushed over. 'Did I hurt you?'

'No, no. It was your kindness that brought the tears.'

The public was gratified with the verdict. Except for Dasrath, other princes taunted Asoka. 'Next time, it will be a finger!'

Asoka was constantly irritated and yelled at Livia when she tried to talk. The injustice rankled him.

Lying in bed looking up at the ceiling, *I can't take it!* thought Asoka, seething with impotent rage, his dream of becoming crown prince over. *Who are you, Asoka? Motherless! A son his father cannot trust? A dandelion stalk? The queen's puppet? A criminal for fondling Sasima's booby-trap?* He was filled with sadness. *Asoka, in this vast jail of Pataliputra, your hands have been cut off. You can never dream of touching the stars.* Suddenly, as if stung by a hornet, he sprang from bed. *I will not be a hermit. I will not be a ghost. I will go to Taxila.* Tears streaming, and stamping his foot, he blurted, 'And I shall be back!'

He tossed and turned all night. Still, he comforted himself. Taxila is where Baba's ascent began. Jail may have opened the door to my destiny. The thought cheered him.

He announced, 'I am going to Taxila!'

Livia was stunned. 'Don't even think of it, Asoka! You must stay here to keep in touch with the public and the army. You'll bounce back. I'll see to it.'

Asoka would not listen. Raising her voice and her fist, Livia yelled, 'I don't want you making emotional decisions.'

Asoka said, 'I can't live here.'

Livia shouted, 'Have you gone mad? I am telling you for your own good.'

Asoka looked at her contemptuously. 'I know my good.'

She persisted, 'What can Taxila give you?'

'Whatever it gave Baba.'

'He was born a pauper,' Livia tried to reason, 'not a prince like you.'

'I have to go.'

Seeing his flushed face, Livia's face fell. Her worst fears were coming true.

'Come with me,' he told Dasrath before leaving.

Dasarath said, 'My life is here!'

'In this prison!'

'What will you do there?'

'Something! Anything!' and Asoka stormed out of the room.

He left the next day.

12

After he left, Livia shut herself in her room. All this time she had clung to her dream of becoming Raj-Mata, despite Asoka's contrary behavior. 'What a calamity! He has walked away from the throne,' she groaned.

By custom, the eldest son succeeded him unless the king appointed another son. A window of opportunity opened between the king's death and the coronation of the crown prince—but only if the Senapati, the Commander-in-Chief, and the army backed the challenger and the public was not opposed. Living away from the capital, a prince had little chance of mustering such support.

When her Greek maid Roxanne tried to comfort her, Livia burst into tears.

'Livia, you are torturing yourself for nothing. His stay here would not necessarily have made him king.'

Annoyed, Livia said, 'What are you talking about? The weak start unraveling in their youth! Look at the crown prince. The King isn't dumb. Asoka has the same quiet courage in the face of danger that my father and Chandragupta had. And he's only seventeen.'

'And when did you see this quiet courage?'

'In his run-in with the cannibals! And in the race!'

Roxanne said, 'But you've always complained about him. Nothing he did comforted you.'

'He's one of those about whom nothing can be predicted, I suspect. Like my father and Chandragupta.'

Roxanne asked, 'Then why lament?'

'But he has to be here!' Livia tore her hair. 'In Pataliputra!'

It was getting dark. Roxanne asked her to eat a little. Livia shook her head. 'I'll vomit if I touch food. You go. I need to be alone.'

She stood sadly looking at the gilded towers after Roxanne left, 'God, I've lost all my worlds! Where do I go?'

She paced, haggard, in her unlit room, staring blankly at the wall, pounding it with her fist. Without the army's support, he'll never get the throne. The thought tortured her.

That night, Morpheus memories jumped out of their grave, whichever way she turned. Skeletons from the past hounded her—her mother in one corner, Nearchus, her lover, in another; Chandragupta, her lord, on the ceiling, and her little Arjan on the wall. She lit a lamp. From her ivory inlaid rosewood box, she pulled out her mother's letters, piled them on the bed and read them one by one, then tossed them wearily on the floor, snuffing out the lamp. She lay down in bed, hiding her face under the soft cover. But memories kept rushing in waves. Half-asleep, half awake, she became bodiless. On a magic carpet, she flew back to Babylon, roamed the Hanging Gardens. *Mother, I see the emerald tiara around your white neck. Lying rapt in your lap, watching your face glowing, I hear father's march to Persepolis and Hydaspes, my eyes weary with sleep. Lift me up mother to your warm bosom, let me cling to you. You put me down like a feather on my bed. Do not leave my room, mama, stay with me, tell me more stories. I feel the warmth of your cheek on mine, my eyes are closing. Only childhood is free of care. If ever, I was an empress then.*

Where are you, Nearchus, child of Apollo, my ageless lover? You stabbed my heart. Your lush green eyes, the free laughter! The stirrings of desire in a body-less mind, silly feelings made sublime by time. You too would have broken my heart, but a part of me will always love you, that heart of a seventeen year old.

The journey to India came before her. *The full moon at night coming up from behind the Hindukush mountains, flooding the snow-capped peaks one-by-one, filling up the gorges and the valleys with an eerie light. Desert and cactus, gorges, the sharp ridged mountains, the forests dark, the oaks gnarled like my twisted life. The wild boar, the hyena, eager to tear me down, like my desires. The charred tall columns of Persepolis, tomb of the "king of kings," wailing in icy winds. The burning of the palace by a Greek king. No more will the feasts celebrate life, the spring equinox. The wall friezes frozen in time, the eyes that once gleamed sit silently in dark and deep sockets. That was Persepolis, dear mother. I am glad you did not see what I saw.*

The little girl lost in the Khyber pass, the tortuous loneliness of its peaks. Camel thorns and dried junipers, the fierce winds, the sharp chips of its stinging rocks sent us flying behind the bluff. And yet at nightfall, the wind so calm a flame will not flicker. Crossing the Khyber, I came upon a new world of bushes and trees, wild animals and birds. And men so different in their plumage, I knew my old world was dead.

Her head throbbing with pain, she got up and began pacing. *After Suba's death Asoka became a brooding child. Slowly, I lifted his gloom. He loved to read the Mahabharata and had a blind faith in the Vedic gods. I told him stories of Greek heroes and Greek gods. I told him he should worship the gods he liked best. He liked Odysseus for his courage, his gift of speech. But he loved Prometheus best, the one who brought fire to earth. His curiosity never ceased to amaze me. One day, he asked, wide-eyed, "Did Brahma not create Greece?" Maybe, but the Greeks think their gods did it. "Hmm" he said, "I will ask the priest." Next day he told me, "The priest says our god has nothing to do with Greece."*

It was four in the morning. Unable to sleep, exhausted, she began a letter to her mother.

I have failed in the second most important duty of a Greek princess—to be the mother of a king. Midway, she dozed off and saw a dream. When she woke, Livia wrote about it.

I saw a strange dream, mother. I was sailing on a raft in a calm sea, the sky azure, the wind soft. The sun warmed my body. Suddenly clouds gathered, the sky darkened and I was hurled on turbulent waves, my raft tossed like a straw. When I awoke, I was on a little island. The sea was calm, children played with shells and sand on the beach; men and women danced to strange strains. Then darkness came at noon, and the voices and music were drowned under the lashing waves. I was pushed down to the deep where monstrous creatures rushed to devour me; shivering in the water, I fought with my bare hands and screamed for life. Then a beam of light rose up from the bottom of the sea, a little boy riding on it whose face dazzled me. Enveloped in the blinding light, I was pulled up through sheets of cold waves, my body trembling while my soul soared. Soon, I was floating in the dark turbulent sea again.

She woke with a start, her skin chilled. *Was he Arjan? Asoka? Mother,* she wrote, *this dream keeps coming back. Now, I understand. He left me on the high sea.* Livia put away the letter.

But now, the dream is over. Like I had no son! I could not fulfill our dream, Suba. You have my word, I will take my own life the day Sasima is crowned king. I will gorge on the same mushroom. But after contemplating suicide for weeks, she decided to wait. *This race will go on to the finish. Always, the weak, the foolish can be baited. Then cut down by the Trojan horse.*

PART TWO

Search for Love

13

Pushyagupta, sixty-five, was an ex-general, an ex-Governor of Taxila, and friend of Chandragupta. Tired of the long, cold winter, he opened his window that morning expecting to see the usual cold, grey skies. To his surprise, the sun flooded his room. 'Today,' he said with a smile, 'the sky is blue, the sun is out, and snow shines like pink gold!'

He quickly threw a wool shawl round his shoulders and stepped out of the door, murmuring, 'These are now my little, my only excitements!' Outside, there was a riot of color: fiery orange, deep red coral, scarlet and yellow. Looking for a perch, flitting from tree to tree, the red-vented bulbul, the laughing thrush, and the green magpie dived, circled and chirped. There was magic in the air. He stood watching, lost in thoughts. *This glorious morning, these translucent leaves unripe, these shy, frail buds bristling for a hurried sip of life, swelling the air with scent—this will all pass away like one breath. How seductive is a spring morning, like the very first flush of love.* He smiled. *Atossa, that day of our first spring together!* Atossa was his wife of forty years. *I see you sitting before the campfire, your chin on your knees and flames dancing in your eyes! What sensations you ignited in my body and mind!*

How life has changed. The hot blood that once scalded my veins now bumps through walls narrow, old and pale. The howling winter winds at night that once drove me into your arms now whisper of the silence.

He began striding to the stables, lost in memories. A pungent smell tampered with his reverie: a manure heap. A horse snorted in the distance. Kamal, his youngest son, was trotting towards him. His seven-year-old granddaughter, Anga, dressed in bright yellow, sat in front bumping with the horse's stride. Seeing him, she shrieked with pleasure. Tenderness came over him. 'She carries the spring with her,' he murmured.

Kamal stopped the horse by his side, and Anga leapt into Pushyagupta's arms. He put her down, afraid he might drop her.

Anga pouted. 'Baba, I want to ride this horse!'

Pushyagupta smiled, 'You will, you will. In good time!'

Anga protested, 'I want to ride it today!'

Kamal pointed to a tree, 'Anga, get me that stick, there...' and she set off, distracted. Pushyagupta's eyes followed Anga. Making gleeful sounds, she was chasing a butterfly.

'A glorious morning!'

Kamal smiled, 'Yes father! Brother will be here soon.'

Pushyagupta gave him a puzzled look. 'Oh, yes, yes...Viswa!'

Memories flared up. He remembered with regret how he had driven his two sons from the house. Viswa, his second, had settled down in Alexandria in Egypt at twenty, and married Itara, a local girl. Radhagupta, his eldest son, had left at nineteen because Pushyagupta would not let him marry the girl he loved, and she had committed suicide. Only after Viswa left did Pushyagupta realize his willful ways. Then he traveled to Pataliputra and compensated for his guilt by building Radhagupta a mansion outside the city. *A mansion for taking the life of my love?* thought Radhagupta.

When Kamal too left for Pataliputra, he got a fright. *Does something in the water and air of Taxila turn young sons into rebels?* He knew racial skirmishes and constant border troubles did not help. Kamal came back a year later. He met with no opposition and was allowed to marry Sonara, a spirited half–Persian, half-Pukhtu girl. Kamal's first son, Bitan, was born and a daughter, Anga, nine years later. Though the priest gave her the name Padmavati, she was called Anga – a limb of Ganga, the goddess river that came down from Heaven to give her bounty to the earth. The baby of the house, she looked a little like the goddess too. From birth she had big green eyes, raven black hair and an unearthly smile.

This spring day, Anga was here to hand out woolen blankets to farm workers. After she gave one to a peasant, he returned with his ten-year-old son, naked and shivering, and pleaded with Anga, 'Pretty miss! You will live a hundred years! Could my son get one?'

Pushyagupta watched her look at the shivering little boy and without a blink, gave him one. Kamal whispered a loud 'no' in her ear.

Back at home, Sonara, her mother laughed. 'Anga, each worker has already been given one. This one is extra.' Anga turned to Pushyagupta, 'Baba, we must give them one more.'

How could he say no to the light of his eyes? 'All right! All right! But only after Viswa arrives.' Hour after hour, Anga waited at the entry gate.

She wanted to do everything Bitan did; it did not matter that she was female and nine years younger. She took lessons in archery, riding, and in Sanskrit too, against the wishes of her mother and the widely held belief that education was the one ornament that not only ruined the looks of females but also their minds.

At long last, Viswa arrived with a camel-load of gifts. When guards opened the gate, Bitan raced barefoot, waving his hands, and shouting 'Uncle is here, Uncle is here!'

Kamal, on horse, dropped his reins and rushed on foot, Pushyagupta hurried to the verandah with his cane, and lead-footed Atossa dragged her arthritic body towards the gate. Viswa ran to hold his mother in his arms. After the embraces, Pushyagupta took Viswa inside.

Playing with children near the farmer's quarters, Anga came running, holding two butterflies, and presented them to Viswa as soon as he sat down. 'Uncle, these are for my cousins,' she said seriously; 'I will get you more. Pack them carefully when you go.' Viswa accepted the gift with a bow.

'Now,' Anga said, 'What have you brought for me?' The green in her eyes gleamed.

Viswa laughed. 'A kiss here first,' he turned his left cheek.

Anga looked at the dusty cheek, rushed out, returned with a dry towel, spat on it, scrubbed the cheek and planted a kiss on it. 'Ma always washes my face before kissing me goodnight!' 'Now, the gift?' she said, hopping with excitement.

'Viswa, you go and wash,' said Atossa and turned to Anga, 'Anga! Be patient.'

'Ma, after all that trouble, she deserves her gift now,' Viswa said.

The wooden crates lying on the verandah were reshuffled and a box was pulled out. Her eyes glued to the box, Anga kept hopping up and down. Viswa took out a bewigged, paddle-shaped doll and a round, narrow-mouthed papyrus basket. It held faience rings and a string of mismatched shells. Ecstatic, Anga gave uncle a spontaneous smooch, and ran out to show the gifts to her friends in the servant quarters.

Viswa had come for three weeks. Everyone sat round him listening to his every word. He described what Ishi, his fourteen year old daughter and Ankhum, his ten year old son, looked like, what they did during the day, the house, and his efficient servants and slaves, what they ate. Pushyagupta told him he was expecting Asoka, a prince, in Taxila for studies.

Viswa looked surprised. 'A prince interested in studies? A crazy one, I guess.'

Bitan asked, 'Uncle, what is their religion?'

'Very different. There are many temples for Re and Amun, the Sun gods. They worship animals and the sun. There are no rituals or fasts, they do not believe in the transmigration of the soul, they just enjoy life. There is no cremation, and the body is mummified. For an outsider like me, religion is fun to watch.'

Viswa sighed. 'Alexandria has everything except the alpine air!'

Kamal took him trekking with his Afghan friends to the Hindukush peak of Lakar Sar and Viswa described the trip to Pushyagupta:

'The route was steep, it took us two days, but the vistas were exhilarating. Ten local Pukhtu tribesmen welcomed us. A rug was spread over dry pine needles on a flat surface at the top, and in the evening, a campfire was built on a bed of small boulders. As the skies darkened, the narrow gorge glowed a warm deep red-brown. In the crisp chill of the evening, men sat rubbing their hands around the fire and wine circulated in clay pitchers. The Pukhtus drank barley liquor. For the evening meal, two sheep were picked up by their feet and tossed into the roaring fire, where their fur immediately flared up, yellow flames leaping like a burst of fire crackers. Their loud bleats stirred the mountains. After the howls tapered away, the disassembled sheep were turned with sticks. Chunks of meat were torn with an ax-like knife, threaded on wooden skewers, roasted on red hot coals and served with Pukhtu flat bread.

After the meal, two middle-aged men with rough skin and long bony faces did a Pukhtu war dance, stirring up dust with their leaps and rapid movements; the others sat in a trance. Very late, we retired reluctantly to our tent.'

Two mummified butterflies ambled on camel-back to Alexandria.

14

On the way to Taxila, Asoka kept asking himself: *How to live? What to do with my life?* It deeply hurt him that his father refused to see him before he left. He had left Pataliputra seething with the anger of a stubborn and opinionated seventeen-year-old and made faces as he rode along on his horse. *Dasrath, a wallflower. Sasima, a bonehead. Marut and Pavan, apple polishers. Tissa—a little twerp.* He struggled to label his father and came up with "Pacifist!" an adjective the warrior class reserved for its worst offenders. Yet, thinking of him softened his heart. *Father, I lost you when I lost my mother!*

He avoided the question, 'And who are you, Asoka?' until he blurted out, 'All balled-up!' The words crystallized in the air. If only his mother were there to reassure him. At her memory, he started crying. 'I am nothing...Nothing! Mother! Nothing!' His promise on her deathbed, "Mother, I will make you proud," flashed in his mind, and he wished she were holding his hand, wiping the tears from his eyes.

For a few days, his head was full of Pataliputra. But with each stride of his horse, the oppressive influence of the palace loosened. Then Taxila raised its head. The best thing about Taxila was that it was not Pataliputra. It was as if he was running away from himself – the grainy wind bristling in his face, lodges that were cold and drafty at night, the tiredness in every bone of his body. But these also had a salutary effect. And galloping for ten hours a day emptied him of anger and self-pity.

He wondered: *What makes man great? The knowledge and wisdom of the ascetics? Prowess in arms, like the legendary hero Arjun's in the Mahabharata? Setting up an empire, like Baba?* Every time he thought of Baba, he murmured, 'But he was a great man. I could never be like him.' Yet deep down, as if buried in sand, lurked a belief that one day he would be just as famous and just as great.

As a prince, he had had an education fit for a prince: Religion, including the Vedas, Sanskrit language and grammar, and *Arthasastra*, state revenue and expenditure; warfare tactics; state administration. But his education was basic. Now he wanted to study philosophy, to speculate about life, nature and the cosmos, and to learn about the Vedic gods, *Upanishads* and the *Bhagwad-Gita*, that would teach him how to think and make him versatile. Like streams from a water fountain, all disciplines at the time sprang from religion. He wanted to learn the clue to greatness.

By the time the hills came in view, the road became windy and steep, and Asoka's youthful exuberance resurfaced. In Taxila at last, the sunny afternoon and the cool mountain air refreshed his bone-weary body. He went straight to Pushyagupta's house. Bitan welcomed him, looked at his tired, dusty face, and said sympathetically, 'Asoka, you rest today and tomorrow! We will talk in a few days.'

After a hot bath, Asoka could not rest in his room. He had never been in a new town on his own. And it was no ordinary town: here his revered Baba had started his ascent to the empire. He stood looking at the snow peaks in the distance, glistening like polished brass in the evening sun. *These are the mountains on which Baba gazed.* He could not resist, and went out riding, having never lived among the mountains. Outside in the frosty air, he thought he was shivering with excitement. He dismounted and when Baba reappeared in his mind, he flung out his arms as if to embrace Taxila, and did a little jig: 'I am in Taxila! I am in Taxila!'

In the yellow light of the setting sun, Persians, Bactrians, Afghans, Greeks and a few locals walked about in loose, colorful robes. Asoka wandered the narrow brick streets with baked-mud houses on both sides, until the stars came out. Lamps began to flicker in windows, and clouds of blue smoke rose in the foothills, in the valley below, and hung in the damp air.

Next day, Bitan showed him around the guest houses, stables, outhouses and the warehouses for storing grain. There were gardens and orchards and pools and bridges; alpine trees lined the road from the entrance gate to the house. The peasants lived in small huts, close to the mud-brick boundary wall, near which pink-cheeked, bright-eyed children played in the dirt, and mothers slaved to feed and milk cows and grow corn and vegetables for the master.

The two friends went out riding through the city. One could buy anything in the markets of Taxila, including young women.

'The city's situated between the Indus river in the west and Jhelum to its east,' Bitan told him. 'The Hindukush mountains are to the north. Taxila was conquered by Alexander, until...'

'I know, I know,' Asoka interjected. 'Baba defeated the Greeks and created the empire.'

'The Greeks, Persians and locals don't live in peace here,' said Bitan. 'Religious and political differences keep them at loggerheads.'

Asoka was surprised. 'They live under one king. Why the animosity?'

'Asoka, look at their history. The Persians, once the most powerful in the world, ruled the North-West of India for two centuries. Then Alexander conquered them. And then came your Baba, who overturned the Greeks. It's bad as a witch's cauldron.'

Asoka said, 'I hope the brew doesn't explode.'

In the days following he explored the city on his own. A rocky precipitous ridge divided the city; north of it were stream-washed vegetable fields and fruit farms, and to the south, deep ravines and rocky knolls, covered with cedar and pine trees. Three major routes passed through the city: the royal road (Grand trunk) to Pataliputra; one to Bactria in West Asia; and a third to central Asia, by way of the Kashmir valley.

Under the pine trees by the Tamara stream in the south valley, Asoka loved to lie and contemplate his life while gazing at the sky, listening to the murmur of running water and the whispering wind blowing through cedar and pine trees.

Taxila's streets bustled with coming and going caravans. Its bazaars were filled with spices, colorful carpets, silks, woolens, perfumes, and tiger and leopard skins. There were rows and rows of food stalls where people ate spicy food, licking their fingers, tears running down their cheeks. Asoka bought a plateful and hurriedly gulped it down. The chilly fumes tunneled through his nasal passages to his brain. With his tongue burning and his head on fire, he ran looking for water, but only time cooled down the heat. As always.

In the bazaars, young Persian, Egyptian and Greek women sat on their haunches, naked to the waist, chins on their knees, ogling men as they passed, their glances promising heaven like the chants of priests. Intermittently they stood up, hands on knees, and start swaying their fleshy hips – like tolling temple bells – to attract both the faithful and the unfaithful. Arab traders touted the loyalty of Persian women, the thrift of the Egyptian and the passion of the Greek. *In foreign markets,* Asoka thought, *they must tout our women's' erotic and culinary skills.*

A few days later, Pushyagupta called him. He had received a letter from Livia, who had stayed with him long ago on her journey from Persia to Pataliputra. She had written to him about Asoka.

'Queen Livia has high hopes for you,' he told Asoka, looking at his big bright eyes, high forehead and firm jaw.

'I am afraid,' Asoka said, smiling awkwardly, 'high hopes and high disappointment go hand in hand.' Just then a pretty girl of seven, her hair and face covered with dust, came charging into the room. She was dragging a white rabbit on lead.

Pushyagupta looked at her tenderly. 'Asoka, this is my granddaughter, Anga. Say hello to Prince Asoka.'

She dropped the leash, dusted off her eyes and took a good look at him. Her eyes widened. 'He! A prince?' She arched her eyebrows in disappointment. 'I thought princes came with red-turbaned soldiers and a loud band.'

Pushyagupta laughed and enclosed her in his arms, running his fingers through her hair. 'Anga, Asoka is not an emperor. He's a prince, come here to study.'

'Oh.' Forgetting what she had come for, Anga darted out of the room.

Pushyagupta asked, 'You like religion?'

Asoka looked down. 'I'm hoping it will help me.'

Bitan arrived to take Asoka to the university. Pushyagupta asked him to come back after lunch.

During the lunch, Pushyagupta asked, 'Do you like Taxila?'

Asoka beamed.

'I love it,' Pushyagupta said. 'Your grandfather and I spent years here before we defeated the Greeks. Taxila has a lot of distractions for the young. So be careful. A Persian friend put it in a poem. It goes:

Taxila, O Taxila! What art thou?

A bird, a beast, or a crust of glorious earth...

Beckoning men to light. Or just delight,

Rolling on your youthful breast.

Taxila was where Chandragupta went to meet Alexander at his court,' Pushyagupta told him, 'but Alexander threw him out.'

'How did he defeat the Greeks?'

'By their own tactics of horse-blitz. We were young and a little foolish but we came out all right.' He smiled. 'Chandragupta had an unconquerable will!'

'How did he know what he wanted?'

'He set his sight on the mountain top and never wavered from that. He believed he was beloved of the gods.'

His eyes wide, Asoka asked, 'Even after Alexander threw him out?'

'That made him all the more determined.'

Asoka sat nodding.

Later, Bitan took him to meet his religion teacher, Bhrigu, son of the famous Chankya who was Chandragupta's prime minister. Asoka expected a bald, lean, tall man, cast in the mould of his father. But under the open door sill before him stood a broad shouldered small man with a head full of hair and small eyes.

'Guruji,' Asoka said, surprised, 'I was only seven when your famous father died.'

Bhrigu smiled. 'He was not always famous. My father was lucky to have Chandragupta as his disciple. As for me, I have no interest in politics. I will die unsung, and that is fine with me.' Fascinated, Asoka watched Bhrigu's nostrils quivering like a bird flapping its wings. 'The rich, the famous,' Bhrigu muttered, 'eat from the same dust bowl as the unknown, the poor.'

Asoka got ready to leave. 'My father hated small kings,' Bhrigu said, 'and their petty intrigues, their endless fascination with aged wine and young women.'

On the way home, Asoka thought of Sasima and the little kings, overstuffed with food, alcohol and conceit. That night and many others, he fasted to prove to himself that he was somehow different.

15

Taxila University was built in the valley amid surroundings of natural beauty. Like a Buddhist monastery, it had a number of classrooms in a row off a rectangular brick verandah that opened onto spacious grounds. Young, curious, eager male minds came from all over India and abroad to study religion here, as well as mathematics, medicine, Sanskrit, grammar, astrology, archery, statecraft, and so on. Students made their own arrangements with teachers who were experts in their field. At a little distance from the verandah stood a majestic banyan tree, hundreds of years old, encased by a round baked-clay platform. Before and after class, students gathered there to chat, to horse around, or to just sit and watch other students. Nearby, a vendor hawked peanuts, guavas and oranges in winter, water chestnuts and sweet lime water in summer. At the outer edge of the sprawling grounds, a few plain brick buildings housed the students. Determined to live without princely privileges like his Baba, Asoka moved into one of the rooms.

Bhrigu was an impassioned teacher. On the first day of class he warned, 'Beliefs that can't stand scrutiny will fall. I always start with Caravaka, the apostle of sensual pleasure. Why? Because the philosophy of pleasure opens the door to the pleasures of philosophy. Odd as it sounds, pleasure liberates the strong and enslaves the weak.'

He spoke as one who had traveled down that road. 'Without the experience of pleasures, wisdom falls to platitudes. In his early life, Buddha was a Caravaka.'

'A materialist, Caravaka's philosophy is simple: there is no God, no heaven, and no soul. Body is the only reality, and pleasure the goal of life. The Vedas are lies, the rituals are lies; their sole purpose is to feed the lazy Brahmins. If a sacrificed animal reaches heaven, Caravaka said, why don't Brahmins kill their mother and father and send them to heaven?'

If *body is the only reality, why was I incarcerated?* Asoka wondered. In his mind, he was not guilty of rape. With his impressionable mind, he quickly embraced the philosophy of sensations. Soon at a party he met Risa, a blue-eyed Greek courtesan with a pretty face. She wore a long black skirt and a tight red choli that, after a few drinks, seemed filled with lots and lots of candy. Excited to meet a prince, she kept touching his body with her breasts. She told him she was eighteen and the grand-daughter of Alexander's General.

Bitan told him Risa had lied and that she was really the granddaughter of a disabled Greek soldier and the daughter of a sheep breeder. She was twenty, not eighteen, and had for four years been the mistress of Kalanos, the Taxila Administrator. Asoka forgave her the lies. 'She is pretty, and like all pretty young women, she's had no time for religion!'

Next day he trotted over in unkempt clothes to her house in the fashionable upper valley. She was waiting for him and came running to open the gate. A stout and dignified woman in her forties opened the door. 'My mother,' Risa said, escorting him inside.

He found no gods in the house. No Zeus, no Apollo, no Vishnu or Siva. He forgot about the gods when she invited him to spend the night. When she awoke in the morning, he was lying awake, anxious, his hands crossed over his forehead. She took him in her arms and whispered, 'I will teach you.' Excited, he exclaimed, 'And I will teach you the Vedas!' She tenderly caressed his lips and kissed him. 'She's so good, so sensitive!' he thought. 'Not like that girl in Pataliputra.'

In the class, he could not get Risa out of his head. 'Why is the Vedic religion so popular?' Bhrigu asked Asoka.

'I don't know,' Asoka said, lost in rather carnal thoughts.

Bhrigu explained, 'Because the Vedas filled our mundane lives with col-orful gods like Brahma, Vishnu, Rudra, Surya, Indra, and others. We love our gods because they are just like us: they enjoy butter, milk, grain, animal flesh and Soma, the salubrious drink, and they sleep with beautiful women. Our rituals keep us in touch with the gods. Our religion has given us rules to run our lives. Men don't like to think, and now they don't have to.'

'What are the sources of this religion?' he asked another student, avoiding Asoka.

'The four Vedas.'

Bhrigu elaborated, 'Written before 1500 BC, only the *Rig-Veda* is relevant to us. Others are ritualistic and meant for the priests. Though the gods have human form, their shapes are shadowy. Originally, the *Rig-Veda* allowed no idol worship, but faced with the Jain and Buddhist religions, whose human founders were becoming gods, the nervous Vedic priests filled their gods with manlike images. Suddenly, stone and wood began to vibrate with divinity.'

'Sun, Rain, and Fire are the first gods in the *Rig-Veda*. The concept of one God emerged later. The hymns were written not for reading but chanting during sacrificial rituals, when animal flesh and other foods were offered to gods. These rituals assured prosperity, progeny, health and longevity.'

If gods expect gifts, Asoka realized, Risa would want some too. He asked Choti-ma for extra money. When she learned the reason, she was displeased, and asked him to return to Pataliputra, and marry the daughter of Senapati, the Commander-in-Chief. 'She'll be good for your future too.' The idea of a woman mending his future was unthinkable to Asoka.

He gave Risa a ruby necklace. She loved it, immediately put it on, asked him how she looked, and standing before a mirror, kept turning, admiring herself, making faces. That night she slept draped around his body like a chewy rope candy. For the next few days, he sat in class craving her scent and the warm soft touch of her breasts.

He began keeping a beard and moustache, to look like a full man. She told him she liked his manly feet and big hands, his muscular, strong body. She said the rumor in the city was that Asoka would be Governor. He kept quiet, praying that Sasima would not be sent, afraid that he might take her away.

He told her that around the sixth century, the *Upanishads* expanded the idea of one god into the Ultimate Reality that inhabits every human

soul and permeates the whole creation. The ideas about the transmigration of soul, 'karma' and the birth-death cycle were also developed later
by the *Upanishads*. To amuse Risa, he told her about the 'Indra and the
Monkey' hymn. In the *Rig-Veda*, Indra tries to flatter his wife, "Your arms
and fingers are so lovely, your hair so long, your buttocks so broad, you are
the wife of a hero." After the *Atharva-veda* declared 'Kama,' sexual desire, a
god, he said, men lost all shame about sex. 'And who can blame them? If
pleasure is god, we are all devotees,' Asoka said, pulling her to him.

One evening he returned from class excited. 'Risa, I have something you will love!' Expecting jewelry, she lay down on her back in dim
lamplight, a small piece of diaphanous cloth covering her navel area.
Asoka lay close to her on his stomach, chin on his hands. He kissed
her breasts and pulled out a few palm leaves from his bag, 'This is the
famous "Creation" hymn!' He did not notice her turn her back to him
in displeasure. Head buzzing, he began:

> *There was neither non-existence nor existence then; neither the realm of space,*
> *nor the sky which is beyond;*
>
> *What stirred? Where? In whose protection?*
>
> *Was there water, bottomlessly deep?*

He paused and fondled her bottom but she pushed away his hand.
He rested a hand on her waist.

> *There was neither death nor immortality then.*
>
> *No distinguishing sign of night or of day.*
>
> *That one breathed, windless, by its own impulse.*
>
> *Only nothing beyond.*
>
> *Darkness was hidden by darkness in the beginning;*
>
> *No distinguishing sign, all this was water.*
>
> *The life force covered with emptiness, until one arose through the power of heat.*
>
> *Desire came upon that one in the beginning;*
>
> *That was the first seed of mind.'*

He stopped and looked long at the hollow of Risa's spine. His own desire stirred, and one hand moved to her breast, the other started crawling toward the hips. She pushed his hands away. Pausing, he gingerly moved one hand till it rested lightly on one breast, thinking, the "creation" feels so cold without the touch of warm flesh. At last, she smiled and let it be. All's well with the creation, he thought.

Poets seeking wisdom found the bond of existence

In non-existence.

Their cord was extended across.

Was there below? Above?

There were seed placers; there were powers.

There was impulse beneath;

And giving-forth above

Who really knows?

The gods came afterwards, with the creation of this universe

Who then knows whence it has arisen?

Perhaps it formed itself,

Or perhaps not.

The one who looks down on it, in the highest heaven, only he knows

—or perhaps he doesn't.

Lying on her stomach, chin on her hands, she said, 'It doesn't...satisfy!'

Softly circling her spinal cleft with his fingers, Asoka ventured, 'Creation is a mystery!'

'That can be experienced!' she said, pulling him down.

'The "spoken word" in the *Rig-Veda,*' he told her another day, 'is identified with Creator.' "Whom I love, I make awesome. (Speech) reveals itself"...as a loving wife, beautifully dressed, reveals her body to her husband." '

'I am not a wife,' Risa said, throwing a veil over her face.

Next day Bhrigu told Asoka that the city had a Governor— Sasima. That evening Risa was dark with rage, 'You said you would be Governor!'

One look at her told him he'd never convince her otherwise. *If only I were the Governor.*

'You're not the one for me.' Risa pursed her lips. 'I've been having these terrible headaches lately from listening to your crap. Who ever heard such profanity at my tender age?' Her face writhing with contempt, she said, 'You have thick lips, large feet and the body of a peasant! You read strange books. You are no prince! You are a prince-ling!'

16

This time he could not get mad or run away. His own powerlessness stared at him, whichever way he turned. It was galling, it was hopeless. And most humiliating, he missed Risa. She'd left an intangible hole in his heart. Loneliness had entered his life.

Filled with self-loathing, he decided to fast. Fasting is a versatile tool, his mother had told him. It punishes the body and strengthens the soul. Given to extremes, Asoka lived on bits of cabbage and rice for the next three months, wandering the valley, brooding, seeing in sensuality nothing but ruin.

Suddenly a misogynist, he told Bitan, 'She left a bad taste in my mouth. Vanity rules all women. They wear perfume like a sword, and think of nothing but the body. To think she hated religion! I had no idea such people existed!'

Bitan nodded sympathetically. 'Strange how religion works. When I was sixteen, I fell in love with this beautiful ascetic woman who didn't change her robe for months. "My religion," she said, "treats the body like dirt." She was too religious.' Bitan smiled.

Asoka said, 'They're all crazed. In no time, she passed from twenty to twenty-eight. She drove me out of my mind.'

'Unfortunate, but predictable. Don't let a woman like Risa affect your life. Grandfather says one bad experience in early life is good for you. And you've had two so you should climb great heights. Now I'm in love with Jaya, and it's very different. Caravaka was wrong. Pleasure's good for the body, but we have feelings too.'

Asoka looked at Bitan with distrust. 'I don't think women know that!'

Hankering to be someone, he buried himself in his studies. He debated with himself, rose early in the morning, watched the goddess

Ushas, bowed to the Sun; when the clouds gathered and lightning flashed in the sky, he became Indra's thunderbolt.

He rejected the *Upanishads* and their endless preoccupation with soul. He found them abstract and boring— too fluffy and tenuous for his worldly needs. He rejected the *Bhagwad-Gita*, which advocated action without the desire for fruit. *The springs of my action will always be the fruit,* he knew. It was the *Rig-Veda* world of gods, who fulfill desire that he eagerly embraced. For two years he read, and searched the scripture for clues to greatness.

In one of his ruminative walks in the valley, brooding over the thirty-three Vedic gods and the reason for the fame of gods, he thought: *They did not create the universe. They came after the Creation, and they claim no moral greatness—some of them are downright rowdy. They kill and lie for power. Indra killed his father to become the god of three worlds. Soma, the intoxicating drink god, is famous because he can exalt and make men feel invincible. Terrible Siva spreads disasters and diseases and kills with flamboyance. The gods are small or great according to their power. First they acquired power, did some good deed for mankind and became immortal. But I don't want to be a god. It's greatness I seek.'*

A thought occurred to him. *These gods were not born with power. How did they get it?* Then it flashed. *They seized it! Indra killed his father. Baba seized power by killing other kings.* 'I got it!' he cried, elated, like the caveman who discovered light. *I can't be a god, but I could be Governor. Maybe even king.*

If I were a god and had one woman here, one there—men would sing of my amorous deeds, he thought. *And if I were Governor, I could have had Risa until I was fed up with her.* It surprised him how nakedly power was worshipped— power that did not enhance a man the way knowledge or wisdom did. *Power is a mask that dazzles the beholder, and deludes the wearer. Clothe a sheep like Sasima in Governor's dress and men kiss his feet, women fall all over him. That's the reality of power. And then there's the reality! Was the mask bigger than the man? Perhaps, because men did not want to let go of it? Perhaps, men become the mask.*

He joined Narad's statecraft class. Narad was thirty-two, a tall, bony man with bulbous eyes and a tuft on his head like an antenna, collecting information from all directions, to predict the rise and fall of kings in the South. This had made him a rich and famous man. A shrewd teacher, Narad sensed a hunger in Asoka. Narad told him about the workings of power using Chanakya's *Arthasastra*, the famous text. "Hungry men kill, and the satisfied become dyspeptic and get killed."

'How was power seized?'

'By patience, preparation and pluck. Keep a hawk's eye. Pounce at the ripe moment.'

Waking or sleeping, Asoka began conversing with gods, convinced they would reveal him the ripe moment.

One evening he went to a gilded hall, where the Brahmins were holding the Soma festival. Soma was the drink that makes "men feel the gods within their veins." All the gods plus some from the public had been invited. In one corner, a man stood completely covered in a black cloak. No one went near him. 'He is Yama, the god of death,' a Brahmin told him. 'He does not care. "They will come, one and all!" says the proud Yama.'

Asoka wandered off to where two Brahmins were serving Soma in small earthen cups behind a large table. Gods stood in a long line in front of the table: Indra (Thunderstorm), Agni (Fire), Varuna (Sky), Sun, the Moon and other gods – scrambling to push ahead in the line, the bigger ones impudently shoving past the smaller ones. One small god, Daksa, was tossed out, and fell flat on his nose. In his eagerness to get Soma before it ran out, he had climbed onto the shoulders of Indra, the top god. 'You don't do that!' a small god told him in passing, without stopping to help him. Asoka helped Daksa to his feet. 'The Soma here is free! No favors to return!' Daksa, the little god, said, straightening his bent nose. Another god overheard. He said, 'Free! Even the gods are not free. Ask any Brahmin!'

In middle of the hall he saw the head of Brahma himself sticking out of a long red tent, mouth half-open, eyes closed in ecstasy. 'What is he doing?' Asoka asked a Brahmin. 'Creation! Creation! And more Creation! Going crazy! Turning the earth into an anthill,' the Brahmin said, laconically.

In another part of the hall, god Vishnu floated on lotus flowers in a golden tub filled with Soma. Surprised, Asoka said, 'You in a tub?'

'Keeping an eye on my children,' Vishnu said, drooling Soma from his mouth. Asoka's eyes fell on a beautiful woman clothed in a black star-studded dress. It was Ratri, the night goddess. *The queen of love and the queen of deception*, thought Asoka, *helping men cover deeds they will disown in the morning.*

He kept looking for Siva. Hearing a drumbeat in the distance, he walked and saw Siva whirling away like the eye of a hurricane to the sounds of Chimta, Dhap, and Damru, his favorite musical instruments. His skull necklace, his blood-dripping-hide, thrilled Asoka. Excited, he joined in, but quickly fell out of step. Asoka woke up in a sweat. 'I danced with Siva!' he said, flinging his body up in the air with joy.

In the magical world of gods where gods performed deeds for fame and glory, the paradoxical Siva fascinated Asoka. Siva is Eros, creator, Siva is destroyer. Siva demands that Parvati, his wife, be a complete ascetic, a yogin, when he meditates (sometimes these spells last a thousand years) and a lustful, panting mistress when he is roused. Siva is imperious. He reduces Kama, the god Eros, to ashes when Kama interrupts his meditation. And Siva has a third eye–the inward eye of wisdom—that he rarely uses. Asoka saw himself in the paradoxes of Siva, sometimes thinking he was Siva.

Gods became gods by taking the amoral road. He waited for his moment, believing he was the beloved of the gods.

17

While pursuing his studies for three years in Taxila, Asoka kept getting the news: Charu had married Sisupal, Visal was fighting in Persia. Livia kept pressuring Asoka to return to Pataliputra. Bitan was in love with Jaya. She wanted Asoka to meet her elder sister, Nachita.

Asoka and Bitan drove in a carriage to the western part of city. Jaya's father was a merchant of Persian and Greek wines who had translated the romance and mystique of imported wines into several fancy marble toilets–his own toilet had a harp hanging from the ceiling on one side of the seat, and a lute on the other.

In one big room, the women appeared, smiling, preened with talcum powder on their faces and lampblack round their eyes. Jaya, eighteen, was slightly built, with big, warm eyes. Her reserve pleased Asoka, and he was green with envy of Bitan. Nachita was taller, with a livelier face. She was under pressure to marry, to clear the path, so her younger sister Jaya could marry Bitan. The whole community was engaged in the noble enterprise of finding her a suitable boy.

Nachita talked freely, asked Asoka about Pataliputra, the city and its people, and he asked her how she spent her days. She worshipped the god Vishnu, she said, and believed in reincarnation and fate. 'What is fate?' he asked.

'Whatever happens is destined to happen,' she said with conviction.

A recent authority on gods, Asoka disagreed, 'We are not puppets flapping our wings in the dark. Our destiny is in our hands. We can soar to the sun.'

'What do you mean?'

His ardor cooled.

He told Bitan, 'She is attractive enough to stir up my feelings, but not pretty enough to dispel my doubts.'

'Doubts? What doubts?' Bitan asked, eager to dispel his doubts.

'That she understands religion!'

'When I met Jaya, I had different doubts.'

'Like?'

'Does she love me? Or does she not?'

Asoka said he'd wait to see his destiny unfold. Still soured by experience, he was plagued by the fear he was not meant for love: *I am not attractive enough, and perhaps I brood too much.*

'My marriage...,' Bitan said, but stopped.

Asoka jumped in, 'When is it?'

'My mother wants it now. But father wants to pay off his debts first.'

The Pushyagupta family had a reputation for great wealth. Asoka was shocked. 'Debts, wedding?' He threw his hands up. 'What's the connection?'

'Asoka,' Bitan hesitated, 'my father's been gambling and losing big.'

Asoka bit his lip. After a pause, Bitan said, 'He was a prudent man until Sasima arrived. Now they're friends and father's drinking and gambling in his company.'

'Can't your grandfather stop him?'

Bitan sighed. 'He tried. He even had me accompany father a few times. I watched the anguish of hope on his face when the dice rolled, and the anguish of despair when it stopped. Baba says father will end up like Yudhisthara.'

Asoka laughed. 'Not get us into the Mahabhabharata war, I hope!'

'I wouldn't be surprised!'

Asoka's eyes grew wide. 'You must be joking!'

Embarrassed, Bitan said, 'Asoka, it's time you met real people and found out what's going on in the city.' He would not say more.

Asoka returned home feeling uneasy. He was not finished with Narad, but putting an end to his studies, he swung into action. With his usual zeal and curiosity, he started mixing with ordinary people and army officials, using his credentials as a disgruntled prince. He was shocked by how much the locals resented Mauryan rule. Persians had lived for two hundred years in Taxila region—it had once been part of the Persian Empire. When describing a Persian province, the Greek historian Herodotus, had first used the name India referring to this region of the Indus river. Then Alexander conquered the Persian Empire, including the Taxila region, and settled a large Greek garrison in Taxila. Afghans, from neighboring Afghanistan, had also been living in this area. Spirited and independent, they detested all rulers. All these different people had a burning desire to overthrow the Mauryas, these rulers with strange gods. That there had been no war for over twenty-five years did not help. The young were restless.

Discontent is ingrained in human nature. Always, the present seems drab, especially when an imagined past looks glorious. Kalanos, thirty-five years and the son of a disabled Greek soldier and Hindu mother, was the Administrator of Taxila. In the new Mauryan Governor, Sasima, Kalanos saw a weak ruler lost in pleasures. Kalanos won Sasima's trust by informing him about the rising discontent and promised to turn the tide by explaining the benefits of Mauryan rule. 'Unfortunately,' he told Sasima, 'your presence is an impediment to peace.' Afraid to aggravate the situation, Sasima moved to Ujjain in Central India. Now, Kalanos began plotting the secession of Taxila.

Kalanos was a swarthy man with stiff black hair and black eyes, and a rough face like a yellow lemon rind. After his mother died at three, his father had married a Greek woman and he had been raised on everything Greek: language, gods, food and wine. Without a wife now, he survived on a couple of Greek mistresses. Curiously, his hair always stood upright, like stiff blades of grass. He had tried oil, water and lard. But his rebellious hair would not be quelled.

The situation took a grave turn. News arrived that Seleucus, the Greek emperor of Persia and father of Livia, had been murdered by Ceranaus Ptolemy, son of Ptolemy, the Greek King of Egypt. Kalanos invited the new Greek King, Antiochus – Seleucus's heir – to invade Taxila. He hoped to become the king of Taxila under the suzerainty of the Greek king.

To incite people against the Maurya rule, Kalanos increased taxes on alcohol and gambling. Protests increased, and looting became common in the city.

To maintain law and order in the region, Mauryas kept an army often thousand men at Taxila fort. Kalanos connived with the Garrison Commander, won the officers over to his side by paying them extra, and promised the soldiers higher pay after the secession. He also started hiring Greek mercenaries.

Asoka rushed to see Pushyagupta, who had been ill for some time.

'Uncle, you don't look well!' he said affectionately.

Pushyagupta smiled feebly. 'Asoka, I am ready to fall off the cliff. Tell me, how have you been?'

'Could be better, without all this talk of secession.'

Pushyagupta became serious. 'A crisis tests the will of a nation just as it does an individual's. One wrong move and you are history!'

Asoka shifted his legs as Pushyagupta continued, 'Things have not been going well. Sasima decamped at the wrong time without taking a firm stand. Now, Taxila needs at least twenty thousand men from Pataliputra to get matters under control.'

Asoka gasped. Pushyagupta shook his head. 'Kalanos smells blood. If the King hesitates, Taxila will be lost.'

Asoka felt grim. 'How did we come to such a pass?'

Pushyagupta stroked his chin. 'I am not sure the King knows all the facts. Today I'm sending him a letter by royal courier.' He added, 'If

Kalanos takes Taxila—which he can any day–Antiochus may move in. His army is massed at the border.'

Asoka felt faint. 'I will take the letter to the King.'

Pushyagupta looked surprised. Piercing Asoka with his pale eyes, he said, 'Come back later today.'

Asoka left that day.

18

In Pataliputra, Livia told Asoka, 'Marut is going to be sent as Governor of Taxila. Now that you're here, you must marry Senapati's youngest daughter.'

Asoka frowned. Marrying his way to the throne was not his idea of destiny. 'Choti-ma, I have no time for marriage. Marry her to Tissa.'

'She's good for you, not Tissa. He wants a beautiful girl,' Livia said matter-of-factly.

Asoka glared at her, thinking, *And I'm the dumping ground!*

'I know you, Asoka. You'll always be obsessed with something. Without my help, you'll end up with a courtesan or a slave girl, like Dasrath. I'll send the proposal today. It's very important you marry her. And leave Taxila alone! You're not the Governor! At least it keeps Sasima out of Pataliputra.'

Asoka looked coldly at Livia. *She's really getting old!* He jumped up impatiently. 'Chotima! I heard you!' He left.

The Council was in session. Asoka left word for Radhagupta, who was now the prime minister. When he returned, Livia was still sulking. He sat down beside her and put his arm around her. Livia's frown disappeared. Tenderly she said, 'Dasrath is seriously ill. Go see him in the infirmary.'

Shocked, Asoka said, 'I am sorry, but I can't see him until I meet the King,' and left abruptly.

Dasrath should have left Pataliputra, he thought. *He should have left Bhairavi. Done something! Anything not to die so young.*

Next day, while the Council was in session, Asoka gave the letter to the King sitting in his high chair. Six lamps lit the big room.

Bindusar read the letter, then read it again. His brows knitted, he left his chair and began to pace the room. 'Revolt? And no word from the governor!'

He turned to Radhagupta, 'Can you read Sasima's last letter?'

Radhagupta pulled the letter from a box and read. "There has been some recent unrest in the city. The situation is under control. I am going to Ujjain for a few days."

The King made a hissing sound and gave Asoka a piercing look. 'Are you done with philosophy, or what?'

Asoka looked his father in the eye. 'Father, for the last few months I've done nothing but meet the public, the army and government officials. I've discussed the situation with Pushyagupta. I am here for your orders.'

The King stood looking out the window. 'Pushyagupta recommends that I appoint you as Royal Representative.'

Asoka was pleased. 'Father, I think...'

'I'm glad someone is thinking!' the King said wryly. 'About the army, talk to Radhagupta.' Asoka heaved a sigh of relief. No warm words from his father. But he felt satisfied. For the time being.

19

Next morning, Bindusar cut short his usual hour-long oil massage, rushed through the bath, and wrapped in a towel, returned to the chamber. Female attendants swooped down, wiped him dry, dressed him and pushed the crown tight over his head. After sending the attendants away, he stood gazing in the mirror—at the wrinkles on his forehead, the bags under his eyes and his sagging double chin. 'The face of the Emperor and the Empire doesn't look so pretty,' he muttered. 'It's under siege from both time and rebels. Decay! Death!' Tilting his head back, he stretched the loose skin under his chin, while still peering in the mirror, until the crown fell and started to roll away. Chasing after it, he picked it up and put it back on his head, mumbling, 'Not easy keeping the damn thing in place!'

He was about to step outside when the door creaked and the chief queen abruptly walked in. Closing the door behind her, she softly said, 'I am sorry, my Lord! I have an urgent item for the Council.'

The King's eyebrows contracted. 'I have no time.'

He was heading for the door when the queen flung her formidable body in front of him. 'My Lord! Call back Sasima. Poor child! He's been sick in Ujjain all this time and didn't even have the courage to tell you, his own father. Let Asoka take care of Taxila!'

Bindusar stepped back. 'Sick? He fled Taxila!' he said angrily.

The queen pressed on. 'Great King, he was seriously ill. I neglected to tell you. What do I know of these things? I apologize.'

When Bindusar's face softened, she said, 'If you think about it, he shouldn't have been sent to Taxila. Your father never sent you away from Pataliputra.'

The King shouted, 'Leave my father out of this!'

The queen hung her head. 'Taxila is so cold! He had to go away for his health.'

Bindusar left frustrated. 'There is always something wrong with these princes! The empire's the last thing on their minds!'

A message was sent to Sasima: 'Asoka will take charge. Return to Pataliputra.'

Reading the King's order, Sasima began to sweat. 'Have I been dismissed?' He stood brooding, blaming himself. 'I should never have trusted that snake, Kalanos. But how was I to know?'

Next day a message arrived from his mother. 'I am worried about your illness. The King wants you back.'

Illness? What illness? There must be a mistake. Baffled, Sasima read the message again, and a smile crept over his face, 'Oh! Mother!' he exclaimed. He was filled with a new admiration for her.

Radhagupta was to lead twenty thousand men to Taxila and Asoka was appointed as Special Representative to negotiate with Kalanos.

Having finished his work, Asoka went to see Dasrath. He had not seen him in three years. To reach the infirmary, he followed the winding garden path north-west of the palace between the fragrant rows of flower shrubs. At the hospital verandah, the smell of medicinal herbs and sweat and blood hit him. Dasrath's room was at the end of the corridor. A male nurse was leaving with a plate of left-over food. The malodor was strong inside the dimly lit room. A woman sat on the head of his bed facing the wall, vigorously massaging Dasrath's scalp. Without a word, Asoka opened the window overlooking the green grounds to let in fresh air, and lit two lamps near the bed.

He now turned to look at Dasrath. A gust of cold wind blew in, waking him. He coughed, slightly raised his head, then said feebly, 'Oh, Bhairavi! Look! Look! Asoka!'

Bhairavi sprang to her feet, rearranged her du-pata and covered her head. Asoka looked at her youthful face to which light had added a patina. Quietly walking to the window, she closed it, blew out the two lamps, and hurried from the room before Asoka could ask her about Dasrath's health.

In the dim light, Dasrath looked like a ghost. *'Death and darkness, darkness and death…,'* Asoka thought, remembering his mother dying in a dark room. A smile settled on Dasrath's gaunt face. *It is as unfitting as a three-year-old girl playing on a tomb*, Asoka thought.

A copy of the *Bhagwad-Gita* lay face down on a table by his bed. Skeleton-like shadows flickered on the walls. Asoka had left a dear brother in good health: the man lying before him had cavernous eyes, and a hollowed face with bulging red veins. Speechless, Asoka stifled tears welling up inside. Dasrath seemed like a ghost of his own excesses. *And yet*, he thought, *there is something magnificent about him, in his unwavering attachment to Bhairavi, in his defiance of the King and Queen. He is more moral than any man I know.* Asoka was covered with shame.

Dasrath's face flickered between pain and a smile; his murmurs were enmeshed in the foam around his mouth. Feebly he pressed Asoka's hand, and turned away his face to hide his sadness.

Asoka sat down on a chair by his bed. *How we played together with Sasima, Marut and Pavan*, he thought, *chasing the cackling peacocks in the rain. Splashing each other with red and yellow water during the color festival. Life was care-free then, like the birds. And now!*

A hopelessness came over him and he sat with eyes closed, feeling alone. Hearing Dasrath mumble, he opened his eyes and stared at him.

'I know Asoka,' Dasrath blurted out, 'I know. For the last few months I have been reading the *Bhagwad-Gita*. She listens when I read. That gives me peace.' Exhausted, his head slumped to the side and he asked for water.

Asoka gave him a cup and said unsteadily, 'Dasrath, I'll soon be leaving for Taxila. Tell me what you want me to do when you're gone.'

He wanted to say, 'Don't worry Dasrath, you'll get well.' But he couldn't. He wouldn't be weak, and admit to his feelings.

'Do something for the slaves,' Dasrath softly said. Then he seemed to gather his strength. 'Will I be re-born a man?'

Feeling silly, Asoka just nodded.

Dasrath lifted his eyelids a minute later. 'You're studying philosophy. Tell me about the *Upanishads.*'

It is neither the time nor place. Why doesn't he ask me about the uprising in Taxila? Asoka wondered. *Or why I'm here? What I've been doing? Why I didn't come earlier? He accepts things so easily. Maybe once hope leaves us, nothing matters anymore.*

Asoka paused. '*Upanishads* are for the ascetics, not for you and me. With luck, you'll be released from the cycle of birth and death.'

'How?' Dasrath's eyes widened in the deep sockets.

'Imagine there are two Brahmas. One, the creator of universe—in space and time, the ever changing—the other, timeless, that which existed before the sun. That timeless Brahma, the "Reality" is also in you. The difference is like the difference between shadow and light. But in that flash in which you see the difference, you can become One with the Timeless.'

'Asoka, I have led a dissolute life. Do you think I can get to God?' Dasrath's simplicity and sadness tore at Asoka's heart.

'You have to believe,' Asoka searched for something comforting to say. 'Perhaps the path of love is possible for you.' He lit a lamp, and picked up the *Gita.*

Let him give up all thought of 'I', force, pride...

...And now again give ear to this my all-highest Word,

Of all the most mysterious,

I love thee well

Therefore I will tell thee (of) salvation.

Bear me in mind, love Me and worship Me,

So shalt thou come to Me, I promise thee

Truly, for thou art dear to Me.

When he looked up, tears were streaming down Dasrath's cheeks. He wheezed, 'Asoka, if God loves men, why do I suffer? Why does Bhairavi suffer?'

Asoka had no answer and Dasrath murmured, 'I made nothing of my life.'

Stiffening inside, Asoka said, 'You lived life your way, that's the best a man can do. The *Gita* says Soul is immortal. It is neither born nor does it die. For the soul, every birth is only a change of dress.'

Smiling now, Dasrath took Asoka's hand. 'I don't know if the soul is immortal. Or if there is heaven. All I know is there is God. And good or bad, I am part of Him.' He had achieved his own salvation at last.

Dasrath opened his eyes and stared at Asoka. A gleam came into his eyes. 'You will be a king, Asoka, I see.' Asoka looked up. *Where was the voice coming from?* On the ceiling, only the shadows danced.

The door creaked and Charu came in with a plate of warm food. Moving the *Gita* away, she put it down there. Asoka pulled the table closer to Dasrath's bed. Feeding him a few bites, Charu smiled feebly. 'Asoka, I heard you have been here three days.' Her forced smile said she was annoyed with him.

Asoka took her hand. 'I had work to finish, Charu. If I visited him first, I could not have done anything.'

Charu's eyes conveyed scorn. Dasrath wobbled his right hand toward her. 'She loves me.' Charu left the room in tears.

Suddenly Asoka felt suffocated. 'I will leave early tomorrow.' He got up, taking Dasrath's hand. 'You look better now.' Outside, the sun was setting. He stood there collecting his thoughts. *Nothing matters to the gods.*

On the path across, he saw Bhairavi briskly walking toward the infirmary, her gaze fixed, a few forelocks, like strands of twisted thought, on her forehead. She held the leads of two apricot-colored puppies bounding in front of her like a pair of spirited horses. *She has charm and above all youth, which is beauty itself*, Asoka thought. *Why does she have such power over Dasrath? Is she Shakti—the female energy? Or Kali, the destroyer?*

She abruptly turned her head, saw him, stopped and greeted him with folded hands. Asoka bowed in bewilderment.

Next morning, he visited Charu. 'Charu, I am sorry for Dasrath.'

Charu broke down. 'If you stay here, he will recover. He has no one but you.'

'Charu, I can't save him, nor can you. Not even Bhairavi.' Impulsively, he said, 'Charu, if he died, you will have just as loving a brother in me.' He kissed her on the cheek. 'I must go, I have to.' Then he hesitated. 'If it were another time, I would have asked, Are you happy? Now, when Dasrath is about to die, our happiness does not matter. Perhaps, another time we will talk of these things that mean nothing...' 'And everything,' he mumbled under the breath.

Charu nodded coldly. It was not that his heart had turned to stone. Doing was everything to him; seeking sympathy was an excuse for inaction and self-pity. From the gods he had learnt there was no pity in the heavens.

After he left, Livia sent a letter to Antiochus, her brother, informing him that her son Asoka, was now responsible for putting down the unrest in Taxila.

But Dasrath stayed on his mind. 'He lost Bhairavi, and now he will lose his life. Why? He hesitated. He always hesitated.' An indescribable sadness gripped him.

In the midst of his pain, Dasrath's words rang in his ears, "Asoka, you will be king." A weakness crept up in his knees.

20

Asoka went straight to Pushyagupta to thrash out the plan he had hatched on horseback.

'I will call the traitor for negotiations, make a conciliatory offer, and have his head cut off by his own guards.'

Pushyagupta burst into laughter, and Asoka frowned.

Pushyagupta became serious. 'Only a twenty-year-old would come up with such a plan. Not that it's not ingenious.'

Shaken, Asoka said, 'His guards and soldiers have to be from the Magadha army—he cannot trust the mercenaries. I don't believe Kalanos has their full loyalty. I need only one conflicted guard to do my bidding.'

Pushyagupta nodded, 'The guards may be loyal but still fail to act. And therein lies the rub.'

'True,' Asoka admitted.

'There is a bigger risk,' Pushyagupta continued, 'You may not come out alive. Kalanos is no fool.'

Asoka said with spirit, 'The alternative is civil war.'

Pushyagupta explained, 'Let us think it through: can Kalanos seize Taxila? Yes. Can he keep it? No—unless Antiochus intervenes. And if Antiochus does intervene, all the Greeks in Taxila—and there are thousands of them—will join him. The Persians and the Afghans will also support him. Taxila will be lost. The consequences will be grave. Just a few miles west of Taxila, is the Khyber pass, the door for entering India from Greece, Central Asia and Persia—the Aryans, Alexander, all took this route. Taxila's occupation by a foreign power will set the stage for a fullblown invasion of the Maurya Empire. All the advantages that Chandragupta obtained by treaty with Seleucus would be lost.'

Asoka sat thinking, a*ll the traitors will have to be killed.*

Pushyagupta saw the clouds on his face. 'Realistically, Asoka, I don't think Antiochus will intervene. Just come to the throne, he needs time to consolidate his power. On his western border Ptolemy II Philadelphus is breathing down his neck. Why open two war fronts and risk losing it all? So Kalanos will come to the table. But you can't give him what he wants, so he'll take your head.'

'What'll he get from my head?'

'Kalanos wants be the Satrap (Head) of Taxila under Magadha suzerainty. He hopes when your head rolls, the terror-stricken Magadha army will capitulate. That'll get him what he wants.'

Asoka pursed his lips. 'I'll have to move fast. And if I fail, only one head will be lost.'

'It is the head of a dear prince!'

Touched, Asoka softly said, 'The risk is still worth it, looking at the stakes!'

Pushyagupta reluctantly said, 'If your heart is set, have it your way. But throw some bait to the guards.' Pleased, Asoka nodded.

Arriving with the army, Radhagupta told Asoka that Dasrath had died. Asoka's eyes became moist. 'He was very dear to me. Selfless and giving, and I could not do anything for him.' He asked Livia to take care of Bhairavi.

Asoka sent Narad as his envoy to Kalanos with the message: "The King is ready to negotiate, but only in an atmosphere of amity. As a gesture of good faith, each party will bring nine guards and twenty-five soldiers. You can choose any site except the Fort."

Kalanos chose the Governor's Hall for the meeting, and demanded that the Magadha army stay fifteen miles away from the city limits. Asoka accepted his terms and a date was set.

Asoka issued instructions to Radhagupta, 'Seal the Kabul border with three thousand men so the emperor of Persia, Antiochus, knows we are not about to roll over. Stop any traitor from entering or escaping the border. When I go into the meeting, have our infantry men in civilian clothes gather on the Fort road. Kalanos must not reach the Fort alive.'

The evening before, Bitan came to see Asoka. Sitting on the floor, he ate from a plate in his hand and studied a map spread in front of him of the Hall and surrounding areas.

Bitan warned, 'Asoka, be careful! Kalanos is ruthless!'

Asoka smiled. 'The food has not tasted so good in years!'

Bitan hesitated. 'Asoka, perhaps it's not the right time. But I had to let you know, Nachita will be married soon. You can still have her, if you decide in the next two days.'

Asoka looked at Bitan, his eyes wide. 'Now?' He carried his food to the window and stood looking at the gathering darkness in the evening sky.

'You gave her no hope.'

Asoka murmured, 'Perhaps! I can't think of her now.'

He came back, sat down and looked at the map again.

He heard Bitan mutter as he left, 'Not one word about Nachita.'

In the morning, Asoka addressed his men, 'Loyal soldiers! Our mission is to get Kalanos' head. Don't be distracted by what I say or do in the meeting. Carry a small knife inside your vest. If I get killed, don't panic or run. Don't leave the Hall without killing Kalanos. You will be amply rewarded.' He added, 'Enjoy your meal and meet me in two hours at the Hall.'

21

Clad in a golden dress and a gold and red headdress emblazoned with the red Royal Crest, surrounded by his guards and accompanied by twenty five soldiers, Asoka appeared in the Hall. It was lit by rows of torches along both sides. His soldiers took their positions behind him in five rows. Five steps up, Kalanos sat on a wooden platform in a gilded chair, his guards behind him and on the sides. He wore a gold embroidered red cloak, his thick neck was lost in his sunken shoulders, and his hair, as usual, stood in rebellion. Both men stared at each other for a while.

After presenting his credentials Asoka said, 'The emperor sends you greetings.'

'Convey ours too.' Kalanos looked amused, stroking his broad chin, staring at him with a faint smile. *Is this the best the Maurya emperor could do?*

Asoka read his thoughts. The door creaked, and a Magadha soldier entered with a deep green emerald necklace laid out on a plate of gold. Kalanos looked down, gazed at it to determine if it was real, then smiled. Asoka picked it up, dangling it in the air for every soldier to see.

Holding up the Egyptian necklace, he said, 'Your Excellency, this is a reward for your services to the King.'

Kalanos gestured to a guard and a tall, thin, young man with a trimmed moustache and tapered short beard came down the steps. Staring greedily at the necklace, he picked it up between his fingers and palm and went back up the stairs, caressing the jewels. With one last envious look, he slipped it over Kalanos' thick short neck.

Kalanos looked pleased, muttering, 'Not bad for the son of a disabled Greek soldier!' He stroked the necklace and smiled. 'The emperor knows the price of peace!'

While Kalanos fiddled with the jewels, Asoka stopped to meet the eye of Kalanos' guards and said, 'The mighty emperor thanks his loyal guards and loyal soldiers.'

He continued, 'God loves the emperor. The emperor loves the guards, and his soldiers. Loyal guards! Loyal soldiers! The King depends on your loyalty as you depend on the King. Let us thank the emperor with a ringing cry of "Long live the emperor!"'

The Hall resounded with cheers. Kalanos watched, uncertain. When the sounds died down, Asoka announced, 'Loyal guards, loyal soldiers! We are here to negotiate peace. So I ask each one of you, including my soldiers, to lay down your arms.'

Seeing Kalanos' eyebrows arch, Asoka hastily added, 'The guards will keep their arms.'

His soldiers walked to the end of the Hall and laid their arms against the wall. Nervously, Asoka watched Kalanos' soldiers. They looked at one another. At last, one broke from the line and slowly marched to put down his arms. Soon, others followed.

Asoka noticed the tapered-beard guard still staring at the necklace. A gleam came to Asoka's eyes.

Asoka proceeded, 'Your Excellency, state your terms for peace.'

Kalanos was ready. 'What does the King have to offer?'

'Your Excellency, I have no authority to make any offer.'

Kalanos had come to negotiate. He quickly said, 'To be Taxila King!'

Asoka's temples turned red. He stared at Kalanos' guards. 'Taxila King!' Asoka repeated, Yes! King of Taxila! King! Of course, King!'

It sounded ridiculous even to the soldiers.

Staring at the tapered beard guard, Asoka slowly said, 'Loyal guards! The King wants,' and added with emphasis, 'the King orders you to sever the traitor's head! The necklace will be your reward.'

Inflamed, his sword drawn, Kalanos leapt from his chair. The tapered-beard, mustached young guard, thrust his spear into Kalanos' back. Pushed by the force, Kalanos fell face down on the last step. Another guard jumped on him, and straddling Kalanos' bleeding back, slashed his thick neck while the first speared him a second time and left the spear deep in his back. Then both soldiers pulled the blood-soiled necklace along with strands of flesh, looked at each other and at the necklace, and holding it high above their heads, ran out of the Hall. Panic spread: Kalanos' soldiers scrambled to get out while Asoka's men rushed to pick up the severed head.

All day Kalanos' head was paraded on the streets. Later in the day, it was hung over a pole in the centre of town. Radhagupta fanned out his army to rope in the traitors. Asoka himself went on a killing spree. For seven days blood flowed in the streets of Taxila as army officers, mercenaries, and their families and friends - most of them Greeks, some Persians - were massacred. 'There shall be no mercy, they deserve none,' Asoka told Radhagupta. 'No Greek, no Persian in Taxila should think of treachery for the next one hundred years.' He pardoned the Magadha soldiers. 'The soldiers are innocent. The officers knew the mischief they were doing.'

22

When it was all over, Asoka collapsed in bed. Emptiness filled him. He brooded. *So many had to be killed. But given the choice between a bloodbath or the loss of Taxila— the most important limb of this empire — it had to be done. Faced with dire situations, a worshipper of Siva turns into a destroyer. Empires are born of blood and sometimes they need more blood to survive. I killed the foreigners with rage, thinking, You are not innocent. You knew the cost of treachery. And yet,* he sighed, *I wish there was no spilling of blood.*

He knew that the persistent emptiness sprang from his longing for tenderness, for love. 'Without someone to hold in my arms, victory feels hollow.'

In time, Asoka's name became synonymous with Bhima, the legendary warrior in the *Mahabharata*, who drank the blood of his enemy after killing him. Preferring order to chaos and killings, the people of Taxila were reconciled. Now they could leave their houses, go out, shop and eat spicy food in the bazaar, sit on their porches in the evenings without fear of being dragged out and knifed. They could tell their children the story of the young prince, and the shining green jewels.

He was not through, yet. His eyes on the mountaintop, he rushed to show the brined head of Kalanos to the people of Pataliputra and to his father, the King. He rode there along the royal boulevard with Kalanos' head on the tip of his spear, high in the air. Citizens lined the streets, wildly waving and cheering, "Asoka, Asoka. We love Asoka!" The horse race swam before his eyes. Drunk with excitement, he appeared at court, bowed and with a flourish, presented the grotesque head to the King on the same shining gold platter on which he had offered Kalanos the emerald necklace. The King's warm embrace told Asoka that he had redeemed himself in his father's heart. He was filled with joy.

That day, the King appointed him Governor of Ujjain. To avoid the perception of hostile rule by the Mauryas, Bitan was appointed the

Administrator of Taxila. He was a local, and unrelated to the King. Every soldier at Taxila's Fort was sent back to Pataliputra, and replaced by soldiers from Radhagupta's contingent in Taxila.

The time had come to bid farewell. Asoka first went to see his teacher, Narad, who had opened his eyes to the working of power. Narad embraced and blessed him. 'You have the daring of Chandragupta.' Then he added, 'May you be the crown prince!'

Has he read my thoughts? Asoka wondered,

Then he visited Pushyagupta. 'You have been like a grandfather to me. I thank you for all the wisdom you gave me.'

Pushyagupta said in an unsteady voice, 'Today, Chandragupta would have been proud!' He smiled. 'And don't worry about wisdom. It comes when pleasures fall—and one day fall they will, from their high horse. I'd trade my wisdom any day for a few of my lost pleasures!' He stroked his white hair, laughing. 'Before you go, I want you to see the Amaltas tree in our garden. Next time you visit, I will be there in my bed.'

Pushyagupta sent for Bitan, but instead Anga, now ten, walked in with a pony tail and wearing a red dress. Fluttering her eyelashes, she said, 'Yes, Baba?' Eyes twinkling, she added, 'Prince, I have not seen you in a while!' Asoka looked at her with delight.

She turned to Pushyagupta, 'Baba, Bitan must be chattering with friends. He's never around when you send for him.'

'I know! I know!' Pushyagupta looked tenderly at her, 'Anga, show Asoka my future home.' To Asoka he said, 'She thinks Baba is the centre of the world.'

'Prince, do you like the Amaltas tree?' she asked walking to the garden.

'It is so beautiful,' Asoka said cheerily, 'when it flowers!'

Dropping his hand, she quickened her steps but Asoka caught up with her. 'Anga, my name is Asoka, not prince,' he teased.

'Asoka! All right, Asoka,' she nodded.

Again, Asoka fell behind. She was waiting for him under the Amaltas tree. 'This will be Baba's home. Every May or June a cloud of yellow flowers will burst to tell him how much he is missed and loved.'

Asoka smiled, 'I'll remember!'

On the way back, they passed by a grove of silk-flower trees. In a gust of wind, a few flowers cascaded and undulated on their journey to earth, floating on a bed of air as if to stretch out the last few moments of their life. With eyes up and mouth wide open, Anga cupped her palms. 'I wish I had four hands!'

Asoka laughed, 'Like the goddess Lakshmi? I like two hands better.' But she had already disappeared.

She was weaving a flower in her hair under a tree, and waiting for another to fall.

Asoka rushed as it fell, and picked it for her. Holding it above her ear, she turned and asked skeptically. 'Asoka, do you know how to pin a flower?' He nodded and she pointed with a finger, 'There, above the ear.'

Asoka gladly complied, and the flower stayed in place. A look of admiration came into Anga's eyes. 'That's good, Asoka! That's good! Bitan is so clumsy. I have to pin it on Jaya for him.'

Bitan was briskly walking toward them and Anga exclaimed, 'There he is! Late as always!'

Bitan explained, 'I was there the whole time.'

Asoka assured him Anga had done a splendid job and told Bitan what she had said. Bitan laughed, 'Oh I see! She is giving away my secrets.'

They turned to look, but she was gone.

The two friends walked back talking about Ujjain.

'On the way to Ujjain,' said Bitan, 'why don't you stay at Vidisha for a day or two with my friend, Kanchan? Here is a letter for him. It will be a short detour.'

Asoka looked skeptical.

'Kanchan loves to travel, tells great stories and,' he smiled, 'has a really pretty sister.'

Asoka laughed, 'Now that's different!'

23

Asoka left for Ujjain when winter had peaked, and spring was still afar. Now he had a carriage, a battalion of horsemen and guards. He moved in an aura of power, like one hovering around the gods. He mused: *Once I disliked the trappings of power. Not anymore.*

Taxila was connected to Vidisha by a dirt road. For most, the chief mode of public transportation was the bullock cart. Farmers traveled long distances on it, asleep on the flat bed wagon or on top of cargo, as the animal ambled along on auto-pilot.

Yard by yard the horse coach rolled, raising dust on the sides. The monotony was soul-grinding. When tired, Asoka slept in the wagon or day-dreamed. *Is my destiny unfolding? Was it Baba's destiny to be emperor? Will it be mine? Certainly it is shadowy like the gods.*

His thoughts rambled on. *My life so far has been a chariot on one wheel. I've never known or aspired to happiness. Only fame and glory.* He thought of Risa, and smiled, *Governor! Ha!*

One day the coachman announced, 'Governor, we are in Vidisha!' A small town situated a few miles northeast of Sanchi in central India, Vidisha's only claim to fame was its proximity to Ujjain, the holy city.

The carriage came to a halt in front of a three-storied house with red and green gables towering above the surrounding high brick wall. Two guards dismounted, opened the gate, ran up the steps, crossed the porch and knocked at the old, wooden double door. A woman's white head appeared through the crack, then receded at the sight of armed men. Watching the nose retreat, Asoka called aloud, 'I've come to see Kanchan!' Like magic, the words pulled the nose out along with the wrinkled face, lighted this time with a toothless smile.

The woman escorted Asoka through a long dim hallway where a caged bird, hanging high from the ceiling, shrieked 'Hello.' Startled, Asoka looked up, 'Oh, hello!' In the narrow hallway, he was overtaken by a cloying perfume. On the facing wall, Vishnu sat smirking in a niche.

The hallway led to a verandah where some weathered wooden chairs and tables sat. A red-necked green parrot in a cage on a table kept repeating, 'You are young, You are young!' The old woman apologized. 'He keeps me company during the day!' She offered Asoka a seat, and disappeared into the open courtyard.

Had he done the right thing to divert his journey? He wondered.

Soon, a tall thin servant, naked to the waist, appeared with a cup and long-necked earthen water pitcher. Asoka had taken just one sip when a stout, short man appeared in a loincloth and open grey vest, giving out the same strong perfume. Between his broad, flat nose and thick upper lip, his untrimmed moustache looked like rampant weeds in a narrow strip of land.

'I am Janakdas, Kanchan's father, you must be Asoka,' the bald man said with great aplomb. Asoka had no time to reply. 'Yes, yes! You must be Asoka! No one comes here except long forgotten relatives on their way to the holy fair at Ujjain, accompanied by a swarm of children so rowdy, so loud, that sitting right here, I get full flavor of the pandemonium at the pilgrimage.'

He clapped and shouted, 'Ho..ho.. ho.' His shrill voice, like a halter, pulled in a shriveled, stooped, dark old man. Janakdas roared, 'Aaa.. Oom! This is no way to welcome a guest! Get some gruel!'

His booming voice sent the servant running. With a delayed smile, Janakdas turned to Asoka. 'You'll be comfortable here! Tomorrow, Kanchan returns.' He sat down on a chair, took out a little wooden vial from his vest, opened it and carefully let two drops fall on his fleshy palm. The jasmine fragrance! Asoka knew. Janakdas massaged the oil on his bald pate, then briskly whirled his palm on his leathery face, and wiped off the last film of grease on his bushy arms. His face now glowed like polished, weathered brass.

'I sell perfumes and incense,' he began, 'As you know, the natural scent of body is completely out of fashion. Older males perfume their bodies to whip up their drooping desire, the young ones to relieve their performance-anxiety. Young females rub it on their bosoms so the males can peek and sniff them first.'

'I also sell lac-dye for women's palm and feet, lip salve, camphor pills, saffron, cloves, and cardamom powder to freshen the morning breath. But it was musk that made me rich: an aphrodisiac extracted from the sex glands of Chinese and Tibetan male deer—a solitary, shy and unfortunate animal. Only the rich can afford the musk. The poor rub with soap.'

'I sell soap too,' Janakdas chuckled behind the weedy patch. 'I'll give you some.' Asoka kept quiet.

Janakdas said, 'Vidisha is a wonderful town. Go out and enjoy it.'

That afternoon, riding on its only narrow dirt road, Asoka passed small thatched roofed houses and shops huddled on either side. In front of mud houses, shriveled women sat on bamboo beds weaving baskets, their uncovered breasts sagging like half-water-filled balloons. On the dust-padded road, bullock carts creaked. Fruit and vegetable vendors, scantily clad around the waist, sat chatting or gazing at the tips of their noses, unconcerned about selling their wares, some nibbling it away to pass time. In front of a yellow-flagged tavern by the roadside, a potter sat baking small clay lamps in a fire pit.

Outside the village centre, Asoka saw a large house with a low mud boundary wall. On the outskirts, he passed small farms. The countryside was filled with the moist air of forest trees. Trotting, cantering, and enjoying the ride, he returned at sunset as cattle herds were returning from fields, their chimes tinkling like random thoughts. Lamps were going up in the mud huts.

At suppertime the family—Janakdas and his wife, and his daughters, Devi, seventeen, and Subha, fourteen— sat on a cotton wool mattress covered with white sheets. The aroma of turmeric and cumin filled the room. As was the custom, the guest was first served with a special beverage, madhuparka, made of honey and curds. The village eatery had delivered for Asoka a specially-cooked spicy goat meat. Food was served in copper 'thalis' and cups, rice with curds, ghee, purified butter, squash, papaya vegetable and chapati, the flat bread.

Asoka sat opposite Devi who looked ravishing in a green choli and red skirt. Every time their eyes met, she blushed, and lowered her eyes. Balls of rice coated with sugar and flavored with spices, were served as desert. Lime water bowls appeared at the end for washing hands. To Asoka's surprise, everyone ate in complete silence. He wondered, *has someone had died in the family.*

After the women left, Janakdas, his belly a little more extended than before, lay down on his side on the mattress, his chin on his hand. Suddenly, he came alive.

'What are you going to do in Ujjain, Asoka?'

'I am going as governor,' said Asoka quietly.

Janakdas swallowed a gulp and quickly sat up. 'Bitan didn't tell me!' For a few moments, his face registered surprise and obsequiousness. Standing up, he said, 'Let us go to the living room.'

That room was locked. Shouting for keys, Janakdas waited, making faces and unintelligible sounds. At last, the shriveled servant showed up and unlocked the room; a musty odor escaped looking desperately for fresh breeze. A lamp was lit, revealing bare walls, flaking mud plaster and furniture dried and blackened by time, clearly from his pre-musk days. Asoka dusted a chair, pushed down on its legs and sat down gingerly. Janakdas threw his weight fearlessly on another chair, which squeaked and staggered before settling down. Janakdas sat a little tilted.

'Isn't it comfortable here, Governor?' Janakdas said cheerfully.

Asoka beseeched him, 'Please call me Asoka.'

Still digesting the food and the title, Janakdas muttered, 'I never had a Governor in my house!'

'A Governor is just another man.'

After a pause, Janakdas said, 'I will give you some musk too. It is not bad if used occasionally.' He looked at Asoka, quizzically. 'Where is your wife?'

'I am not married.'

A spark came into Janakdas' eyes. He quickly left the room without a word and returned a few minutes later with a mysterious smile. 'Governor, I'll tell you an interesting story. When word spread that musk is good for a man's sex life, demand mushroomed and the price went through the roof. Poor animal! For a few kicks, shakes and jerks, men strip it of life. Perhaps sex is like religion—men will believe in any damned lie. Sometimes I feel like a priest of sex.'

Asoka sat amused as Janakdas went on. 'I ask Kanchan, Why keep running to distant lands? For excitement sell goat glands. For more excitement sell more animals' glands. There is no money in adventure.'

'Where does he go?' asked Asoka.

'Kandahar, Herat, Alexandria. He has seen more places than I.' Then, remembering he had never been out of Vidisha, he said, 'I don't need to go anywhere. The glands come to me!'

'Young men should see places.'

'The world is a scary place if you have nothing to sell.' Janakdas' fatherly concern seemed genuine. He came to the point. 'Governor, when you get a chance, advise Kanchan to get his hands dirty in sex glands. I don't have time to run after every animal.'

'Let him travel and get it out of his system.' Asoka felt awkward advising anyone. Advice is easy.

Janakdas said, "Our Dharam Sastra, Righteous Code of Conduct, says you should obey your parents.' He followed the old precept: Invoke religion when all else fails.

'Our Dharma Sastra says a lot of things.' Asoka felt on firmer ground. 'But a man has to do what he has to do.'

Asoka fell asleep as Janakdas went on about his great discovery of musk gland. When he awoke an hour later, Janakdas was still rattling on. Asoka got up yawning and stretching, and mumbled, 'I will talk to Kanchan.'

'Governor, we had a very interesting conversation!' Janakdas said, shaking his head. Then added, 'I'll send someone to show you your room on the second floor. I recommend a walk in our garden. You will be...gland.'

In his room, Asoka opened the window and stuck out his hand: it was cool but not cold. Jasmine fragrance came pouring in with the gentle breeze. He went down. In the garden, it was quiet and dark under the half-moon. In a window on the third floor a lamp flickered, where, perhaps, in the dim light, the master was performing some pre-sleep chore, his head buzzing with animal glands.

Suddenly, Asoka heard footsteps in the back and reflexively reached for the small sword inside his vest. In the shadow of a tall tree backlit by the moon, a dark figure was moving towards him. When it came out of the shadow, he saw Devi standing there.

She is beautiful, Asoka thought, admiring her glowing face in the moonlight. A warmth came over his body. 'Devi! You?'

She whispered, 'Governor, do you take milk?'

He nodded, and said in a hushed voice, 'Would you like to walk with me?'

In the pale light, he saw her blush. 'I saw you,' she softly said, 'and just wanted to...talk.' Then she whispered, 'I love to walk in the garden at night but I'm not allowed.'

'Why?' he asked, surprised.

'Night is dark,' she said innocently.

'I am with you.' He put his hand on her shoulder. 'Don't be afraid!'

She raised her face up and he saw the moon in her eyes. He took her hand, and asked warmly, 'What do you do during the day?'

'Learn Sanskrit,' she whispered, 'and help mother with chores, though we have lots of servants.' She added, 'I perfume the house with incense every day.'

They walked up and down. And then, standing under a huge banyan tree, Devi said in a hushed voice, 'Our family treasure is buried under this tree. For bad times.'

Delighted at her innocence, he smiled. 'Don't tell that to anyone, not even me. I might return one night and take it all away.'

She looked at him as if he could not do such a thing. 'What is a governor?'

He explained, and she asked, 'Where?'

'Ujjain.'

'I have never been there,' she said wistfully.

'You'll like it.' He pressed her hand. 'It is a religious place.'

'So I hear.' She looked in his eyes.

'O! It's late.' she said, suddenly pulling her hand away. Near the house, he drew her close and kissed her. She hastened to the door, turned and looked at him for a moment, then disappeared into the house.

Back in his room, Devi filled his thoughts. Her trust and innocence. The feel of her hand, of her breasts, lingered like the fragrance of jasmine in the house. *'Does she love me? Does she love me not?'* he asked himself, suddenly remembering Bitan.

He stood by the window. The moon was hidden behind diaphanous wandering clouds. A knock at the door startled him. Devi entered, her face silvery pale in the moonlight coming through the window. She put a gold pitcher and a cup on the table by his bedside. 'Water!' She wiped sweat from her face with a corner of her dress then asked in a trembling voice, 'Do you want something else?' He gazed at her silently, and she hung her head.

Before he knew it, he was holding her in his arms. She stood in his embrace, eyes closed, face up, lips trembling and he kissed her long. Loosening his grip she slipped away, blushing.

Next morning he wondered if it was all a dream. His heart was full of commotion, so after the morning meal, he went for a long walk.

Kanchan showed up at noon. 'Sorry I missed you. Would you like to go deer hunting?'

In the nearby forest, the friends caught sight of two fawns nibbling plant shoots. Suddenly, out of sheer exuberance, the fawns began chasing one another, heads up, heads down. In the midst of their frolic, Kanchan downed one with great panache. After returning home, Asoka skinned, basted and roasted the meat. Devi set the table. Some of Kanchan's friends joined in the feast. Late in the evening, after the friends had left, Asoka and Kanchan sat before the campfire in garden and talked. Asoka asked, 'Why isn't Devi married yet?'

'Father has no time apart from glands. And a good boy is not just going to walk in and ask for her hand!'

Asoka changed the subject. 'Your father told me you had an accident on a caravan trip.'

Kanchan became agitated. 'I knew it! He must tell everyone who steps through the door.'

That night, Asoka opened his window and stood looking out. Not a leaf stirred. On the table in the corner sat the long-necked, round-hipped pitcher. Thinking of Devi, Asoka grasped the bottom with cupped hands, threw his head back, and gulped down the water straight from its golden lips. Moonlight blotched a wall in the room. *She is the one,* his heartbeat said.

'I don't know her,' said a voice.

Another said. 'You know enough!'

The idea of having a pretty young woman by his side enchanted him. The voices kept clashing. 'Choti-ma would reconcile herself to it.'

'It would be rash.'

'I never felt like this about Nachita. But then she was not half as beautiful.'

He kept tossing and turning in bed, half-expecting Devi to come to him; once or twice when the wind blew, he woke with a start, looking at the door. It was a long, lonely night. He asked for his morning meal in the room and stood thinking by the window. *Tomorrow I'll leave, and days and months will go by. When I return here ...she'll be gone.* The thought distressed him.

He was still lost in thought when there was a knock at the door and it opened softly. Without turning, he said, 'Please leave it on the table.'

'These are from our garden,' said a female voice. He turned. Devi was taking out two half-ripe guavas from inside her choli. She put them on the table and made to leave. Asoka ran and closed the door.

'Devi!' he said as if in sleep, taking her in arms, and lifting her chin. 'Devi, if I asked for your hand, would you say "yes"?'

Her jaw dropped as if she was suddenly standing naked before him. She covered her face and a muffled sob escaped her. He pressed her to his chest, and she nodded "yes" smiling through her tears, then freed herself, and ran away.

After five days in Vidisha, Asoka had the woman he craved. Before he left for Ujjain, he couriered a letter to Choti-ma telling her about Devi, and apologizing for his unseemly haste.

24

Asoka's letter stunned Livia who read it over and over. Letter in hand, she called for Roxanne, then shouted at her, 'How many times have I told you not to arrange flowers in my room without checking first with me?' Roxanne had been doing this for years.

Roxanne looked surprised. She hesitated then started to turn away. Livia shouted, 'Don't just leave! Get me a glass of wine.'

Roxanne handed her the cup. 'What is it, Livia?'

Livia burst into tears. Roxanne put her arms around her until Livia calmed down.

'He should have married Senapati's daughter. He keeps doing these foolish things. How's he ever going to be king?'

But it was not about Senapati's daughter. What shocked her was that Asoka had not invited her. She felt pushed aside, if not by Asoka, then by life. It was no consolation that no one else was invited. Next day when her emotion dulled, she thought, *how ironic! My husband didn't come to my wedding and my son did not invite me to his.* She knew he never consulted her, or anyone else in his decisions. Yet in the matter of his wedding, she did not expect to be ignored.

She calmed down in a few days, then it struck her that she was no longer a participant in life. She had become a mere spectator, an outsider. It was human obsolescence—the diminishing usefulness of every life after the reproductive years. It hurt. She liked Asoka's independent spirit but not when it affected her. One thought, though, consoled her. *He is going to need me, he is not yet king.*

25

Asoka left for Ujjain the day after the wedding. His bride was dressed in a gold embroidered skirt, and wore lampblack around her eyes, sandalwood perfume on her neck, breasts and navel, and henna on her hands and feet. On every limb she was covered with jewelry and gold where it was possible to hang or strap it. Drawn to her scent, Asoka sat beside her in the wagon, enjoying her head wobbling on his shoulder as she slept, delighting at her half-open mouth, salivating at nothing. The wonder of a woman! The warmth, the mystery!

He did all the talking, little though it was. *It is too early for her to talk,* he thought. Gazing at the sky, he could not help wondering whether he had done the right thing. Perhaps, it was the bridegroom's remorse after the wedding. He dismissed those thoughts. *She is lovely, and the deed is done.* When restlessness returned, he mounted his horse and lashed it.

When the couple reached Ujjain, spring was not far behind. Situated on the river Shipra, the city had a mythical past. Gods and demons had churned the ocean in search of 'Soma'–the elixir of immortality. When the nectar was recovered, the gods seized the vessel and ran off with it with the demons in hot pursuit. A mad scramble ensued across the skies; in the melee, four drops spilled over Hardwar, Nasik, Prayag and Ujjain–transforming them into the holiest of holy places. Every few years, people assembled there in large numbers to dip in the holy river that would send them to heaven.

Avoiding Sasima, Asoka camped at a little distance from Ujjain then went to take charge from him. Handsome as ever, Sasima sat in a large room with a high ceiling, on an embellished high-back chair– his little throne – with his feet up on the table. Though the sun was out, the windows were closed, and several lamps lit the room. Sasima had had the chairs opposite him removed. Four female guards stood around holding a large umbrella over him.

As Asoka stood facing him, Sasima stared for a long moment, then came round the table, patted Asoka on the back and returned to his seat. At last he mocked, 'My brave brother! How handsome you look!' He clapped for a chair. 'Why are you standing? Sit close to me.'

'I accept the gracious compliments of my handsome brother.' Asoka sat down opposite him, his attention caught by a strange wooden statue standing behind the throne. It had a man's head hanging between the thighs and man's genitalia at the top. Asoka could not stop gazing at it.

Sasima was in mock high spirits. 'Brother! When will I see the beautiful bride! Won't you invite me to a scrumptious dinner?'

Asoka replied, 'Perhaps we should delay the meal, dear brother! I don't even know that the bride can cook a meal fit for the crown prince.'

Sasima nodded. 'There are two kinds of brothers—the brave and the ambitious. You are brave, I hear. Ambitious? I hope not. When I am emperor, I will need brave brothers.' He stared at Asoka questioningly, then restless, he stood up. 'Will you be loyal to me, Asoka?'

Asoka shifted his legs. 'Are you not my elder brother? Have I not been loyal to you?'

As Sasima got up again and embraced him, Asoka smelled alcohol on his breath. 'I will protect you,' Sasima said raising his right hand from the elbow, like a king. 'Xander! Xander!' He called out loudly, 'My brave brother is here.' To Asoka, he said, 'He is my philosopher-guide.'

This was the fashion at the time for kings and nobles to maintain a philosopher or two at their court. Alexander the Great had taken an Indian philosopher to Babylon with him.

Sasima got back in his chair. 'Xander is the best. A thinker, he spends most of his time standing on his head.' Turning to the statue, he said, 'Xander thinks God has not played fair with man. Though the head sits on top, it is a slave to the limbs of sex, gluttony and desire. Now look at Xander's model of man. Private parts sit atop the blubbery belly, fidgeting in the wind. Belly bears down on heart, the constant troublemaker. Below the heart, notice the poor slave, the jelly-filled hard shell, lying at the foot of its masters—hanging between the thighs, plotting its next wile or deceit.'

Sasima began to laugh, then grasped a rope attached to the head. 'If God was honest, that is how man should have been made. Of course, he would look funny. Now watch,' he said, jerking the rope, 'the scheming head lurching from thigh to thigh, from thought to thought. That is Man! The Real Man! To understand man, you have to look at him from the thigh up. And this is best done by a headstand. That's how the headstand began. But now men do it to straighten their topsy-turvy world.' Then, pointing to the statue, he said, 'Now tell me Asoka, is that not man? The jewel of Creation?'

Asoka sat listening and wondering, with his hands crossed inside his vest, one on knife.

Sasima gave Asoka a piercing look. 'Is Xander right?'

Asoka only smiled.

Just then a stout middle-aged man entered the room wearing an army helmet to his brows, strapped to his chin. On his small round face, his rather long, red, hooked nose looked like a very small bird, the "red munia," perched on a pale apple.

'My name is Xan...der,' the man squeaked, taking off his helmet and exposing a bald pate. He sat down on the floor with legs crossed, staring at Asoka, threatening a headstand by his look.

'Not Alex?' Asoka teased.

'You got it,' the man said, looking pleased. 'The Alex of Alexander—his head and his heart—was all screwed up. Look what he did to Persepolis!' Like an overly full bladder, Xander relieved himself by going into a headstand. From that vantage point, he continued to stare at Asoka.

Asoka stared back. *A mad man?* he wondered. *A clown? Certainly not a philosopher.* 'Are we both looking at the real man?' Asoka teased.

Xander's mouth widened in a smile and his lips stirred, but words failed. He tried again and this time came tumbling down. Came a voice from the floor. 'That's right!'

Asoka saw Sasima watching him. He nodded when Sasima asked, 'Do you understand, Asoka?'

After Asoka left, Xander warned, 'Beware crown prince! His eyes are shifty.'

'They will be fixed when I'm King,' Sasima said curtly.

26

Asoka threw himself into his job. Each province was carved into several administrative districts. Each district included hundreds of villages, each administered by a rural officer—the Rajuka—who in turn was assisted by a Yukta, the record-keeper. Several ancillary officials assisted these officials.

The district officer—the Pradesika—was responsible for law and order and collection of revenue. Asoka asked the Pradesikas to set aside a fixed time to hear public grievances. He expanded his spy network to report on corrupt officials, remembering Chanakya's warning, "It is possible to configure even the path of birds flying in the sky. But not the ways of government servants who hide their dishonest income." He punished corrupt officials who at first dismissed him as a zealot who would come and go. When he did not let up, things began to change - slowly.

To increase both revenue and production, the Pradesikas had to be enthused. Asoka started to meet them periodically with their families at his mansion, and Devi became a vital part of these meetings. It took a heavy toll on her. Even days before the event, she often complained.

'I don't like these gatherings.'

Asoka was surprised. 'Why?'

'I have to plan the menu, order, check and issue provisions, make sure the servants are not wasting or stealing food. The servants love the ghee. You should see how quickly it disappears. They are all thieves!'

'Devi, you have a large staff,' Asoka said, 'Make one person responsible for the event.'

'Easy for you to say,' Devi said, unconvinced.

The public liked the young Governor despite his strange ways. Not lost in pleasures, he was willing to listen to them. Everybody who was anybody— successful businessmen, high central government employees, high army officials – invited the young couple to their homes. Enjoying his power, Asoka liked it but Devi whined, 'The parties are a drag. Everyone hangs around you. Especially the women.'

Things at home were not going well. Like the juice of a cut sugarcane stalk, his feelings for Devi were drying up fast. She spent most of her time decorating the mansion, and evenings had become an exercise in silence so he took to riding his horse after work. On one of these rides, an idea flashed and he approached Devi, 'Learn horse riding!'

Devi looked aghast. 'What's wrong with the horse carriage?'

'It moves like a funeral march.'

But nothing he said convinced her.

He would not give in. He dragged her to the stables and pointed to his horse. 'Look at that statuesque head, that broad chest, those sculpted haunches. Wouldn't you love to kick that big ass?'

Devi covered her nose. 'The odor! I can't stand it.'

On their way back to the mansion, he cast sidelong glances at her. *How she's aged! She looks so ordinary!*

He started to take long trips into distant territory, going as far as the gulf of Kutch where Kanchan accompanied him on fishing trips to the sea. Kanchan introduced him to oysters and Asoka loved these "chestnuts of the sea" and had them shipped home in seawater barrels.

He travelled the countryside to address the Rajukas who had never seen a governor before. Asoka lectured them, 'The villages are our wealth. Help farmers produce more. Every farmer should pay one quarter of a good crop, rather than one sixth of a bad crop as they now do. We win if they win.'

The Rajukas pointed out that the farmers spend money on animal sacrifices and rituals to please the rain gods, and have no faith in seeds or canal water. Furthermore, instead of doing something about their miserable lives, they constantly curse and blame those who live with them.

'Work with a few. When they succeed, others will follow,' Asoka exhorted the Rajukas.

It frustrated him that there was no room for him to make policy changes as all the laws were made by the centre. The peasants did not trust Rajukas, who to them were grim reminders of the king's dark power to tax.

At the end of the year, Devi announced she was pregnant. The news pleased and scared Asoka. *My life is in a whirl and the future so uncertain*, he thought. He was camping at Seogarh when Mahinda was born and he rushed to see his son, but after the initial surge of love a shadow came over him. *I have fearlessly pursued my desires until now*, he thought, *Will I have to give them up?* Scared, he consoled himself: *he will follow his destiny and I mine.*

27

The revenue collection increased but the farm production still lagged. Then Asoka's familiar demon returned as he was out riding. *Running from village to village here, I will die unheard, unsung. There is no glory here. This work is fit for Tissa. He'd be happy with it. But I lack resources to reach the mountain top. Even fifty thousand soldiers will not do. I'll have to gamble. But how? I will think of a plan, and guard my secret in the darkest chamber of my heart where even the sun cannot see. If only I can sit in Baba's august chair, the floor of heaven will be touching my head.*

When a crisis occurred in his fourth year, he forgot everything. The rainfall was scant and the hungry peasants pinned their hopes on the following year's rain. But an even greater disaster followed — a severe drought struck the land. The fields turned rock hard, the pastures cracked and the livestock stopped yielding milk.

Asoka toured stricken villages and everywhere he saw sunken eyes, hollow cheeks, stomachs pulled back to the ribs, and legs turning into reeds. The farmers prayed endlessly, and kept doing havans, rituals, to please the rain gods. Old men complained that while they starved, their sons spent huge sums of money on religious rituals and gifts to priests.

The real culprits, Asoka thought, *are the rain gods*. All summer, the fiendish sun spewed fire. The clouds— false, feckless, impotent— blustered, tantalized with empty thunder and vanished without a rain drop. Ponds turned into dry holes, streams into serpentine paths of dirt and rock. The peasants had already eaten their goats, buffalo and sheep. All they had left was an ox to plough the field and a cow for milk. In dire need, some farmers killed their cows.

In the central region, the situation was even worse. People there were eating boiled burls and bark. He saw children reduced to skeletons, chewing on dry branches as if on bones for a few shreds of meat.

Honest farmers stole scraps of food. He opened the stored corn pits, but that was not enough.

One day, when assuring the farmers they would get additional corn, he heard the loud wails of a woman. When these continued, he went to the nearby hut. Beside herself, the woman told him that having gone without food for five days, her children had begged their father to kill them and end their misery. The family had decided to perish together, but after killing his children, the man went insane and killed himself, leaving her to suffer alone.

When he returned home that evening, Asoka was shaken. At dinner there was fresh yogurt, hot buttered plump chapatis and roasted birds wrapped in bitter leaves, and rose apples, mangoes, and sugar coated rice balls. Devi, having sat all day in shade dressed in white muslin, kept complaining of the searing heat. He felt sick in the stomach.

And there in the fields, the famine—the demon of starvation and death—is crazing the arid soil, he thought, *tearing up the peasants' callused feet and grinding away their flesh.* Nauseated, he left the table, his meal untouched, and ordered that simple food be served until the end of the drought.

The food items in his warehouse he distributed to the villagers. He admonished Devi, 'We can't bury our heads in the sand and just watch others suffer. The gods put us through difficult times to test our strength.'

The drought terrified him. He relieved the villagers from paying taxes in affected areas and ordered the garrison to dig canals and cut forests on the plateau to build new settlements— farming could be done there with little water. He even sacrificed a bull to appease *Indra* and *Varuna*, the gods of rain. All to no avail.

"As you sow, so you reap," he had read in the scriptures. The drought shook his faith in the gods. Asoka asked himself: *what sin these poor starving farmers had committed? Could all the villagers have sinned equally to suffer the same fate?* He questioned the ways of Karma. Once he had believed religion had all the answers. Now he was not sure.

At the end of the year, his daughter Sanghamitta was born. The stress of raising two children, his long travels during the drought, and their arguments at home had exhausted Devi. Tired and unhappy, she left one day with the children to live with her mother at Vidisha. Shattered but not defeated, Asoka vowed to go on. Yet often he thought about his son Mahinda and little Sanghamitta. He knew they were in loving hands and getting better care than the nurses could provide.

Luckily, for him and the people, the rains returned the following year. Once again, the countryside was dressed in bright green, like a bride. Life began to look... well... like life. The streets and fields resounded again with children's joyous screams.

28

Asoka had now been the Governor of Ujjain for seven years. Pleased, the King conferred on him the additional title of Governor of Taxila. Bitan was doing well there, so Asoka was to keep his seat in Ujjain. Asoka decided to visit Taxila.

Bitan invited Asoka's old friends Visal and Sisupal to join them in Taxila for his visit. Tissa accompanied Visal. Livia had asked Tissa to consider Anga for his prospective bride. Most of the kingdom now expected Asoka to succeed the King. So did Asoka.

To acquaint himself with the army and local officials, Asoka arrived a month early. By the time Tissa and Visal arrived, the spring was about to end. Sisupal arrived a few days later. The friends assembled at Bitan's house on a sunny morning for breakfast: apples, grapes, dates, curds, honey-coated wheat balls, eggs, bread and Kasaya, an intoxicating drink made from rice meal and flowers. They ate and caught up with one another's lives.

A big scar on Visal's pale left cheek—a memento of a battle in Persia—became a conversation piece. Visal described his life.

'I fought a few battles, returned to Pataliputra, landed a good job in the cavalry and got married. Now I have a son and a daughter. What next? Weight going up, hair falling, youth missing. No time for anything but ageing. Eating garlic, herbs and barley, walking for fear of losing virility, but irregularly. Life getting crazier. Birthdays arrive uninvited, like dear relatives; the juices of the body turning rancid. My spirits undulate at the intimations of mortality. I wait for friends to meet in the park for walks, but some turn up in the funeral ground. I keep considering different possibilities for my funeral—as a Brahmin, Sudra, rich, poor, Greek, Persian, Hindu or Jaini—hoping that variety, the spice of life, will keep me ticking.'

He paused for water, then continued, 'Then there is the grave question of how I am to be distributed after cremation—in the air or in the river? Why not land in the greasy hair of some drunken slobs at a wedding party? But I'd prefer my ashes be turned over to urchins, who can chew on my bone fragments for nourishment. That would be charity— my first and last. There's no time for giving while I'm running around.'

'Wow! Giving away your entire body to charity! What generosity! What timing!' Smiling, shaking his head, Asoka added, 'A grave predicament!'

Bitan said, 'But the aged don't have to act like twenty year olds. Why climb a mountain on a stretcher? Go stargazing on stilts?'

Asoka said, 'Let's get off these distant things. Tissa, tell me the news.'

Tissa reported that Choti-Ma had obtained Bhairavi's freedom and keeps talking about a visit to him at Ujjain. Tissa peered at Asoka with his small eyes. 'And I have to tell you something— I'm friends now with Marut, Pavan and Sasima. I no longer live under your shadow, big brother! I don't mind if Sasima loves alcohol and women. He's a gentle soul and the King is very fond of Sasima's seven-year-old son, Nigrodh, who's more fearless than anyone of us. He is something!'

Asoka's eyes widened. *Has he sold his soul?*

Sisupal reported that he had converted to the Jain religion, had two children, and was now the Forest Minister. Visal told Sisupal that by looking at him, one would think he must be eating elephants.

Asoka quipped, 'Sisupal likes to throw his weight around.'

Sisupal asked about Asoka's parade march in Pataliputra, with Kalanos' head on the spear. Asoka laughed, 'I was just playing the good son.'

'I'd say you were playing the successor son!' Tissa caustically interjected.

Had Sasima been pumping him up?

To clear the charged air, Visal asked Asoka, 'Tell us about your adventures.'

'Adventures?' Asoka said. 'I deal with bureaucrats — the tombs of the spirit, the epitomes of mediocrity, the mules of empire! Their self-interest always comes first. Of course, each thinks he's brilliant!'

Bitan teased, 'Asoka, be fair. They run the empire.'

Asoka backed off. 'True, some are dedicated.'

'And what have you been doing, Bitan?' asked Visal.

'I married about the time Asoka left for Ujjain,' Bitan replied. 'Then my grandfather died. Two years later, my wife and child died in childbirth.' The air turned sad.

To lighten things up, Bitan said, 'Well, we had three happy years. After her death, my grandma said, "When a spouse dies, man loses his empire, and the woman, her centre." I wrote a play about her based on the love story of Urvashi and Pururavas in the *Rig-Veda*.'

Asoka asked, 'What's the story?'

'I'll tell you this evening,' Bitan said, getting up, 'Let's go for a ride in the valley.'

After an exhilarating day followed by rest and a swim, the friends sat down in the garden to eat and drink around a campfire. At a little distance, a servant turned meat on hot coals. Asoka went to see what was cooking and returned with a smile. 'Peacock meat!' He told Bitan. 'You didn't forget!'

He watched the sparks fly and thought about his children.

Just then, Anga appeared in the distance with a large clay pot in her hands. Sixteen now, she wore a green top and bright red skirt, her hair carelessly flung over her shoulders. Her large eyes shone in the flames, like emeralds. A servant with two pitchers of wine followed her. Asoka could not take his eyes off her. *How beautiful she has become! Her lips are like wild red berries!*

Filling the air with her scent, she greeted everyone. Putting the pot on the table, she took the lid off, and the spicy aroma of goat meat wafted out. Anga's eyes met Asoka's admiring gaze and she let her eyes linger, then smiled at him.

Smitten with a desire to hold her, Asoka thought, *What a smile! My God! So ravishing!*

Anga teased, 'Asoka! You have been hiding in Ujjain!'

With blood rushing to his temples, he blurted out, 'Anga, you look such a lady!'

Anga's cheeks turned red. Throwing her head back, she glanced at Bitan, as if to say, "Don't treat me like a child." She turned.

'You must be Sisupal?' and he bowed, getting up from the chair ever so slightly.

Speechless, Tissa sat entranced, watching her.

'Oh, I forgot, Anga, this is Tissa,' Bitan apologized, 'Asoka's younger brother.'

'And a friend of the crown prince,' Tissa reminded, curtly.

Asoka said, 'Anga, sit here close to me! Tell me, what have you been doing?'

Blushing again, Anga sat down and throwing her hair back with a flourish, said, 'Philosophy, music, horse riding!'

'Philosophy, music, and horse riding! No goddess in our pantheon does it all!'

Anga smiled shyly. 'I go riding with Bitan and sometimes with father. When I gallop, they slow me down. That's no fun.'

Asoka blurted out, 'Ride with me tomorrow!'

A frown appeared on Tissa's face. Asoka ignored it.

Anga's eyes lit up, then she hesitated. 'Let's go early, so we can be back for the morning meal. All right?' She glanced at Bitan. She knew that without his support, her mother would put her foot down.

'Perfect!' Asoka exclaimed, still awash in her smile.

A servant announced that Anga's music teacher was waiting. 'Oh, I forgot!' She turned to Asoka, 'Don't forget!' She rushed out waving, leaving behind in the empty chair her form, her scent, and her smile. Asoka's eyes followed her until she disappeared.

Bitan said, 'She wants to do everything. She wanted to go to Alexandria with me, so I ended up not going. Mother wants her to marry but she refuses — two more years of philosophy, she says. She was Baba's princess, and now Ma and Pa are having a hard time.'

Asoka couldn't resist. 'They should be proud of her. She'd be a jewel in any king's crown,' he said. *My crown.*

Tissa sat glowering at Asoka.

Bitan changed the subject. 'Asoka, do you remember the Amaltas tree?'

'Of course!' *Where I pinned a flower in her hair,* Asoka thought.

'Last year, when the tree blazed, she sat under it for hours. She said she talked to grandpa. She's decided to be buried under an Amaltas tree.'

Eyes wide, Visal asked, 'How old is she?'

Bitan told him.

'So young and full of death!' Sisupal commented.

'What's so special about the tree?' Visal asked.

'She says its blazing color is like life, like love,' said Bitan. 'She ridicules the idea that the dead take on a body in heaven, and live there forever.'

The food was served as the flames gamboled. Full of rich food, and good wine lubricating their bodies, young heads began to levitate in the clouds of love.

Visal described his experience in Persia, 'On the war front, months pass and you don't see a single woman. Only alcohol provided a little relief. But after a victory sex did flow like water.'

'To me power is gambling, alcohol, and woman,' Sisupal said, 'all rolled in one.'

Bitan philosophized, 'Power turns us into its slave.' He turned to Asoka. 'What do you go after?'

Asoka hesitated. 'The woman of my dreams!'

'Oh?' Visal was surprised. 'Not just any woman! What happened to the good old horse, and Sophia, the love of wisdom?'

Asoka said, 'They all sleep in the same bed.'

Baffled, Visal asked, 'Why women? Why now?'

'It's not about women. It's about life. There's more to life than meets the eye.'

'See!' Visal mocked, 'Asoka has to philosophize even about sex!'

Asoka became serious. 'Sex, family, religion, don't make life perfect. Sex is like an oyster. Consider: the shell gives no clue to the soft flesh inside—heaving in wavelike motions, awaiting touch; there is something earthy, strange and mysterious about the oyster, the quaint taste, the lingering, soporific smell of marsh land and the sea.'

He continued, 'The oyster is good but not good enough! I want the pearl, the pearl that grows out of the humble, lowly oyster. Out of those ridiculous, coarse, fleshly motions!'

Sisupal shrugged his shoulders. 'What's the point?'

Asoka replied, 'The passion of flesh is the pearl!'

Visal said, 'Life offers other things!'

'What else is there?'

Wringing his hands, Visal said, 'Nothing has changed! Ask Asoka to show you a horse's arse, and he will deck it with flowers and incense and tell you it's a shrine. I regret I asked.'

Asoka smiled. 'You can strip the shrine down to what you want it to look like!'

'Tell us about the play,' Visal said to Bitan, 'That would be simpler.'

Bitan yawned, 'Surprisingly, my story is like Asoka's.' He got up. 'We'll do it some other time.'

Sisupal and Visal left, Asoka and Bitan started walking in dark toward a small building lit by a lamp behind the house.

Tissa followed them. 'Can I join?'

Asoka replied irritably, 'Tissa, leave us alone.'

Tissa persisted, 'Why? What's so private?'

Bitan came to Asoka's rescue. 'We have to discuss work, Tissa.'

Tissa taunted, 'Sounds like a conspiracy to me!'

Frowning, Asoka said, 'Yes. It is a conspiracy!'

In the study, Bitan told him, 'The King is seriously ill.'

'I know,' Asoka said. 'My misfortune is I can't even go see him. Choti-ma wrote that if I do, the queen will think I have come to change my father's mind, and cut me down like a weed. It makes me very angry.'

Bitan comforted him. 'Asoka, even if you go, there's no certainty you'll reach him in time. At least your last memories of father are pleasant!'

'True!' Asoka thought of his father's last warm embrace.

Afterwards, they talked about the succession to the throne. Before parting, Asoka told Bitan, 'I'd hoped Tissa would help me. But not anymore.' After a moment, he said, 'I'll need two thousand cavalry and one thousand infantry.'

Bitan looked surprised. 'That's too little, Asoka.'

'Another twenty thousand will make no difference. I have no choice but to play dice.' Bitan shook his head.

Grimly, Asoka said, 'I am still sorting out the plan in my head. And myself too.'

Bitan comforted, 'I know it's not going to be easy.'

'Everything's so complicated.' Asoka thought of Anga. 'And still undecided.' Getting up to leave, he suddenly asked, 'Bitan, why didn't you remarry?'

Bitan looked surprised. 'The way we were, there's no re-marrying!'

'People do it all the time.'

'People do all kind of things. One can marry five times and not know love. I'm not saying love is all spiritual. It's as physical as life. But like life, it's more than just the body.'

Asoka reflected. 'If you marry, love may yet come.'

Bitan sighed. 'I will, when I forget her!'

29

A little before sunrise, Asoka reached Pushyagupta's mansion in the foothills. Anga's chestnut horse was waiting outside. She had been watching from her window and came running out, wearing a leather helmet strapped to her chin, a leather dress to her knees and leather leg guards—like a Greek soldier. Her eyes were shining and her face flushed in the sun's first pink rays. She stood on the porch, fluttering her eyelashes; she crooned, 'Here I am!' She smiled impishly.

Blood rushed to Asoka's heart. *Something happens to me when she smiles.*

Grinning, he held his hand out, and she clasped it tightly and mounted her horse. His spine tingling, Asoka flung himself on his, settled in the seat, straightened himself and turned to take another look. Just then, his eyes met Bitan's. He was standing by the window overlooking the porch. "She is impetuous, handle her with care," his look pleaded.

Asoka walked his horse alongside hers to the gate, now and then casting her a loving glance. She was aglow with the pleasure of youth. Now out of the gate, spurring the horses, they trotted down the spiraling road. Anga rode her stallion fearlessly. Taking one more look at her in the pink rays of the sun, Asoka thought of the '*Ushas,*' the dawn, in the *Rig-Veda, With her lovely face, she awakens us to happiness.*

Under the gaze of her lover, Anga radiated like the *Ushas* under the Sun. The streets were awakened by the rhythmic tapping of hooves. White clouds drifted into the valley below, turning glowing red, pink and purple. On their right stretched low inclines, undulating rocky hills with craggy rocks, filled with sparse shrubbery and a few solitary trees.

Further down, they passed two cypress trees leaning toward each other. The trees had been twisted in that wilderness, and pressed closer by westerly winds but not yet touching. It was believed they were the spirits of two young lovers who had died in each other's arms.

He could not help looking at her; she caught his glance and smiled. *The way my heart beats when I look at her, at her lovely smile,* Asoka thought, *I know I am in love. Will she love me? She is the first bud of spring, I a summer leaf. And yet, with no other woman have I felt so young or so excited.*

They cantered in silence until the road widened. The mouth of the valley lay before them, a flat stretch of land reaching out to the horizon in distance. The horseflesh quivering under his thighs, Asoka spurred his horse towards the Haro river and began to gallop. His brown horse's thundering disturbed a foraging wild pig which scuttled for cover in the corn field. Then without slowing, he turned his head and saw Anga's spirited chestnut horse on his heels, darting headlong, leaping over gullies in long strides. Soon it was galloping beside him, running stride for stride, trying to thrust his nose in front and ahead of Asoka's horse. In a wink, Anga pulled ahead, her helmet falling loose, her dark hair fluttering in the breeze, and waving a hand with a shriek of joy.

This time, she turned her head and cried, 'Catch me Asoka, if you can!'

The words reverberated and resounded in the hills. *The gods have spoken and by God, I shall!* thought Asoka, spurring his horse, feeling he was flying on clouds– the white mud huts and corn fields blurring in front of him and racing backwards.

Down in the valley, the sun and the clouds played hide and seek, the morning first silvery grey with a hazy chill, then warming and turning soft reddish-yellow. In the distance, the streams shimmered like silvery serpents slithering in the sun. It was as if two parallel valleys existed side by side–only one visible at a time. With Anga in view, the valley seemed filled with her warmth.

After an hour of galloping, the terrain became uneven; Hathial Spur rose from the hills in the distance. Asoka now overtook Anga, slowed, and came to a halt.

Anga reined in her horse. 'Asoka! Please don't stop,' she implored.

But Bitan's look was in his mind. 'I am thirsty, Anga,' he said, dismounting.

Tethering the horse to a boulder, he walked to a nearby pond filled with white lotus flowers. He plucked one and held it up. *This flower aspires to, but can't match, her virginal beauty*, he thought. He walked his horse to her. Still seated on hers, Anga was gazing at Bhir monastery in the distance.

She turned when Asoka called, and ambled her horse towards him. With a lingering look in to her eyes, he handed her the flower.

Surprised and delighted, she twirled the stem between her fingers, inhaled its delicate fragrance, and looked tenderly at him, then at the velvety white leaves. She smiled. 'So beautiful, so fragile, like the morning.' With the cool velvety white petals, caressing her lips, then her cheeks, she asked coquettishly, 'You like the lotus flower?'

Now Asoka smiled, looking into her eyes. 'When I was nine, I used to sneak to a pond in our garden in the morning to eat lotus leaves. My mother caught me one day and forbade me. She said it's a sacred flower.'

Anga pressed a petal to his lips, 'Here!' she said playfully.

Asoka kissed the white petal, looking at her. 'Some other time!'

Anga plucked a petal and rolled it up like a betel leaf. After a bite, she stuck her tongue out. 'I will never be a lotus eater.' She pointed, 'Have you seen that monastery?'

'No.'

'I can take you there. Would you like to?'

'Some other time, Anga. Remember the morning meal!'

'I can do without it. And you can eat the lotus leaves!' She said playfully.

'We'd better go,' he said, gently. 'Another time.'

In a daze on their way back, he decided to declare his love.

'Anga, do you really want to spend another two years on philosophy?' he asked, heart pounding, as he rode alongside her.

She became serious. 'I do. It makes my mother very unhappy.' She looked into his eyes.

Was it philosophy itself or her mother's unhappiness that drove her? He couldn't decide. 'Anga, I love...,' and was suddenly struck by the thought, I may be dead in a year. He paused, '...your decision.'

'*Where shall this end? Next year I'll know,*' he told himself, closing his eyes. All he wanted now was to hold her in his arms forever.

They climbed the hill. As they approached Pushyagupta's house, Asoka looked up at the mountain ridges touching the skyline above the floating white clouds. Soon the silky white wisps converged on the horizon, covering the sun and the mountains, until a slight chasm in the clouds unveiled a single peak between heaven and earth—like it was the centre of the universe itself. Mesmerized, Asoka glanced now at Anga, now at the lonely peak. In that instant, he knew their destinies were somehow bound together; the sound and the echoes he heard in the hills would chime in his mind to his dying day.

30

After his father's death, Viswa made a trip to Pataliputra in March 273 to settle his financial affairs. He brought Ankhum, his eighteen year old son with him, and his friend Semat who was nineteen. His father was Viswa's business partner in Alexandria.

Wearing a purple embroidered robe, Anga had hurried to the outside verandah. 'You're all covered in dust,' she told them.

Viswa introduced Ankhum, then Semat. 'I guessed you weren't my cousin,' she smiled at Semat.

Then Viswa saw Atossa at the entrance. Pushing the young men aside, Viswa rushed to embrace his mother, 'Ma, so good to see you!'

Atossa tried to coax her failing eyes to glimpse her son's face, feeling and stroking it with her fingertips, pausing at his forehead, nose and lips. Anga stood aside, watching, smiling.

Ankhum came forward, as if pulled by her charm, and lightly embraced her. 'Anga! All these years I have been hearing about how pretty you are! And now I can see for myself!'

Semat hesitated for a moment, then stepped forward and taking Anga in his arms, pressed her to his bosom like a long-lost friend. Flustered for a moment and her face red, Anga laughed and gently pulled away.

Anga escorted her grandmother inside and everyone sat down in a large hall. Viswa had a hard time recognizing Anga. Etched in his mind was a dark-haired, bright-eyed little girl. But now, sat before him a greenish-eyed, beautiful young girl with a self-conscious smile. He felt her warm spittle on his cheek. After refreshments, the guests left to rest.

At the evening meal, Viswa sprung a surprise.

'Ankhum's name has been Alexander for some time, but we call him Alex.'

Bitan threw his hands in the air. 'And we've been talking about Ankhum all this time! Why the change?'

Viswa put a hand on Alex's shoulder and explained with affection and pride.

'The Greeks rule Egypt, so we didn't want to saddle him with an Egyptian name.' Then he stood up, bowed and said with a flourish, 'Ladies and Gentlemen, here is Alex—my handsome Greek boy!'

Everyone clapped. Alex, his ears red, said, 'An Egyptian is Egyptian by any name! Every time I meet a Greek girl at a party, she looks at me and immediately asks, "Where are you from? Nubia?"

Viswa turned to Semat, 'And this is Alex's best friend and my partner's son, Semat. After eating a lot of hot curry at our house, he is now a zealot. He even likes the smell of the Prakrit language. He kept us entertained en route with his flute and harp.'

Loquacious by nature, Semat turned to Alex. 'But you do to those Greek girls—I mean, all right?' Semat could follow the Prakrit language, but had a funny way of speaking it. Alex blushed and glanced at his father from the corner of his eye.

The following day, Viswa got his gifts out. The first he gave to Anga – an exquisite collar of gold with cloisonné work, set with lapis lazuli, amethyst and turquoise. Anga's eyes widened until she jumped from her chair, hugged her uncle and planted a kiss on his cheek.

Viswa laughed, 'Anga, no cheek-wash this time!' and Anga blushed.

'It is a late dynasty design collar. I gave one to Ishi when she was married. This will be our wedding gift to Anga.'

Sonara frowned at Anga. 'If I can get her to marry!'

Anga glared back.

'I have another small gift for our beautiful Anga,' Viswa said affectionately. He took out a mirror of polished bronze. Its handle was carved in the shape of a naked Egyptian servant girl holding a bird, suggestive of love and beauty.

'Uncle,' Bitan teased, 'you should have brought with you the groom too!'

Blushing, Anga looked at Semat, who was watching her and they both smiled.

Viswa announced, 'I plan to stay three months this time. Alex wants to take horse-riding lessons which are not available in Alexandria. And Semat wants to learn Prakrit.'

After breakfast the next day, Bitan, Alex, Semat and Anga went for a walk in the orchard.

Bitan walked with Alex and Semat swerved at Anga.

'Semat, what do you do?' Anga asked.

'I want to be scribe, then I don't like it' he replied.

'What is scribe?'

Semat's eyes widened. 'You don't know scribe?'

Arching high her eyebrows, Anga shook her head. 'No!'

'I tell you, scribe is boss, he sits in cool shade and writes, others work.'

Anga was charmed by his manner. He did not like making necklaces with his father, he told her, and wanted to go to war, the thing that men do. After a while, they changed walking partners. Alex told her about his sister. Anga asked what she did. 'Wipes children's noses,' he said contemptuously, 'and cleans the house.'

Anga overheard Bitan asking Semat if he would like riding lessons. 'Yes, Yes. Everyone here on high horse.'

She noticed when he started taking lessons in horse riding and Prakrit language and within just a few weeks, he was out cantering on flat grounds with Alex.

One morning in early June, Semat came looking for Anga. She was sitting in the courtyard in a yellow-green robe with her book lying face down on a table. She was helping her mother to chop vegetables. Sonara sat, feet propped up, on another chair.

Semat said, 'Anga, come riding with me.'

Sonara's brows arched. 'Where's the trainer?'

Pushing the vegetables away, Anga got up scowling at her mother and said, 'Let's go.'

She came back in her cavalry dress. Sonara gave her an angry look, but Anga just shrugged and left.

On the flat ground, they broke into a long stride. 'You are doing well!' Anga cried.

Semat bragged, 'Now I can beat you!'

Anga smiled. 'We'll see!' Making eyes at him, she spurred her horse, then slowed remembering she had to watch him. A few minutes later, she looked back. He was losing the saddle grip and she trotted back. 'Semat, sit tight!'

After a while she got tired of watching. Overtaking him, she shouted, 'Semat, I'm going for a gallop, you take your time. I'll wait for you past the sharp bend in the road.'

At the bend, she stopped and waited. Soon he appeared, his legs flung wide, laughing, waving wildly and galloped past her. Anga shouted, 'Semat, horseback is not the place to horse around!'

On the way back, she followed him, admiring his ride. She sped past waving, her body arched to tease him. Semat kicked the horse and started galloping behind her.

Anga waited for him at the turn. Semat was nowhere in sight. She retraced her steps and sighted him at last—not upright on the saddle but lying flat on the ground. His horse stood nearby, snorting. Semat's face was contorted with pain, he had broken his right ankle.

It was a sunny day, and she knew the countryside well. She did not panic, and waited for a passing wagon. Two horse wagons were coming her way. She waved frantically, pointing to Semat; the drivers looked at her and Semat and drove past without stopping. Now she tried to pull Semat up on her horse but he was too heavy and she gave up. 'I'll get a wagon, Semat,' she assured him. 'You stay tight.' and she made for home.

Bitan and Alex brought him back to the house.

Anga felt guilty and Viswa's plan to leave at the end of June was now in jeopardy. The injury worried him. He said, 'If he can limp by then, I'll put him on camelback so he can lie down, sleep and watch the stars at night.'

A physician bandaged the ankle, pushed it against the wall to measure the pain, then declared, 'It will take him three months to walk.' He seemed like a magician to Anga.

Viswa frowned. 'I'll have a caravan pick him up. I have to leave.'

'Can Alex stay?' Bitan asked, not happy to take on the responsibility.

'Alex wants to go,' Viswa said. 'He is missing his mother.'

'I think he's missing his girlfriend,' Anga said with a smile.

Viswa laughed, 'These things happen.'

Of all people, Semat seemed the least concerned; he was happy sitting up in bed with his broken leg to the side and feeling rather detached from it—playing the flute, and watching Anga in the garden from his window.

Viswa and Alex left in early July and Bitan got busy with his work. Feeling responsible for Semat's condition, Anga sat by his side for long stretches, reading philosophy or Sanskrit drama, translating it to Prakrit for him. He liked her to read Afghan love poems to him. Sometimes, she played the harp, he on the flute.

His eyes were always searching her, his face lighted when he saw her. She sensed his excitement and it excited her.

One day Anga came with her harp and sat down on the floor by the side of his bed. She said, 'Semat, today you play harp. I'll play the flute.'

Motionless, Semat just stared at her. At last he spoke, 'Anga, I can go on looking at you forever.' Blood rushed to Anga's cheeks, she got up and started towards the door.

'Anga, I've something for you,' Semat said in a honeyed voice. 'Come to me.' Anga went to the chair on which he reclined, his right leg on a footrest., He took a red hibiscus and white jasmine bracelet from a basket and Anga's face lit up.

'Give me your left hand,' he said softly.

She extended her hand, and he pulled her to his chest and kissed her cheeks.

He whispered, 'Please don't be angry, Anga. I fell in love the moment I saw you.' Her body swelled up with blood and when he kissed her again—for a long moment—she could hear her own heartbeat, and fell limp on his chest. He kissed her lips, her eyes, her nape. Then taking her hand in his, he put the bracelet on her wrist.

She gently pulled away and tried but failed to play the flute, her hand, her whole body trembling. She made for the door, turned back, went to him, planted a quick kiss on his cheeks and ran out, her face red with pleasure and excitement.

Next morning, on her way to her philosophy teacher, she tiptoed to his room and kissed him. He embraced her. 'Anga, I think only of you.'

In the weeks following, Anga confided her love to him, and the two pledged to be bound forever. When she was away, he composed poems and read them to her.

She tried to avoid her mother. But not for long.

That evening Sonara sat down with Anga. 'Anga, your father and I want you to take interest in the kitchen. You will need it when you wed Tissa.'

Anga's face fell. 'Tissa?' she stammered.

Calmly Sonara said, 'Asoka's younger brother who came here to see you.'

Anga's face went red. 'You should have told me!'

'Your father told me yesterday.' Sonara turned her face away, as if she was lying.

'Mamma, I am not going to marry for two years,' Anga said tearfully.

'You are already late. I should never have listened to you.' She dropped the ultimatum. 'You must stop seeing Semat.' She added, 'I have noticed your unnatural happiness.'

Anga ran out of the room in tears. Next morning, she went to see Semat. 'Semat,' she said cautiously, 'I am soon to be married.'

Semat's face fell. In a raised voice, with nostrils quivering, he said, 'You come to tell me now!' and he burst into tears.

Anga motioned to keep his voice down, but he kept shouting, 'Get out, get out, I don't ever want to see you.'

Miserable, she left but returned that afternoon, and finding the door ajar, quietly entered. Semat was lying on the bed, his head buried in the pillows, body shaking with sobs. 'Semat!' She gently whispered. At the sound of her voice, he sat up and wiped his eyes.

'Who is the man?' he sniveled.

Anga did not think. 'Prince Tissa, but I...'

'Prince!' he burst out, his body shaking, 'So that is what it is! Now I know. I am nobody. You tell me, "I love you!" and I believe you. You play drama. Get out!' He and his Prakrit were falling apart.

Hurt and surprised, Anga cried, 'Semat, listen. I don't want to marry him. I want to marry you.'

Semat put his fingers in his ears and turned his face to the wall.

Sobbing, Anga mumbled, 'Semat, let me explain. I am desperate. I love you, only you. I had come to tell you what my mother told me, not what

I felt. I told you as soon as I heard. I only want you, Semat, only you—not Tissa or anyone else.' She held out her hands. 'Only you! Only you! Semat!'

A smile broke through Semat's tears. Forgetting his foot, he jumped up to embrace her and promptly fell down. Laughing, Anga fell upon him. They stayed like this, laughing between cries and tears, then Anga helped him back to bed.

'It was my mistake,' Semat said. 'Come with me to Egypt.'

Anga's face fell. All she knew was that her uncle had stayed back in Egypt for Itara. But living there had never occurred to her.

'You are thinking of an excuse?' Semat asked sarcastically.

'Semat, I will go to the end of the world with you.' Anga gently said. 'But I want you to stay here with me. Everyone—my mother, father, Bitan—will agree in the end. I will make them agree. Oh, we will be so happy!' She kissed his lips.

'If that makes you happy, I will stay. I just want to be with you.'

'I want you to be happy. I'd leave everyone if that is what you want!' She smiled through her tears.

Semat began to cry. 'No, no, I will stay.' He took her in his arms.

That evening, Anga went to her mother. Lowering her eyes, she looked at the ground. 'Mamma, I don't want to see Tissal.'

'Tissa, not Tissal,' Sonara snapped.

'Doesn't matter!' Anga snapped back.

Sonara yelled, 'Are you crazy? Look me in the eye. Tell me you can be happy with Semat, tell me he can give you what you are used to in life. He is nothing. Nothing!' She spat on the floor, her tongue hanging out.

Trembling with rage, Anga shouted back, 'You think "those things" will make me happy? I cannot live without him!'

Controlling her anger, Sonara said, 'I will tell you this: You will not marry him!'

With scorching eyes, she glared at her mother. 'I am going to Alexandria!' Anga started for the door.

Sonara shrieked, 'I wish you were never born!'

Anga ran out crying.

For the next few days, the two headstrong women fought. During the lull between storms, each mulled things over. Then they stopped talking.

After a couple of days, Sonara went to Anga. 'Think with a cool head, Anga. You want to ruin your life for a good-for-nothing boy? Have you taken leave of your senses? You have all your life before you.'

'My life is over!' Anga said curtly.

An awkward silence filled the room. Sonara said, 'If that is the way you feel, I want to make sure your love of two months is for real.'

'Five months,' Anga jumped in, 'I fell in love the day I saw him.'

After much back and forth, the terms were settled. Anga would not go to Alexandria and she would also not see Semat for six months. At the end of the trial period, they would be engaged and wedded a month later.

A surprise awaited Anga: Semat had been moved out of the house to the farthest guest house near the boundary wall. Their movements were carefully watched. Still, Anga and Semat kept up a pace of torrid letters carried secretly by her maid. Defying her promise, Anga tried a few times to meet him secretly in the garden at night.

Then Tissa arrived from Pataliputra. Anga was furious and refused to see him. Her mother explained that despite sending a messenger to Choti-ma saying Anga was seriously ill, Tissa insisted on rushing to her side to nurse her, certain she would want to marry a prince. Only when Bitan told Tissa the full story did he return to Pataliputra, vowing to find comfort in religion, and not place his happiness in the unpredictable ways of womankind.

Then a new fear raised its head when the maid told her that a courier had been sent to her uncle in Alexandria. Now she dreaded that he would come and take Semat away.

31

Livia continued to take care of foreigners' lodging, food and other amenities in Pataliputra, keeping a low profile. Through her hard work and energy, she had earned the King's respect.

Around this time, a scandal broke out. It involved the Textile Commissioner who was responsible for providing work for young widows. The state provided yarn which they spun, and collected their wages. Weavers wove it into clothing, bed sheets and other household and commercial items. If they did not perform the job, workers could lose their thumb or fingers. The Commissioner was using helpless young women for sex and household work. One of the victims told her story to Bhairavi, who told it to Livia, and it reached the King. The Commissioner was dismissed; Livia was given the additional responsibility of that position.

Livia's work brought her in frequent contact with Radhagupta, now the Prime Minister. Livia made an effort to mend relations with the chief queen, but failed. After Asoka's ride through Pataliputra with Kalanos' head, the queen was convinced that Livia and Asoka were conspiring against Sasima.

The King's health was rapidly deteriorating, and succession was on everyone's mind. The army was divided into doves and hawks, and the hawks had favored Asoka ever since he had put down the Taxila revolt.

The King himself had wavered after the uprising. He discussed it in the Council but found that Gajadhar, the Senapati, strongly supported Sasima. Without his support, the succession would not be orderly. Then there was the queen. He dropped the ball.

Livia was aware of Asoka's standing in the army. She knew he had Radhagupta's support. Since Asoka could not come to see her, she decided to go to Ujjain. She even went to the queen and asked her permission. The queen gave no answer. Livia decided to surprise Asoka.

He was out on a field trip when she arrived. When he returned, he found Livia sitting in the courtyard talking to a servant girl. 'Choti-ma! You didn't inform me!' and he embraced her. He had not seen her for seven years, and she knew she had markedly aged: she had wrinkles on her neck and under her eyes, grey hair, and her cheeks had lost their glow.

Sensing his disappointment, Livia said, 'That's what happens to neglected mothers.'

'But I like what I see.' she added. 'Your body is fuller, though you no longer have boyish looks. You look imperious, like your grandfather. But you have a better nose.' Then, 'Where is Devi?'

'With her parents.' Asoka told her the story. A fleeting sadness came over her, then she grinned. 'You'd be in big trouble if she were Senapati's daughter.'

Asoka showed her around. 'It is good,' she said wryly, 'but a Palace it is not.'

For the next few days, she visited the markets, bought meat, vegetables, fruit, and cooked for him. It pleased her that unlike Chandragupta, Asoka enjoyed Greek food. She didn't talk much.

Walking in the garden one afternoon, he said, 'Choti-ma, you've been so quiet! Unlike you.'

She was startled. 'I have a lot to talk about. I've just been waiting for you to ask.'

The tall Mimosa trees cast long shadows in the garden, and guards were pacing in the distance. To avoid them, she went inside and told him about the politics in Pataliputra. 'Where do you see yourself in the picture?'

Asoka looked away. 'Choti-ma, I have been away so long from Pataliputra!'

'That is what I was afraid of,' she said. 'I know you too well, Asoka. You will never be happy just being Governor. You were born to sit at top.'

Asoka seemed grimly quiet. Where was his old love of politics, she wondered. 'Everyone knows the king wanted to make you his heir.' Livia exaggerated.

'Well, nothing has changed.' There was sadness in his voice, as if he had been disappointed.

Livia frowned. 'It is not the time to vacillate, Asoka.'

Asoka said irritably, 'Choti-ma, I don't want to talk about it.'

As the widow of Chandragupta, she knew when to push and when to fold. She let go—this time. In the next few days, Asoka talked to her about everything but the succession. He made a mistake in Devi, he told her, she was stuck up in her ways.

Frustrated, Livia said, 'Asoka, you keep skirting the only issue that matters. Despite being Governor, you have not learnt to listen. In people with responsibilities, a deaf ear is a dangerous trait.'

He looked embarrassed. 'Choti-ma, please know that it is not out of arrogance or pride. Other people's advice does not matter to me. I listen only to my inner voice.'

The words "other people's advice" stung her. She controlled her anger.

'You can at least hear me out, even if it is an outsider's advice.'

'You're right, Choti-ma.'

'I don't understand your indifference to the throne. Have you forgotten your mother's wish? Her treatment by the queen? Your own treatment at the hands of the crown prince? And what about Chandragupta's promise to me that my son will be king?'

'I wish I were in Pataliputra,' Asoka said, looking out of the window.

His evasiveness inflamed her. 'You think the throne will wait for you? It's not your horse.' She pierced him with a look. 'Do you have what it takes to be king? Have wine and women turned you into Sasima?'

He bristled. 'That is a lie. A big lie! I am no Sasima!'

She attributed his ambivalence about the throne to his not want-ing to kill Sasima. He still had not said what she wanted to hear and remarked contemptuously, 'I don't know how you put down the upris-ing. Perhaps, it was Radhagupta. You have the morality of the man in the street.' Then springing on him like a tigress, she said, 'Where was your love for your brother when you rode with Kalanos' head through the streets of Pataliputra?'

Panting, she paused to recover her breath. 'God Indra killed his father for the throne. For Greek gods such deeds bring glory! Haven't you noticed the strong kill the weak and take what they want by force? It's the law of the jungle! It's the law of the world! Who are you? A sheep in tiger's skin?'

Asoka's face twitched. 'It is not the killing I dread. I killed plenty in Taxila. But Sasima is not a traitor, and he has more right to the throne than I. As for Indra, he is a god! He made up for his patricide by giving the rains to mankind.'

'You can do plenty when you are king.' She waved her hands in the air. 'Let's end this discussion here and now. I didn't come here to listen to your preaching.' She locked herself in her room and stayed there for two days, refusing to eat.

On the third day, Asoka stood outside her door, 'I am not leaving until you come out.' When she opened the door, her eyes puffed, Asoka said, 'Choti-ma, we are fighting over nothing. You've told me nothing that I do not already know.'

She asked for water and after taking a sip, said, 'Think with a cool head, Asoka. There is no love lost between you and Sasima. When he is king, you'll be dragged through the streets till dead.'

Asoka still kept quiet, his head low.

She added, 'Cowards, jabbers, men without worth, wallowing in the ankle-deep splendor of their birth, thirst for the blood of every adver-sary. Forget yourself! Think of the empire. How long do you think Sasima can last? The Queen can fool the King but not the vultures hovering around, ready to devour him. I've seen the hungry look in

Senapati's eyes. Does Sasima's life mean more to you than the fate of the empire?'

He sprang from his chair, his face dark, and began to pace. 'Choti-ma, I will die before I let anyone touch the empire! But I don't want to sit here discussing with you, like a murderer, whom and how I should kill. It is vulgar. Words mean nothing to me. My actions spring from my nature, not from fear or greed.' He sat down, still shaking.

His expression and his response softened Livia. Suddenly she felt assured. She went to him, and running her fingers through his thinning dark hair, said, 'I have a hunch you will do all right. You only need a good woman. And...the empire.'

There was nothing left to say.

A few days before her departure, she went to Asoka in his study.

She stood at the door, hesitating for a minute. 'Asoka, I have to tell you something.' Asoka asked her in and pulled up a chair.

'Radhagupta and I have become lovers,' she said, averting her eye.

Asoka gasped for air and reached for water, as if the earth moved beneath him. Sitting with his eyes closed, anger, even disgust, crossed his face. She sat turning a book, now and then looking at him, waiting for his words.

At last, he said coldly, 'Why did you have to tell me?'

She avoided his eyes. 'Because you should know.'

Silence. Then, 'I am forty nine. The flame of love has died in me. But not the desire for some warmth on dark cold nights.'

A longer silence ensued. When she looked up, his face had changed. There was sympathy, even love in his eyes. Softly, he asked, 'Choti-ma, why not marry?'

'I will, after you become king,' she said calmly.

He thought for a moment and then said, 'What if that doesn't happen?'

'It will,' she said like a clairvoyant. 'And yes, stay with Radhagupta before you enter Pataliputra. He will be waiting for you.'

Shortly before she left, she said, 'I've brought with me your grandfather's sword. I thought you would want it.'

Asoka looked surprised. 'What about the one you gave me?' His eyes seemed to accuse her.

Livia bowed her head, 'That was a fake, to keep your dream alive.'

That day she put the sword onto his open palms. 'It belongs to the successor of Chandragupta Maurya. It belongs to you!'

Two days later, she returned to Pataliputra.

32

It was a sunny, cold afternoon in Pataliputra. The streets hummed with people, horses and ox carts. Only ten days remained before the celebration of the crown prince's birthday and anticipation showed on every face. The preparations had been underway for months. Along with animal fights to the death, wrestling was the most popular public event. A large enclosure had been set up in the festival grounds. Two finalists would emerge out of several contenders. The crown prince liked to match two bodies strutting about in T-strips in the sanded arena, each grappling the rival's upper body, raising it, whirling it and pounding it against the ground. Although the winner received cash, the crown prince awarded a handsome consolation prize to the loser on the side—depending on the level of his body's demolition.

The event was widely announced. Colorfully dressed men walked up and down the streets in clown's caps, playing tambourines and exciting the crowds: 'Come one, come all! Watch two mounds of flesh grapple, jab, and swirl and pound each other like two rhinoceroses butting horns in the heat. Watch ribs crack, eyes bleed, retinas detach, brains discombobulate and pulverize. Enjoy the fearfully muscular bodies disintegrating before your eyes. Walk away untouched, unhurt by the mayhem as from a trip to the zoo; flex your muscles at home standing before the mirror, making faces, glorifying in your prowess. It is a great chance for excitement outside of bed: maybe the only one you'll have.'

Inside the Palace though, a different scene was playing out. After the usual morning meal, Bindusar complained of dizziness. Staggering to his bedroom, he fell down and had to be carried on a stretcher. Physicians, priests, and soothsayers swarmed to administer their special medicines, taking credit if the King as much as groaned or squeaked. Priests gathered around his bed. They lit a sacred fire in the room, and Vedic hymns were chanted to exorcise the evil spirit in the air, quickly clogging the room with smoke. The priests took turns, so as not to miss the sumptuous royal lunch or their long afternoon naps– and did some chanting in between. Two days later the King's breathing stopped. The second Mauryan emperor lay dead.

Women huddled in palace corners, worrying, whispering about their future. Disgruntled palace servants prophesied the Mauryan dynasty's end. Loyalists went about their usual chores as if nothing had happened. It was believed that the body of the dead soars to the realm of eternal light: it travels in a celestial car, or on wings of the soul to the heavenly abode; there it recovers its former body in a glorified form, and resumes living happily in Yama's abode. Yama, the first human to discover "the path of the fathers," was the king of the World of the Dead, and also called the "Leveler." In the *Mahabharata*, sage Narada describes Yama's heavenly abode: "In that fair domain it is neither too hot nor too cold...Nymphs dance and sing to the piping of celestial elves and merry laughter ever blends with the strains of alluring music...Yama sometimes plays the flute, sometimes drinks Soma and even offers the drink to the faithful. The unbelievers he commits to hell."

Minutes after the King's death, a lot more Brahmin priests swarmed into the room than were employed in the palace. They knew it was not a moment when one worried about or could keep count of the expenses. To reach Yama's abode, the Brahmins claimed, it was critical that the cremation rites be performed only by Brahmin priests. Otherwise the survivors would pay a heavy price: the soul of the dead would hover around them and plague their existence.

Amidst the Vedic chants, Bindusar's body, except the face, was washed and covered with white linen. Family members filed in to bid farewell, officials and important public figures followed after them. At night, the body was put on a horse wagon and led to the cremation ground by Sasima, the deceased's eldest son. Hymns to Yama were melodiously recited. A pyre of sandalwood stood ready, prepared by a Chandala– the outcast at the cremation ground– to burn the body.

A cow was prepared for sacrifice. To prevent its experiencing the fear of death, a secondary victim, a Billy goat, was placed by its side. The goat was led, kicking and bleating, to immolation, and sacrificed to God Agni– Fire– with the invocation, 'The goat is your share; burn him with your heat.' The idea was to let the goat take the heat and spare the pain to corpse. The cow was then sacrificed to meet the needs of the dead in heaven.

Bindusar's corpse was then put on the pyre. His face was covered with the omentum of the cow– the membrane which envelops the intestine - symbolizing its body. An invocation addressed the dead: "Gird yourself with the limbs of the cow as an armor against Agni, and cover yourself with fat and suet so that he will not embrace you with his impetuous heat." It was believed that the sacred fire– the god Agni– was the courier between the human and the divine world. Agni received the corpse– together with other foods– purged and purified the dead body of sins and evil, cooked it, made it worthy of god's meal, and then conveyed it to them.

Sasima took away the bow– the symbol of a warrior– that had been placed over the body of the dead Bindusar. The widowed queen, dressed in white and without jewelry, walked to the dead body. She lay down to the left of the corpse on the pyre. One of the priests addressed the dead. 'O mortal king, this woman, your wife, wishing to join you in the future world is lying by the corpse; she has always observed the duties of a faithful wife; grant her your permission to abide in this world and relinquish your wealth to your descendants...' Sasima proceeded to the pyre, took his mother's left hand, and escorted her away.

The pyre was now lit. A prayer was made invoking Agni not to scorch or tear asunder the dead man's skin or limbs, but to convey the mortal as an offering to the fathers– after the flames did their work. "Agni, consume not this body to cinders; nor give it pain..." the prayer said. When the fire grew spirited, a Soma oblation was made to Agni, to be conveyed to Yama. Yama loved the Soma. The crackling body was then left to burn to ashes and bones.

It was believed that by the power of invocation and ceremony, the dead man's impure corpse became, at the end of the incineration, one of the fathers to whom the oblation is made. It was like a magician's trick by which the sacrificed became the recipient of the sacrifice. Other rituals were performed to purify the living participants in the ceremony, so the separation between the dead and living was complete.

On the way back, the mourners were asked not to shed too many tears. Tears, they were told "burn the dead." Before returning home, the priest asked them to cleanse themselves by bathing in the Ganges. Sasima and the other princes reached home around three in the morning. At the palace door, they rinsed their mouths with water in which neem tree leaves had been soaked, to purify and disinfect their bodies. They inhaled the smoke of sandalwood at the threshold to symbolize their severance from the dead, and to protect them from the wayward and unpredictable ways of the spirits.

Following the King's death, Sasima's birthday celebrations were cancelled.

33

The King's death was announced the following night by relay torches on highway-posts to the public and officials of the empire.

Around eleven at night a courier came to inform Asoka. He felt a stab in his heart, though he had been preparing for this moment for some time. *I could not even touch my father before he died!* He was lost in thought. The courier interrupted, 'Governor, can I go?' Asoka nodded absentmindedly.

Agitated, he went out for fresh air, then returned disoriented and went back to bed but could not sleep. His head throbbed, and his heart fluttered. The wind strengthened and whistled through the house, flinging open, then slamming the windows and doors. He shouted at the servants, 'Shut the windows and doors tight.' Frightened, the horses neighed and whinnied in the stable.

He went back out and stood looking: clouds were gathering in the sky. 'Father, you should have died later!' he said, and went back to bed. He fell into a dream: the palace was in flames, Baba whispered to him, "Asoka rise!" He awoke and leapt from the bed, crying, 'A warrior I was born, a jackal I will not die!'

His loyal guards, trained for this day, gathered in the mansion compound. Lightning flashed in the sky, wind and dust were blowing and soon rain came pouring down. The wagon harnessed, he told the driver, 'We are going to Pataliputra. Now!'

The wagon started rolling, an iron lamp flickering violently at its side. 'Whip the horse,' he ordered the driver. After only a few miles came the thought, *If I am killed, Anga would not know of my love.*

'Take the first road to Taxila,' he ordered the driver. Astonished, the driver slowed down and turned to look at his master. Asoka was annoyed. 'The first road to Taxila!'

For the next two hours it rained hard. Unable to sleep in the din of the storm and rain, he thought about his father. *Father was a large shade tree. Now I stand alone in the sun's blazing heat. Strange how hostile the world suddenly seems, my ties to brothers already feel weak. No one is ever ready for a parent's death. I used to resent his distance, but now as a father myself, I know lack of time is not lack of love. He tried to do his best as a father and as a King.* His heart warmed at the memory of their last embrace.

The rain stopped, and he fell asleep. Soon he was awakened by the screeching of birds in the purple-grey skies. Looking out of the drawn shades, he thought of Anga, and felt comforted. *How tender is the color of the sky before sunrise, like her youthful face. Like the hopes of a young bride.*

Soon, a bright sun came up. The horse carriage passed through the flat landscape, raising dirt. The road seemed endless, the monotony broken only by a few tall trees that sprang up now and then on the roadside. His thoughts wandered. *Ambition! How many have fallen into your cobweb? The young, the foolish, the daring, even the wise! You are a runaway horse, a fever of the mind that does not abate, though the raging river floods subside; you are a leach that sucks a man's blood and gets bolder and fatter with each bite. You are the rope of a man's twisted dreams that keeps lifting him up by neck until, feet off the ground, he hangs by his own noose. The ambitious man wears clothes of hypocrisy, and a toothy smile. But there is a nobler kind of ambition that lifts a nation and sometimes mankind. Without it, gods are not gods and kings not great kings.* Anga reappeared before him and he asked himself if love was loftier than ambition. *I don't know yet. Ambition is man's face to the world,* he thought, *love, his entrails, his flesh and blood.*

These ruminations continued until ragged and unshaven, he showed up seventeen days later at the door of a surprised Bitan, on a late afternoon in November.

'You chose the longer route?' Bitan asked.

'I remembered I'd forgotten some important things,' replied Asoka.

Bitan told him about the family crisis. 'She is such a headstrong girl.'

Drained of blood, Asoka turned pale. Alone in his room, he thought *it would not matter now if he lived or died.* Then he remembered: *She is not yet wedded. She is still mine.*

When he asked about the men, Bitan replied, 'I have already dispatched them to Pataliputra. I drew them from the garrison.'

'From the regular army?' Asoka asked, surprised.

'Yes.'

'We had talked about mercenaries.'

'They started asking inconvenient questions. I asked Uncle Radhagupta and did what he advised. They are regular army men and will get lost in the crowd. No one will suspect a thing. I chose Persians, Afghans and Greeks—the men who hate Sasima. The officers will follow your orders—they're getting paid extra. No one knows about the mission except Purandas, the Assistant Army Commander. He will meet you at Uncle's house.'

Asoka wrung out a feeble smile. 'You did exactly what Kalanos did!'

Bitan smiled. 'With one difference—I did it for the empire.'

At suppertime, Asoka asked to see Anga. She came dressed in a black kaftan and a black vest, like a widow-in-mourning, and greeted Asoka with a forced smile. *She looks so pale,* thought Asoka. *Even in pain, her beauty shines, if delicately.*

She sat down with a sideways glance, looking lost.

The sun splashed purple and red in the evening sky above the mountains. When Bitan asked her to play the flute, she politely excused herself. Asoka yearned to hold her in his arms and bring a smile to her face.

'What have you been doing, Anga?' Asoka asked after an awkward silence.

'Nothing much.' She gazed into the distance.

Asoka said, 'Anga, I am going on a perilous journey. I may never see you again. My journey would be bearable if you would sing.'

Baffled, she looked at him, fidgeted for a while, then, after a long silence and in a trembling voice, said, 'Asoka, I will sing. I will sing for you!'

Darkness had crept in. A fire was started and one dry log immediately caught flame and lit her beautiful, sad face. She looked at him, and he saw the flames trembling in her eyes. A gleam came into his eyes, then passed away at the thought: *She is not mine.*

'This is Bitan's favorite song,' she said, 'Semat liked it too. It is about an Afghan soldier, who falls in love with a girl drawing water from a well. He watches:

> *Her flaming-red skirt,*
>
> *Her silken, golden hair,*
>
> *Flutter like desire in the evening air.*
>
> *Their eyes meet. The water-filled pail drops from her hand. He cries out:*
>
> *Will she be mine before the battle-cry?*
>
> *Will I die dangling my stick to the sky?*

Anga sang with great emotion, and the singing seemed to exhaust her.

It is my song too, thought Asoka. *If only she knew. For her, I'd gladly give up the empire.*

Suddenly he thought of Semat—*a stranger, a nobody, a 'mleccha', the untouchable. He had no right to steal her! If only I could make her happy,* he anguished. Then a surprising thought came to him. *Even if that meant letting her go to Semat.*

Anga left abruptly. Bitan and Asoka sat silent. *And I came all this way,* Asoka thought, *to tell her of my love!*

He poked at the fire. The flames were down to a flicker, and his shadow flitted on the ground. Stirring the embers, he said, 'Bitan, I have a favor to ask.'

Bitan looked at him through the dark brown patch of night.

'My children are in Vidisha. If I am killed, their lives will be in danger. Please send for them until the situation stabilizes.'

Bitan nodded. 'Asoka, it's going to be a long journey. Get some sleep before you leave in the morning. Also, I've made arrangements for your men.'

Before leaving early next morning, Asoka handed him a bundle. He said, 'Regardless of what happens, I will not need these now. Send them to Choti-ma.' He added, 'And yes, I am also leaving the carriage behind. I will be on the run!'

Bitan said, 'I have given some beards, moustaches and body paints to your men.'

The friends parted in sadness, not knowing if they will see each other again.

PART THREE

✦

The Path of Power

34

Chaos ruled in the streets of Pataliputra following Bindusar's death. The Greek, Persian and Afghans soldiers sent by Bitan assembled in the streets, protesting against Sasima and demanding Asoka be their king. Watching the crowds from the third floor of the Palace, Sasima turned to Purohit, the chief priest. 'What's wrong with these men? They are behaving like the soldiers of Taxila.'

The Purohit lifted the turban from his head. 'Crown prince, it will quiet down when your coronation date is fixed.'

The queen suspected Livia's hand in the unrest so rumors were spread about Asoka's atrocities in Taxila, and Varsha was paraded in town, sitting in an open palanquin. The Purohit was asked to perform an animal sacrifice to destroy Asoka. The Senapati was told to turn Pataliputra into a fort. 'It is Asoka's head,' she warned, 'or your job.'

The Senapati knew Asoka had left Ujjain. What route would he take? There were two possibilities – the shorter Ujjain-Pataliputra road or the longer Taxila-Pataliputra route. One hundred cavalry men were sent to look out on each route to find out, and special checkpoints set up near Pataliputra on the rivers. A special squad watched the city gates. 'Now,' Gajadhar boasted to the queen, 'Asoka can enter the city only if he's dead.'

The men at Reotipur checkpoint– ninety miles west of Pataliputra on the Ganges – expected Asoka to take the Ujjain route and they hoped to get a special reward. They fidgeted for forty days. At last they had a break– a party of five cherub-faced monks in orange robes approached. Watching them, Ramadin, a soldier, got a strange feeling. A stout broad-faced guard with long hair, he searched their bags and found only rice. Yet he noticed that the men kept shifting their legs.

He lined them up and got them to take off their robes. Their inside pockets revealed knives in banana leaves and not Buddha's sermons, as the monks had claimed.

Now the monks were lined up in their undergarments. A handsome monk caught Ramadin's eye, which gleamed at seeing an unusual bulge in front. His desire stirred, Ramadin walked the monk to a secluded tent, sat down, and prepared to view nature's happy aberration. Eyes shining, he softly said, 'Pants down!' Ramadin's face fell with the undergarments and he walked away feeling cheated. After a few yards, he realized that he had forgotten to search the monk. Returning, he found the monk still standing there, covering his parts with a long banana leaf running from his navel to the ground.

The search of the undergarment's inside pouch revealed a treasure of a different kind— one gold armlet, a ring with royal insignia, a pearl necklace, and Asoka's personal seal. Forgetting his own disappointment, Ramadin ran to the Chief, shouting, 'I got him, I got him!'

The Chief gathered ten soldiers who had recently seen Asoka, and asked them to identify him. In the line-up, all the soldiers pointed to the same broad-shouldered monk with a broad forehead, large eyes, a receding hairline and a pox mark on his left cheek.

'We have our man!' the soldiers shouted jubilantly. The Chief stared at the monk—his gaze intense enough to transform any man into Asoka. Then the monk was charged with being Asoka. But he changed his story. He said he was neither a monk nor Asoka—just an ordinary man. The scar on his scalp troubled the Chief. The soldiers were reassembled.

'Does Asoka have a star-like mark on his scalp?' the Chief asked.

'I'm certain he has,' Ramadin replied, 'though no one saw his shaved head. If you put a goat's hair cap on him, he'd look exactly like Asoka.'

'Sure?' the Chief asked, afraid of making a mistake.

'Absolutely,' his men said.

'Me too!' announced the Chief, eager not to be left out of the reward.

The Chief took Ramadin aside, 'He is a prince. Give him his own tent. At night, quietly sever his head. Here,' he said, handing him a sharp axe. 'And don't talk to anyone about it!'

The deed done, the head and the body were stuffed into a wooden box and rushed to the Senapati. The Senapati quickly buried the box in his backyard and sent for Sasima. 'Take a look,' he advised.

Sasima stood watching in the yard, arms crossed on his chest, brows furrowed, and his nose wrinkled. As the soil was removed, the stench sent him running inside. Senapati followed him. Sasima asked, 'You've made sure?'

'Of course,' the Senapati replied, twirling up the ends of his moustache.

'And you're absolutely sure?'

Irritated, the Senapati snapped, 'I am not a fool. I am the Senapati!'

Sasima looked at him. 'O! Yes. Yes. But do get rid of the head and the body. You and I should not be seen near it. Announce that he was killed in the forest by a bandit.'

As he climbed into the carriage, Sasima thought of his nagging mother. He stuck his head out of the window. 'But don't remove the checkpoints yet nor the men at the city gates.'

Sasima rushed to tell his mother the good news. Always suspicious, she asked, 'Did you see the head?' 'Of course!' replied Sasima. 'And you were satisfied?' Throwing up his hands, Sasima put Asoka's personal items in her hand. She examined each one minutely. A smile spread across her face. She was thinking of Livia.

When they heard the news, all the soldiers grieved and the public was shocked at Asoka's premature demise. The Purohit advised Sasima to cremate the body with proper Vedic rites so that Asoka's spirit would not harass him at night. Sasima asked the Senapati, he assigned it to the Chief, and the Chief passed the job. The buck stopped at Ramadin.

Ramadin took the coffin to the cremation ground. Chandala, the man who cremates the bodies, was hulk of a man with a long moustache and long hair. He carefully looked at the body and the head. 'What's his name?'

Stepping three steps back from the Chandala– the Untouchable– Ramadin replied, 'Asoka, a common prince.'

'The trouble with Royalty is that they lose their heads,' the Chandala observed, impudently. And added, 'I see a lot of flies. Where are the Brahmins?'

'Stop jabbering! Do your job!' Ramadin said sharply.

The Chandala held out his palm. 'Two cremations, two gold coins.'

Tossing two coins on the ground, Ramadan hurried out.

35

At the start of his journey Asoka was depressed. The world looked a dark place to him: his father was dead, his mission dangerous, and he was a hounded man. As he rode through the winding cobblestone streets on a cold, cloudy day, everything seemed shrouded in grey— the snow-clad mountains, the tall alpine trees, the flowerless vines, the once-enchanting lotus- pond, and the valley. Even nature seemed against him— an icy wind was blowing and the sun remained hidden behind the clouds. Bare branches spread out against the sky like twisted wire-mesh. 'Leafless, tangled, like my love!' he grumbled.

He couldn't gallop; he was paying no attention to the horse, his trot was erratic, as if he were riding a donkey. He started raving. 'My desire for the throne has sapped. I should have told her of my love that day in the valley. Why does she hold me in thrall? Is it her beauty? Her unearthly smile? The way she kissed the lotus leaves looking at me? I know there was love in those big eyes! And she sang for me!'

He realized he was not going fast enough. 'How will I reach Pataliputra in time? But why should I rush? I have no one. I don't need to live. My father is dead. My brother wants to kill me. I have been dead for years to my children. My mother is not my mother. Yesterday I was a governor, today I'm a fugitive. And the woman I love loves another man.'

His ravings ran much faster than his horse. 'I want to takeover an empire defended by six hundred thousand men. My army is three thousand strong. And I have not even seen it. It is out there some-where,' he said, pointing to the sky, 'like that pear-shaped cloud. There! Good for one minute's sprinkle! I am the greatest lunatic in this empire. No madhouse will touch me. And I am very, very tired. I am going to lose my head, if it's not gone already. But how does it matter? If I'm killed, I'll rule in hell. There is no heartbreak there, and no limit on craziness.'

Another thought followed: *If I lose my head, how will I woo her? The dead do not embrace. I have to hold her in my arms. When she comes before me, the throne turns cold and the world becomes warm. In the Upanishads, man becomes God, free from before and after. And in love, man becomes sensation, and time is obliterated.* He touched his head. *This head has to be saved. To woo her, to win her. And to make love!*

Suddenly his horse stopped to piss in the middle of the road, turning a natural function into a public performance, as a horse, being horse, sometimes does. Jolted, Asoka reprimanded himself. 'No dreaming until you reach the Palace! This is just the beginning.'

He started to gallop and at last his horse caught up with his hopes.

Chandragupta had built the Royal Road from Taxila to Pataliputra for fast communication and rapid movement of the army to the border. It was mostly flat terrain and crossed several big and small rivers. Most of the boat bridges were in various stages of repair. Of his fifty men, Asoka had assigned a team of fifteen to ride as his advance guard. Fifteen were at the rear and twenty accompanied him. All carried their food provisions on horseback. After crossing southeast Taxila, the party tackled the formidable Jhelum River. When a suitable depth was found, they forded the river at night and the party camped on its south-east bank near the Royal Road. Early in the morning, Dhanur, a young soldier, led an advance party of fifteen to forage for food in the little town of Bucephala, founded by Alexander the Great in memory of his valiant horse.

Near Bucephala's only little market, a party of seventy-five Magadha soldiers was camped by the roadside looking for Asoka. Noticing a party of men looking for food, they stopped them for questioning. Dhanur slipped away with two men to tell Asoka but twelve of Asoka's men were captured.

'Did you count the number in their party?' Asoka asked, stroking his recently grown beard.

'About twenty,' Dhanur said.

Asoka told him to go back, mix with the Magadha soldiers, and kill the captain but only if he discovered Asoka's presence and came after him. To avoid detection, Asoka immediately crossed to the west bank of the Jhelum, deciding to forsake the highway and taking instead a forest trail. Marching through the forest, they speared three sharp-tusked grizzled boars or Varaha but the Brahmin soldiers refused to eat their flesh. For them Varaha personified the third of the ten avatars, or incarnations, of god Vishnu. Asoka explained to them that Vishnu, the god of preservation, would want them to live, not die, so the men relented. They made faces as they swallowed little chunks of boar meat, and sometimes threw up.

The trail had slowed their pace so they forded the river at night to the east and got back on the highway. Dodging the pursuers, they pressed on for two days without stopping, despite many difficulties. Some rivers had no boat bridges. The horses swam through, and the men felled trees and crossed on rafts. Food was always scarce. Twelve men short, they separated into parties of two and four and quickly bought whatever they could in the villages. Some days they lived on edible bark. Soon they camped on the west bank of Sutlej river near Phillaur town. An advance party was sent out to check the east bank. The men were surprised to spot Dhanur walking in the bazaar, arm-in-arm with the Magadha soldiers. They rushed back to inform Asoka, who wondered, if they knew about his movements? That night, as three men watched by turn, others slept lightly, ready to decamp at a minutes' notice.

To Asoka's astonishment, Dhanur appeared a little before midnight. He said, 'King, last time, the Magadha soldiers were tipped off by a villager. I learned that they unhorsed our men and left them to wander in the forest. At present, they are unaware of your movements. I've made friends with the captain, and cook for him. This evening the captain returned laughing to his tent with a broad-hipped woman. I think he'll spend the next few days here with her.' Dhanur kept calling him king.

After Dhanur left to join the Magadha soldiers, Asoka picked up a handful of dirt in his hand. *I am the King of this much land!* he thought.

It alarmed Asoka that the Magadha soldiers were hot on his heels. 'Regardless of the captain and the broad-hips, we have to move,' he told his men. They immediately left, riding all night and the next day till noon, then stopped for half a day to rest the horses. That night, Asoka crossed the river, returned to the highway, rode all day and all night at breakneck speed, without stopping for food. He hoped to leave behind the pursuers once and for all. In their haste, one man crashed into a tree, and two fell from their horses, breaking their legs. When the party set up camp for the night, a horse was killed, skinned, and roasted on a greenwood fire, filling the area with smoke. Languid with hunger and fatigue, the men tore the half-cooked flesh into large chunks and devoured it, then slept like logs.

Long rides, lack of sleep, and hunger were taking their toll. Every time a soldier collapsed dead, he was quickly buried. If wounded, he was left in the nearest village at the mercy of the villagers, and forbidden to speak. A horse without a rider was quickly killed to avoid it falling into enemy hands.

Passing through the village of Kurukshetra, Asoka paused to look at the sprawling field where, a thousand years before, the famous *Mahabharata* war was fought between the Kaurava and Pandava clans. He bowed in reverence to the great warriors Arjun and Bhima.

After another round of grueling days, Asoka camped at night on the banks of the Jamuna river in the village of Vrindavan. This village had a special meaning for him. It was here that Lord Krishna grew up a shepherd boy, played his flute, dallied with young milkmaids, and stole their clothes while they bathed in the river. Sitting up high on a tree branch, he dangled their skirts and choli when the nude maidens returned from the river, dripping, shivering, begging for their clothes, their cheeks red under his amorous gaze.

Lying on the riverbank, and thinking of Anga late into the night, sadness overtook Asoka: *on this cool sandy shore on hot summer nights, Krishna would make love a thousand times to his beloved Radha, moonlight nuzzling her breasts.*

Asoka left Vrindavan before sunrise. When the sun came out, Asoka turned to check if the Magadha soldiers were on his tail and fell from the saddle. He quickly got up and continued, though for a few minutes the road and the sky changed places before his eyes.

Happy that they had covered so much ground, the party rested for a day at the ancient city of holy Prayag, situated on the confluence of the Ganges and the Jamuna rivers. They washed their muddy feet and sandals, and swam and frolicked in the Ganges. Asoka had vague memories of coming on pilgrimage to the city with his mother when he was six or seven. Unexpectedly, Dhanur joined them at Prayag. He had left the Magadha party at Kurukshetra.

'There, the captain decided to wait for you, while cozily spending his time with the broad hips. One of his men,' he added, 'had fed the captain wrong information.'

Passing Varanasi—the timeless city, the city on whose Ghats old men came to die to attain heaven—Asoka hoped to reach Pataliputra soon. To his dismay, at Buxur he learnt of the checkpoint on the Son and Ganges rivers near Semariya, manned by three hundred guards. Surprised by the number, he wondered if his luck had run out. The men now proceeded cautiously, he in disguise.

At a little distance from the checkpoint, three men sat for two days as mendicants by the roadside, observing the guards. They noticed the guards fell asleep at midnight and woke up around dawn. Though Asoka was unaware of it, perhaps the news of his death on the Ujjain route had lulled the men, or perhaps the chilly nights kept them in their blankets. Anxious, he decided to take the risk. On the third night, five horsemen cleared the checkpoint first. Twelve were to go with him on foot, two hours before dawn. The rest were to follow an hour later.

That dark, cold night, four men appeared at the checkpoint carrying on their shoulders a dead man on a plank of bamboo poles. Eight walked behind chanting, 'Ram Nam Satya Hai'— God is Truth, God is Truth. Their chants, though not loud, woke two of the guards. Tightening his blanket around his shoulders, one sat up yawning and rubbing his eyes. The other berated the men, 'Leave the dead in peace!' The pall-bearers said nothing, but lowered their pitch.

'Who is this man?' one guard asked.

'A grand man of our untouchable tribe,' Dhanur replied. 'My ninety year old great-grandfather from the village of Daner, where he will be cremated.'

The guard looked at the pall-bearers suspiciously, 'I hear no cries, see no tears.'

'Crying is easy! When a man— however great or grand – lives to be that old, children's tears also dry up with his skin and bone.' Dhanur stepped closer to the guard. Breathing right in the guard's face, and with one hand on the shroud, Dhanur said, 'Let me show you the corpse!'

Wrinkling his nose, the irritated guard bent back. 'Take it away.' Drawing the cord to open the gate, he joked, 'He will burn well!" And as an afterthought, added, 'With fewer sticks too!'

After they passed the gate, Dhanur mumbled, 'He burns best with his own fuel!'

The funerary men continued their long strides, wobbling, stumbling, and tossing Asoka's body from side to side on the plank under the white shroud. Poked by sharp edges, Asoka lay numb with cold, his cerebellum pulverized. Playing dead will be a new experience! He'd told himself. Now he was not so sure.

The city was still a considerable distance away. After another mile, Asoka rose from the dead on the bank of the Ganges. After a bath at this lonely spot, he traveled barefoot as a peasant, carrying on his head a long loose sack of vegetables that dangled over his ears and below his eyes.

Only twenty-seven men had survived the ordeal.

36

Seven days remained until Sasima's coronation. In the mansion built by his father outside the city, Radhagupta paced in his study around midnight. *What's happened to Asoka? He should have been here by now. The fickle public is already salivating at the prospect of the feast. In a couple of days they won't care if an ass is tossed on the throne.*

But something also kept whispering, *He will come, he is resourceful. He killed Kalanos without the army. He crushed the uprising quickly.*

Radhagupta snuffed out the lamp and stood looking out of the window, as he had for last few days. On the long approach road to his house, he had had lampposts lit for the last thirty days. His loyal guards at the gate knew not to stop any man from entering the gate. It seemed a night like any other.

Too wound up for bed, Radhagupta re-lit the lamp and sat at his desk reading his favorite chapter from the *Bhagwad-Gita*, where Lord Krishna tells Arjun to act without attachment to the fruit of the deed. *Right now, just when I need it most, all this talk of detachment seems hogwash,* he mused. Lost in thought, he did not hear a knock at the door. Then startled, he dropped the holy book, and rushed to open the door. In the trembling light, a bearded man stood before him in rags, covered in dust from head to toe. But the man's eyes shone like the flame of lamp in his hand.

'Asoka!' Radhagupta embraced the weary traveler joyously. Then he quietly said, 'Prince, go wash, eat and get some sleep.'

Next morning, they talked. 'Purandas, the deputy army chief, is waiting for your orders.' Radhagupta said. 'He'll be here this afternoon.'

'I'll go tomorrow night,' Asoka said, after a pause.

'You don't need to. Purandas has a great plan.'

'I can't leave the job to any other man.' Asoka said. He remembered Sasima's betrayal by Kalanos.

'You'll be taking an unnecessary risk.' Radhagupta looked displeased.

'One night. One chance. That's all I have. If I challenge Sasima and kill him, the public will forgive me in the end.'

'Prince! Stay out of the city. What if Sasima escapes or hides in the city and shows up the next morning? There'll be a bloody war. Who knows how many heads will roll? Most of the army supports Sasima. And you have only three thousand men.'

Asoka looked into his eyes. 'I'm betting Sasima will lose his nerve after the Senapati is killed.'

'I don't agree,' Radhagupta warned. 'Sasima can be stubborn!'

'Purandas' plan is not perfect. His story that Marut killed Sasima for the throne will not hold water when I emerge as king. People aren't dumb. I'll forever stand condemned in their eyes, and my own.'

Driving his chariot to the city next morning, Radhagupta kept rehearsing in his mind the difficulties he faced. *Senapati's watchdogs stand snarling at the gates. Of course, the Palace guards will be told there is an internal squabble between the princes, and they must keep out. But what if some idiot among them loses nerve, pulls out his arrows and starts shooting Asoka's men? The bloodshed will get the army out and hell will break loose. But this prince is so cocky, so foolish! He may doom us both.*

Next morning, Asoka himself drove Radhagupta's chariot into the city dressed like a peasant— a turban to his eyelids, his right eye heavily circled with carbon, his chest bare except for the sacred thread, and with a butterfly moustache and Greek whiskers. At the city gate, the guards stopped the chariot to open the heavy doors. Radhagupta's breath became fast. *The guards are so slow!* Then he noticed one of Senapati's watchdogs staring at Asoka. Trembling, Radhagupta prepared for the worst, not daring to look the guard in the eye. A few seconds passed but it felt like an eternity. The man turned away and resumed his chat with his fellow guards.

The chariot came to a stop outside Radhagupta's office building. Asoka followed the Prime Minister, holding his lunch bag. Radhagupta hastily climbed the stairs to his second floor office and quickly sent his own guard on an errand. Locked in Radhagupta's antechamber, Asoka lay down on the floor, heaving a sigh of relief. Livia dropped by during the day and brought him food. She told him that Bhairavi, now a Palace guard, would meet him at midnight in front of the Princes' Palace.

A few minutes before midnight, Purandas opened the east gate. Streams of soldiers began filing into the city. Purandas marched toward the Palace and unlocked the back gate. The soldiers circled the Palace and stood guard.

Inside, only five officials lived in the Palace Complex—the Prime Minister, the Purohit, the Senapati, the Treasurer, and the Chief of Palace Guards. The Prime Minister's house was empty. Radhagupta had been living outside the city for some time.

Around midnight, five men took charge from the day guards at Senapati's house. Senapati's regular night guards had been sent to the Prime Minister's house outside the city.

After dispatching his men to the Senapati's house, an anxious Asoka stood leaning against a large tree in front of the Princes' Palace, waiting for the men to return. It was quiet and dark, and a sickle moon hung in the sky. His mouth dry, he heard the beat of his own heart; every hoot of an owl or screech of a bird startled him. *I have been close to death before, but tonight the stakes are so much greater than my own life. Should the Senapati escape, I am dead. But I will not let despair raise its head. If only I had won her! It is easier to die without the throne than with the uncertainty of her love!*

A bird shrieked in the distance. He heard footsteps behind him. Startled, he turned, his heart pounding wildly. He drew his sword.

The men climbed the porch, and one of them knocked softly on the door. The Senapati was snoring with abandon after a hearty love bout. The first few knocks were lost in the loud vibrations of his soft palate. Then his wife woke, sat up in bed and shook her husband by the shoulder. Unable to open his eyes, the Senapati drawled, 'Hmm, haa... Who...What?'

'Someone is at the door,' his wife whispered in fright.

He cocked his hand behind his ear, and began to doze off again when his wife shook him hard. He growled, 'Where are the stupid guards?' Knock knock. Louder this time. He sat up and started to call them, but heard only his own voice. 'Rogues! Asleep again! I'll hang you all,' he shouted. 'They might as well be dead!'

His wife softly reminded him about the neighbors and he got up. 'Perhaps it's that crazy crown prince with some new-fangled plan hatched by his senile mother!' His wife handed him his robe and he walked to the door tying the cord, and picked up a sword. 'Who's there?' he asked sharply.

'Asoka,' the cheeky Dhanur replied, pulling faces in dark.

'Asoka?' he repeated, fully waking up. 'Asoka who?'

'There's only one,' Dhanur replied, puffing his cheeks.

'That one is in deep sleep!' the Senapati sneered from inside.

'This one is wide awake,' Dhanur smirked, standing on one leg.

The Senapati's irritation mounted. 'Asoka is with Yama!'

'Asoka is your Yama!' Dhanur said, thrusting his sword into the belly of the night.

The Senapati was now trembling with rage. Drawing his sword, he cracked open the door to peep. One man kicked it open; two others seized him by the neck, pinned him down, stuffed his mouth with rags, and severed his head. Then the men entered the house, stuffed rags in the mouths of his wife and children, tied their feet and hands behind their backs and escaped into the night.

Sword drawn, Asoka strained to see the shadows of men moving towards him. Then he remembered! They had been sent to the Senapati's house. He recognized Dhanur passing under the lamp. 'Done,' he whispered in Asoka's ear. Involuntarily, Asoka's eyes turned up to the heavens. He wiped his brow and thanked the goddess of the night. 'The greatest danger has passed.'

Leaving fifty soldiers to guard the front, Asoka went to the back entrance of the Palace where Bhairavi was waiting for him. She opened the backdoor. In the courtyard, looking up at the sickle moon in the sky, Asoka told himself, 'dark deeds are best done in the dark when desire takes on flesh.'

Crossing the verandah, he stood at Sasima's bedroom door. Soft moans and groans of love came from the room. Gently tapping the door, he heard clothes rustling, and the bed creaking. Then he heard footsteps behind him and startled, turned to see a young boy, eight or nine, wrapped in a blanket, walking toward him. The boy stopped a few feet away in front of the next door, and stood watching. Asoka went to him and whispered, 'What is your name?'

'Nigrodh, Sasima's son,' he answered fearlessly. 'Who are you?'

'Oh, I came to see Pavan,' Asoka whispered.

'He is in the next apartment. Go out of the courtyard and turn right.'

'Thanks,' Asoka patted the little boy on the back, 'You are a handsome boy. Now go back to sleep.'

The little boy went in, leaving the door ajar.

Agitated, Asoka stood outside Sasima's room, mumbling, 'Why does he have to go urinating, like an old man at night?'

He knocked again. Suddenly, the door opened and a half-naked woman bounded out, clutching a baby in her arms. She disappeared into Nigrodh's room.

Asoka entered Sasima's room. Covered with a white sheet, a body lay in bed, the toes sticking out. With the tip of his sword he gently poked the sheet near the neck and whispered, 'Sasima, I am Asoka. Get up! Pick up your sword! Fight!'

He stepped back, sword drawn.

The sheet quivered. Nothing happened. 'Sasima, only cowards die in bed,' Asoka exhorted, bending over the sheet. It quaked like a leaf. Someone was breathing hard. 'Let's get it over with.'

A trembling voice came from under the sheet, 'I am not Sasima!'

Contemptuously, Asoka said, 'When the day of reckoning comes, sinner becomes saint. Say your prayers, Sasima!' The little boy's face jumped before him and he had an urge to run, but instead thrust the sword with both hands into the sheet, ripping it. A cry rent the air and blood spurted out, streaking his face. 'So warm! The blood of a cold man!' Asoka mumbled, horrified.

He wiped his face on his arm and ran outside. Bhairavi was waiting. Asoka had forgotten to check if Sasima was dead. He sent in a man, who soon returned. 'King, you killed Marut, not Sasima!'

'Damn it!' Asoka wrung his blood-spattered hands and his face flushed with remorse. 'I did two wrongs.' He turned to Bhairavi, 'Sasima must not escape. He has to be with the queen! Take these men and capture him. Don't let the queen stop you. I will be with Choti-ma.'

He turned to his men. 'Three of you go and take Pavan prisoner. Don't kill him.' The killing of Marut had shaken him.

He stopped under a lamp. He had expected blood on his sword, but not strands of flesh. He shivered. *How could I use my grandfather's sword for this dark deed?* He hurried to the Nandi lake to wash it. He stood looking wistfully at the water, where he had swum countless times as a youth. *I can't foul this lake with his blood!*

Briskly he walked over to the Ganges and stood on its bank, looking into the dark waters. *The Ganges shimmers, but I have thrust a pale sickle into her womb! We played with wooden swords here and fell dead with our eyes half-closed. How I have changed! What is it in nature that makes a monster of us?*

He took off his robe, waded into the cold water to his thighs, and washed the sword, running his fingers over the hard, cold surface. One spot felt sticky. He took off his clothes and swam to the middle, scrubbing it hard in the strong current, then washed some more. He swam ashore and wiped the blade against his thigh, turning it back and forth until he could see moonlight glinting on a blemish-free surface. He dressed and started toward Choti-ma's apartment.

Cicadas chirped in the distance, and frogs croaked nearby. He heard a boat splashing, making waves. There was no cheer or spring in his stride. His tongue was parched, his mind numb. *Even a wrong deed I could not do right*, he thought, tortured. He looked up. The sky was clear of the clouds.

It should have been a foggy night!

37

Standing by her window, Livia said to Roxanne, 'It is a dark and beauteous night; the breeze is heavy with fragrance. Spring is about to come into my life. The moon's face is arched to break into a happy song. The gods eagerly await the drink of enemy's blood. I could die of happiness. And yet, a shadow lurks in my breast!'

With her hair piled high, she wore all her jewels, and was dressed like a queen in a green silk Chiton gathered at the waist with a gold belt. Ever since Suba had said it went well with her olive skin, she liked green. Her eyes shone like the eyes of a cat at night.

Roxanne smiled. 'I am so happy for you. When Asoka left, you'd given up on him.'

'I know, I know. How was I to know the uprising would sink Sasima? Asoka is a natural. I was naive then, thinking that he needed my potion to get the throne. Now I know. Ambition is not a decoction anyone can drink, and behold, he turns into a king! You have it or you don't, like my Nearchus' green eyes. But I like to think I unlocked his mind to possibilities.'

'You think he will conquer the world?'

'I would like him to sweep at least through Persia. Then I, the magnanimous older sister, can ask my son to forgive my dear brother's life.'

'I thought you loved your brother!'

'Of course! But love is not rustproof. He hasn't sent me any wine in ages.'

Roxanne went to the window, and craned her neck. 'I don't see a thing in the distance. It is going to be a long night. I pray he returns.'

Livia frowned. 'Pray! Have you gone mad? Of course he'll return. I know all the secret passages, all the byways of the Palace. I have wandered in them. I'll kill the queen; I'll kill Sasima and the last Maurya if he doesn't.'

'It won't be necessary, daughter of Greece, Princess of Persia.'

Roxanne brought out some wine. 'Let's drink to his success. It will help us pass the time!'

'In the old days, I had Chandragupta and wine before going to sleep. A warm drink of lemon and honey will do tonight. I have to be awake.'

Roxanne called a maid for the drink. 'You're right. We should not be found in each other's arms when the king returns. But we have so much time on our hands! Oh, I know. You promised me the story of your life. It will keep us on our toes.'

'From beginning to end?' asked Livia.

'To the end!'

Livia sat up in bed against the wall, and Roxanne pulled up a chair by her side. 'It happened in my last incarnation,' Livia said, closing her eyes. 'A Greek princess, I was only seventeen, lost in my dreams, and waiting for my prince in Babylon. Just the thought of having a young man close to me sent blood rushing all over my body. In the enchanting terraced Hanging Gardens, I spent many an afternoon alone with Nearchus, a distant cousin, staying with us for military training. Those gardens, built hundreds of years back by the great Nebuchadnezzar for his beautiful Persian queen, Amytis, were perfumed by their love and mine.

'Then one day my gossamer world went up in flames. I was to be sent away to India and married there to the Indian Emperor.' *That day my world, my laughter, my games with Nearchus— all were scattered like spring blossoms in a storm*, Livia thought. 'I was angry at first, then cried for days on my mother's chest.'

'Unknown to me, I was in love with Nearchus, his golden hair and green eyes. In the Hanging Gardens we played the game of "See and

Tell" with the plants, and the winner could ask any favor. During the day, I'd get the name of a plant, and later score over Nearchus. I would punish him with a long, long smooch, imagining he had covered my body and was whispering the magic words. Just the thought made me giddy. And now, I'd never see him again. The thought tortured me.'

'My mother told me that my father was defeated in north-west India by Chandragupta Maurya, and had to concede even Kandahar and Kabul in Afghanistan, parts of Baluchistan and Herat and had to give me away by a treaty. He was not happy, but Chandragupta promised that at fourteen my son would be declared crown prince.

'Later, my brother Antiochus, who was present at the tent where negotiations took place, told me that when Chandragupta asked father for my hand, father asked him for five hundred war elephants in return. Chandragupta was the victor and did not have to give anything but Chandragupta was eager for me and told father, "You will get your dumb, fat elephants."

To be traded for elephants was funny. But going to India was not funny. And not seeing my parents again was not funny.

'For me, the unreal had become real. It was as if the moon had landed on our roof and whisked me away on a beam. But I was not about to give up. At the earliest opportunity, I told Nearchus and his face fell. In that instant I knew he loved me. Without a word, I burst into sobs. He kissed away my tears and with his voice trembling, said, "Livia, I have had no time to think about our marriage. To consider it now would be a terrible idea."

'He rejected my idea of eloping to Athens and I was crestfallen; he lacked the courage to stand up to my father. But how could I blame him? My father was emperor of Persia and very willful. By custom, he had an absolute right to marry me to whomever he pleased.

'I continued to sulk, but at last submitted to my fate. A few days later, my mother came to me and took my hands. "You are such a silly girl! You are not the daughter of a donkey-breeder who can marry any fool; you are the daughter of the emperor of Persia. You have to marry the conqueror– it is the royal way. You'll laugh when you hear about my strange marriage to your father. After the defeat of the Persian King Darius III, Alexander compelled ten thousand Greek soldiers to accept Persian wives. He wanted to breed a new race of men fit for his world empire. Eighty top officers, including your father, were also told to marry Persian noblewomen in a mass wedding at Susa. Happy or miserable, everyone took his bride home. Alexander's wishes would not be flouted. The daughter of a defeated noble, I was at a low point in my life. But when I saw your father, my heart fluttered– he was so handsome! I was lucky. Even if he'd had one eye and limped, I would have had to marry him. And he was no emperor then." My mother sighed, then with a forced smile, said, "If your father had won that damned war, I would be welcoming an Indian princess for him."'

'Her words brought me no cheer. At last, she hung her head and said, "Livia, you have no choice...I had none."'

That day is etched with a red hot iron in my mind, Livia thought. *I remember it all – mother's dark green silk dress, the round plump emerald necklace, her wrinkled, weary face.*

A tear rolled down Livia's cheek, and the warm sensation brought her back to the room. She attempted a smile. 'I have been happy. I don't feel that way now! Certainly, not now.'

Roxanne caressed Livia's hand and Livia took a sip of the drink, now cold. 'When I saw him, I liked his imperious look. He was so strong and yet so tender when he held me in his arms. I was in awe of him. When I came to Pataliputra, I asked myself, Who is this man, this conqueror of India? Later I came to like his confidence and determination. He was a real man.'

Livia paused, pulling at the threads of memory.

'I was now resigned, and decided to make of it what I could. And then it flashed, what about the marriage that I had always wanted in the midst of my family and friends? I rushed to my last resort– my mother.'

' "Child," said my mother, "if he came here, you might not have a kingdom to go to. And he is coming to Taxila to escort you. Given the distance and my health, your father has forbidden me to attend the ceremony at Pataliputra. Antiochus can't go because he is the crown prince. One of your cousins will join the wedding." '

'Inconsolable, I fell asleep. I dreamed that I was in bridal dress with a crown of fresh flowers round my head. Astride a white horse, I saw my groom's face hidden behind the wispy clouds. As the horse came closer, I recognized Nearchus floating in air, his arms reaching out toward me. Just then I heard my mother's shrill voice and I woke with a start. Even in my dream, I couldn't marry him!

'Then an idea occurred to me: what if I married an image of Chandragupta here? I was excited and ran to my mother.

'At first she was aghast, but finally the idea took hold. She too liked the pomp, the ceremony. We realized no human could substitute for the king, and an animal would be insulting so finally, we settled for a statue. When my father heard of it, he was angry at first, then, afraid of delay, he became reconciled to the idea. "He urgently needs the elephants," my mother told me.

'Elephants! Elephants! And I am the one getting trampled, I thought.

'A royal sculptor was summoned. A stone statue would take months, and porcelain would be too fragile, so we settled on a wooden figure. I wanted it to look it happy, but majestic. Antiochus and the generals described the King to the artist.

'Then we ran into a problem. A statue could not sit down and get up during the ceremonies. My marriage plan was in jeopardy. Then my brother Antiochus, ever creative, suggested the statue be made in parts—head, torso, thighs and legs— and joined separately by movable iron bars. Not perfect, but it would work.

'Slowly Chandragupta began to emerge from the log. His hair and moustache were painted black, and his dark brown eyes were polished to a shine. I wanted him to smile when I looked at him. But he sat unimpressed, unmoved. I demanded a softer demeanor. Poor sculptor! Like most Persians, probably he had never smiled in his life. So we found a happy artist who invested the statue with a smirk, the best he could do. Now he seemed pleased at having me as his bride.

'A wedding date was set and my mother and I sat down to discuss the ceremonies with a priest. He said that the duty of a Greek wife was to produce a male heir. We were told that the betrothal ceremony, engue, was done by the treaty. Ekdosis, the bride's ritual bath, banquet, music and dancing, and gamos - the giving away of the bride— would be performed at Babylon. But the most important ceremony would be performed in Pataliputra: after the couple has been showered with nuts and dried figs, the bride enters the bridal chamber, the door is closed, and the women outside sing an epithalamion – a marriage song– in shrill, high-pitched voices, to drown out the bride's cries as she is deflowered.'

'On the wedding day, while I shivered in the cold, ritual bath water, my hand-crafted husband sat through it without a twitch. Later, sesame seed cakes were served to the guests. In the evening, torches were lit and music and dancing began. I danced as never before. A condemned prisoner dances most vigorously the day before his execution, Nearchus had once told me. The gaiety filled me with sadness as I was to leave at dawn the next day. I did not sleep, and my mother kept bursting into tears. She teased me, saying that once I reached India, I would forget her and dear father.

'On the dreaded morning, my mother took me to Ayapana, the house of Ahur Mazda, the Persian god. With tearful eyes, she asked him to give me a son who would be king. I bowed, and prayed for my happiness.

'Outside the house, I stood wrapped in the early morning haze. The journey I was about to undertake was long and arduous— through desert, mountains, snow, icy winds, narrow passes and dangerous gorges. I was embarking on a journey to death, I felt. Perhaps in leaving her familiar world, every bride goes through a little death. I was consoled by the thought that if I were to die, my wedding ceremonies would become my funeral rites.'

Something distracted her.

38

'I heard a knock!' Livia looked around.

'It's the wind under the door.'

'O! All my life, I've waited for a knock on my door!'

'Not anymore! Livia, this is the last night!'

'Oh, yes.' Livia resumed. 'Wrapped in the golden bridal robe, I kissed my father, hoping to see a little softness in his eyes. Not a word or a look! In my growing up, he had never said a harsh word to me, but he always kept a stony face; showing emotion to him was a weakness. Later mama wrote that after I left, he did not sleep for three nights.

'On a sunny, sultry morning in early July, I left the house that had been my world. Accompanied by my husband's statue, I sat in the decorated horse carriage. In the distance, the splendid Ishtar gate stood unmoved. A crowd of relatives, friends, servants and slaves surrounded the carriage. My eyes searched in vain for Nearchus. He hated goodbyes. My mother's face kept appearing before me. In my mind I had rehearsed the departure many times yet when the moment came, I broke down. I touched my husband for a little comfort, but recoiled at the hot touch. How I wished I were sitting next to my real man.

'Months later in Pataliputra, I got the statue out on a whim and showed it to my Lord. He was amused. "Impostor!" he said, "He had the nerve to wed my bride!" Gazing at its flat groin, he said with mock relief, "Thank God he couldn't consummate the marriage!"

'I had asked my father to arrange an Indian historian and a Prakrit language teacher but the search team for a historian returned empty-handed. "Though philosophers and priests litter the country," the team leader told me, "we found no historians." When pressed, he said, "The Brahmins, the only learned class, have no time to spare from amassing wealth, though they ask people to devote all their time to improving their lives after death."

'Prakrit was the language of Pataliputra, and I was lucky to find a teacher. A man named Raman arrived by mule from Taxila, with a small bundle under his arm. "All my belongings for my earthly existence," he said. He had travelled with caravans between India and Persia and was fluent in Persian. In the wagon where we conversed, he would explain the Vedic philosophy, which, to him was loftiest in the world.'

'We passed through rugged mountains and desert. A unit of my father's army escorted me to Kandahar in Afghanistan where the Indian Emperor's territory began. Megasthenes, a friend of my father, joined us in Kabul. The difficult journey gave me time to reflect on my life. After the Khyber pass, everything changed—the skies, the people, the trees, the wild animals, even the birds. It knew my world was dead. But what would the new world be like? Would Chandragupta love me? Would he live long? Would I have a son? Would he rule over India?'

Livia was tired and paused.

'We still have a couple of hours,' Roxanne said, eagerly.

Roxanne accompanied Livia as she went out to see if the army had surrounded the palace. A sickle moon hung in the sky, and all was quiet. She came back to her room.

'What happened in Taxila?' Roxanne asked.

'I stayed with Pushyagupta, then Governor and a friend of the Emperor. When I heard my lord would be arriving in a few hours instead of two days as I had expected, I quivered. One of the maids was touching up my face. I ran when I heard the guards shouting. "The emperor is here." The mansion shook as if an earthquake had hit. Spears clicked, clanked and thumped the floor. The door creaked, and gilded soldiers filled the room. I peeped from behind the heavy dark curtains. Was he handsome? And then I got a glimpse and my heart stopped! He had broad shoulders, a large forehead, big eyes, a twirled up moustache, and hair brushed back. He looked manly and distinguished. Only I found his nose a little too broad. Come to think of it, I had never thought about the nose. But it was a nose I could live with.

'I quickly disappeared. Only one thought now possessed me– he is the emperor and I his queen. When he called me in, I staggered, trying not to fall. He embraced me. "Welcome to my country, princess!" My weariness and reservations melted away in that one long moment. A strange feeling overtook me– a longing to stay pressed in his arms. He sat there for a few minutes, refusing to eat, then he took me out to show me Taxila in his special four-horse wagon which had a long, comfortable seat for two.'

'He held my hand to help me climb in. It was a beautiful day, sunny, crisp and cold. I sat beside him, not knowing what to say, enjoying the sun, the morning breeze, and looking at the mountains in distance. As we drove to the rocky, precipitous ridge dividing the valley, he kept fiddling with the curtains. The naked trees looked so beautiful against the sky and my head buzzed with strange thoughts. He started to name the trees, but I heard nothing. Suddenly, he went silent, and gazed at me as if he had never seen a seventeen-year-old girl and I basked in his gaze.

'He took me in his arms and kissed me. I sensed his impatience when, with a flick, the curtains came down. My impulse was to resist, but I was not going to fight the emperor of India! I closed my eyes and entered a world where I had not been before.'

'Over the next two days, Chandragupta was engaged in business with the governor and other administrators in Taxila. Then we started our journey to Pataliputra. I thought of my mother's marriage when she'd travelled with my father from Susa to Babylon. What happened on that journey? Now I knew. By turns I was euphoric and sad as she must have been.

'We had our honeymoon on the run and I no longer needed the distraction of the scenery. My world was filled with new feelings and sensations. Once in Pataliputra, my priest completed the remaining ceremonies. Then blushing under his white beard, he sternly told me that

I was ready for the final stage of the Greek wedding. And I thought, I'd heard no loud chants in the carriage, and now it's too late!'

My arrival at the Palace created a sensation. Perhaps Chandragupta Maurya's two queens had expected a plain, plump princess, but this pretty young queen devastated them. Determined to find fault, they belittled my breasts, declaring them unattractive because they were smaller than their own. Yet my youth made them despair. "A beautiful woman of thirty-five can't compete with a young woman of seventeen," one of them whined to my maid.

'My life with Chandragupta was far from bliss. He was not an easy man, which made the other changes—people, customs, food, court life— even tougher for me. He was dedicated to his vision of unifying the country. He would talk about Chankya and other officials about whom I knew nothing. He assumed that just being the wife of the emperor should be enough for my happiness. His other two queens had told him so. If I saw him for an hour twice a week, I felt lucky. Every day, I waited for his knock at my door.

'I found it hard to converse with him. Often, he would walk out in the middle of a conversation. If I cooked, he would ask his cook to prepare something. The second year was even worse. Even my simple questions, he answered sharply. Like, "Dress as you please." Or, "Why discuss everything?" '

'I decided to fight back. If I gave up on him, he might lose the little interest he had in me, and I was not going to pack my bags and head back to Persia. I wanted to convince him that besides my bed, he could share a good conversation, even a laugh with me, and that I had good mental equipment too.

'Remembering my mother's admonition that the purpose of a Greek princess's life is to "rule over the emperor," I learnt about his food pref-erences, his habits and his interests. I struggled to acquire proficiency in Indian dishes, in learning the details of hunting and politics— subjects that fascinated him. He was pleased and gave me what no one else had: my own quarters with a separate kitchen and staff where he became my regular guest. Only later I realized he did it to protect me from a jealous chief queen who ruled over the kitchen.

'Megasthenes was a great help at this time. He had a wonderful collection of stories and was a great conversationalist. That he was also a historian impressed the King. The two would sit late into the night talking about the things men talk about—raunchy jokes, sexual exploits, hunting, and wars, and uproarious laughter accompanied their drinking late into the night. Slowly he led the King to accept my interest in state affairs.

'Megasthenes advised me to order and design the King's robes, and to select wine at dinner. At first, when I poured wine, Chandragupta wouldn't ask me to join him, but then, after a couple of years, he always did. A few cups of wine made me feel extra warm for him, and want to feel his furry chest. He enjoyed that immensely.

'Chandragupta's second favorite activity was drinking wine. He liked to drink in the evening with his favorite queen; he preferred the wines of Persia and Greece, which my father regularly sent him. He always returned the favor by sending my father silk or jewels. He followed a rule in drinking wine: never more than four cups. Sometimes I would offer him a fifth cup when the going was good, and he'd wink at me and smile. "I am no longer a twenty-year old stud. And I have to keep my lady happy."'

'I asked my mother to send Persian embroidered silk robes, waistcoats and embroidered leather shoes for my lord. He soon grew fond of the Persian style and sent local tailors for training in Persia.

'With Megasthenes' assistance, I began to talk with ministers and grew familiar with court politics. I would venture my opinions, even if unsolicited. Chandragupta would not comment, but he listened carefully.

'After two years, my ship began to turn around. He came to recognize that I could discuss politics and philosophy with him. He liked it because he could let his guard down with me. He told me he wanted to unite India, and it vexed him that Kalinga and a few other states in the south were still unconquered.

'Megasthenes told me I must meet Chankya, a living legend. What a sly man Chankya was! I don't think he liked me or any female, much less one who was eager to challenge him. At first, his looks frightened me. He never smiled, and his eyes shone like the eyes of a wolf on the prowl. Clean-shaven, his head was as smooth as the bottom of a frying pan and in the middle of his big head stood a stiff pigtail that looked like the tail of a monkey on the run.'

'Chankya had written Arthasastra, which I read and I was amazed by its breadth and scope. It told me all about the King's administration, the treasury, tax system, civil and criminal law and punishment; war strategy, war preparation, and foreign policy. Then I understood why a simple teacher from Taxila had become Chandragupta's Prime Minister. The man was a genius!'

Suddenly Livia rose and looked anxiously out of the window.

'It is not yet midnight,' Roxanne said. 'We have ample time.'

Livia continued. 'We'd make the usual small talk in bed. I loved to put my head on his chest, and it relaxed him. He'd then talk on and on, sometimes as if he were on stage delivering a soliloquy. I always listened intently, interjecting a question or two to assure him I was not asleep, that I cared. He was a man who always wanted to do the right thing—he had strong ideas about what was right– but one who also had a soft side.

'One day, he asked me if it had been difficult for me to leave my parents. What could I say? "I am sorry," he said, "but I have nothing to apologize for. Those are the customs of war." At least he'd thought of it! He explained his impatience in Taxila, "You know you were my war booty."

' "And now?" I teased.'

' "My lovely Queen," he said, kissing me.'

'Chandragupta loved life. After oil massage every morning, he would go for a vigorous ride - a love of his from his military days. He told me the cool breeze and the morning sun reinvigorated him. He aimed to rule with wisdom and strength.

'For an emperor, he was humble, as if he had never forgotten that once he too was just an ordinary man. He knew too well the downfall of Darius III, the Persian Emperor, and cited it as an example that no king was invincible. Once, talking of Alexander's victory over Porus, Chandragupta's anger flared up. His voice quivered as he said, "Future Alexanders will not dare to cast an evil eye on my united India. Ambhi, that traitor! If he had not kissed his ass, Alexander would have been thrown out of India like a kitchen rat."

'The last two years of my marriage were my happiest. In the fourth year, I was joyously pregnant. One day he came in excited. "I am going to attack Kalinga. My army is ready and strong; my health is excellent and I have you, dear Livia. I feel invincible."

'I was scared. It pained me that he would be away when my baby was coming. With teary eyes, I asked him to wait.

'His answer surprised me. "I'll talk to my ministers." '

'I was thrilled when he delayed the campaign. He already had two sons including Bindusar, but I knew he wanted a son from the Persian princess, the grandchild of the Emperor of Persia. Always practical, he said that child would secure India's north-west frontiers for a long time.

'The birth of my son Arjan was celebrated in Pataliputra as if he were the crown prince. I summoned a wet nurse from Greece. But when Arjan was six months old— just a month or two before the planned attack - the emperor told me that he felt ill and had lost his appetite.

'He became obsessed with death. For a while I paid no heed thinking it a passing phase. But it did not stop. One day I broke down. "I don't want to hear about your dying." I cried. "How will I live without you?" But to no avail.

'One day, as we were lying in bed, he astonished me by putting his head on my chest. I felt happy like a mother, but something inside me felt his terrible burden. I did not ask questions and just stroked his head. He would tell me when the time was ripe.

'A few days later, he sobbed uncontrollably on my chest. I tried to comfort him but when he didn't stop, I cried with him. Words couldn't say more.'

'He calmed down. "Livia, I don't want to die!" he mumbled.

'I kissed his tears. "You are not going to die, my Lord." I, a frail woman - what else could I say to an emperor?

'His voice kept breaking. "Livia, my time has come. I have been so happy. That I will die without conquering Kalinga does not hurt. But that I will not live to see Arjan grow up– that does. And you are so young!"

'Chandragupta was incapable of lies or exaggeration. My head was reeling and I sputtered, "My Lord, what are you talking about?"

'Calmly he said, "I have an incurable disease. Livia, I have only three months left."

'I fought with him. "Why didn't you tell me before?"

'"Every day I came to tell you, but I lost my nerve. My physician checked and rechecked." '

'I collapsed in his arms.'

' "I am sorry, Livia," he repeated, "I am so sorry."'

'That evening, the room was lit but the air was dark with pain. I remembered when the news had first broken of my leaving Babylon for India; then, it had seemed that I would never be happy again but that fantasy had melted away. Now my life was coming apart and I had never felt so helpless.

'I went to the room where Arjan was sleeping and his innocent face broke my heart. I stood listening to his breathing in that silence, thinking of death. I picked him up and felt life stir within me. I cannot let myself go under, I thought. I have my son. I will bring him up, the son of Chandragupta, the grandson of Seleucus, to be the future king of India. I will think of my life tomorrow. And I dropped down on my bed.

'I would walk around as if I were dragging a dead body. Wherever I looked, I saw couples in good health. What a terrible sight, I thought.

' "A King's illness is a state secret," Chandragupta told me. "The transfer of power must be smooth and orderly." In the next two weeks, he abandoned the throne and crowned Bindusar King.'

Livia stopped to regain her breath.

Roxanne looked grim, and asked, 'Were you with him at the end?'

'Yes! We went to the Nepal foothills where he spent his last days. He was brave to the end. Every time he put on his robe, I cried. There were only bones left. Increasingly he discussed religion with a Jain sage in the area. My only satisfaction is that he died in my arms.

'I did not have much time to mope and cry after Chandragupta's death. My trials made me even more determined to bring Arjan up as...,' Livia hesitated, wanting to say 'the future king of India,' but she stopped herself. 'When he died...' She choked up.

Roxanne offered her a drink.

She took a sip. 'I can't go on...'

She got up and went to the window. Outside it was dark and silent. She came back and lay down on the bed. 'I am tired. I will nap before Asoka arrives. If I fall asleep, wake me up at the whisper of his steps.'

39

Raj Purohit, the royal priest, lived only a couple of houses away from the Senapati, the army chief. A light sleeper, he was awakened by strange sounds from his neighbor's house. Throwing a woolen shawl over his shoulders, he picked up his gold-handled cane, threw a turban on his head, and went out. Close to the Senapati's house, the sounds grew louder. He went through the open gate, climbed up the steps, and on the verandah, discovered Senapati's severed head, lying in a pool of blood. Horrified, he went in, untied Senapati's daughter and son and rushed to see the queen. *Who would kill the Senapati?* he wondered. *Not Tissa, not Marut, not Pavan. Asoka! It has to be Asoka.* He recoiled in horror. *He is not dead?*

On the way to the Palace he saw the cavalry and infantry taking up their positions. He leaned heavily on his cane to save himself from falling. He was the only man—other than the King and Sasima— who could enter the queen's apartment. A lamp flickered outside her chamber, and two young female guards lay sprawled on the floor fast asleep. He bent over one, his beard lightly brushing her cheek. Feeling a rat scampering over her face, she sprang up mumbling obscenities. Seeing the Purohit, she hung her head.

'I have to see the queen! Now!' said the Purohit.

The queen emerged pale-faced, arranging the disheveled brown folds of her robe over her bosom. The priest stood, and raised his shaking right hand in benediction. Looking at his ashen face and shaking cane, the queen slumped in a chair.

'Queen, the news is not good! The Senapati has been killed.'

The queen collapsed on the floor. The Purohit knelt down, and put his hand on her head. 'There is not much time, Queen! Sasima's life is in danger!'

As if hit on the head, the queen sprang to her feet.

'There is some plot afoot. The cavalry has surrounded the Palace. We must get Sasima out. He can inform us later of his whereabouts.'

He had barely left when the wet nurse to Sasima's infant arrived, sobbing. 'Prince Marut has been killed.' The queen heard and did not hear. She ran to the King's bedchamber. Sasima had been sleeping there for the last few days. His guard said Sasima had gone to the river for a pleasure ride with a woman.

She rushed a guard to find him, another to his bodyguards, yet another to harness the horses while her mind was reeling. *Who'd kill the Senapati? Asoka? I never believed he was dead.* Livia flashed in her mind, and her fists clenched. *Is she sleeping with Purandas? Visal? Radhagupta? I will claw her heart out,* she vowed, clutching at her chest.

A guard brought more bad news. 'Pavan has been killed.'

She paid no attention this time. *How could I be so blind?* She rushed to Livia's quarters holding a naked sword. Halfway down the hall, she realized that Sasima's life had not yet been secured. She turned back and waited impatiently for him and kept pacing. Half an hour seemed like an eternity to her. When he showed up at last, she flew into a rage. 'While the throne sinks, you dally with whores!'

Sasima was taken by surprise. 'It's a bluff!'

'Bluff! That could be your last word.' She dragged him to the King's chamber, gave him instructions, packed his clothes, and put gold coins into a pouch.

Sasima resisted. 'This is ridiculous! I will not leave Pataliputra. I have the army's support.'

'You...have the army's support!' she sneered. 'Is the Palace surrounded by your supporters? You said Asoka was dead! And you don't even know your nurse has been fornicating with Marut in your bed!'

Sasima was outraged. 'Was my child there, too?'

'Fool!' said the horror-stricken queen, 'Must you piddle while the sword is closing in on your throat?'

Sasima was totally disoriented now. 'I have to see my son.'

Instead, the queen took him to the secret stairway in the King's chamber, and thundered, 'Run for your life!'

Meant for such dire situations, the underground passage opened near the Ganges. She did not embrace Sasima or say goodbye. At the riverbank, four bodyguards waited for him. He fled.

Blood-lust raging in her heart, the queen walked with her two big female guards to Livia's apartment, like a general leading an army of two.

A guard knuckled at the door. Rubbing her eyes, Livia jumped out of bed, flung open the door, and opened her arms. 'Asoka! King! My son!' Her face contorted when she saw the queen. Before she could speak or run, the sword was inside her chest.

Falling, Livia gasped, 'You? Bitch!'

'Vermin! Slut!' the queen fulminated, 'I will watch you bleed to death! You will not see that traitor Asoka, king. When he comes here I will drink his blood!'

Livia raised her head and hissed, 'You ...go...burn... in hell! Asoka... will rule.' Her head dropped to floor and a smile spread across her face.

Further enraged, the queen raised her hands to stab her again, when Bhairavi stormed in, shoving the guards aside, and thrust her sword into the queen's chest. The queen fell over Livia, in an awkward, involuntary embrace.

The guards had turned on Bhairavi when, suddenly, Roxanne appeared with a drawn sword pointed at them. Immobilized, they exchanged glances that said, 'Let's get out of here!'

The queen lay dying. 'Dasarath!' said Bhairavi, stabbing her two more times, 'To lighten your sorrow!'

'Forgive me, Suba. We got your wish,' Livia mumbled, 'And my pride. Forgive me.' Her eyes were fixed on the ceiling.

Roxanne tried to comfort Livia. 'What more can life... give...me?' she murmured, and her head jerked off to the side, one hand around the queen.

'I saw the queen coming.' Bhairavi cried. 'I ran... I ran but failed.'

Roxanne consoled her, 'In the end, she found a little happiness.'

When Asoka arrived, he embraced Livia's bloodied body. 'Choti-ma, you could not see me on the throne. The irony of it! After what you suffered. How could the gods deny you a little happiness? I should have anticipated the queen's rabid rage,' he kept saying, 'Now I have a mother's blood on my hands.' He wept. 'Am I cursed? Must those I love die young?'

The search for Sasima proved futile.

40

Even Asoka's supporters were outraged by the Palace killings. Overnight, Asoka had turned into a Rakshasa, a demon. And ironically, in his flight, Sasima became a hero. The Cavalry had declared its support for Sasima. Purandas, now the Senapati, kept a lid on the Infantry, but the revolt continued to grow. A civil war threatened Magadha, the name by which the kingdom was known.

Unnerved, Asoka called on the Purohit, regarded as the upholder of Dharma, the Code of Righteous Conduct. 'Our Dharma requires that Sasima be given a fair chance to get back his rightful throne,' the Purohit advised, adding, 'Give him at least eighteen months to return.'

Asoka had always aspired to be a great king and to rule with honor and bravery, never through moral depravity. Had Sasima been killed, the finality of death would have diffused the general moral outrage. People forget and forgive when they have no choice.

'I thought that by removing a weak prince,' he told Radhagupta, 'I acted in the interest of the empire!'

'That is not the perception,' Radhagupta said. 'Now people face a dilemma. Is Asoka moral? He also killed Marut and Pavan! You must give the public a reason to forgive you.'

Asoka told the Purohit to announce that scriptures required Sasima be given eighteen months to reclaim the throne, but out of remorse, Prince Asoka had agreed to grant him three years. The announcement appeased some, others stayed doubtful. The concession he made reflected his concept of fairness: Sasima! Take the throne by your valor and wit. But not as your birthright. He realized it would be difficult, if not impossible, for Sasima to make a comeback. The odds favored him this time. A gambler, he took his chance.

A few days later, Roxanne gave him a letter from Livia.

Son,

I will be gone when you get this letter. It is horrid but true: I poisoned Suba. I went mad; I could not live without you. I could not live without a son. Or die like an orphan. I had to be Raj Mata. I hated that woman, and could not bear seeing her as Raj-Mata. Every day I regretted the deed. But what I did, I would do again. Life gave me no choice.

Please don't hate me. Think of the young girl whose youth and dreams were smothered by a mighty King— your Baba. There is no reason why things happen in life. Someday you will know our happiness comes from living by our passions.

Mother Livia.

The revelation shocked him. He despaired. *Mother, I lost you to Choti-ma's pride.* His mother's face, when she lay dying, haunted him for days. That he was the cause of her death grieved him to no end. Nor would she have approved of the Palace killings. *I grieve for you, mother. But I'm glad you were spared the gruesome sights. I am not a murderer, mother. Forgive me!*

His anger at Livia softened as he reflected on her life and the sacrifices she had made for him. *Choti-ma, you gave me so much affection, and suffered for me. You even gave up your life. Someday, I will be worthy of your sacrifice. You were a warrior to the end!*

He brooded. *Choti-ma never found happiness. Did she love Radhagupta? Could she love? Starved of love, hungry for power?* Looking at his own failed marriage, his unfulfilled love for Anga, he wondered, *Is that what is driving me to these deeds?*

Trembling, Tissa approached Asoka the morning after the killings. 'Asoka, let me set your mind at rest. I will become a monk, if you want me to.'

Asoka was angered and surprised. 'Tissa, do you think I'd kill my own brother?'

Tissa stood looking at the floor. Irritated, Asoka asked, 'You said you were Sasima's friend. Do you know where he has fled?'

The question surprised Tissa. He kept quiet.

Angered, Asoka suspected Tissa knew more than he was saying. 'Tissa! If you don't trust me, perhaps you should go.'

'I will,' Tissa said, voice shaking but eyes cold. He joined the Vaishali monastery soon after.

Broken-hearted at Livia's death, Radhagupta sought retirement from public life. Asoka implored him to stay. 'Radhagupta, this is a very trying time for me. Choti-ma would have wanted you to help me out.' After a long period of mourning, Radhagupta relented.

Later, he told Asoka the story of the unfortunate monk. 'It was part accident, part design. The idea occurred to Bitan after you handed him the bag at Taxila. He found your exact double. He sent the man with his companions to hand over the bag to queen Livia.'

Asoka shook his head. 'Sacrificed for nothing! How cruel!'

'His family has been compensated.' Then Radhagupta asked, 'How did you cross the Semariya check point? I heard it was leak-proof.'

'By attending my own funeral.' Asoka told him the story.

'But what if the Guard had asked to look at the dead man?'

Asoka laughed cynically. 'How many guards would leave the warmth of a bed on a cold night to look at a dead stranger? My body was painted black, my hair and beard white, my cheeks drawn in between the teeth. I had a sword under my back and a horse behind me.' He sighed. 'If I'd had to run, I'd have lost the empire. But I would have returned. I learnt something though. Even after death, the body is jerked around!'

Sasima was always on his mind. He dreaded the day when a stranger would appear in the court, take off his wig, pull down his beard and announce, 'Look at me. Look again, Asoka! I am Sasima, the crown prince!' Barbers were appointed to check visitors carefully before allowing them entry to the court. The Secret Service patrolled the border and scoured Kalinga. Rumors circulated that Sasima had been sighted in Bactria, Nepal, and Kalinga. His ghost was everywhere.

Sasima haunted him. *I can kill the man but not his ghost*, he agonized. *Why has Sasima not returned to claim the throne? That is what I would
have done.*

Gradually he strengthened his Secret Service, purged the army of
officers loyal to Sasima, organized sports for the soldiers, and reminded
the officers that he had saved the empire from the secession of Taxila.
Knowing that nothing wins loyalty of the army like a raise, he increased
the soldiers' pay.

Winning the public's trust turned out to be more difficult. Sasima's
absence reminded the people of Asoka's ambition. But the three year
waiting period helped. Asoka invited community figures to court,
addressed small assemblies, and told them he had acted in the interest
of the empire. Above all, he expressed remorse. He attended public festivals, opened a Palace kitchen to the public on Samaj– a festival when
hundreds of animals were killed for spectacle and sport. The public
loved the pomp and show, so Asoka began to go on hunting trips. But
his best ally was time.

His personal life was a much bigger mess. He missed his children–
Mahinda and Sanghamitta– but Devi would not part with them.
'They need a father, not a King,' she said. She had become a Buddhist
lay person like her mother and the children were being brought up
as Buddhists. Time had given him perspective. Asoka did not blame
her now. He blamed his haste. He persuaded Devi to join him at the
Palace as chief queen. She assumed another name — Asandhimitta —
as royal women often did. Now he hoped to see his children in the
Palace.

When they arrived, he was shocked. Sanghamitta, now seven, was a
vivacious, happy girl who ran around in simple clothes and two braids,
and fluently recited the Buddha's sermons. Mahinda, with his round
chubby face and his shaven head, looked more like a monk than a
prince. *If I am killed*, Asoka worried, *I'll have no heir to carry on this empire.
Mahinda shows no interest in the throne.* More distressing was the idea that
Sasima's son Nigrodh will take over the empire. That fear set him off
on a new trail.

Love or no love, the dynasty comes first, he decided. A girl was found—
Karuvaki, the granddaughter of a Commander in Chandragupta's
army— willing to bear him a son and then return to her parents. *I'll be a
stud for the empire,* he mused, *if that is what it takes.* Asoka hit the bull's eye.
A son named Tivara was born in ten months. When the time came
for Karuvaki to leave, she fell into shaking sobs. Asoka felt guilty and
told Karuvaki she could stay to be near Tivara. She remained as the
second queen, relieving some of his burden by attending the endless rituals for the kingdom and for the health of new prince. She
assumed the name of Tissarakka, as if the Palace had changed her
whole persona—which it did.

His quest for greatness had brought him struggle after struggle,
and nothing but emptiness. His flame for Anga continued to burn
steadily. The lonelier he felt, the more he missed her. It was a vicious
circle. He often thought of Bitan's words, "You can marry five times
and yet not know love." He longed to whisper soft endearments in
Anga's ear, and to hear, 'Asoka, I love you!' No woman had whispered
those words to him.

Anga became an obsession, as power had been at Taxila. The morning they had gone out riding together had taken on a life of its own.
He never tired of inquiring after her. Bitan told him that when Semat's
father rushed to Taxila to take him back to Alexandria, Semat had
promised Anga, 'I will be back.'

'She'll wait until he shows up or she drops dead,' Bitan said.

Often Asoka asked himself, *When will this nightmare end?*

But bad times, like good ones, do not last forever. Within three
years, he received a pleasant surprise: Sasima had been sighted in Tosali,
Kalinga. The news soon spread that Kalinga's King had killed Sasima
when Sasima attempted to take over his throne.

41

A heavy burden had been lifted from Asoka's mind. He had paid his dues. The Purohit determined a coronation date in the early spring of 269. Preparations began in full force. The vassal chiefs of Herat, Kandahar, and Kabul, along with the King of Kalinga, and the governors of Taxila, Ujjain and other regions, were all invited to the coronation. Invitations were also sent to Antiochus, emperor of Persia, and Ptolemy II, emperor of Egypt. Asoka asked Bitan to come, and to bring Anga with him if possible.

He would now be king but there was no joy in his heart. The years of uncertainty, the constant fear of Sasima's appearance, the recalcitrant army, the distrusting public, his trouble in getting his children to the Palace, the disappointment in Mahinda, Choti-ma's murder, the knowledge that his mother was murdered by Choti-ma, the Karuvaki episode, his yearning for Anga, all had taken their toll. Asoka constantly questioned himself and agonized over his failings. *If I had thought things through, so much suffering could have been avoided. Why didn't I anticipate the chief queen's rage after the Senapati's death? Choti-ma should not have been in her apartment that night. And there can be no excuse for failing to find out where Sasima had been sleeping. I made facile assumptions. Was my mind castrated? Did killing Kalanos easily turn my head into lard? How could I think I was above mistakes? I've so many flaws. How will I be a great king? Not just great. But the greatest! I'd send a minister to the gallows if he made one such mistake.*

What troubled him most was his inability to win Anga. He constantly upbraided himself. '*My grandfather set up this empire before he was thirty. I am thirty-one and I have not won a single war. But first I have to win Anga. Once I thought power is everything, as it is for the gods. The gods can have all the women they want but they don't care about love. Disrobing a woman does not uncover her soul. Why is power not good enough for me?*' He brooded further. '*Without her, my sorrow runs deep as the waters of the sea. I long to hold her and look into her eyes, and see her soul lovingly gazing at me. Only then will my pleasure touch the Himalayan peak.*'

But as the coronation date drew near, his thoughts turned to the throne. *Power is all I have now and I will use it to the hilt.* He went to the Purohit to learn the extent and the source of king's powers.

'In the beginning there was anarchy,' the Purohit explained. 'Gods and demons were always at war. To achieve victory, the gods realized they needed a king. Once they chose one, the tide turned in their favor, and the demons lost because they were disorganized.'

'So the king rules by divine right?' Asoka said.

The Purohit hedged. 'Only the Brahmins are the representatives of gods on earth. The king can claim divine right for purposes of war. He can tell the soldiers, "Fight to the death and you will go to heaven." The king can also pretend to be seen in the company of gods – with his secret agents masquerading as divinities– and appear to be on intimate terms with them. Seeing the king in divine company, the soldiers will fight to the death.'

Surprised, Asoka asked, 'Is that what kings do?'

The Purohit gave an all-knowing smile. 'Since time immemorial!'

Asoka was incredulous. 'And the soldiers believe it?'

'Listen!' said the exasperated Purohit, 'Who can doubt the king is favored by the gods. How else would he be king? Look at the ordinary man. Sitting on a sagging bed, chewing on starchy meals, looking day after day at the face of the ageing wife, every man readily believes the king is divine. The king has power, splendor and beautiful women. What more do the gods have?'

Asoka sensed envy in the Purohit's voice. 'But you said the king's power isn't divine! So how can he be a god?'

Impatiently, the Purohit said, 'What's the difference?'

Asoka left more confused than ever. *These priests talk from both sides of their mouths. And want me to believe every word!*

42

Pataliputra, the city of flowers, always looked beautiful. The roads were clean, people were prosperous, they wore colorful clothes, and food was plentiful. But on Coronation Day, the city took on the special glow of a bride. The towers of the city and the Palace were polished to a shine. One thousand wooden columns were erected on the roads and decorated with fragrant flowers that also covered the city's gateways, towers and arches. The Royal road was carpeted with blossoms and frankincense. Red and yellow banners flew over the windows and roof-tops. Torches tall as trees sprang up along the Royal Avenue to light up the festivities into the night.

Men and women dressed in their best. Balconies and windows swarmed with people. Women from distant villages with babes-in-arms squatted on roadsides. Young girls—plump, skinny, tall, short, fair and dark—painted their faces, and tried out different ornate hair designs, each assured by her mother that she looked divine. Young men perched high in trees, nibbling peanuts and puffed rice. Old men walked around wearing ill-fitting old clothes and fading memories of their youth. Even the Buddhist monks came out in droves to watch the spectacle of a lifetime.

The majestic Maurya dynasty throne stayed in the court hall. In the main Palace quadrangle, under a gold roofed pavilion on four jeweled pillars, a fig-wood throne sat on an altar. Next to each pillar stood tall gold vases filled with blue and red flowers. Army officers in red, olive and green paraded the Palace grounds, visibly proud. The public brought offerings of plants, flowers, clothing, ivory objects and food grains to the future King. These were displayed in a separate pavilion and in yet another, the armor used by Chandragupta in the war—including the royal armor— was placed on show.

The Royal elephant stood near the fig wood throne pavilion. On it sat the royal mahout, in a gold embroidered red turban and a white waistcoat. The elephant was painted all over: the head, ears, eyes and trunk in yellow, green and red colored leaf motifs, the plump legs and short tail covered in golden thread. A six-stringed gold bead necklace hung around its thick neck. With its small beady eyes and its creased, loose skin, the elephant looked a little like an especially fat dowager. Nearby, the royal horse stood caparisoned in similar splendor, its front leg slightly raised and curved inward to enhance its majestic look. Its painted face resembled that of the long-faced royal priest. Self-importantly, the Brahmin priests moved with raised eyebrows and grave expressions. They had sacrificed in the preceding weeks hundreds of animals to ensure the long life of the king.

The ceremonies began in the Coronation consecration pavilion. Before a select audience of guests and nobles, Asoka shed all his finery—his jeweled necklace, gold armband and bracelet—and changed into a simple white cotton garment round the waist. Then, to the sounds of the royal orchestra, the lustration rites began. While Asoka held a black antelope's horn in one hand, the priest moistened his naked upper body with lustral water made up of seventeen kinds of liquids: water from rivers, ocean, and springs, plus honey, ghee, and the genital fluid of a calving cow.

He made offerings to various gods. To the good-natured King with his kind face and melancholy eyes, the priests presented a bow and four arrows, symbolizing victory in all directions. The King took three steps forward onto a tiger skin—identifying him with god Vishnu, who covered earth and the heavens in three paces. Then he took part in a symbolic battle and a chariot race, threw dice three times, and performed various magic rites as directed by the priests.

Then the Purohit, reading from scriptures, addressed the King.

The sovereign lord has been born, the eater of the folk (power to tax) has been born, the destroyer of enemies, the protector of Brahmins, the guardian of law, has been born...Here I seat thee for...peaceful dwelling, for wealth, for prosperity, for the welfare of the people.

Then they sprinkled consecrated water on his body.

The King makers—the priests— administered the oath. 'Let us proclaim him King!' 'Be it so!' the audience called in loud voices.

After the consecration ceremony, the Brahmin priests, dignitaries and officials filed past the King one by one, sprinkling drops of water on him from a conch-shell. A military salute was given by twenty-four decorated elephants that raised their trunks, and trumpeted, as they passed the King.

Next, the King came down from the fig wood throne and made obeisance to the holy powers—the Brahmins. He donned his regalia and mounted the gilded four-horsed chariot. He was now presented to the public amidst clapping, cheers and the deafening roar of the trumpet. Asoka's eyes searched the crowd for Bitan and Anga, and spotted Bitan in the distance waving to him—all by himself. He felt a stab in his heart. Where was Anga? Had she already left for Alexandria?

Led by an orchestra and a chorus of dancing girls, flanked by officials, the white parasol and the royal flywhisk, Asoka's chariot slowly marched along the Royal road, behind it the royal elephant moved with its inimitable stately gait, gently rocking the two exquisitely dressed queens in the Howdah. The chariot turned back at the northern city gate, and his mind strayed on the return to the Palace. *Within the next ten years, ruling over a united India, I will have the glory I covet. I'll be immortal. With ten years of wars still left in me, I'll give my neighbors a taste of their own brew.*

At the Palace, the dignitaries surrounded the new King. For the first time, Asoka sat in the Hall on the gilded Mauryan Dynasty throne. Upholstered in silver and gold cloth, with ivory-inlaid wooden legs with lion claws, it was a high-backed armchair, decorated with ivory, jewels and gold-inset animals. As per custom, the King used the royal golden seal for the first time, proclaiming the release of all prisoners in his kingdom. At the thought that his Baba, the great Chandragupta Maurya, had sat on the same throne, Asoka's hair stood on end. The words 'Mother, I will make you proud', rang in his ears.

Then he heard Choti-ma's words, "You need an empire... and a good woman."

Where is she?

43

Celebrations continued into the night and Bitan waded through to the crowd to congratulate him. Asoka embraced him eagerly. 'Where is Anga?'

Bitan broke the bad news, 'She joined a Buddhist nunnery two months ago!'

'Nunnery?' Asoka stammered, his face, white.

Later that evening, Bitan explained, 'Semat left three years ago around springtime. He joined the army in Egypt. Until a year ago, he kept sending messages, then the letters stopped suddenly. Anga thought he was going to surprise her. The next thing we learned, he'd been killed in the war. Anga was devastated. For six months she stayed in bed. When she recovered, she decided to become a nun and no one could stop her. She is in Taxila monastery. I visit her periodically hoping to bring her back but she always says, "I want to forget everyone and everything. Now my Lord is the Buddha."'

It was the day of his triumph. Yet, at the end of it, Asoka collapsed in bed. This hollowness he knew well. *How awful to lie in bed staring at the stony walls, the cold ceiling!* He remembered the night in Taxila, when, after putting down the revolt, loneliness engulfed him. Suddenly, he was furious at her. *What is she to me? I think of her all the time and she keeps being silly. A nunnery! Of all places! I must stop thinking of her.*

His resolution lasted about an hour. Like a piece of dry wood floating in ocean waves, she kept bobbing up in his thoughts: her sunny large eyes, mischievous look, head turning smile, and even her sad song. She *is now unbound,* he told himself. For a moment, hope flashed then frustration took over. 'She inspires so much love and yet she's unconscious of it.' She haunted him. When he met Bitan the next day, he announced he wanted to go and get Anga from the monastery.

Bitan was aghast. 'Asoka! You will hurt yourself if you go. First, she must feel tenderly for you. Imagine your going there! The emperor himself! She resents pressure. Any and all pressure. She'd suspect my hand. She might even commit suicide.'

Asoka turned pale. 'She'd do that?'

'That's Anga!' Bitan said sadly. He paused. 'Give her a year or two! She's such a romantic girl. And so intense! Give her time to reflect on the Buddha, and then write to her. If you're lucky, she may yet come to love you.' He sighed. 'It's been a stressful time for us all, particularly for me. Mother is disgusted with her. But I was so depressed after she left, I tried Buddhism. It didn't work. I was desperate and went to the Kashmir valley. The beauty of the mountains and the lake calmed me. It is a paradise on earth, a place to hide in grief.'

'I have to put my administration in order,' Asoka said. 'That will take time. I can't leave Pataliputra now. To me, paradise is wherever Anga is.'

The next day, Asoka met up with Bitan. 'Bitan, I need people in my Council who can tell me the truth— not what I want to hear. Will you be my treasurer?'

Bitan was surprised. 'Asoka, I need to stay near Anga.' But he agreed to stay on as governor of Ujjain and Taxila.

The evening after the coronation, Asoka also met Kalinga's King. Long ago, he had visited Asoka's mother and Livia in Rajnagar at Vaitarni. Asoka still remembered the cannibals. The old King had with him his latest acquisition—Sunanda, a bosomy twenty four year old with sensuous lips. She had large round eyes and kept smiling at Asoka.

His hair all white, the King bowed obsequiously to Asoka. Sisupal, now the prime minister, came with him. Sisupal averted Asoka's eyes. Asoka congratulated him on his new title, and talked about Charu and the children.

Before he left for Taxila, Bitan told him, 'Sisupal wants me to recommend him to you for a minister's post in government. He told the King you're a good friend.' He added, 'He thinks you'll listen if I ask.'

Asoka laughed. 'Just like Sisupal! I did talk to Visal about him. He is unpredictable, and sly, we concluded. We're better off with him there as our man. Kalinga is the entry to our kingdom from the south-east and only second in importance to Taxila.'

Asoka tapped Narad, his statecraft teacher, to join his Council as Head of the Secret Service. The old Purohit who had bitterly opposed Asoka was allowed to retire. In his place, he appointed Shivdutt, a learned younger Brahmin. Historically, the Purohit was the most important man in the Council, after the Prime Minister. In Asoka's Council though, the Purohit lacked such eminence, because the King himself was well versed in scriptures.

Asoka filled his court with learned men from many fields—cosmology, astronomy, logic, mathematics, epistemology, music and physics - all considered branches of religion. Bandhu, the astronomer, assisted the Purohit in setting the dates and time of sacrificial rituals. He also kept a lunar-solar calendar to forecast eclipses so that nothing important would be initiated on those days.

In the tradition of his ancestors, surrounded by ministers, ambassadors, foreign dignitaries, and military chiefs, Asoka lived in the shadow of divinity. He loved pomp and splendor, cultivating every form of luxury and art. He began converting the wooden Palace walls to stone, and all the sacred edifices in the city were rebuilt. To enhance the glory of his dynasty, he started work on the great Hall— the showcase of the empire— where his court met, and foreign dignitaries were received. It was to be a building more glorious than any in Greece, more wondrous than Persepolis had once been.

One hundred polished sandstone pillars, twenty feet high, were erected in the big Hall, with twenty carved niches for lights spiraling down the pillar. Processions of nobles and hunting scenes were etched on the stone walls. The ceiling was gilded and Persian carpets covered the floor. When completed, the Hall glittered with two thousand stars. Its exquisite workmanship prompted some foreign visitors to conclude that the King had unearthly spirits at his command.

Sitting under the canopy of gold-threaded tapestry in the Hall, wearing his gold and silver-embroidered heavy robe, and his glittering Mauryan crown, Asoka felt like a minor god. Every day he appeared in the great Hall as the ultimate Court of Appeal. In the criminal appellants, he looked for repentance, humility and truth, and came down hard if he thought they lacked those qualities. He loved to throw parties: peacock, his favorite fowl and a delicacy, appeared regularly on the table. Overnight, whole villages of peacock-farmers sprang up around the city. Now every fashionable rich person began serving peacock dishes.

Asoka cultivated his passion for hunting, a sport that his Baba loved and was dear to the people. He would emerge from the Palace astride his elephant, the royal parasol above his head, surrounded by bodyguards– spearmen and young females with swords– carrying his standard and flywhisk, with colorful bunting waving around him in the breeze. An orchestra of conches, gongs and drums preceded him. On the day of royal procession, the road was marked off with ropes. It was death for spectators to attempt to breach the fence. Nobles on horsebacks followed, helpers trailed on foot leading hunting mastiff dogs– the breed loved by the Greek kings. In the Mahabharata, the Pandava brothers make their final pilgrimage to heaven with a leashed mastiff. The masses loved the spectacle and cheered wildly.

Asoka had learnt in the *Vedas* that the universe was shaped like an egg and divided into twenty-one regions, of which earth was seventh from the top. Below it were regions of the 'Nagas'– serpents– and other immortal beings. The lowest seven regions constituted 'Naraka' – hell– through which tormented souls passed or lived in eternity.

The world fascinated him. He asked Sahdeva, the court cosmologist, to discover the entry points to the various regions above and below the earth. 'The entry doors have to be within our borders, since they are mentioned in our scriptures.' For two years Sahdeva travelled around the empire, but came up empty-handed.

Vague descriptions in scriptures did not satisfy Asoka so he asked the five most learned men in his court to discover the answers to the following questions: Where is heaven? Where does Indra live? Where is Yama? What are the soul's properties? Where are my father and grand-father after their deaths?

For eighteen months, the wise men wandered the earth, searching and asking questions. Then they reported. 'We found nothing more than what is already in the scriptures.'

Could Scripture be wrong? wondered Asoka.

He invited Upagupta, the head of the Buddhist Sangha, to shed light on the soul. 'We live in a changing universe,' said Upagupta. 'The law of change and decay applies to every person and everything. Therefore, there can be no immortal soul.'

Asked to clarify, the Purohit said the soul was not made of matter, but of divine light, the same as god. Thus it was immortal and unchanging.

Asoka could not reconcile these contradictions. 'Could it be there is no soul?' he wondered aloud in his court. 'If so, there's no heaven to go to.' Everyone summarily dismissed that possibility and he let his faith decide. *My grandfather had a soul, he thought, and my father had a soul, and I have a soul. Our religion can't be so wrong.*

In the midst of all this, Anga haunted his thoughts. He imagined her sitting on her throne by his side, her eyes sparkling under the crown, on her lips a subtle smile of love and pride. In the midst of a meeting, a hunt, or a meal, the thought would occur to him, *What's she doing now?* When he thought of her in the monastery, an ineffable sadness would envelop him and linger on for days.

The thought of her alone could not contain his restlessness. As governor, he had once thought the throne would bring him great-ness. Now he knew. *I do not feel great. Only victory in war can bring death-defying fame.*

He called his Council and asked Senapati Purandas for a map showing all the unconquered territories. Purandas gave him a map. 'This was prepared a long time back for your grandfather, after his victory over Seleucus.' As Asoka was turning it over, he added, 'For forty years there has been no war. Our men and equipment are rusting. For the glory of empire and your fame, we need a war!'

Whichever way he turned in the map— to Afghanistan, to Kashmir and Nepal, and northeast, to the bay of Bengal, to Mysore in south— the land was already under his rule.

He frowned. 'Well, not much to conquer. What's left? Small and contiguous states in the south— Cholas, Pandyas, Satiyaputra, and Keralputra. I can conquer them in just one short sweep.'

Purandas said, 'You've left out Kalinga.'

Asoka said, 'That hornet's nest! Right now it's stable. It'll be annexed, if the situation changes. Let's finish off other states first. When we get Kalinga, the question will arise: What next?'

Radhagupta intervened. 'That decision can wait, Great King. Meanwhile, we should take the opportunity to modernize our army. Alexander proved that elephants and chariots are now obsolete.'

'That will take three or four years!' said Purandas.

'We are a great power,' Asoka nodded. 'We can choose when we attack. How would you modernize?' he asked Purandas.

'The infantry has bamboo and leather shields, two-handed swords, spears, and bows. We need several infantry divisions with longer spears, small straight-cut swords, metal shields, metal helmets, scale armor, and thrusting-pikes. Our horses are old. We need young horses. Our cavalry needs to drill to develop strength of seat.'

'And the cost?' asked Asoka.

Radhagupta replied, 'We'll reduce the infantry by one hundred thousand, limit the elephant corps, and eliminate the chariots. The savings will cover the cost.'

Asoka said, 'I like the plan! Also, get good topographical maps.'

44

In the sixth century BC, Buddha had founded the first religious order in history, the Sangha or the Vihara, a community of yellow-robed followers. Buddhism appealed to a rising class of merchants who resented the dominance of the Brahmins and the Kshatriyas– part of a rigid caste system. Anga left home at twenty and went to the Sangha in Taxila, determined to dedicate her life to the Buddha. Bitan also had toyed with Buddhism after his wife's death but decided against it.

The Taxila monastery was situated on a knoll at the foot of the Hathial spur to the southwest of the walled city of Bhir Mound, and north of the Tamra stream. It consisted of an inner court with several small buildings, a promenade and cloister for afternoon walks, a large tree, a clear water pond, and one just for lotus flowers. Small cells around the courtyard housed eleven monks and five nuns, including Anga. The single-story mud brick buildings housed a refectory, a tailoring room, a provision store, the dining hall, a kitchen, two bathrooms, a drug store, and an infirmary.

Each Vihara was run independently. Decisions were made by consensus, and arrived at by motions, resolutions and a quorum. On the days of full or new moons, monks and nuns met in the Assembly Hall to declare their steadfastness to monastic discipline, and to confess to any offense committed the previous fortnight. Lay people also participated in a fortnightly ceremony called Uposatha, where they would give rice or scraps of food or other gifts to the Sangha, to earn merit for the future life. Everyone at the Sangha pursued a rigorous course of "right discipline"– yogic concentration, and an ongoing examination of one's thoughts, words and conduct.

Like other nuns, Anga shaved her head, put on a saffron robe and abandoned family bonds, including any desire for children. She learnt that death was as real as life. Upasila, the head, told the monks, 'We don't know whether we will wake up tomorrow. The certainty of death liberates us from the anxiety of possessions. And frees us to experience existence as pleasure.'

Anga accepted the hardships of her new life. Her sorrow had faded but not her desires and she tried to repress them through meditation. But her eyelids still fluttered at memories of physical love and her heart longed for romance. She strove for a union with the Buddha, imagining that all her feelings and thoughts would dissolve in the flame of divine love. She prostrated herself, closed her eyes, and rubbed her forehead on the Lord's feet. Exasperated with her progress, she often sighed, Buddha! I am lost as ever!

If I were a man, she thought, *I would cut off the parts responsible for these feverish visions.* Sometimes, she woke up panting from making love in a dream, sometimes sobbing from frustration. *Lord, it was not my fault that I fell in love. Why am I being punished?* Sometimes she told herself that she had sinned. *Perhaps I'd suffer less had I not been carried away.* Her cheeks burned when she remembered what had happened one night. *It was wrong! Very wrong!*

She told her suffering to Priyambada and Ansuiya, two nuns who had become her friends. Priyambada was young and reflective, while Ansuiya, with her long, sad face, was older and warm. Priyambada said, 'Anga, you did not sin. In youth, our body is our heart. It shows us the way of love! Buddha is compassionate. He will show you the right way.'

Priyambada had had a similar journey before coming to the Vihara. Realizing all bodies crave love, Anga thought, *I loved Semat but it was not unique, it happens to everyone. And it's not the end of my life.* She felt released from Semat's hold, and able to open her heart to the possibility of divine love, or human love, as yet unrevealed.

She reflected. *I cannot love Buddha without knowing love, without connecting to life.* In the pounding of her heart, and the unabashed yearnings of her body, she heard this call to life. Yet it left her utterly confused. Part of her wanted to return home, but pride stood before her like a fortress wall. She had denounced her family, and promised her life to the

Buddha. *Those were horrid years!* she admitted to herself. *It would be the same all over again. I should be ashamed even to think of going back. I will find His love. I must. One day Buddha's love will come flying like a dart and pierce my heart.* At that moment, she was sure, she would faint with ecstasy.

She told Ansuiya, or Suiya, as Anga called her, 'Am I just my body? I see flowers and go into rapture. A handsome monk's smile sends me up in flames. It scares me!' Anga started crying.

'Anga, it takes time,' Suiya said, holding Anga. 'It took the Buddha six years to steady his mind. Just don't waver in your faith.'

Anga wiped her eyes. 'I'm never happy anywhere. I'm always somewhere else!'

Bitan visited her every month. His visits reminded her that life was passing her by and that she was going nowhere. Resolving to be firm, she told Bitan to stop coming.

When Suiya came down with a fever and lost consciousness, Anga nursed her in the infirmary as if Suiya were her mother. She did it out of love, and because the Buddha had said, *You, O bhikkhus, monks, have neither a mother nor a father who can nurse you. If...you do not nurse one another, who, then will nurse you? Whoever, O bhikkhus, would nurse me, he should nurse the sick.*

Anga spent many a night by Suiya's side, applying cold press to her forehead, offering her water in the night, and cleaning her pot. She experienced a strange peace in giving. From then on, if any nun fell sick, Anga became her nurse. This was the only time when her thoughts did not run wild and she was at peace. Still, it frightened her that she might die without knowing love.

She completed a year at the Vihara and rejoiced. It had been a long year. Within days, a courier arrived with a letter from the King. All letters were directed to Upasila but the courier insisted he had been directed to deliver it only to Anga. Called into the Assembly Hall, Anga arrived looking haggard and pale. Upasila told the courier to hand her the letter. After sending him out, Upasila glared at her. 'A letter from the emperor! After you've read it, turn it over to me.'

Stunned, Anga rushed to her cell to read.

Dearest Anga, Bitan told me you that are in the monastery. After a year, I have not yet recovered from the shock. You wanted to be a nun and for a year a nun you have been. But now it is time to leave the Sangha.

Anga, I love you. I want you. I loved you before anyone else came into your life. Say 'yes' to me, Anga, and I will rush to Taxila. You'll come here as the queen of my heart. My love waits for you—Asoka.

Anga's temples throbbed. The day they'd gone horse riding together swam before her. She still felt the cool silken touch of the lotus petals on her cheeks. Is it possible? The Emperor! In love with me! She read and re-read the letter, trembling all over.

She tried to calm herself like a good nun. Sitting crossed legged and closing her eyes, she tried to meditate. *Lord Buddha, show me the path.* But Asoka kept fluttering before her. Suddenly, she remembered. She ran outside and asked the courier to come back the next day.

Then, she took the letter to Upasila. Waiting for his reprimand, she stood before him, head down. Upasila turned pale. He put the letter back in her hands and said sternly, 'Obey the emperor!'

Anger flashed in Anga's eyes. 'Revered One,' she said forgetting the rules, 'that is not for you to decide.'

Hurriedly, Upasila got up and left the Hall.

Again that night she prayed to the Buddha. He too had been tempted by Mara before his enlightenment. *Am I on trial? But I'm so weak, Lord,* she cried. Love had knocked at her door. *But I am not looking for an escape. To receive his love, I have to love him from my heart. And Buddha may yet come!*

She tossed and turned, crying all night and her hands trembled when she sat down to reply. *How should I address him? Should I just use 'Devanampiya' (dear to the gods)?* It was the honorific title for addressing a king. *But it sounds so sterile. I called him Asoka. Now Asoka may be too familiar.* She paced a while then came up with the word "Piyadassi", meaning "of gracious appearance", or "the gracious one". She liked its resonance.

She wrote, as if she were touching his face.

Piyadassi Raja Asoka, I'm greatly honored by your sentiment, but I am under an oath to Lord Buddha. A nun I am, and a nun I wish to remain. Your humble servant—Anga.

Afterwards, her body ached.

Suiya comforted her. 'Don't torture yourself, Anga. Go to him. Much better than burning in the monastery.'

The courage it took to refuse the King energized Anga. She wrapped the letter in a red cloth and put it away in a corner of her cell, under a small stone. In the Uposatha, she confessed to breaking her celibacy vow in thought.

Asoka whispered all night from under that little stone. "I will bring you here as the queen of my heart!" He had touched it, she thought, and the thought haunted her. She struggled not to hold it in her hands. But one night, longing for his body, she impulsively pulled it out, kissed it and put it under her pillow. From then on, every night before going to bed, she caressed it, and read it.

When Bitan came to see her against her wishes, she smiled. With blood rushing to her cheeks, she asked, 'How is Asoka?' Stunned, he gazed at her in silence. Her face was more serene than he had seen in years.

Her love for the Buddha had transformed into love for Asoka. She didn't know this but Bitan sensed the change. It showed on her face. Gently he said, 'Every letter that Asoka sends to me about state business ends with this one sentence: "Though she is not here with me, she is always in my thoughts."'

A sadness came over her, and she struggled to keep her eyes dry. At last she broke down. 'Ask him to forget an ordinary nun like me.'

Bitan wrote to Asoka about her extraordinary inquiry.

When Asoka received Anga's refusal, he was shattered. He read the letter several times for any sign of love. He saw resignation in it, not rejection. He was not surprised and tried to console himself with the thought, *she's not a scheming nun, not one to come running when the emperor sends for her! She knows of my love, it'll happen. And it must!* He remembered the horse ride, with the peak in Taxila shining through the clouds. *My love, like a vine, will wrap around her.*

He also fretted: *How much longer will I have to wait? Will she love me? Will she come?* He wanted to write but refrained, remembering Bitan's words "Sow the seed and wait. You can't rush a plant, much less the plant of love."

Waiting was not easy as patience was not one of his virtues and before another year had passed, he sent her another letter.

Anga, how many times have I seen you in my dreams? I am never happy but when you are in my thoughts. Every hour I wonder what you might be doing. Every morning in the Ushas, the goddess of Dawn, I see your beautiful face. Come to me, Anga! Come soon!

The letter made her giddy. But now she was afraid of impulsive love. She decided to look inside herself instead. After several days she wrote back,

Lord Asoka, I think a lot about you. But I am still committed to the Buddha. I will pray for you.

A tear fell on the letter. She carefully wiped it, but the stain remained. When Asoka opened the letter, he immediately noticed it and jumped with joy. *She loves me, she loves me!* He felt like a sixteen year old in the first throes of love.

Every night Anga read both letters before going to bed. Though the first was falling apart, she carefully glued it together with pine resin. Not a day passed when she did not yearn for him. The nuns who had been living long at the monastery without any hope of human love, now amazed her. But she wanted to make sure she loved Asoka, and not the King.

One sunny afternoon, sitting under the huge Pipal tree, she looked in her heart and asked herself, *Would it make any difference if he renounced the kingdom?* The answer was unequivocal. *I would be just as happy, even more. He will tend the garden, I, the house. Taxila will be our little paradise.*

One day the bell rang for prayers but she heard only the last ring. She did not go to the Assembly Hall, and just sat crying. Later, a monk came by. 'Sister, you did not come to the prayer hall! Are you sick?'

Feebly, she sniffled, 'Yes.'

Lying by the lotus pond on her stomach one afternoon, her chin on her palms and the deer grazing about, she reflected.

I have been unjust to Asoka. I love him yet I tell him otherwise. My devotion to the Buddha has reached its limit. How do I declare my love? Her eyes lit up. *I will write and seal it, and Bitan will send it. But I can't do that from the Vihara. I am under oath here. It would be like adultery. I must free myself from my vow.* She watched the flowers and the grazing deer. *Lately, my thoughts have not been under control. In the prayer Hall, I avert my eyes of monks lest they read my thoughts. When I walk, I stumble. I am so afraid to be in love again.*

She walked over to the clear water pool, stood on a rock jutting into the water, leaned forward and looked at her reflection. She was shocked. *In this robe, I look like a sack of rice!* Unconsciously, she gathered the front folds to one side, smoothed the crinkles over her chest, tied a knot, and looked again– the two ripe lotus buds now stood out. Pleased, she stood watching when a gust of wind startled her. She blushed, and looked around, stealthily.

Priyambada and Ansuiya were passing by, they noticed, and walked over. Pointing two spread fingers at her bosom, Priyambada teased. 'Are you going to receive the emperor tonight?'

Anga's cheeks turned red.

Suiya fluttered her eyelids. 'Priyambada, what's happening to our friend?'

Arching back, Priyambada stuck out her belly. 'This!'

Anga turned away, embarrassed. 'I have to water the ivy!'

'You are the ivy, Anga!' said Suiya.

'Don't just stand and tease!' Anga pleaded. 'Come, help me.'

Priyambada and Ansuiya laughed and walked down with her.

Next day, Anga went to Arhat Upasila. She kept her eyes on the ground and her head down. 'Arhat, I have fallen in love!'

A year earlier she had spurned his advice.

'Again? Who is it this time?' For a moment anger showed on his face, then he softened.

'Will the Lord forgive me?' Anga asked in anguish.

Gently, Upasila said, 'The Lord is compassionate. Go and live your life the way it was meant to be lived.'

Joy surged in her heart and tears came to her eyes. She bowed in reverence.

Holding up his hand in benediction, he said, 'You may return to the laity.'

45

Anga returned home and after a few months she had put her life back together: horse riding, reading, music and philosophy. Ruddiness returned to her cheeks. Her hair frustrated her —it would not grow fast enough. She looked like an army sergeant so Bitan got her a real hair wig from Alexandria.

Bitan prepared to join the Treasury and Anga was going with him. She wrote to Asoka. *My heart is already yours! But for the first few months, I want to live with Bitan. What do you think?*

It has been a long wait. I can wait a few months more, if that's her wish! thought Asoka.

Sonara was giddy. She went about gleefully telling the relatives, "My daughter is going to be Empress!" To Anga, she said, 'Remember, the wedding must be performed at Taxila.' Anga just smiled mysteriously.

Bitan and Anga reached Pataliputra in late spring and lived in Bitan's house in the Palace complex. Asoka wanted to throw a party to welcome Anga, but she refused. 'I can't leap from solitary meditation to the centre of people's attention.' So he threw a party for Bitan, inviting all the ministers, high officials, foreign diplomats, even their wives. Anga was nervous.

The day of the party, the Grand Hall glittered with lights. Shadows danced on wall carvings of flowers and trees. Men and women were dressed in gaudy colors, and their painted faces looked like the heads of owls, pigs, dogs, hawks, and horses, screwed on human shoulders. An assembly of strange animals it was. Even before wine was served, people wafted in their own stratosphere. The orchestra played for two minutes, and then a beaming King arrived. A loud cheer went up in the Hall. No one could remember Asoka looking so happy.

A few minutes later Anga entered in a dark blue silk dress with a border of gold, fastened by a gold chased brooch, her lush black hair piled high, like a queen's. Around her long golden neck, she wore an Egyptian collar with red, green and dark blue jewels– blue for the night sky, green for new growth of the seasons, and the red for life. Suddenly, the royal orchestra broke out in song. Awed, the crowds yielded an aisle for her. At her request, Bitan walked one step behind, alongside the new envoy from Babylon and his charming young Greek wife.

'She is so dainty, so pretty, the music must be for her,' men whispered.

Someone asked the envoy, 'Who is she?'

'A princess from Persia!' he smiled.

Rapt in thoughts of the Vihara, the music escaped her and she glanced about her apprehensively as she walked– not one face was familiar. *The whole evening is before me!* She turned back, panicked, to look at Bitan, who gave her a reassuring smile. Cups of water were passed round, and she lunged and seized one. Clutching it, she took up a corner. Now she looked around. People were drifting about, trying to look important, nodding at strangers, laughing in dribbles or in sounds like falling rocks. Near the entrance door stood three men in distance, looking hopelessly lost. She felt a little better. From the corner of her eye, she caught sight of a fashionably dressed man who was whispering to a second fellow standing nearby, pointing at her. Anga quickly gazed into her cup, swirled it, and took a slow sip, sniffing the bouquet of fresh, sparkling water. *My god! It hasn't even started,* she thought. Her eyes searched for Asoka and spotted his crown. He stood mobbed by ambassadors and their wives.

Scantily clad young females passed the wine around. She took a cup to bide her time. Asoka noticed her and waved, gazing at her as he talked. She smiled back with love-filled eyes, her heart pounding. Leaving the mob, he came up and embraced her.

'Welcome to Pataliputra! Everyone is eager to meet you, Anga,' he said, pressing her hand. Her head began to spin. Just then, Radhagupta came rushing in, as if he had news of a fresh Greek invasion. Asoka apologized, 'I'll be back soon, Anga.'

Alone again! she sighed. The man who had pointed at her was elbowing his way through the crowd and flashed his shining uneven white teeth at her. He had an olive complexion and lush black hair. Self-conscious, she turned her head away.

'I am Dionysius, the Egyptian ambassador,' he said, standing in front of her. He was about thirty, with a sharp nose, small eyes and a square face. He bowed until his head was close to the floor.

'You are absolutely beautiful...ma'am...'

She was flabbergasted, but managed to say, 'Thank you! I am Anga.'

He rose slowly and straightened his back. 'What a lovely name! I have not seen you before. Your husband must be new to the city.'

Anga took a sip of wine. 'I'm not married.'

Dionysius's eyes lit up. 'How delightful! I mean not that you have no husband but that you are not married. You know what I mean. I have not come across a single beautiful woman in Pataliputra. I mean,...a beautiful woman who is single.' His smile lifted his cheeks and turned his eyes into slits. 'Do you speak Greek?'

'Oh! no, no. No!'

'No matter. I speak Prakrit. Rather, I try. All the pretty ones here seem to be taken early. Then they turn frigid. I mean they do not move— I mean they do not mix. Look at me, thirty one and still unmarried!' He stepped back to see the effect of his announcement.

She stood sipping wine, looking into her glass.

'I want to invite...' He stopped, followed her wandering eyes.

'What did you say?' she turned her head back.

His unrestrained pleasure in himself amused her. In her head, she composed his obituary: *Here lies the man who did not meet a beautiful single woman.*

She saw Bitan in the distance. 'Excuse me,' and slipped away.

Bitan stood talking to Visal whom she remembered coming to Taxila with Asoka. 'Anga!' he smiled. 'Bitan just told me you were here. Do you like our city of flowers?'

Anga answered politely. 'A little flashy. But I'll get used to it.'

Just then a man came hurrying up to Visal. 'Two army guests are having a fist fight.' 'Excuse me.' Visal rushed away to control the rebellion.

After the guests left, Bitan, Anga and Asoka sat sipping wine. Anga blushed under Asoka's gaze. 'Anga, the first time I saw you in Taxila,' he said, 'you were around seven. You came running into the room, looked at me, and ran out, saying, "Grandpa, you said Asoka was a prince! But I see no carriages and red turbans!"'

'I don't remember,' Anga stammered. 'Shows how foolish I was even then.'

Asoka laughed. 'And so charming!'

Asoka took her hand. 'Anga showed me around your garden!' He turned to Bitan. 'Tomorrow, I want to show her the Palace gardens.'

The next day, she arrived wearing emerald earrings and a bright yellow cotton dress. She looked like a spring flower. Lunch was served under the cool shade of a wide tree but Anga ate little. Asoka joked, 'You don't like the food!'

Anga laughed, 'I'm still getting used to eating more than once a day, Devanampiya.'

The word jarred. 'Anga, we agreed long ago that you'd call me Asoka.'

She said with a twinkle, 'I can live with Asoka...,' then added, and 'Piyadassi' ' A tender look spread over his face. She knew he liked that name.

After lunch, Asoka took her around the gardens. 'Tell me when you get tired, Anga.' Hand in hand, they passed the equestrian statues carved in polished stone, guarding the main Palace gate, and the lion carved on the grand Hall entrance pillars.

'You must love animals, Piyadassi,' she teased.

'I do—when they arrive carved at the table,' he grinned out of sheer exuberance.

The gardens surrounding the great Hall were open to the public. To the east of the Hall were the King's private quarters, its pathways lined with tall trees and flower shrubs. The grounds to the west had a lake, and a serpentine pond, filled with lotus flowers. To break the monotony of the flat grounds, a man-made island, Kamarupa, stood looking forlorn in a lake called Nandi. A curved wooden bridge led to the island. Peacocks strutted there with glistening purple-blue-green feathers. A few pigeons fluttered their wings now and then, cooing in contentment.

Asoka said, 'I have to show you a special tree.'

He led her to two Amaltas trees in full bloom near the island. Seeing the flowers, Anga was overcome by sadness.

'Perhaps I should not have brought you here.'

'Oh no, I love them. They are my old friends.' She sighed. 'It was so long ago!'

'To me, it feels like yesterday.'

'It's getting late,' Anga said, looking at the sunset.

'Tomorrow, we'll walk to the river.'

The next evening, Asoka said, 'I remember the great sunrises in Taxila. The sunsets here over the Ganges are just as magnificent.' He lifted her into the royal boat. The touch of her body, her scent, made his heart race. He kept rowing, eyes on her face, glowing in the pale evening sun. At the south-west turn of the river, he anchored the boat and they walked barefoot on the warm sand. The sun was setting on the distant horizon. Enraptured, they watched the unearthly embrace of the river and the sky. The fiery red sun gently penetrated the trembling river, spilling red, orange and pink in its eager body, flushed with pleasure. In a few minutes, the agitation over, the sky turned a purplish tint, and the river took on an unearthly glow.

Asoka clasped Anga's waist from behind, and resting his chin on her head, inhaling the scent of her hair, he was transported to a world of feelings unsullied by thought, it was as if he was clasping pleasure itself! And beauty more ravishing than any goddess. He stood lost in an eternity of love.

She caressed his hands. Then a gust of wind blew a speck of sand in her eye, and she rushed to splash water on it. Asoka planted a lingering, warm, moist kiss there— and it soothed her.

Taking a palm-full of water, he splashed a few drops on Anga's face. Trembling, she filled her hands with water, splashed it into the air, then joyfully jigged to catch the falling water drops on her face, laughing. Asoka watched her, enchanted.

Both felt the magic moment would last as long as the river flowed, as long as the sun came up in the sky. Ah! The ecstasy of this moment! Of young love! The timelessness of it all! More delicious than the wines of Persia and Greece, more perfumed than the frankincense of Babylonia!

But oblivious that time, that great spoiler of love, would stop at nothing.

They savored the colors, the beauteous evening. Then he sat down on the bank, his arms enveloping Anga, her feet playing with gentle water waves. When it turned dark, they returned, and he sadly watched her disappear into the tarnished silvery dusk.

Next evening, playing with water on the riverbank, Asoka said, 'Anga, I have known you since you were seven. But there are things about me you don't know.'

'Asoka! I remember the beautiful hibiscus flower you pinned in my hair!' Anga teased.

Asoka became serious. 'I want to tell you everything.'

Lying on the sand on her stomach, chin propped on her hands, she looked at him with her large eyes. 'I feel I've known you forever. But still, if you want to, I am listening!'

Asoka started. 'When I was eleven, we—my mother, Choti-ma and Tissa—went on a pilgrimage to Vaitarni. We had our bath and that afternoon, without telling my mother, I took off to explore the forest with Tissa. Tissa went back to the camp, but I ran into cannibals. They were sacrificing by fire a boy about my age. When I tried to save him, I was captured and tied to a tree. I vowed to kill the barbarians when I became King. Had Tissa not returned with Radhagupta, I too would have been sacrificed. That day, I killed a man and lost my innocence. But the killing, the blood on my hands, left a stain for a long time on my mind. I had nightmares. My mother did a havan to rid me of my demons.'

Anga sat up and took his hand. 'To lose the innocence of childhood like that! How terrible!'

'The burning body of the youth sometimes still flashes before me. I can't think of Kalinga without thinking of blood.' He paused, then continued. 'Soon after, my gentle mother died. My father became distant after her death, and I felt like an orphan. Now I know why children become estranged from their fathers when the physical link with the mother is severed. I blamed the chief queen and Sasima for my loss and I grew up having no one to please but myself.

'Choti-ma loved me in her own way, but she was not my mother. She was obsessed with seeing me on the throne. To Choti-ma, killing a man was like killing a cockroach. To my mother, killing a cockroach was like killing a man. Choti-ma told me a lot about the Greeks. They question everyone and everything, and consider revenge killing a noble deed. Alexander's mother killed his father so Alexander could be king, she told me. Strange story! That night I dreamt Sasima stood tied to a tree, and I set fire to his body.'

Anga reacted, 'You could never do that, My Lord.'

Asoka took her hand and pressed it affectionately. 'Why should Sasima be the crown prince?' One day, I asked her.

'"Who else should be?" Choti-ma asked me.'

'The ablest prince! I thought I was the ablest prince. Words and ideas always fascinated me. I argued with the priests. What God could want an innocent youth's sacrifice? The priests complained to the queen; she told father I had no respect for religion. As if he wasn't already annoyed with me.'

'Then I won a horse race with some luck, and some pluck and the victory went to my head. Like mad, I wanted Sasima's girl and I had her. Then I was unjustly convicted of rape. Fed up with Pataliputra, I left for Taxila. Like my grandfather, I came into my own there. I fell for a courtesan but she threw me out because I failed to make Governor. Suddenly I saw I needed power. I turned to philosophy and religion, not because I am religious, but to unlock the secret of power, and to find out if power is greatness. When I read about the power-grabbing Vedic gods, I put aside my squeamish feelings my mother had planted in me. I hardened myself at the feet of Siva, the Terrible.'

Anga protested, 'Piyadassi, you can't go against your nature!'

Asoka smiled. 'I don't know,' he said. 'Anyway, my teacher told me power is seized, not granted or conferred. Sensing my opportunity, I killed the Taxila Administrator and became Governor. In an instant, I became perversely bold and wise.'

'Now my dreams took on flesh. I quietly raised a small army. That evening when you sang to me so beautifully in Taxila, I left on a perilous journey. I entered the Palace at night, and killed the Senapati. But things went awry, and I killed Marut in Sasima's bed by accident. My men killed Pavan, and Sasima escaped. What is worse, the angry chief queen killed Choti-ma. That Marut and Pavan were killed, still troubles me. I grieve for Choti-ma. Later I learnt that she, not the queen, killed my mother.'

Anga was shocked. 'How could you still love her?'

'I didn't find out until after her death, but by then, it was too late to be angry. My heart goes out to my mother. She lost her life because Choti-ma had no son. Sometimes, I curse myself. But I can't forget what Choti-ma did for me. She loved me, if strangely. And she paid for her ambition.' He sighed. 'Caught up in the excitement of imagined glory, sometimes we commit deeds that haunt us for life.'

Anga looked directly into his eyes. 'So who is Asoka?'

'More evil than good. Or rather, both evil and good. I chose the path of power, the way of gods. The evil in me is my ambition. Sasima and I could not have lived in the same empire. But the good in me is my love for you. That evening in Taxila, I was so moved by your sorrow that had Semat appeared, I would have walked away for your happiness. Love is glorious but also sinister. It can dredge up demon in us, as well as the god.'

He bent down, pressed her to his chest and kissed her forehead. Anga gazed tenderly at him for a long moment. 'Asoka, I see only love in your eyes.' She paused. Then she asked, her voice trembling, 'Can you forgive my folly?'

Asoka smiled softly. 'I was angry for a while, then sad, very sad. But remember, I myself had fallen for a courtesan at seventeen. It gave me an understanding of our hearts.'

It was dark. Anga got up, dusted off the sand, and kissed him on the lips. Tearfully, she said, 'How I wanted to run into your arms when I received your second letter. I was afraid of succumbing to impulsive passion, so I tested myself by fire for a year. But your love is my life, Asoka. I want to be your Parvati, your Sita. If I lose your love, I would not want to live.'

Asoka folded her in his arms. 'Anga, you are the one. The one for me.'

46

Anga loved horse riding. They'd leave in the evening and return around midnight. One such late afternoon, they took a forest trail in the south-east of the city and went on for three hours. On the way back, thunder clapped and lightning flashed. The terrified deer sprang to their feet, and wolves ran to hide in their dens.

As the first raindrops fell, Anga cried, 'Piyadassi, the monsoon is here!' Since childhood she had believed that forests were infested with man-eating 'Rakshasa'—demons— at night.

'Those are fairy tales,' Asoka comforted her. 'I've never seen one in my life.'

The rain started to pour down. Dripping, they dismounted and waited under a tree. Asoka took off his waistcoat and put it on Anga. Lightning flashed and he saw a wide-canopied Banyan tree with pillared arms, and rain sloping down its foliage to the ground. They ran to it and stood watching the rain, Anga in Asoka's arms.

Whenever the lightning flashed, the many trees of the forest were revealed— all washed. Mimosa, gardenia, aloe-wood, laburnum and kachnar, shrubs and creepers of peacock flower, hibiscus, exora, purple wreath, golden shower and moonbeam. The rain slowed down, and leaving the Banyan tree, they found they had lost the forest trail, and Anga's horse kept getting tangled in the low branches. All four directions seemed to have been erased by the heavy rain and a timeless forest existed shrouded in damp darkness.

Dripping heavily, Asoka scrambled to find another Banyan tree as the rain had slowed down. Through the leafy screen, he sighted a flickering light in the distance and Anga and Asoka exchanged happy glances. In that darkness, the now visible, now hidden, the quivering oil lamp flame became their towline. Each time the wind blew, the flame trembled and dimmed, and each time the swaying branches obscured it, their hearts sank.

Then lightning flashed, and in that instant, a shining white hut sprang up not too far from them. Instantly, Anga was transported to the old Vihara. Oblivious of the rain, she felt herself melting in the fire of love.

In those days, many ascetics— the Sramanas—lived in forests, subsisting on berries, fruits, nuts and rice, wearing only deerskins or tree bark. Anga and Asoka now reached the hut. On the porch stood a three-legged potbelly iron stove and firewood was stacked against the wall. Asoka wiped the rain from his face. 'Anga, I'll find out if it is a hermitage or a den of thieves.' He drew his sword and knocked.

'Who is there?' asked a female voice. The door opened and a little girl stuck her head out, then closed the door again.

'A traveler and his wife!' Asoka replaced his sword.

Anga now joined him and called to the girl, who emerged wide-eyed.

'What is your name?' Anga patted her back affectionately.

'Shakuntala.' She seemed amazed at the sight of this beautiful woman.

'Where is your father?' Anga asked.

'Visiting a friend,' the girl smiled.

Shakuntala went in, lit another lamp and held it up to Anga. Her eyes brightened. 'Who is your father?' Anga asked.

'Rishi Janakraj.'

'And your mother?'

'I have no mother.'

Surprised, Anga asked, 'Are you an ascetic's daughter?'

'No. He found me and my sister at this door. We are like his daughters now.' 'Can we stay here tonight?' Anga asked.

'Oh, yes. We have two rooms. One here, the other there.' Shakuntala pointed to a grove of trees out at the back. 'That's where we both sleep.' She explained, 'This is my father's hut. I fell asleep, but woke up to perform the evening prayer here.'

Holding the lamp, she showed them the rectangular room. It had a small window that was closed. Two blankets lay on a bamboo mat. Next to it, a deerskin was spread for meditation, and beyond the deerskin, a cotton mattress lay against the wall. A water jug and two chipped cups sat in the corner on a small table.

Shakuntala went bounding to her room and returned dripping, carrying towels and sheets. She went off again and brought boiled rice, fruits and a red hibiscus flower in a banana leaf basket. She put the basket on the mat and gave the flower to Anga.

Asoka dragged the iron stove near the door and lit a fire. Anga stood wrapped in a sheet and dried her hair over the fire. Asoka rubbed her back, then stood outside the door drying his cloak, with a towel round his waist.

'You're not afraid to be by yourself?' Asoka asked Shakuntala, lifting the towel a little, to direct warm air to his wet behind. Suddenly, a flame leapt at his front.

'Piyadassi! Anga blurted, 'Be careful of fire on your...!' Her cheeks turned red. Amused, Asoka smiled at her, and Anga lowered her eyes. Shakuntala spread the banana leaf with fruit and rice. Still blushing, Anga asked, 'Shakuntala, do you have company?'

'I have my twin sister, a deer and a fawn,' she replied, innocently.

Anga took off her gold bracelet. 'Shakuntala, don't hesitate. Take this gift for your wedding. Now go to bed.'

She left and Anga, now dressed, and Asoka, still wrapped in the towel, sat down to eat. 'Not exactly a royal meal!' Asoka teased.

'It is,' Anga smiled. 'The meal of the emperor and his queen!'

The meal over, they talked, stoking the fire.

Spreading out the sheets and the blanket, Anga took the cotton mattress. Asoka opened the window, extinguished the lamp and dowsed the logs, filling the room and the porch with the aroma of pine and smoke. While the smoke cleared, Asoka stood in the doorway looking out. Nothing was visible behind the curtain of streaming rain. Each time the lightning flashed, he saw the foliage of the forest glitter, and turn silvery.

At last Asoka lay down on the bamboo mat. The wind howled outside, but he heard only Anga's gentle breathing. His own became faster. Only a deerskin divided them. He sat up in bed, and craned his neck to see Anga's head on the pillow facing the wall, her body covered with a blanket. His eyes caressed her hair and her bare white neck, and blood rushed to his head. The desire to kiss her overtook him. Naked, he crouched on all fours, and crossed the deerskin like the Rubicon, then lowering his head inhaled her scent, and whispered in her ear, 'Anga, I can't sleep.' She turned, her eyes shining with love. With a faint smile, she looked into his eyes and lifted the blanket. He slipped in—feet first—lightly touching her navel, her thighs, her calves, till he lay facing her.

Tightening the cover over him and enclosing him in her arms, she softly whispered, 'Are you warm, my love?'

Pressing her close, he caressed her back and kissed her, her body melting in his arms. Outside, the rain pounded the parched earth; the earth panted, emitting a fragrant vapor. His lips wandered over her eyes, the inside of her neck, her firm breasts— like a spring shower falling lightly on golden marigolds, he lingered on her smoldering lips. There was nectar and ambrosia in each sip, each bite. His head swirled with her scent and the warm sensation of her skin. Blood flooded every vein, as flash floods fill a valley. His consciousness of the night, of the rain, of the dark, silvery forest, of the pine scent, began to ebb and her throbbing, silken warmth began to warble in his veins. Void of all thought he whirled, rollicking into a stratosphere of unsullied pleasure, his consciousness receding back in time, till it dissolved in a blinding light: matter exploding into pure energy. Nothing existed then. Neither he nor Anga. He did not hear her faint cry of 'My Buddha!'

How long he remained in that blissful non-existence, he did not know. Then, awareness, like a lotus flower, began slowly to uncurl, and a universe began to form around his consciousness. Once again the rain tapped softly on the roof and the wind whispered to him; he felt the thin veil of the dark wet night falling around his, and her voluptuous nakedness. From nonexistence to existence, he awoke as a floating cirrus, entwined to an ember on earth, listening to the tapering rain with languorous senses, more asleep than awake.

In the haze of flickering darkness, they gazed at one another lovingly and he felt the light, warm caresses of her fingers on his flanks. A sense of oneness seized him; he kissed her eyelids, her lips, and pressing her warm breasts to him, clasped her tighter, as if the duality that had crept between them in the last few moments was unbearable.

When the rain stopped three hours after midnight, they left the hermitage. Picking up the crushed red hibiscus flower from the bed, Anga dropped it lovingly in the vase of her breasts. A few days later, the two were quietly wed in the Palace temple.

47

Anga moved into Livia's apartments, away from the other queens. Of the dozens of personal maids who had waited on her, she let all but two go. 'I don't need a string of harp players to wake me in the morning,' she told Asoka, 'I don't need maids to wipe my face while I am still yawning in bed. I don't want maids to bring me flowers– I like to pick my own. It's funny seeing maids waiting outside the toilet with sandalwood soap, ready with rosewater and frankincense - toilet may be a ritual, but sacred it is not. The morning oil massage is too greasy for me– I'd rather meditate in cool, crisp skin. With four women escorting me to my bath, I feel like a prisoner being hauled to her cell. And I'd rather massage my gums, clean my teeth and paint my lips myself, than feel like a patient on the operation table.'

Asoka understood the nun in her. Indulgently, he asked, 'What else?'

Mischievously, she said, 'I don't want a maid rubbing scented saffron musk on my breasts!'

'Perhaps you'd rather the emperor did that?' he asked with a smile.

Her face became serious. 'If the emperor wouldn't mind!'

Asoka laughed, 'I'll never finish the job.' He paused, 'You really want to do everything yourself?'

Anga replied, 'No. The maids can paint animals around my belly button and on my behind.'

Asoka gazed at her skimpy green Choli and the floral skirt round her small waist. Kissing her bellybutton, he said, 'Oh! I'd love to do that!'

Their love blossomed like spring flowers as she exorcised the ghost of his loneliness. She never went to bed without fresh flowers by the side of her pillow, and she had a soft lamp light burn in the antechamber at night. She played Veena, a stringed musical instruments, before going to bed to get him in the mood. In the morning she woke early to be around him till he left. Every evening she wore new jewelry to please him. She spoke with disarming openness, and when he took himself too seriously, made fun of him.

The two were so rapt that the first winter, spring and summer passed without their knowing it. He finished Kamarupa Island, the artificial hill in the middle of the lake that Chandragupta had started for Livia for relief from the summer heat, but had left incomplete. It became their love nest. On its gentle slopes now grew flowering shrubs and low plants kept moist in the summer to provide a cool breeze. Anga loved antics, and glowed in his presence. If she saw a gossamer-winged butterfly, she went chasing it. Nothing gave her more pleasure than catching one. 'See!' She'd wave her hands with child-like delight. Lifting her up in his arms, Asoka would always say, 'You are my butterfly!' When she tired and felt hot, she took off her clothes unselfconsciously. Laughing, they fell together into the flower bed and would lie in each other's arms, dozing off in a delicious languor.

At other times she baffled him. Some afternoons she sat in the garden reading the Buddha's sermons, and would swim in the lake alone sometimes after he fell asleep at night. Twice a week she observed silence from morning to noon. She told Asoka, 'Only in silence can I discover and reshape myself. Those who talk do not know. Those who know do not talk.' Sometimes on those mornings he teased her simply by moving his lips.

Their second spring in Pataliputra was glorious. On afternoons they capered on Kamarupa Island. She would improvise a silly rhyme, and he would recite the refrain. Her favorite was:

Anga: For long I was dirt,

Oh, how it hurt!

But a pea-head I was not,

I was...a regu-lor!

Asoka: See! Now, I am an empu...roar.

Anga: I drank and I rocked

I knew it could not last

But learning was hard.

I was such a stumbler.

Asoka: Who cares! Now I am an empu...rear

Anga: Of all things in love

I wear a garden glove

Oh I am such a fumbler.

Asoka: But overall, I am an emp-error.'

These capers inevitably ended in love-making.

'How did a nun,' Asoka teased her once, 'learn to make such passionate love?'

'Praise be to Buddhism!' she said tongue-in-cheek.

'Buddhism?'

Then she told him a story, 'Once there was a conference of leaders of different religions. They wanted to decide which religion gave to its adherents most happiness. Each leader had one question to answer: How would you comfort an inconsolable bride, who discovers on her wedding night that her husband is a eunuch?'

'The Vedic priest said, "O unfortunate woman, do havans, rituals, pray day and night. If your karma is good, it may yet shoot up like a cactus in desert. Don't give up on havans, they are your only hope. After all, it can't get any worse."

'The Jain leader said, "I feel sorry for you O deprived woman. Starve your body to cool down the passions. That too is a release."

'The Ajivikas leader said, "O unlucky woman, it was all pre-ordained! Acceptance of fate brings resignation. And resignation makes you religious! Now religion is not bad if you can't have that!"

'It was the Buddhist's turn. "That's life, woman! Don't just sit around and moan. Find happiness elsewhere. Take charge and run from the man who doesn't have a thing."

Asoka burst out laughing. 'You devil!' he said, folding her in his arms.

48

Like his father and his grandfather before him, Asoka loved hunting and Anga always accompanied him. On one trip, he killed six deer and a bison. And hundreds of animals were shot by the nobles. He looked at her proudly, hoping for a word of approbation.

But she was unhappy at the carnage. 'Asoka, everyone knows you're a great marksman. But animals are not just food. Even the buffalo is endearing with its slow gait and silly face.' Asoka was disappointed. 'What are you saying?'

'Piyadassi, you wouldn't burn down a forest. So why kill indiscriminately?'

Asoka laughed. 'Anga! Animals exist to be killed.'

Anga's face fell. 'Animals are not criminals. They are just helpless.'

Asoka pressed her hand affectionately. 'Don't think about it. It will only hasten your wrinkles.'

Another day, Asoka killed a deer and she refused to eat it, though she loved deer meat. He was surprised. 'What's wrong?'

'The deer looked at me just before you shot it,' she said sheepishly.

Asoka laughed. 'Next time, look the other way.'

Curious about her ideas, one day he asked, 'What attracted you to Buddhism?'

'I was pushed to the wall and had no one to go to but Buddha.'

'Why the Buddha?'

'He was so handsome! Imagine, a twenty-eight-year old athletic prince with a beautiful wife and an infant son, who gives up his life of luxury to go begging for food. How he must have missed his son and his wife, and the joys of their love-making!'

Asoka did not like that she took to the Buddha because he was handsome. 'So why did you give him up?' He asked coldly.

Gently she stroked his cheeks. 'I wasn't ready. And then you came along.' She pulled Asoka's ear playfully.

'Did you get something out of it?' he asked, happy now.

'I learnt to think for myself; to take one day at a time.'

He said, 'I don't like Buddhism. How can one give up desires? Desires are our life.'

Anga laughed. 'I would not want to convert you.' She snuggled close to him, 'I wouldn't want my Lord to be a celibate monk.'

Asoka looked into her eyes. She seemed to be a believer and a skeptic at the same time. 'The Buddha must have been a gambler,' he said suddenly. 'He could have lost both worlds. I could never give up the pleasures of a King.'

'Piyadassi, the hero is always a gambler, and a trailblazer!'

49

Another spring came and went. For some time, Anga had been pressing him to take her to the Kashmir Valley, a neglected part of the empire, distant and without a good road. She never asks for anything, thought Asoka and decided to please her. He also wanted to see for himself the vulnerability of his northern frontier against the tribes, and if it needed to be fortified.

Radhagupta warned him, 'It's unwise to go there. The roads are narrow, winding and hilly. It may take months. And hostile tribes are there.'

But Asoka was not persuaded and sent fifteen thousand troops in advance. A party of nurses and physicians was hastily assembled to cover the contingency of Anga's pregnancy.

The party left in early winter so as to catch the carpet of flowers in mid-spring. Bitan was at the head. Two separate sets of tents were carried for the King—one for the next stop. Asoka and Anga's beloved horses—Puskar and Niguna – also had their own tents. Every elephant, horse, mule, and camel, carried food provisions or personal royal items. Ganges water was carried on camel backs in water skins; hundreds of slaves carried delicate items like pottery, and the fig wood throne. Every day couriers delivered state developments by relay.

Bitan described the Kashmir Valley. 'The region is mountainous, with deep, narrow valleys and high, barren plateaus, drained by the upper Jhelum River. It has forests of pine, fir and tall deodar trees. The valley was once a huge lake, called Satisar after Siva's consort, Sati.' Bitan grew euphoric. 'If I were a monk, I would wander in its mountains and valleys.'

A camp was set up at Jammu. Unfit for mountain travel, the camels had to be left there. The sweltering sun, the hilly roads and the steep climb tired the horses. Many fell exhausted, and some died. Men drank what little water they had left, mixed with lime and rock-hard brown sugar. The hope of cool mountain air kept everyone going. The royal couple crossed the precipitous ridges and narrow downward slopes on the back of sure-footed elephants. After Banihal, the weather changed markedly. The cool wind brought a smile to every face and Bitan announced that they should be there in an hour. Everyone sat up for a vision of paradise and no one was disappointed. Encircled with snowy mountains, the large green lake was an emerald set amid sparkling white pearls. Overwhelmed by the sight, Anga pressed Asoka affectionately.

After resting for three days, the royal couple went out sightseeing. The land, the people, even the sun's rays were different. The beauty of the local women— peach complexioned, with almond eyes, sharp noses, and innocent faces—surprised them. Anga said, 'It is unearthly here. Even the sun shines with a soft glow. Like the light in the eyes of a woman gazing at her infant!'

The serpentine Jhelum River had created islands in the valley. There the locals grew fruit and vegetables. Flocks of sheep, goats, yaks, and ponies foraged on green hills. On the terraced slopes, people grew rice, maize, millet, lentils, cotton, barley and peas. The people spoke the Dardic language— Indo-Aryan in character— derived from Sanskrit. It pleased Asoka to see that Siva was their most popular god.

Several caravans from central Asia regularly passed through the valley. The bazaars were filled with wool carpets, copperware, leather robes, shoes, and small boxes made of walnut wood. Long-bearded men walked about in loose long robes. The party discovered a new spice there— a stiff, wire-like yellow spice—called saffron. It was used for coloring clothes and perfuming milk. Anga bought some for herself and for Suiya, who had left the monastery and joined her at the Palace as her companion. Anga also bought two silk-like waistcoats made of a special soft goat's hair.

The beauty of the Valley and the gentleness of its people impressed Asoka. *They are not barbarians, they worship Siva,* he thought. So instead of ordering a massacre, he set up a garrison there to protect the border. There in the Kashmir valley, he founded a new city—Srinagari (Srinagar)— to commemorate his visit, and ordered a temple for Siva.

50

An exhausted royal party returned in late summer. Anga had developed a cold in early autumn that turned into a bad cold and low fever. Her physicians recommended a daily steam bath for recovery. Engineers devised a three-story steam-bath building accessed by an indoor stairway. On the third floor, a long wooden bench was placed in a room lined with plaster-coated animal hides. An iron grate in the floor let in the steam from water boiling in the room below. The first floor door opened onto a swimming pool. In a few months, she was cured.

That spring, Asoka decided to take Anga out for a chariot ride to cheer her spirits. He sent for her and waited below on the last step of the Palace terrace. With her head covered to her eyes, she appeared in deep green on the large platform and seeing Asoka waiting, hastened down, her eyes gleaming. She is weak, she may fall! thought Asoka, and taking the steps two at a time, caught her at mid-terrace, and carried her down in his arms, gazing into her eyes.

Her face red with embarrassment, Anga whispered, 'Piyadassi, put me down! The guards are watching!'

He grinned. 'Anga, I live in a fish bowl.'

He saw the surprised guards exchange approving glances. One of them said, 'Our emperor is in love!'

The other said, 'I heard her call him "Piyadassi." ' Later, out of affection, they started addressing Asoka as Piyadassi.

Asoka put her down in the chariot, and starting the horses, turned to her with a twinkle in his eye. In a hushed voice, he recited his favorite lines of the 'Ushas' hymn from the Rig-Veda:

Like a wife,

Unveiling to her lord, with conscious pride,

Beauties which, as he gazes lovingly,

Seem fresher, fairer, each succeeding morn.

He noticed Anga's eyes tear up. 'What's wrong, Anga?'

She wiped her eyes. 'I could die this moment in your arms, Asoka. I am so happy. And yet,' she added, 'my happiness frightens me. The gods are jealous!'

Asoka laughed, 'You're talking like my mother.'

She hid her face in his chest.

She had this guilt about her good fortune. She had known the agony of love, the pain of loss, she had seen suffering in the community around the Vihara. Despite her own ecstasy, the wrinkled faces of hungry children and starving women sprang before her eyes. Sadness took over her.

She resolved to start an orphanage for the disenfranchised, the low caste children in the city. When she broached the idea, Asoka vehemently opposed it. How could his queen spend time outside the Palace with the poor? It was not that he was opposed to the orphanage. But he opposed her going out, and her involvement in it.

'Then let the children come here,' she said.

He tried to dissuade her. 'Anga, the world is filled with starving people!'

Anga's face fell. 'Piyadassi, do you have contempt for the poor?'

Asoka protested, 'I have contempt for their rigid ways. That's the reason they suffer. I saw that in Taxila. They don't even know their own religion.'

Anga was indignant. 'What choice do they have? The poor live in a dark well. They don't even know the sun is out there. You yourself once said religion keeps cannibals in the dark.'

'Well, their religion preaches violence and killings. Ours doesn't.'

Anga pleaded, 'Piyadassi, I can't be happy if I just watch and do nothing. When others suffer, we suffer.'

Though not happy, Asoka relented at last and an orphanage was opened in the city.

There, children received food and toys and learnt a craft. Anga became attached there to a twelve-year-old boy, Sewak. He ran to her as she got down from her carriage, and touched her feet. She knew he adored her. Vocal and intelligent, he called her 'Rani-ma.' The boy explained to her, 'My name is Sewak. And, Rani-ma, Sewak means servant. I am your servant.' Alone of the two hundred children, he followed her like a pet dog. Once his teacher admonished Sewak, and told him not to bother the queen. Sewak's face fell, and he stood away from her, sobbing. Moved, Anga went to him, caressed his back, and told him he could see her anytime at the orphanage.

'Where are your parents?' she asked him one day.

His eyes teared up. 'I have no father. My mother died when I was one. I have no brothers or sisters.' Then one day out of the blue, he said, 'I want to die for you, Rani-ma.'

'Does he understand what he said?' she asked.

The teacher explained, 'Sewak thinks he must die to prove his love.'

She told Asoka who laughed. 'I hope he finds a woman worth dying for.'

Constantly, Sewak asked Anga questions about her parents, brothers and sisters, and how the children lived in the Palace.

'He is curious,' she told the teacher, 'full of energy and always cheerful.' She gave Sewak the old clothes from children at the Palace but realized she could not show favor. So all the children were given clothes and toys. One thing led to another. When Anga realized there was no place there for sick children, a physician was appointed and rooms added to serve as a hospital.

Happy in love and with her inner-self flourishing, she yearned to see a smile on every child's face. On Asoka the effect of happiness was different. If he could, he would have stored her love in a gold box like a miser, and watched the rising mound of his treasure with pleasure-filled, greedy, eyes.

Yet, for the first time in life, his world was complete. Always introspective, he often wondered whether the lust for power arises from the absence of love. Was Choti-ma's obsession with becoming Raj-Mata the result of a life void of love? He asked himself if power was a filler for love. For himself he knew, that power was good but not good enough. It satisfied him, but what gave joy was the mysterious power of love.

One day Bitan casually asked, 'Asoka, how is life?'

'Wine and honey!' he chirped, 'Every day before sunrise, I hear the nightingale sing on our windowsill.'

Bitan smiled but with a twinge of envy.

51

The news of Anga's pregnancy made Asoka euphoric. Acting on the popular belief that only a happy mother gives birth to a happy child, he had the best musicians in the city move to the Palace to play whenever she wished. She also liked plays, and Kausal staged a different play from the Mahabharata every three weeks. One of her favorites was Savitri who, by her charm and persistence, wins a reprieve from Yama for her husband, after his death. Every morning for an hour Anga listened to sermons for the benefit of the unborn's moral development.

Despite a difficult pregnancy, she gave birth to a healthy boy— Kunala. Many animals were sacrificed in havan, and festivities lasted for fifteen days in the city.

Asoka had not yet declared a crown prince, but Devi had not forgotten his journey to the throne. A few days after Kunala's birth, she asked Asoka to declare Kunala the crown prince. 'Mahinda, the eldest, is the natural heir but he wants to become a Buddhist monk.' Amid great rejoicing, Kunala was declared crown prince.

To celebrate his birth, Bitan's play Pururavas and Urvashi— based on a story from the *Rig-Veda*— was produced in the Palace. Pururavas, a mortal, falls in love with an immortal nymph, Urvashi. She agrees to be his consort but warns him that she'll vanish if she ever sees him naked. Pururavas was unhappy but promised to comply. One night as they make love, lightning flashes, she sees it all and vanishes instantly.

Heartbroken, Pururavas searches for her everywhere. One day he recognizes her in a lake, swimming with other nymphs, and implores her to come back. "It is all over; after four years of sex three times a day, I am sated," she replies, and disappears.

In the *Rig-Veda*, she stays immortal, but not in Bitan's version.

The Chorus comforts Pururavas. "The immortals don't care for love. Its sex they want. The mortals want both, because love makes them feel immortal."

"How can the gods not want love?" Pururavas cries out. "How could Urvashi not want love after four years of glorious sex?"

The Chorus replies, "The fault, dear Pururavas, is not in love, but in immortals. The young, the powerful, the rich, think they are immortal. And they just want sex, not love."

Pururavas pleads, "Just tell me how to get her back."

The Chorus advises, "Convince her that love is to sex what wine is to a meal. What butter is to bread. Send her fresh flowers. Tell her you are going mad. Numb her mind."

Pururavas follows the advice, and Urvashi returns to him. Her celestial companions taunt her. "I prefer the excitement and fever of a lifetime," she tells them, "to an eternity of mindless existence. Why, in heaven there are no lovers. No poets. And no philosophers!"

Leaving the Hall, Asoka said to Bitan, 'I like what you did. Only love can change us!'

PART FOUR

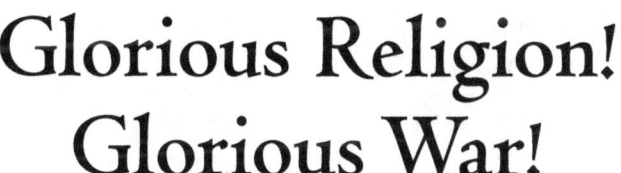

Glorious Religion!
Glorious War!

52

Four years after Asoka's coronation, Narad, the head of Secret Service, had surprising news for the King. 'The old King of Kalinga has been found murdered in the palace along with the crown prince. After adultery, murder, and betrayal, Sisupal is about to marry Queen Sunanda, and become king'

Radhagupta shrugged his shoulders. 'What's new? The man with lust for power will stop at nothing. What's amazing is that he always sees god's hand in his rise.'

Narad was rushed to Kalinga to observe the changed political landscape. With him he took a team of secret agents— prostitutes, monks, ascetics, and plain clothes men. Within a few months, he reported back. 'Kalinga is in turmoil. Queen Sunanda gave birth to a prince and Sisupal promised he could become crown prince if she took care of the old King. She obliged. Now he's married her, though he is already married to Charu, your sister. But Sisupal lacks a power base: royal birth, military or public support. He was not even born into the Jain faith. Though he has shaved his head like the Jains, the masses want him out.'

'What religion do the people follow?' Asoka asked.

'When the Aryans invaded India two thousand years ago, they Aryanised the north but were late in reaching Kalinga,' Narad explained. 'So the Jain religion moved in there and is still predominant. Strangely, the Jain God is not divine, it's 'Jina', the perfected human soul. You know the black marble statue of Jina in our temple here in Pataliputra? It was stolen over a century ago from Kalinga. Now it's a sore point in our relations. Sisupal has promised the public he will bring back the Jina.'

'Who is the true heir to the throne?' asked Asoka.

Narad continued, 'The burly mustached Mahabali. He's the Senapati and Queen Sunanda's brother. He has the backing of an impressive army: an infantry of sixty thousand, a cavalry of one thousand, seven hundred war elephants and two hundred chariots. He has spread the rumor that Sisupal murdered the old King. Sisupal panicked and ran to his Prime Minister Nauchand, a Mahabali-hater. Nauchand advised him to throw God into the ring.

'When I reached Kalinga,' Narad continued, 'Sisupal had a convenient revelation— God had told him that he was destined to be Kalinga's King. That appeased the masses. "If God talks to him," the ignorant, the poor and the religious fanatics said, "he is good enough for us." However, others— merchants, landowners and educated Brahmins— were not impressed. They will support Sisupal on the condition that he will grant them land rights and mining concessions.

'Sisupal believes he can persuade you to return the Jina,' Narad added. 'That would make him a god. His Prime Minister Nauchand, a lean man of sixty, has returned with me to plead his case.'

As the emissary of a vassal state, Nauchand was warmly received. 'Kalinga is your strongest subject state,' he told Asoka. 'I ask you to donate our ancestral god Jina to us.'

Surprised, Asoka said, 'Nauchand, Jina is also our god.' He added, 'I think Sisupal needs Jina to save his neck.'

Nauchand folded his arms. 'A just King like you should return the stolen Jina,'

Asoka sprang to his feet. 'Nauchand, you know that after defeat, Kalinga lost all rights to Jina, and it is our god too.' He sat down. 'Kalinga wants to go to war over a piece of stone?'

Nauchand's face turned red. 'King, Jina is no stone. Jina is our God.' He added, 'Sisupal is not only your friend, but the husband of your sister. Would you abandon him?'

Asoka thought for a moment. 'I can't betray my people.'

Nauchand ran out of arguments, pleas and threats. 'Great King! If war comes, you will be fighting against Kalinga God.'

Asoka rejoined. 'Magadha is not without gods!'

Nauchand went back empty-handed.

53

A usurper of the throne, without royal birth or military support, will resort to desperate acts, Asoka knew. Putting aside his plan to annex the unconquered small states, he told the Council, 'We have to annex Kalinga first. It's in turmoil.'

As ever, Bitan was the prudent voice on the Council. 'Should we go to war over the Jina?' Asoka felt himself flush. He revealed that Sisupal had secretly given asylum to Sasima for three years.

After a pause, Bitan said, 'To you personally, it was treachery. But in the end, Sisupal did not help Sasima.'

'Territorial gain is an excellent foreign policy objective,' Narad said.

'Big fish eat small fish,' Radhagupta, the war hawk, said. 'It is time we annex Kalinga.'

Bitan would not give up. 'Why not install Mahabali by sabotage?'

'Bitan, the horse is out of the gate! People are clamoring for the Jina. Barbarians don't understand peace,' Asoka said.

Bitan shook his head. 'Kalinga already resents Magadha's rise to power. A war will only increase the people's hatred for us.'

'Once the war is over, Kalinga will share in our prosperity,' Asoka replied. 'The past will be forgotten.' He turned to Purandas, the Senapati. 'When will we be ready?'

'We're just waiting for the last one thousand Persian horses for the cavalry and some odds and ends for the infantry,' Purandas said. 'We're almost there!'

54

When news of war preparations reached Sisupal, he faced a dilemma: go to war against the mighty Magadha, or hand over the throne to Mahabali. He loved power, and hated Mahabali. That made his decision simple. However, the treaty with Magadha forbade military expansion.

Nauchand advised, 'Toss away the treaty. Go to war. If you win, you will become a god. And if you lose, you may still keep the throne, as Porus did after losing to Alexander. Every winner needs a proxy to rule the conquered land.'

'Our King will bring back the Jina!' the priests announced in the temples.

The message spread like wildfire. Overnight, Sisupal became a national hero. Confident now, he sent for the Senapati. Caressing the rosewood arm of his royal high chair with one hand, and holding toddy in the other, he told himself, '*At last I'll get Asoka.*' When the tall, muscular Mahabali appeared in his court dressed in a red uniform, Sisupal smiled. 'I have to tell you what happened last night.'

Mahabali sneered. 'I have no interest in your dark thoughts or your dark deeds.'

Sisupal's felt his face turn purple. Putting down the toddy, he said loudly, 'God told me to wage war!'

Mahabali looked astonished. 'That will be suicide.'

'God said, "Your devotees will bring you victory."'

Mahabali narrowed his eyes. 'The old, the sick, the unarmed will bring victory?'

'Mahabali! Mahabali!' Sisupal said impatiently, 'There is power in numbers. Five hundred thousand men on God's mission cannot lose!'

Mahabali rolled his eyes and pounded the table. 'We can't fight with ill-trained, ill-equipped men! But...'

'No buts. This is straight from God.' Putting his feet up on the table, Sisupal leaned back on his chair. 'We shall win. Asoka has no moral courage. He's drowning in sensual pleasures.'

Mahabali went pale.

Sisupal noticed and asked sarcastically, 'Are you afraid?'

Mahabali stayed calm. 'The men have to be equipped and trained. Where is the money?'

'Of course! The money! Of course. I have a great plan! I am immediately suspending the payment of tribute to Magadha. Also, I am going to levy a tax of three pana on each head of the family. Every married woman will contribute five palas (each pala 37.76 grams) of silver. Young women, old men and children will plough our fields. Our ironsmiths will produce swords in large numbers. Every soldier will get a sword.'

Having expounded his grand plan, he waited for applause. The Senapati sat lost in thought, stroking his chin. His voice was steady. 'Beware the war, King! One of the heads you save may be your own.'

Sisupal barely restrained his anger. 'I follow the higher being's command.' Suddenly, his eyes closed and his head dropped to his chest. A moment later he opened his eyes. Noticing Mahabali's face had turned dark, he said with glee, 'God just talked to me!'

55

Lost in war details, Asoka stayed late in the Council or worked and slept in the room adjoining the Grand Hall, meant for emergencies. He did not see Anga for days. Disregarding the usual queenly custom of turning the newborn over to a wet nurse, she was immersed in breast-feeding Kunala. She was jealous of Asoka's increasing interest in state affairs and it was a part of him she wanted to understand. After a few days, she sent for him.

'There's nothing the matter!' he told her.

But her feminine intuition said something was amiss. *Could it be me because I've been breastfeeding Kunala?* She broke down. 'I'm not attractive to you anymore!'

Asoka assured her, 'Anga, do not say that! Kunala is dear to us.'

Anga frowned. 'You don't tell me about the Council deliberations anymore.'

He did not want to discuss the war with her. *I need glory. Glory is a king's quest for immortality. She may not like the war, but she'll love the victory. She'll be queen of all the mines and land. When I uncover a cartload of diamonds at the foot of the palace terrace, her jaw will drop, and she'll rush to embrace me.*

'Anga, once I loved that beautiful face,' he said evasively. 'Now I love all of you—even your changing moods. Kunala is a handful and I don't want to burden you.'

'Burden? Have I ever complained?' Her voice was trembling. 'Tell me everything. I have to know.'

He told her about the looming crisis, and her face turned dark. 'What have you decided?'

'To annex it.'

'What about Charu?' she immediately asked.

He told her that the State comes first and that Sisupal wanted him to return the Jina. But he couldn't.

Anga pleaded, 'Piyadassi, correcting an old injustice will only add to your glory.'

He countered whatever she said with, 'I am a hunter!' or 'I am a warrior,' 'or 'Baba would be proud.'

Her eyes filled with tears. 'I don't doubt that. But Baba fought wars to end wars. The empire is strong enough now to live in peace.'

He turned his back on her and left. She was angry.

That night when he came to the bed, she was not there. He did not remember her ever being so angry. Surprised and remorseful for having walked away without a word, Asoka went to the antechamber to say "I'm sorry." A lamp flickered on the corner table. She was asleep on her side, wrapped in a blanket. He stood watching her face, musing. *Untouched by power! Oblivious to glory! Like a child!* He kissed her on the head, and went back, murmuring, 'No music tonight!'

Around midnight, he was woken by the sensation of soft, warm caresses on his back. It took him a few moments to realize that Anga was in bed. He lay with eyes closed, motionless, enjoying the warm touch, the caresses. Then his breath quickened, and sensing he was awake, her fingers moved to his navel. He quickly turned and enclosed her in his arms.

In the morning, she said, 'I am your conscience, Piyadassi. Please forgive me!'

Asoka kissed her. 'Anga! I know you are worried. But lust, gambling, and alcohol send more men to their graves than wars. I'd rather die on the battlefield than in bed.'

Anga was silent then said softly, 'Piyadassi, I admit love has made a coward of me. But I won't let my fears or my conscience stop you from doing the right thing.'

He tried to explain. 'Anga, I am a warrior. Our gods are warriors. The *Rig-Veda* says those who fight and die in battle go to heaven.' He looked into her eyes. 'But I love and admire the gentleness of your soul.'

'How amazing that war is still part of our social order,' she said. 'We have love, children, music, theatre and poetry! And then, Wars! It's madness. Who are we? Nature's blight or freak?'

Asoka smiled. 'Anga, it's the way of the gods. The way of the states.'

Having got her to acquiesce in war, he faced another hurdle. Women accompanied kings on war campaigns, and she wanted to come with him. He wanted this too, but he was afraid. 'You are fragile, Anga. The journey is hard. Kunala needs you here.' Then he paused. 'And certainly, the war will not be pleasant.'

But she was stubborn and highly strung. 'Nurse will take care of Kunala,' she insisted. 'I want to be by your side. I couldn't survive if something happened to you.' When Asoka resisted, she declared, 'I'd rather die with battle scars than stay back and live.'

Asoka capitulated and she promised not to leave the camp during the fighting.

Deep down, he was pleased. He remembered the day of victory in Taxila, and the day of his coronation. *Having Anga by my side on the day of victory will bring down the gods to revel with me.*

56

Chandragupta Maurya had created an efficient war machine: an infantry of six hundred thousand, a cavalry of thirty thousand, three thousand in the elephant corps, two thousand chariots, and a Navy of seventy ships and ten thousand men. The Army was organized into battalions, companies, regiments and divisions. Most of the soldiers came from the professional caste of warriors and were almost equal in numbers to the farmer class.

Months before the march, divisions of the army filed through the city streets to drum up public support for a war tax. In the streets, large numbers of women sat making bandage rolls. Half the grain harvest was impounded by the army and after two years of war preparations, the army was ready. Based on projections that Kalinga's infantry numbered sixty thousand, Asoka took an infantry of fifty thousand on the war campaign, and all thirty thousand of the cavalry. He also took eighty elephants and a unit of a thousand men specially trained to attack elephants.

Weaponry included swords, shields, bows, arrows, spears, javelins and lances, artillery, ballista, battering rams, and other siege engines. While the army did not have the magical weapons that rained fire and death as described by the poets in the *Mahabharata* and the *Ramayana*, the infantry had poisoned arrows and incendiary missiles—fireballs and arrows with incendiary tips. Sudras and slaves carried the soldier's rations and arms, often weighing as much as sixty pounds.

The army was followed by a Commissariat consisting of supplies, equipment and men. Bullock trains carried food, water, arms, spare parts and camping equipment; and mechanics, foragers, astrologers, diggers, carpenters, surveyors, engineers, ironsmiths, cooks, storekeepers, priests, butchers and helpers. There were bards to entertain the troops, and heralds to carry messages to the enemy, color-bearers for war signals, and trumpeters to announce battles and victories. A mobile hospital, complete with physicians, veterinarians, medicine makers, nurses and medical supplies, also accompanied the army.

For fifteen days preceding the departure, the Purohit did havan, sacrificing hundreds of animals. All loved flesh; there were no vegetarians among gods. Military might alone was not enough for victory. The gods too, must be on your side, the priests said.

On a cold February day in 261, the army left for Kalinga. It marched throughout mid-June, and set up camp near Tosali, the capital of Kalinga, to wait out the monsoon. Every day Asoka mixed among his men inquiring after their families, having started the practice to inspire his troops. From a rich army-supply merchant, Asoka's Intelligence learned that Sisupal was preparing to field his army at Dhauli, a few miles south of Tosali, so as to get an edge for his elephants and chariots. The merchant also said that Sisupal had raised an additional army of over 400,000 religious fanatics, telling them, 'With thousands of lives before you, give just this one to your God Jina.'

To be close to the war-field, Asoka moved the campsite ten miles south of Dhauli and fortified it with a ditch and stockade. A tent-hospital was hurriedly set up east of Dhauli.

After the rains tapered off by the end of August, the hot sun baked the ground dry. In less than a month, Kalinga's army began to assemble on the Dhauli grounds at the foot of two small hills.

57

It was late at night, crickets chirped in the distance and most of the soldiers had retired to their tents. A few sat round a small dying campfire: Sewak, the sixteen-year-old orphan, who had wanted to die in war for Rani-ma; Madhatter, twenty-three, a Vaisya artisan; Kausal, the Sudra actor, in his thirties; Nakul, the eighteen-year-old son of Cavalry Commander Visal, who had left a pregnant wife back at home; and Panda, a shaven-headed, thirty year old Brahmin artisan and cynic.

Kausal stirred the embers. 'In a few days, we may all be dead. Let us re-live the pleasant memories of the march and the summer camp, to give ourselves comfort in our dying moments.' He turned to Sewak. 'Begin with the march.'

Sewak said, 'I am an orphan. Fatherless, motherless, caste-less, rudderless, and homeless. Until now. Now, the Orphanage is my home. I'm an ironsmith apprentice. At thirteen, I decided to become a soldier. I saw a lot of professional soldiers walking around with their young "mistresses." I did not know what they did with mistresses, so I asked. Then, the world looked so funny. To think we are no different than the monkeys!

'On the day the march began, I saw the imperious King in his royal chariot, dressed in red and blue and wearing his jeweled crown, waving goodbye to his people. His eyes shone like the jewels. The splendor of his dress! He looked like a god. I was in a fantasyland watching the cavalry, the infantry, and the elephants! Each division's flag— with its own animal and color— fluttered in the wind. And I was part of all this!

'The army was a motley crowd of different castes, tribes and guilds. Most soldiers were between sixteen and twenty-five. Though I was not yet sixteen, I got in by lying about my age. No one knows an orphan's age but I knew from an uncle. I came from the guild of ironsmiths. Others were from the artisans, carpenters and other crafts. But the largest number was professional soldiers– the Kshatriyas. When I found out that slaves will carry our arms, I thought, what luxury!

'Soldiers came in all sizes and colors. Some Dasyus from the south were so black they disappeared into the night. I think I am fairer than most, particularly after soap and a good scrub in the Ganges. Almost as fair as the Kshatriya. But not quite. They say their complexion makes them superior to us, the dark skinned men. I doubt it, but I can't prove them wrong.'

'I saw long lines of soldiers' wives waving to their husbands in the crowd. All had tears in their eyes. I knew their fate. After the goodbyes, they'll head back to their husbands' homes to wage their own wars: explain to their children where their fathers went; comply with the thousand demands of their mothers-in-law; cook, churn butter, winnow the grain, grind wheat, bring water from the well, clean the house, make cow-dung cakes; keep endless fasts for the welfare of their absent though well-fed husbands, and on and on. And if their husbands were to die, God help them! Then the widows' ill stars would be blamed for their husbands' death by the mothers-in-law. The widow will become a leper in her own home. People talk about the bravery of the dead soldiers, but dying is easy. It is the death in life– hour after hour, day after day– that is scary. For me, death will be a release from a life I never asked for.' He wiped his eyes.

Then he resumed. 'We took the royal southern route built by Mahapadma Nanda, who was ruler before Chandragupta. I had never heard of Kalinga before joining the army. Now when I think of Kalinga, I think of hilly tracts and jungles, fertile valleys, swift rivers, streams, and long stretches of coastline. I think of coconuts, salt, fish, and cannibal tribes. I saw all this as I was passing through Giria, skirting the dense Hazaribagh forests teeming with wildlife, and at the Rajauli camp. There we also learnt to make toddies from palm fruit. On the way, we sang war songs and listened to war stories.

'Soon spring arrived. Blossoms, fresh shoots, fragrant air! Passing through villages, we watched the new young animals sprinting about, children frolicking alongside buffaloes in ponds, sometimes riding on their backs. Children stuck their smiling faces from windows and waved. That's when I knew that I'd never had a childhood.

'After the villages came vast stretches of forest land. Once we saw a tiger less than a hundred feet away, majestically crossing the road. We all stopped, and it went quietly away. We heard wild elephants in the forest, trumpeting their existence. And at sunset we saw the cattle tinkling their bells.

We camped at Ranchi Fort where a communication centre was set up to relay messages between the capital and the army camp. From Ranchi, we passed through low hilly terrain from the Singhbhum to Horomoto. Long marches and never enough rest. We'd march for days from morning till evening, then rest for two days. Many slaves fell unconscious by the roadside, only to be flogged by their soldier-masters. Poor slaves! Many of them died. Had I not become a soldier, I too, would be lying dead somewhere by the roadside.

'From Bonaigarh, the road meandered alongside the Brahmani River, the second largest in Kalinga, which transported our supplies. A garrison was set up on its north bank, near Bonaigarh. My sergeant ordered me to stay there but when I told him I knew Rani-ma, he let me go. We camped at Barakot on the east bank of the river and rested for seven days, swimming and fishing, sitting up late at night, getting drunk, telling tales. Then we began the final leg to Tosali through Gogwa, Bajrakot, and Rengali to Talcher. The terrain became lush, with deeply furrowed valleys, rolling hills with trees, fields of mustard, maize and rice. In the coastal areas, we bathed in the ocean and got drunk on toddy at night.

'We grew beards, moustaches and long hair during the march, to feel part of the wilderness. Then the weather became warm and we began to sweat so we cut off all our hair. When cool breezes and showers cheered us, we'd burst into song. The march, the heat, and the foreign land created camaraderie among us. Now we laughed at every joke, at our castes and our odd-shaped bodies. Always, we talked about food. When we had a good meal, our spirits soared. Alas! Such days were rare. Friends said I was an orphan. I replied that an army on the march is no better. No father, no mother. No relatives.'

'Near Jagatpur, we reached the Mahanadi River, deep and swift. The vistas changed. Alligators basked on the river banks, their eyes glinting red in the sun. Some of us shivered with terror and I wondered what would happen if an alligator were to walk up the road and greet me with open jaws like an old friend. No laughing matter! To cross the swift river, one row of horses and elephants was stationed upstream, one down, to catch men who were washed away. Quite a few men did, but everyone was rescued.

'By the time we approached Tosali, we could tell by the clouds, the smell, the breeze, that monsoon was near. No armies fought during the monsoons on the soggy ground. Archers could not press the bow with their feet, and the cavalry could not charge. So we waited until the ground was again dry.

'I am looking forward to my death. Only then Rani-ma will not forget me. She is my goddess. More beautiful than any. The day she stroked my back, I sat entranced. Until then, I had known only kicks and whacks and slaps on my face and body. Now I knew paradise.'

It was Madhatter's turn to speak. 'Sewak, at least an orphan is a human being. Look at us; we're only members of a caste. We are born in one, marry in the same, and die as Brahmins or Sudras. Even the corpse has a caste. I never knew I'm a human being. And I've never thought of others that way.'

'I'm a stone cutter and Vaisya by caste. We don't live by an honor code or seek glory; when my chisel falls on the stone, I hear the tinkle of silver coins. Once after a havan my small gift so outraged the priest that right there, he invoked God to destroy my home and wealth. Lucky for me, I was already penniless. I'd lost my farm after paying interest at five percent per month to the village lender. Just because I am a Vaisya. As a Brahmin, I'd have paid interest at one and one half percent. From what I earn as a soldier, I am going to buy back the farm. Oh, I'll be so happy!'

Madhatter talked about camp life. 'I loved summer camp at the Udaigiri and Khandagiri Hills and nearby. Flanking a narrow pilgrim path, the bony sandstone hills rose straight from the coastal plain. A fork in the road led to a Jain temple at the top of Udaigiri Hill. These grounds were once covered with tropical forests. But over the centuries, most of the trees had been felled for fuel and mud-huts. A pass was issued to each soldier to control exit and entry from camp. The rules were strict: back before midnight. No liquor inside camp. But we always managed to smuggle a tummy-full of toddy.'

'The monsoons arrived with much dust and bluster. We ran from our tents, faces up and mouths open, to taste the first warm raindrops. The heat abated, but the rains brought grasshoppers and insects and a constant feeling of dampness. Evenings buzzed with mosquitoes, flies and chatter. The insects were constantly sneaking into our nostrils, ears, and other delicate places; but I never figured out what they were looking for so persistently. Even the Jain soldiers— forbidden by their religion to take any life— killed them lustily. And in the evenings, moths gathered in thousands around the oil lamps, as if not to miss the death convention.'

'Every day, we drilled from early morning to mid-afternoon. Sometimes we hoped for reprieve, but the rains mostly came at night or in the late afternoon.'

'The camp changed the forest's ecology. Practitioners of the oldest profession set up shop. By day, they sold mangoes. The vendors themselves looked like over-fertilized, over-ripe, giant-sized mangoes— round, fleshy-nippled, tough skinned and inside, pink. It always surprises me how men spend more time picking mangoes— looking, smelling, and squeezing— than in picking their wives. I know one is taste, and the other function. But still.'

'After we brought it home, the mango was then disrobed in anticipation of great pleasure. Delighting in its touch, we sank our teeth in the soft, juicy flesh, savoring it, smothering it, reaching down to the centre, licking, lapping, making sounds of enjoyment, until it looked like a tired hairy bone. A good mango was pure delight. But often it fell short of expectations. Still, remembering the good times, we kept going at it. A diminished mango was better than none.'

'My friend, Kalyan, a timid, short, pudgy soldier from Taxila, played with the ripe mangoes, fantasizing. But I was clear: for me nothing less than a mango vendor would do. So I went looking. When I returned, Kalyan, my friend asked, "Did you like any?" '

'"Too circular!" I said, wrinkling my nose. But time, like light, changes human perception. Within two weeks, Bunda, my round mango seller, metamorphosed into "delectably plump." I sheepishly described my first encounter. "Her beastly breasts snarled, and snared me in the thicket of desire!" A few such encounters changed my psyche. I became loquacious and happy. I'm planning to take Bunda home and raise a family of six.'

'In their spare time, different soldiers pursued different interests. Some made bamboo beds; others played the lyre or horn. With my friend, Panda, the shaven-headed Brahmin artisan, I stumbled upon some caves. His nose was so bony, I joked that he must have chiseled it with his own hands, notwithstanding the difficulty. We patiently carved curvaceous females on rocks, including a scene of the abduction of a faceless young woman. She had consorted with Panda in a dream, but hid her face behind a cover. "Which country was she from?" I asked, and he laughed.'

'"Maidens on the rock?" shouted the outraged army priest, a joyless man, when he found out. I guess joy and priest do not mix because he is full of God. As penance, Panda was ordered to carve Ganesha, the elephant-headed god. To spite him, Panda made Ganesha's belly big as a wine vat. The priest screamed, "That's an insult to God!" So Panda had to operate on the belly, which earned him the nickname, "Vaidya—doctor–Ganesha." '

'I teased Panda. "God has a great sense of humor. Look at mans' knobby knees and animals' faces! And look at this whole business of creation! Our bodies, our lives, wrapped around an extendable little thing. God would enjoy a little desecration." "Fools! Think!" God would tell the fanatics, "It's your conduct that desecrates me!" '

Now it was Nakul's turn. 'I am eighteen, a Brahmin by birth, but a warrior by profession. I grew up fantasizing about wars. I've been married for just a year and I've left my pregnant wife behind. But I would not miss this war if I had to leave three pregnant wives at home.'

'I love theatre so Kausal and I started one at camp. In my mind, frivolities push back thoughts of death. For female roles, we conscripted young female nurses and cooks. Every three weeks, we enacted a play on an open stage. When a heavy downpour came—and it often did—everyone ran inside, the colors streaked our faces, and we looked like clowns.'

'Then we announced "The Game of Dice." The whole camp was excited. It is a story from the *Mahabharata*, and tells of the righteous Yudhisthara, the eldest of the five Pandava brothers. Notwithstanding his righteousness, he gambles away to his cousins, the Kauravas, his family's wealth. Desperate to win it back, Yudhisthara then stakes his four younger brothers and loses them. Then he stakes their one and only common wife, Draupadi. Again, the same result. Perhaps, the righteous have no commonsense and plenty of incompetence. '

'Flying high, the Kauravas order their booty, the beautiful Draupadi, to appear in the gaming hall. She refuses and is dragged in by her hair. As punishment, they order her to be stripped naked so she prays to Lord Krishna to protect her modesty. In one of the famous scenes in the *Mahabharata*, yard after yard of her sari unwinds and gathers on the ground, but the last yard always stays around her slender waist. For this infuriating prank, the angry Kauravas blame Lord Krishna.'

'Our play began in full moonlight. White wisps of clouds drifted in the sky, and the bamboo stage was lit with torches. Draupadi was dragged in, and the stripping began. Every eye was glued to her belly button. It was like the devotees were waiting for the 'darshan'— the vision of God. Then came a swift tug, and Draupadi stood naked. But something was missing, and we rubbed our eyes. "It's a boy! You cheats!" the soldiers shouted. To avert a riot, the Chorus came running, "Miracle! Miracle! Lord Krishna has done it again! A little differently though! But who are we to question the ways of the Lord?" ' The soldiers went to bed angry and unappeased.'

Panda was asleep when his turn came so Kausal woke him. 'What's the point?' he said, going to his tent.

58

Two days before the war started, Madhatter, a Magadha soldier, went to visit his sister Kali, who was married to Aswin, a Kalinga soldier. After the meal, the discussion inevitably turned to war. Madhatter complained about Kalinga's King, 'All this over a piece of stone?'

Aswin's face turned red. 'Asoka is evil!'

A shadow passed over Madhatter's face. 'Pass some toddy,' he said to Aswin. Madhatter took a sip. 'Do you think killing the enemy is good karma?'

Aswin became agitated and pulled at his hair until a handful came out. At long last he replied. 'The agony is in the doubt.'

'Thousands will be killed, maimed, widowed, orphaned,' said Madhatter. 'Still, the doubt will remain.' Aswin just sat glaring at the wall.

Madhatter turned to his sister. At twenty-eight she seemed run down and haggard. Her daughter, seven years old and skinny, played with a rag doll in the dimly lit room while her one year old son sat sniveling in her lap. Before leaving, Madhatter opened his rag bag and gave small gifts to the children. Outside, he murmured, 'Am I going mad? Or just catching up with the world?'

59

The war was creeping closer. On the morning before, the soldiers sat by their tents repairing, sharpening, and polishing their armor, or scrubbing the horses and elephants. Panda turned to Kausal. 'How did an actor get into this mess?'

The feminine-faced Kausal grinned. 'Every life is a mess and an actor's life is only more so. I'll die without knowing who I am. I have been Rama, Ravana, the demon, Krishna, even Sita, in my days. This war may be my final act. Whether I live or die, at least I'll earn respect.'

'Respect for killing?' Panda grinned. 'Who respects a dead man?'

'I'll get a half-decent burial!' Kausal clarified.

'For killing?'

Kausal said, 'I don't like killing. I'm only good at slicing watermelons with my sword.'

Panda laughed. 'Believe me Kausal, men are no different! Think of man as descending from the distinguished family of gourd. When cracked open, both the watermelon and men's heads give out red juice. To the sword, man's throat and chest are no different. After all, for purposes of war, you are not the son of an old mother, not the husband of a young wife, not the father of a toddler. You're just a sword!'

Nakul, eighteen, sat nearby listening and polishing his armor. 'Kausal,' he interrupted, 'you don't love killing? Then why come to war? No one goes to war to die! To die, go to the holy cities of Kashi or Prayag by the Ganges. That's where the old men go!'

Kausal counted six whiskers on Nakul's chin. 'Nakul, you are a dear friend. I hope your whiskers keep growing!'

Eyes shining, Nakul smiled. 'Kausal, I am made of steel!'

Sitting next to Nakul, Drona spoke. 'I have these terrible headaches. And war is the best painkiller I know!'

Kausal grinned. 'Drona, you'll love your headaches, if you get back home!'

At noon, Shivdutt, the royal Purohit, started a havan on the camp-grounds. With his long face and long nose, he could be mistaken for a horse. Every few minutes, he would dump scads of wood sticks, ghee, melted butter, incense and other flammable material into the altar fire to the chant of 'Swaha!' as if to satisfy the craving of the flames—as if the flames had a bottomless belly. Smoke filled the air and the red-eyed soldiers coughed and wiped away tears. The priest recited hymns in a voice that rose simultaneously from his mouth and his nose. Nothing to him was definitive. Even the words of the hymns were incomprehensible to all, and no one seemed to care: is not God beyond words? Though sacrificed to feed the gods, the goats and the bulls were in fact devoured by men. Ambiguity on ambiguity. The havan ended with Shivdutt recit-ing part of the *Rig-Veda* hymn to Arms: "...With the bow let us conquer all the corners of the world..."

Then he came to the point. "Fight to the death! In Yama's heavenly abode, maidens await you!"

Every young soldier was surprised and delighted. Those who were feeling drowsy, sat up. Suddenly, death did not seem all that dread-ful. Wiping their swollen eyes, dreaming of a smoke-free heaven, they bowed to the priest for revealing the fastest way to fulfill their desires.

After doing his job, the priest retired to the waiting feast, and the state now took over. Late that afternoon, on the open ground near the camp, the soldiers were pampered with good wine. It tasted much better after they learnt that the Kalinga soldiers would have lowly toddies. To excite the soldiers to heroic deeds, the throats of hundreds of oxen were slit in full view. Some soldiers became ecstatic at the sight and some even borrowed the long knife to try their hands at butchery. But pos-sessing only man-cutting skills, they made a mess. In the rising smoke of roasting flesh, many saw their own burning bodies.

At dusk, hundreds of torches lit the ground. Buttressed with wine and tantalized by the aroma, even the vegetarians stared at the color and texture of moist pink flesh. Lustily, they pounced on rice and red beans and some forgot they were vegetarians. If an insect or a moth sneaked in, some gulped it down, mistaking it for a half-cooked cumin seed. All through the evening, the soldiers joked, horsed around, and boasted. "War is in my blood! I am fighting for Magadha glory! I love my country so!" Each believed what the other said, yet each was ashamed of his own unspoken feelings.

In a corner, Panda stood reflecting. *These simple acts today will affect their future lives. By sacrificing their bodies, the bulls will be born warriors in their next lives. Those who slit the bulls' throats have forfeited their claim to be reborn as men. They will keep coming out of the birth canals of goats and sheep for centuries. But the real heroes of this feast are the little insects who unwittingly became the soldiers' meal. In one giant leap—escaping thousands of births as lowly species— they will bob up from the amniotic fluid as crying humans.*

Later in the evening, the soldiers sang and danced. Despite their revelry and their swagger, the shadow of death flickered in every mind.

60

The day had arrived. An hour before dawn with the first trumpet call, soldiers lay squirming in bed, staring out at the dark blue skies. Sweating in his crowded tent, Kausal woke with a start. 'I dreamt I was killed,' he told his friend in the next bed, who pulled up his sheet and drawled, 'May your dream come true!'

Anga had not slept and was up before dawn. After Asoka put on his tunic and scale armor, she dressed in red like a bride. Then with trembling hands, she applied a vermilion red 'tilak,' a red mark worn on the forehead, to send him off to war, and garlanded him while praying to the Buddha. As he turned to leave, her eyes were glistening with tears.

Since she'd heard that Kalinga would be fielding four hundred thousand soldiers, she had been having a recurring dream in which Asoka was seriously wounded in the war. He laughed it off when she told him. 'Anga, dreams are just our hopes and fears. Don't worry, I'll return in one piece. It is the Kalinga soldiers that will be mincemeat.'

He's so blithe, she thought. After he'd left, she fell on the bed and cried bitterly from a sense of helplessness and diffused sorrow. It was as if something was wrong with her life. It had been building up for weeks within her, and congealed into an ominous foreboding.

Asoka met with his War Council. Ramdev, the Commander of Elephant Corps, advised that in light of Kalinga's elephant force, it would be safer to attack the enemy at night but Asoka disagreed. He rode his horse Puskar, to within a mile of enemy lines. In the morning mist, near the two little hills rising against the sky, masses of Kalinga army darkened the horizon.

In an hour, the men preened and dressed, and assembled in the kitchen tent, ready to go. They had an early meal, and carried a few pieces of bread in their pouches, and water in skins— enough to carry them through the day, or to the end of their lives.

Sisupal looked forward to victory. He had chosen the sprawling Dhauli field, located south of the narrow meandering Daya River, for tactical reasons. The gentle downward slope of the land gave him the advantage for his elephant and chariot charge. He fielded his army starting at the foot of two hills from where the slope began.

Perched on a royal elephant, Sisupal took up his position at the centre of his infantry. He was surrounded by guards and wore full regalia, with a yellow flag, a green parasol over his head, and his gold-silver sword at his side. He planned to foil the fearsome Magadha cavalry with his elephants and chariots alone. His two hundred elephants stood in two rows at the front, twenty-five feet apart. Each carried three archers and a mahout on its back in a Howdah. Weighing seven to eight tons, these war-elephants could charge at an impressive twenty miles an hour. On their flanks, Sisupal placed one hundred chariots spaced fifteen feet apart. His five thousand cavalrymen stood behind the chariots.

Sisupal's infantry consisted mostly of hastily trained Jina devotees. Three hundred thousand men, arranged in three squares of a hundred thousand each, were behind the elephants. One hundred and fifty thousand foot soldiers were kept in reserve. The light infantry—with bows and small swords—fronted the heavy infantry with their own spears and swords. The infantry included thousands of young boys with smooth chins, excitedly waving their hands and stomping their feet as if they were at a carnival.

Sisupal addressed his officers. 'Brave Kalinga soldiers! Remember, you are fighting for your God. We have numbers on our side. And God. The Jina cannot lose.'

Observing Sisupal's lines, which stretched far beyond the breadth of his own lines on both sides, Asoka surmised Sisupal's strategy. Once the Magadha cavalry was destroyed by Sisupal's elephants and chariots, he planned to advance his infantry, and grip Asoka's lines on all sides in a "bear hug."

Asoka relaxed. He ordered his army to stand at ease as he went on a reconnaissance of enemy lines from up close, trotting up and down the field. It became clear that he could not use his cavalry as long as Sisupal's elephants faced him. So he deployed sixty-four of his own elephants facing Sisupal, spacing them ten feet apart, in eight files, eight deep. So closely placed, they'll go charging through the wide spaces between Sisupal's, he mused.

He now positioned his forces: one thousand special archers, equipped with incendiary missiles, flanked his elephants, in twenty columns, fifty deep. He left the rear open. On the wings, ace archers, fifteen thousand light infantry, and equal numbers of heavy infantry behind. The light infantry would disable the enemy with a hail of javelins, and arrows; the heavy infantry would then move in to finish the job with swords and spears. Twenty thousand infantry he left in reserve.

Ten thousand cavalry stood on the left, five thousand to the right. Fifteen thousand horsemen were left in reserve.

Formations completed, the enemies stood facing each other at a distance of about a mile. Years in the making, the encounter would have the finality of that moment when all the wedding ceremonies are over, and the guests have retired. Only the man and the woman stand facing each other. No more prognostication, procrastination, peregrination or obfuscation. Just convolution. And contumulation – lying together in the same tomb.

Asoka addressed his officers. 'We shall win. Don't let the enemy numbers intimidate you; an army of ten thousand always crushes a crowd of one hundred thousand. Remember, each of you has to kill only five of Kalinga's men.'

He looked up at the sky for propitious signs. 'God! Turn the sun's rays into spears. Baba, I see the keys of Kalinga in your hands. Fill me with the fire that burned in your veins! Give Magadha victory and glory!' His hair stood on end as he thought of his grandfather in the field with him. As if it was a magic wand, he fondled the ancestral gold-silver hilt of his Baba's sword.

He gazed at the majestic elephants, vermilion red on their fore-heads, flags fluttering in the breeze; and then at his archers in red, and at his brave horses, restless, like the fiery steeds of the gods.

He stared at the Kalinga army and his nostrils flared. *Cannibals! Barbarians! For years I have been waiting for this moment. Get ready to die!*

The awesome scene from the *Bhagwad-Gita* swam before him: *At the sight of his cousins and uncles standing in the enemy lines, Arjun lays down his arms. Lord Krishna exhorts him to pick up his arms and fight. Fighting is your duty as a Kshatriya. 'They are already dead', he says, and shows Arjun his cosmic mouth, at the deep end of which men are revealed lying dead on the ground— even before the war began.* Suddenly inspired, Asoka saw hundreds of thousands Kalinga soldiers lying dead before him on the Dhauli ground.

A herald rode out to the enemy lines and declared war by cast-ing a bloody lance upon the enemy soil. Trumpets, drums and conches blared, thundered, putting fear in the enemy's heart. To the sound of martial music, the Magadha elephants started their lumbering advance.

At that moment, a street dog, about nineteen inches high, strayed onto the field. Hobbling about in the open space between the two armies, its tail between the legs, it clearly did not descend from the warrior line of dogs. It glanced at one army, then the other, and loudly barked. The martial music stopped and the elephants halted in their tracks. The soldiers stood at ease, amused. But the dog seemed in no hurry. It strolled up and down, stopped, gnashed its teeth and growled, like a General at his troops. Then slowly, it began to retreat. On its way out, it encountered two bushes, one tall and scraggly, the other leafy and stout. The dog stopped by the younger bush—stuffy and swollen— raised its hind leg, and let out a furious stream.

A Magadha soldier was irritated. 'This is no time for frivolities! I'm going to kill the dog!' He drew his bow, but his friend next to him gently put his arrow back in the sheaf. 'It's a bad omen to kill a dog before killing an enemy soldier. On the battlefield in the *Mahabharata*, the armies stood for days waiting and watching Lord Krishna, taking his sweet time to deliver his long sermon, the *Bhagwad-Gita*, to Arjun. Poor dog! He will be done in a few minutes.'

The dog stopped at the edge of the field, and looking displeased, howled, face up. Watching from the sky, Yama, the god of death, heard in the howl strains of men's soaring spirit. But the soldiers heard a dirge. The dog then quietly bowed out of the field, tail between its legs.

The martial music recommenced, and the little grey hillocks started to lumber again. An astonished Sisupal watched sixty-four elephants marching toward him, and wondered, *Do I summon my elephants and expose the cavalry? Or do I let them pierce my lines and come charging at me?*

The Commander read his thoughts and shouted, 'It's a bluff.'

The elephants rumbled to within shooting distance of the archers, then suddenly picked up speed. The Commander frantically shouted, 'It's no bluff!' He waved to the mahouts who raised their iron goads in the air and mercilessly thrust them into the elephants' raw neck wounds that were kept open for the purpose. Like a swarm of newly hatched turtles scrambling to the sea, two hundred elephants began to run towards the centre.

The Magadha archers opened fire, aiming incendiary missiles and fireballs at or between the elephants' eyes. Like humans, elephants panic when they see fire up close. They also panic when their masters lose control of them. Disorientated now, the elephants turned on their own men and pandemonium ensued in the army. In panic, the mahouts began hammering chisels into the elephant's spines in order to split them, so that they would collapse to the ground. Howling, many elephants fell. Others, whose spines were not yet severed, went berserk with pain and anger. The Magadha soldiers now started spearing the mahouts, and the elephants, which were falling like huge boulders in an earthquake. Some started lifting soldiers up in the air with their trunks, then pounding them hard on the ground in rage.

Kalinga's cavalry was now sheltered only by chariots. Hoping to draw these out, the Magadha cavalry began its tactical charge, and a thousand hoofs simultaneously hit the ground. Sisupal signaled the chariot attack. With trumpets blowing and drums roaring, his drivers loosened the horse reins, shaking fists in the air and raising a war cry. Two hundred chariots galloped to destroy the Magadha cavalry in its path.

The Magadha horse column had trained for such a contingency. The riders slowed their speed, and kept watch as the chariots gathered momentum, like snow rolling down a mountain in an avalanche. When the chariots came close, the Magadha horse columns swiftly parted just enough to let the Kalinga chariots sweep past them. Once inside the columns, the Magadha cavalry began firing on the drivers and horses. Arrows and spears rained down. Drivers jumped and horses snorted, neighed and reared in the face of the onslaught. Chariots skidded, collided, and overturned. Amid the din and roar of men and animals, everywhere on the field lay torn harnesses, broken shafts, wounded horses and wailing drivers. The Kalinga chariot offensive was over.

The elephant rampage was still in full swing. Infuriated, elephants trumpeted and bulldozed soldiers from both the armies. Some engaged in tusk to tusk fights. For two hours they zigzagged and howled, terrorizing soldiers of both armies until the damage was limited by severing their trunks, slashing their spines, and repeatedly spearing them to deep silence. Hundreds of Magadha soldiers were killed in the melee. But Kalinga's elephant menace was contained.

Now, Kalinga's cavalry stood unprotected. Asoka attacked the right flank in concave formation, Visal the left in a wedge. With no stirrups then, the riders kept their seats only by drill and experience. Kalinga's bamboo armor— its shields and metal-tipped arrows— was pitted against Magadha's metal. Though the Magadha onslaught was furious, the ferocious determination of Kalinga's fearless men made up for their poor equipment and lack of training and experience.

Still, Kalinga's horsemen were falling like dominoes; the right flank was routed in the first hour. Asoka wheeled to see how Visal was faring and found him struggling to hold his lines. After he attacked in a wedge, Mahabali, in a skilful move at the last minute, had regrouped his horses in a concave formation, trapping Visal in a pincer movement. Horses thundered and reared and for an hour, a fierce battle raged. Magadha's losses were mounting.

Asoka called in his cavalry reinforcements. To relieve the pressure on Visal, he attacked Mahabali's rear. Visal's men breathed a little easier and quickly regrouped to attack. War cries rent the air. Pressed from front and back, Mahabali's cavalry was slaughtered. The battle was over even before the reserves arrived.

With his elephants taken out, his chariots destroyed and the cavalry over run, Sisupal, still hopeful of victory, now launched his infantry attack. Hundreds of thousands of his men began to advance in close formation. The sight of vast numbers of humanity about to fall upon them, sent shivers down the spines of the Magadha soldiers. It looked like a locust attack as arrows rained down on them in thousands. The Magadha men struggled to hold their lines. Even bleeding or wounded, Kalinga's soldiers continued to fight bravely with arrows, swords, and even bare hands until they fell dead. The Magadha infantry was forced to pull back.

Asoka saw his men in distress. He rushed to cheer his troops, waving fists at the enemy lines, then rearranged his men. The heavy Magadha infantry, with their sixteen-foot spears, metal armor, shields and swords, moved to the front; the light infantry to the flanks, from where it fired arrows at enemy lines. The sixteen-foot spear division, clad in armor, advanced like a wide, multi-pronged sword, and the long spears began to mow down the Kalinga soldiers. Kalinga's spears and swords were no match against the enemy's powerful thrust.

Kalinga's Senapati then changed tactics. He threw thousands of his men on the long spears to tire out the Magadha men. The battle turned into a war of will against deadly fire-power. When one Kalinga row was cut down, another row of men appeared with crooked yellow teeth and bloodshot eyes, raising fists and war cries. The battleground became a vast Vedic altar of roaring fire, into which, like havan material to the sound of 'Swaha,' Kalinga soldiers were getting dumped to the chant of 'Jina.'

Asoka saw his forces were in danger of falling from exhaustion. When the twenty thousand cavalry reserves arrived, he sent for his infantry reserves for support. Visal divided the cavalry in two divisions. Each simultaneously attacked the left and the right wings of Kalinga's infantry from the rear. Asoka attacked the rear centre. A fierce, indecisive battle raged for several hours. Mahabali, defending the centre, would not yield his lines. Angered by his resistance, Asoka pulled back his horses, regrouped in a wedge, then charged like a speeding battering ram. The force instantly breached Sisupal's centre. With his forces scattered, Mahabali read the writing on the wall. He told Sisupal to surrender and save thousands of lives.

Seated under the decorated umbrella atop his royal elephant, Sisupal sneered. 'A leader must stay the course in the face of mounting losses.' He signaled for infantry reserves.

Asoka galloped through the gap created in the centre, and lunged towards Sisupal. Raising his right arm, tilting his body back and to the side, he threw his javelin like a missile. Mahabali saw the javelin fly, hissing through the air, and shouted, 'Watch out, King!' Sisupal ducked and saved his neck, but the javelin went through his right ear and scraped the right side of his face to the eye, before it fell on the ground. Sisupal winced in pain. He felt his face, then looked at his open hand—it was drenched in blood. Disorientated, he threw himself onto his horse and took off, his guards in tow.

Angered, Kalinga's soldiers turned on Asoka, shooting en-masse; an arrow pierced the left side of his armor, grazing the muscle over the scapula. His soldiers surrounded him. Irritated and bleeding, Asoka shouted, 'I am not hurt. The battle has yet to be won. Don't stop killing!' Sisupal had escaped amid the commotion.

The news of Sisupal's escape ran like wildfire. The man who promised Jina had abandoned the ship. The will of Kalinga soldiers was now shattered and they started running towards the thickets, the groves, the Daya River, and toward the little hills. Confusion, chaos, pandemonium, and panic spread everywhere. Thousands and thousands men were running in all directions dumping their bows and spears, their turbans flying off the head, unrolling on the ground; their feet clapping the ground soaked in blood. The men jumped over the bloodied bodies and the corpses, tripped over broken spears, kicked their way through fallen arrow sheaves, and stumbled over cut up elephant bodies, and dead horses– some lying on their backs, all four feet up. In trying to go through the unending maize of severed heads and limbs of man and animals, many slipped, fell, and got run over. Thousands turned and began running in the opposite direction on seeing Magadha soldiers in distance waiting with drawn spears. But there was no place to hide. The Magadha infantry had ringed the field, and the cavalry formed an outer circle to catch the men escaping from the inner ring. Dhauli had become a killing field.

The Kalinga soldiers did not know how to surrender. Only when their glum-faced officers raised their hands, did the hapless men throw down their swords or other gear. Yet, in the frenzy of killing, thousands and thousands of unarmed soldiers were slaughtered. By evening, the surrender lines stretched to Tosali and white wagons moved in to haul away the corpses and the hacked bodies.

Kalinga's rout was complete. Every elephant's spine had been slashed and hundreds of elephant trunks lay scattered all around, like phalluses of a mighty god after an orgy. Thousands of horses— men's friends—lay dead, their eyes saucer-like, their faces convulsed, their bodies twisted.

Faint with fatigue, and with his face smeared with dust and blood, Asoka returned to camp before sunset. No king had ever won such a resounding victory in war. In the late afternoon sun, he wondered how many of the enemy would see the sunrise. His right ear bled from the thunder of war cries, the neighing of horses, the blowing of trumpets. At camp, he quickly dismounted and when he saw that Anga was not at the entrance of the royal tent, he went to look for her. The wife of the victorious king always welcomed the Lord at the door and proudly wished him hundreds more such victories. For Asoka, immortality was at hand.

When a guard told him that Anga had gone to the hospital, he was stunned. The guard repeated himself. Asoka's face turned red with anger and disappointment. To win the greatest war in this land and she's not here to embrace me? Asoka had given the Master Guard orders not to let Anga out of the camp. Flailing his horsewhip in the air, and with his eyes flashing, Asoka shouted, 'Bring the traitor here.'

The Master Guard came to him, shaking as he stood before him, his head bowed. Trembling with rage, Asoka lashed the man's face from side to side. 'Speak, Master Guard! Speak!'

'Great King! I tried, but...' The Guard's legs gave out, and he collapsed at Asoka's feet. 'She said she would not be stopped, she had to go to the hospital.'

Dread filled Asoka and dark thoughts crowded him. To *nurse the bleeding, the dying, the mutilated?* He turned to his personal guard, 'Flog this traitor to death.' But as the Master Guard bent to say his last prayers and the first lash cracked his bare back, streaking it with blood, the memory of his own flogging flashed before Asoka along with the kind words of the Warden. "Did I hurt you, prince?"

'Stop,' suddenly Asoka said, hurrying to his tent.

A carriage was sent for Anga.

Female attendants swooped down to scrub the King's wound. A nurse applied herbal paste and put clove oil drops in his ear. Without the salve of Anga's healing touch, he felt no relief but sat scowling. 'To return wounded from the war,' he groaned, 'and not be nursed by my queen because she is out nursing the soldiers!'

61

Angry, he paced his tent, hands behind his back. Abruptly, he decided to survey the battlefield. On the way, he whipped his horse until it baulked, snorted and reared but the master paid no attention.

In the pale light of the setting sun, Asoka stood at the edge of Dhauli field. As far as the eye could see, the sprawling field was covered with corpses and carcasses: cut-up, mutilated, grotesque. Blood, raw flesh everywhere, on each face and body, and on the ground. Like a tornado fells trees in a forest, dismembered bodies lay in disarray. Horses and elephants lay in pools of blood, slashed, their bodies torn apart. Wherever he looked, there was no life. The carnage took his breath away.

He reflected. *It is one thing to kill a thousand men and another to wipe out a whole generation.* The stillness of the vast space before him, filled with the severed heads, torn-off limbs, and rotting flesh sickened him.

Something came over Asoka. He dismounted to look closer but his feet became soaked in blood. Repulsed, he remounted and rode through the field, his eyes on the dead. There was horror on those faces, horror in their eyes. The rising stench was already unbearable. What was he searching for? *If at this moment the dead came back and looked at themselves,* he thought, *they'd vomit, and take to their heels.*

To distract himself, he went to watch the sunset over the Daya River. Stuffed with dead bodies, the river intermittently stopped and then slowly flowed red far into the distance. Darkening the skies, vultures and crows shrieked with excitement. So much blood? So many bodies? His head reeled and he shut his eyes.

Darkness was falling from the sky and Asoka turned back. On the way, he came upon a dead white horse that looked like Niguna, his horse. Flies had settled on its face. Asoka got down. How beautiful it must have been in life! The horse seemed to glare at him with an accusing look. 'Is this how you love?' Startled, Asoka whipped his own mount and looked back over his shoulder fearfully.

His eyes fell on a soldier's smashed face that was covered by a thick veil of black ants. He consoled himself with the thought that dead soldiers go to heaven. Was there any sign of soul on their faces or in the manner of their dying? But he saw only terror on their faces.

Do animals and men meet the same end? The horror of it! There is no bravery, no honor, no dignity in these deaths. These men are not going to heaven; they were butchered. Disfigured, tortured. He saw guts spilled out of bodies, heads hanging by few threads. *Is this the glory I seek? Is this my road to immortality?*

A lifeless, pale moon hung in the sky. *Just this morning everything was magical. My heart beat with joy and pride! The young men assembled dressed in their best, as if to attend a wedding feast. And now! That festival has turned into a vast cremation ground. Nothing stirs here. This morning, heads, hands and legs were in the right places. And now? I am in the land of the dead. I stand alone here with those two little rocks! How did a day so fair, turn so foul?*

Overcome by nausea, surrounded by darkness, his knees trembled as he rushed back to camp. He kept weaving his horse between the corpses filling the ground, and splashing through puddles of blood. *There is no escape now from this hell*, he thought.

Like spirits of the dead, hundreds of men and women now began to enter the field, flickering lamps in their hands as they searched for their loved ones. They stopped and lowered their lamps to swollen faces, cut-up bodies, moved on, stumbling sometimes over the corpse of a stranger. Their cries pierced the night.

Darkness now shrouded the dead. Asoka's thoughts were interrupted by the unceasing wails of a woman in the distance. He spurred his horse. A severed mustached head sat in a woman's lap, illuminated by her lamp; hunched over it, she stared at the puffed-up face and tenderly stroked the lips with one hand. Asoka had the urge to run, yet stood petrified. Rocking, she lowered her head and kissed hard the swollen blue mouth, as if in a fit of strange passion. Then she raised her head, looked up and shrieked.

Moved by her anguish, Asoka dismounted. 'He fought bravely!' he said softly.

She stroked the grotesque face, without looking up. 'I needed him,' she sobbed, 'not his bravery!'

Quickly Asoka remounted.

'God! Give that demon, Asoka, the pain he has given me!'

He heard her curse. Darkness clutched Asoka. Light went out from his eyes.

62

Hysterical, Anga returned to the camp in blood-spattered clothes, her face a ghostly white. Suiya struggled to hold her. 'Anga! Control yourself! Don't disgrace the Buddha!' she pleaded.

Shaking with sobs, Anga cried, 'So much horror! How could God create such a world? I don't want to live! Suiya, choke me to death!' Suiya tried to hold her close. 'My lord has never fought a war before; he could not have known the horrors of war. Buddha! Kill all embryos in the womb!'

With the help of three maids, Suiya took off Anga's clothes, bathed her, robed her, and changed her sheets. Anga collapsed on the bed. She would not eat.

Asoka returned shaken. *I have more blood on my hands than there is water in the Ganges,* he thought. He went to look for Anga—for a caress, a loving look, a touch of her hand. He found the bed empty. 'Anga!' he called out, searching the dimly lit antechamber. There, she lay asleep on her side, her hands between her knees, her cheeks pale and tear-stained. Gazing at her anguished face, he forgot his own pain, and love surged in his breast. He bent down, kissed her on the cheek, and whispered, 'Anga, come to bed!'

She turned over, pulling her knees up to her chest. He gently tapped her waist, then shook her elbow. She did not stir. Annoyed, he stared at her. *She should not have left the camp.*

The woman's curse rang in his ears. Before him, she kept kissing the ghastly severed head. He shook his head, then said, 'Where is my Queen? My Anga! Wake up, Anga! Wake up!' She turned over again.

He carried her to the bed and threw a blanket over her feet. As if in dream, she mumbled, 'No, Asoka.'

The woman kept kissing the severed head's swollen purple lips. 'Anga!' he shrieked, pulling down the blanket. 'She sleeps like the dead!' Frantically he pulled her by the ankles until her naked hips rested on the edge of the bed. 'Wake up, Anga!' he said, holding her legs up by the ankles.

Eyes still closed, she cried, 'Don't spear me, Asoka!'

'Spear me?' he mumbled hoarsely. Sliding down the golden pillars of her flesh, his eyes fastened on the crown of her soft arch and desire dizzied his head. He pushed her knees to her chest. Anga woke, and sat up in bed, to hold him away with her hands. Her eyes widened. In the pale moonlight falling from the tent's high window, she saw Indra's thunderbolt, and her insides quivered. 'The terror!' she gasped, then looking at his white face in the dark, mumbled, 'And the pity!' falling back on the bed.

When he saw the severed head enter her womb, he shrieked. Anga lay motionless, sobbing.

He fell asleep with his chest against her back and one hand on her breast. In a minute or two he awoke, and drowsily whispered, 'Anga, are you all right?'

Between sobs, he heard her say, 'I want to die.'

He sprang from bed as if stabbed in the chest. In his robe, he looked out of the door. The air reeked of the dead, and the pale moon had disappeared. He listened to the hoots of the wood owl and the constant shrill cries of excited crows, then he slumped next to her in bed, his body aching and his swollen eyes almost shut, numb with pain.

In the morning, Anga was still asleep in his arms. He pulled his aching hand out from under her head and lay awake. When she awoke, he said tenderly, 'Don't ever think of death!'

'You think only of yourself,' Anga said bitterly, wiping her eyes. He lay wondering, with eyes closed, *What does Parvati do when Siva returns home in a bloody hide?*

He stood up and watched her, lying there with her closed eyes, and her arms crossed on her forehead. The gentle breeze kept bringing the dead inside the room in waves. His heart quivered with shame and he went out to order the men to quickly dispose of the dead in the river.

'The river is still choked. Several men are pushing the bodies with long logs,' a soldier said, as if speaking of a clogged sewer line.

Impatiently, Asoka ordered, 'Stack them! Burn them! The dead have taken over the living!'

The sensation of burning and vomiting took over his body. To clear his head, he took a horse-ride to Pipli town in the blazing sun. When he returned in the afternoon, he went straight to the antechamber. Anga sat on the bed with her back to him, wearing a crumpled, purple robe. Suiya was doing her tresses but left when she saw him. Anga sat without turning her head, even when he lightly kissed her on the nape, his lips lingering there awkwardly.

She sensed his pain. With the back of her hand, she caressed his cheek and he sat holding her for a long time in silence. At last, she turned to him, weeping. 'I had asked Dhanvanti to tell me if Sewak was injured. When I heard he lay dying, I rushed to the hospital. Sensing I was there, he opened his eyes slightly and struggled to smile. Then he died in my arms. After that, I could not leave the wounded.' Asoka kissed her forehead and quietly walked out of the room.

63

As soon as the battle began, the Magadha war hospital was filled with men howling in pain—their necks slashed, spears inside chests and stomachs, legs and hands dangling by strands of flesh. The tent reeked with the smell of blood and open flesh. Flies swarmed on the wounds. From one end of the tents to the other ran physicians, surgeons, nurses, helpers, and priests, lost in the land of the dead.

The hospital tents were set up in a light forest, a few miles east of the war camp. War rules prohibited attack on the white wagons, which hauled the wounded and the dead from the battleground. Beds were laid out in long rows inside each tent. A crematorium was located close by for those who did not make it and a kitchen for those who did. Separate tents nearby housed the physicians, nurses, cooks and helpers.

And how many, exactly, came streaming into the hospital? Nakul, Visal's son, the bony Madhatter, shaven-headed Panda, and the handsome Drona. In the next couple of hours of battle, the long-faced Adeva, the actor Kausal, and the orphan Sewak, were joined by hundreds of others.

When a patient arrived, Dhanvanti and the other physicians observed his condition by taking his pulse and turning up his eyelids, and then determined the appropriate treatment. Irreparable and rotting limbs were sawn off and tossed out of the window onto a heap. The nurses then washed the wound, applied an anti-inflammatory herbal paste, and bandaged the patient.

Nakul had been shot in the knee and chest. He was quickly operated upon, then bandaged up and moved to a bed where he lay unconscious for two days on a blood-spattered sheet. A broken arrow had lodged in Madhatter's stomach. Without an influential father, he waited two days for an operation. Panda, a Brahmin, had been hit in the neck.

The arrow was removed, the wound washed, and he was bandaged and put to bed, unconscious.

His face, neck and stomach battered by arrows, and unconscious, Sewak kept mumbling 'Rani Ma...Ra..ni...ma.' Angered by this, the priest sent him straight to the cremation ground.

Rambha was one of many assistant priests. Walking up and down death row, he kept drumming into the soldiers' ears, 'Soul is immortal. You're headed for heaven!'

Adeva groaned, 'But I am in hell now.'

The priest lost his patience. 'Stop it! You want heaven or not?'

'Heaven! Honor! Medals!' Adeva sputtered in agony, 'All lies! Big lies!'

Rambha roared, 'Those are the glories by which we measure your life!'

Later that night, Visal came to visit his son. 'Nakul, don't die while I breathe!' he cried. He pleaded with the gods, 'Take my life in his place. What will I tell his mother when I reach home, and her eyes search for him?' Before leaving, he told the nurse, 'Reema, my life is in your hands!' and she glanced at Nakul, lying there like a crushed flower.

Ayurveda– the science of longevity– was the main system of medicine at this time, and war medicine held a special place. To treat the wounded and the disfigured, special surgical equipment– consisting of twenty types of knives and needles and thirty probes– was used. Buddhist monks often served as medicine men. A Buddhist text declared that garlic, for instance, prolonged human life to one hundred years.

The ultimate Vedic drug was Soma– an intoxicant juice extracted from a plant that was believed to confer immortality. But Soma was no help to broken bodies. Instead, the chanting of magic rites from the *Atharva-veda* was supposed to heal by exorcising demons. Light, fresh air and water–especially water—were regarded as efficacious remedies. The *Rig-Veda* spoke of one hundred and seven healing plants but did not enumerate; such knowledge was kept secret by the Brahmins.

That night, owls hooted and crickets chirped, and the breeze shifted between the malodors of flesh and boiling herbs. The stench of death filled the tent and the bullock carts kept hauling corpses to the dump. Freshly cut logs slowly smoked the dead. The priests kept stuffing god in the dying ears.

The buxom young nurse with sensuous lips, Reema, was a child widow. At midnight, she awoke from a nightmare. She had dreamt of her death, and unable to sleep, went back to the hospital. At the entrance, an oil lamp flickered, and two male guards slept locked in an embrace. Inside, the wounded groaned. When she saw Nakul, her heart pounded. She thought him handsome and laid her head on his chest. Electrified, Nakul opened his eyes, smiled feebly, and sank back into a coma.

Kausal woke with a start as she passed his bed and his consciousness flickered. *When the moment came, I could not fight. The sweat, the pressure to piss, the diarrhea. Then boom! Someone chopped off my left arm from the elbow. I fell. Last night, the captain said he saw me kill two men. I am embarrassed to be turned into a hero! Now I know the heroes!* Kausal saw his child's face before him. *Courage is not in killing but in living when all hope has gone.*

A searing pain pulsed through Nakul's ribs. 'I must be alive,' he screamed, his right leg on fire. In the hospital, he had discovered the sensation of being alive. It was unlike just breathing. His expectant young wife Rukmini's face kept floating before his eyes. At night, he cried. *I will never hold her in my arms again.*

The next day, a physician checked his purple leg. At the surgery station, Nakul lay tightening his haunches, clenching his fists, and grinding his teeth. He squeezed his eyes when the axe fell, then he saw his leg being flung out of the window. 'This Nakul will never walk his child,' he sobbed.

With a scarf covering her nose, Reema came to dress his oozing stump. He looked at her. *Rukmini...?* And lapsed into a reverie. *She is pretty...her lush tresses on my chest, her serpent-headed silver bracelet...caressing my spine.* He woke up in a sweat as Reema was talking to Kausal. He closed his eyes. *Two coconuts swayed on a palm tree.* His eyes followed Reema when his condition improved but inside he crumbled with doubts. *Her face will fall when she sees my stump! Could she love a tottering one-legged man? Making love would be painful.* He wiped his tears. *Reema? Her breasts are pointed, but my head splits with pain when I look at them.*

A hard rain one night gave rise to the stench of dead fish. Madhatter was jerked out of unconsciousness and found his hand clutching his own nose. Where am I? A serrated knife seemed to be scraping at his spine. He buried his face in his pillow. *Those humid evenings with Bunda...how her mangoes throbbed in my eager hands!* But now...he only wished for death.

As soon as his consciousness returned, he started cracking jokes. When his neighbor said he was about to die, Madhatter pointed to the sky, 'Pa, your son is coming!' The man died the following day, leaving behind two sons and a wife. *How was I to know?* Madhatter lamented as he dried his eyes.

Panda writhed in constant pain and made a confession to his Brahmin neighbor. 'I am terrified of death. At home, when others lay dying, I would say "Not to worry, you'll go to heaven." Now I know!'

A nurse brought yellowish water that smelled of rotten fish. In horror, Panda asked, 'Cow or horse urine?' She thrust it into his mouth without ado. He complained to Madhatter, who was miserable himself, and he turned away, saying, 'Who said life is perfect?'

When he heard that Panda had died, Madhatter's first thought was that he wouldn't have to pay Panda the two panas he owed him. But he soon forgot about the panas, and cried.

Two days later Madhatter died.

64

For lack of medical care, thousands and thousands of wounded Kalinga soldiers died on the battlefield. The dead were stacked in several large heaps, dowsed with incendiary material like turpentine, and set on fire. Chandals, the professional cremators, with flames sparkling in their eyes and their dark bodies glistening with sweat, kept tossing dead bodies, severed heads, limbs, and logs into the fire. In the erupting volcano, bones detonated, flesh crackled and logs exploded like fireworks celebrating Siva's dance of death. Tall columns of smoke and billowing clouds soon covered the skies. Stars flickered like glow worms through the smoky clouds at night. The acrid smell of flesh spread as far afield as Tosali, Utkala and Dantpura.

Strange-looking men wearing tree-bark skirts, their faces hidden behind bushy beards and shoulder length hair, wandered the field turning over the bodies with irons as they looked for edible flesh. Black vultures with white down on their breasts, black beaks and lappets on their necks, descended in hordes on Kalinga for a leisurely feast, until, eyes glazed, they fell exhausted to the ground. Bearded vultures from distant lands hurried to gourmandize, feeling what Alexander must have felt on seeing the treasures of Persepolis laid out before him. Into chests and cavities hollowed out by the vultures, cats moved in to rest.

Overnight, Tosali became a ghost town. The temples were boarded up, the shops closed and the streets deserted. While most Magadha soldiers, stunned by the massacre, stayed at camp, some went looking for loot and excitement. They plundered the city, kicking open the temples and stripping the gods of jewels and finery.

In the centre of town near the Jain temple, some old widows hawked palm drinks and roasted meat. A toothless old woman stepped into her alley with her three grandchildren— one in her lap— to buy vegetables. When she saw the carnage in the street, she started to turn back but three soldiers caught her. They dragged her into the street, tore off her silver earrings and nose-ring, snatched the little boy who was clinging to her chest, and cut down the two children. Then they raped the old woman.

A soldier raised the little boy in the air to dash his brains on ground, when the child stammered, 'You won't... kill me?' Winking, the soldier handed him over to a friend who took the child to the temple, stabbed him and left him bleeding on the steps. The soldiers then went in search of fresh excitement.

A little distance from the temple, four Magadha officers sat drinking toddy, telling raunchy jokes, and watching the plunder and rape. One short, fat officer took an ivory elephant from his vest and dangled it in the air, crooning, 'I collect Kalinga elephants.' The other soldiers clapped.

Another took out two silver Ganesha statues. 'The shop had only two. These people are so poor.'

At another stall, several soldiers sat eating meat and drinking. One said, 'That old woman had so much meat in her cart! And so cheap! At first I was suspicious. Then I said, Oh well! It's their meat!'

The soldier who had knifed the child now joined the group. He croaked, 'That was my sacrifice to the Jina!'

'Let's not lose our heads,' one soldier admonished.

The braggart grabbed the soldier's collar and a scuffle ensued. Two other soldiers jumped in to make peace. One shouted, 'Look! Look! There! There in the alley!' Everyone turned. The copulation of two donkeys was in full progress and a ten-eleven year old boy was pounding his fist on the male donkey's rear to push him in deeper.

At another stall, a soldier told his story. 'Yesterday, I brought a young boy— not more than fourteen— to my bed. Really, quite cheap! The idea came to me when he lay naked on his stomach prostrate before me, begging for favors, as if I were a god. I liked his fleshy hips. After the deed, I thought, "No god could do more."'

At another table, two young soldiers sat sipping lime-honey drink. 'I watched my brother crushed to death by an elephant,' one sobbed.

His friend comforted him. 'You also lost an eye.'

'But I'm still alive!'

The news outraged Asoka. 'First the carnage! And now this?' he fretted. The men who had killed and raped were executed. The plunderers lost their hands. Those who sat and watched and did nothing were stripped of their slaves, and made to carry their own equipment on their backs on the journey home.

65

What was left of the Kalinga army was in shambles. Along with several others, Kalinga's defense minister crossed over to Magadha. It became clear that Sisupal was hiding in his fort. He had rebuilt the town on the site of an old fort, built around the time of Mahabharata war in 1400. On his birthday in November, it was reported, Sisupal would ride his elephant to the Jain temple for worship at around noon.

To avoid further bloodshed, Asoka ruled out a siege or an assault on the fort and decided to mine the south-east fort wall near the temple. To avoid raising suspicions, during the day the army built a mobile tower, hinged ladders, battering rams and the catapult. At night they excavated an underground chamber and filled it with dry pine sticks, lac, metal powder, wax, sulphur, saltpetre and turpentine.

On the appointed morning, Sisupal appeared with Queen Charu. She was overladen with gold, even for a queen. Sisupal also sat on his elephant in full regalia under the royal umbrella, bedecked in pearl necklaces, arm bracelets, and pearl earrings. Power to him was still sweet. He liked to make the crowds wait. His elephant Gamini, decorated in splendor, lumbered through the admiring crowds like a plump bride. Casting contemptuous glances at the creatures below, Maggu, the mahout, felt like a minor god in his white tunic and bronze threaded turban.

The tinkling bells and the slow, syncopated movement of the elephant induced drowsiness in the royal occupants. Suddenly, there was thunder. Startled, Sisupal looked up at the blue sky. 'Is it going to rain?' he asked his loyal driver, Maggu.

Maggu studied the sky. 'Very likely, my Lord!'

More explosions followed. Sisupal smelled turpentine in the air, and before his eyes the south-east wall crumbled and soldiers streamed in. He looked for his horse to escape, but realized he was inside his own fort.

People stood trembling, expecting an angry God to appear in the sky until they saw the Magadha soldiers. They surrounded Sisupal. Standing on soldiers' shoulders, a herald announced, 'Soldiers, put your arms down! Don't try to escape or you will be killed.'

Every Kalinga soldier surrendered without a shot.

Shaking, Sisupal raised his hands. The elephant lowered itself and the King stepped down. He was stripped of his gilded weapons which he had never used. Charu stood sobbing at a little distance.

Asoka addressed Kalinga's soldiers. 'Brave soldiers! I promise prosperity to Kalinga.' He turned to Sisupal, 'How should I treat you?'

Sisupal was ready. 'As a king.'

'After you betrayed a friend?'

When Sisupal vehemently denied the charge, Visal called a guard.

'Do you know this man?' Asoka asked Sisupal.

Sisupal lowered his head.

'You sheltered Sasima for three years!'

'Forgive me, Great Asoka!' Sisupal stared at the ground.

Asoka turned. 'Brave soldiers, you served your King well. Did your King serve you well?'

'He is a coward! He betrayed us!' a chorus went up.

'A King who runs from the field surrenders his fate to his soldiers.'

Charu ran to Asoka, 'Stop Asoka! He is my husband!'

Asoka nodded sympathetically. 'Charu, he is an enemy of Magadha.'

Asoka turned back to the Kalinga soldiers, 'Your verdict?'

'Death!'

When a few men spat on Sisupal, Asoka said sternly, 'Stop! He is a King, and must die like a King. I ask two of you to come forward.'

To his surprise, Mahabali, the Senapati, stepped up. Asoka handed him a sword.

'Wait,' said Sisupal, turning to Asoka. 'You are responsible for the war.'

Asoka turned red. 'Sisupal, death makes you bold!'

Mahabali thrust the sword into Sisupal's chest, and he fell to the ground glaring at Asoka. His soldiers cheered, though a few now sobbed.

Mahabali addressed the soldiers. 'Forgive me. My love for my sister Sunanda turned me into a coward. Had I done this deed early on, Kalinga would have been spared this bloodshed. Ambition is a national misfortune in a usurper and weak king.'

Mahabali turned the sword on himself but Visal jumped in and grabbed it.

'Mahabali!', said Asoka, 'only cowards die by their own hands. Please honor me by serving your great land.' And he appointed Mahabali Administrator of Kalinga.

Ashen-faced, Asoka regarded Sisupal's body. 'He was a friend!'

Visal said, 'No, a traitor!'

'Cremate him like a King!'

'Great King, it has been a long day. Go and rest now.'

'There is no rest but in death!' Asoka answered wearily.

Over the next few days, Mahabali turned over the keys of the city and the Treasury to the victors. A horde of gold, silver, precious jewels and diamonds was seized. Grain, young widows, unmarried women and cattle were turned over to Magadha soldiers as war booty. In sympathy for the enemy dead, Asoka decided not to celebrate his triumph.

Before leaving Kalinga, Asoka went to Charu to express regret for Sisupal's death. Apologizing, he asked her to accompany him.

Charu fumed, 'You've taken all of Kalinga's gold. My gold. Kill me, and take my dead body.'

Confined to bed since the end of the war, Anga was roused now. She went to see Charu who sat in a small dark room with no light, mourning.

'Charu, I know you are in pain.' Anga pleaded. 'Think of the children. When the Magadha army leaves, Kalinga's soldiers will kill them.'

Charu sobbed on her shoulders and Anga cried with her. At last Charu relented.

66

The army's march home began in winter. The skies were a tarnished silver, the plateaus and the hills a dull grey, and the terrain bleak. The brush alongside the road was brown and straggly and the trees were gnarled and leafless. Village after village, field after field, was deserted, with not a single young man to be seen. Kalinga had become a ghost land. When the army passed, little children ran inside, peering at them with fearful eyes from behind the half-closed windows. Hunger, desolation, and despair showed on the faces of every woman and child, and old men dried their eyes at the memories of their sons.

The Magadha soldiers recalled the euphoric march to Kalinga. To their young minds, war had seemed an adventure, and something heroic. They wallowed in its imaginary glory. In the heat of battle, they fought bravely and by any measure, had achieved a great victory. Yet now that it was over, victory seemed hollow. Who can rejoice when so many had been killed. *We were young when we arrived. Now we are weary and old.*

The soldiers grieved for their friends killed in the war — men who were once strangers. And worse, they grieved for their enemy. They asked, 'We saw no enemy on the field, and yet we killed and killed. Were we blind? Drunk? Or just stupid?' A strange love for the enemy had taken hold. But curiously, it only added to their pain.

These were simple men. At all times simple men carry their consciences with them. But in a soldier, conscience is a troublesome thing. Reasonable men push it aside with distractions; unreasonable men smother it with the mud and dirt of blind self-interest. But simple soldiers lug it, like their genitals, even to the war front, where it is totally unnecessary and subject to grievous injury. No herbal paste or bandage will heal something so shadowy.

The men marched quietly with bowed heads. They cracked no jokes, and sang no songs. In their minds images of dead men, burning

men, swarming flies, clouds of blue smoke, kept turning round. The
stench of dead flesh would not leave their nostrils. Mired in Dhauli's
red-brown marshes, they had nightmares. And alienated, they lived a
numb, desire-less existence.

Anga gazed blankly at the dull grey sky, her body jolting against
the carriage window. *From woman's labor comes a child, from man's sweat, corn.
But from war? Only hurt, pain, and death.* In her heart, she did not blame
Asoka. *He is a King!* she reasoned. Yet her horror was not diminished.
When Asoka spoke, she would look at him and keep silent. Much
as she tried, she could not bring herself to smile or cast him a loving
glance. Sometimes, taking his hand, she pressed it to her bosom—more
out of habit than feeling. Often she sobbed that she was still alive, and
wished that she had killed herself at the monastery. A wall of the dead
had arisen between her and Asoka.

Asoka was pensive. *Wars have been with us since the beginning of time. Have
other kings felt what I feel? Men die from pestilence; men die from fire and flood. Men
just die from living. But there is something rotten in so much mayhem and violence. It is
a mockery of manhood, of glory and pride. That day, looking at the dead, I felt so small.
Who am I? I asked myself. Every time, a voice said, 'A murderer! A butcher!' It has killed
all my pleasure in the flesh. O how frail is man! How pathetic in his thoughts! We are
all corpses wound with motion and speech! A stab in the chest is all it takes to uncoil our
spring. O Anga! You were so right. But why did you have to come? I will bounce back.
I have to. I am a man. I am a Maurya King. I am Asoka!*

PART FIVE

Suffering
and
Happiness

67

The fog began to lift from the minds of the men as they neared Pataliputra. The clear blue skies and the sunlight helped to exhume, as it were, the long buried faces of family and friends from the recesses of the memory and they smiled when the city's shining towers appeared before them.

Unprecedented crowds turned out to get a glimpse of the victorious emperor. As his chariot entered the city gate, a deafening roar went up as if a god had descended to earth. People had been long preparing for his welcome. A hundred trumpets rent the air as Asoka entered the city gate. Euphoria filled the air, the streets were carpeted with flowers, and young women, married and unmarried, greeted the returning soldiers with uninhibited embraces. With his white hair glistening in the sun, Radhagupta garlanded Asoka. 'Great King! The Vishnu, preserver of this empire, you are now also the Siva, destroyer of Kalinga.'

These were heady days. Magadha was now the greatest power on earth, with its far- flung empire and vast resources. People were glad to be alive— the days were giddy, the nights bacchanalian. For seven days the Palace kitchens were thrown open, and the public feasted on deer, cows, oxen, goats and sheep. Pataliputra became a carnival city.

Through it all, Anga struggled to keep up a cheerful front. She was proud of Asoka's victory, his resounding welcome, and the glory he had brought to the Mauryas. Had she not travelled with him, she would have been as delirious with joy and pride as everyone else. But she had seen the patient on the operating table. Even when the meat chunks came dressed in saffron yellow or red chili gravy, to her every piece seemed to have an eye that stared at her. Unable to look at it, she rushed to her room, overcome with nausea. Asoka noticed her plight and followed her. 'Anga, we have to get out of Kalinga!' Embarrassed, she hung her head. *'What's wrong with me?'* she admonished herself. *'I should be happy! And I...am. I am!'*

Nightmares and heart palpitations kept her from sleep. Severed human limbs appeared in her dreams. She spent hours rubbing her hands, dunking her head in cold water, and scrubbing her body over and over. The pink of her cheeks had turned white. She sat for hours in the garden twisting lotus flowers and uttering, 'To mud...to mud...the burning red river, the bulbous cupola, the bird perched on the eye.' She would crush the petals with her hand, humming, 'I've carried her corpse too long on my hands ...ding-a-ling.' Then she'd laugh. Her laughter broke Asoka's heart.

Every physician in the palace was called in. Each diagnosed a different ailment: imbalance of humors, demon attack, food poisoning, heatstroke. One prescribed spa baths, another asked her to eat almonds boiled in oil. Each brought his own prepared decoction. To exorcise her demons, all agreed upon continuous chanting from the *Atharva-veda*. A verandah in the palace was turned into a den of priests. First thing in the morning, Suiya would read her Buddha's sermons to calm her mind.

Something worked. Anga slept better and her appetite improved, though the shadows lingered on. Once she even went horse riding with Asoka. Relieved, he rewarded the priests and physicians with gold and cows. To cure her pale skin and her melancholia, he asked Suiya to take her out on long walks.

One day she told Suiya, 'Even the thought of meat repulses me now.'

'Anga, every pleasure in the world is at your feet.'

With tears streaming down her cheeks, Anga sighed. 'When I sit down with him to eat, I feel like a stranger. In the hospital that day, I thought that he was drowning in a river of blood. To build this empire, my grandfather fought alongside Asoka's grandfather. He filled our world with music, and love, butterflies, and flowers. But he never talked of wars.'

Anga shuddered. 'For months after Semat's death, I saw corpses in my dreams. Corpses walking, laughing, crying all around me. When Asoka talked of war, I'd see an ocean of corpses at night. When I was sick that winter, Asoka often cried. But that did not stop him from filling Dhauli with corpses. To see Sewak— that gentle soul— gored and chopped up like that! That's what we do to life! To our happiness.'

'Anga, think of the King. Think of Kunala.'

Anga sighed, 'The agony is that we've parted ways. He is not the same. Nor am I. He's lost his cheer and become temperamental. On the journey back, he sat so quiet, his face pale. Every time I looked, he was gazing at the sky. Not once did he ride his horse or smile. It broke my heart. If only he'd leave his grandfather alone. He keeps pumping himself up, like Hanuman, with Maurya glory and the glory of war!'

Suiya put her hand over her mouth. 'He is a King, Anga!'

'Also a man! Only once in all these years, have I seen him go wild,' Anga said, with a tear in her eye.

Suiya probed, 'What did he do?'

Anga closed her eyes. 'Too painful to remember. Too painful to speak.'

Suiya took her hand. 'Anga, we live in an insensate world. War is as real as death and disease.'

Anga looked scornfully at her. 'We don't choose death and disease!'

'But wars have always been there!'

'I should've stayed back. I cannot live without his love. A flower dies when its color leaves!'

'Anga, try to keep cheerful. It will pass.'

'Cheerful?' Anga said. 'A silent grief lives under the ice.'

Suiya sighed. 'Take hot baths, go riding. The sweat and heat will vaporize your memories.'

Anga closed her eyes, swaying her body from side to side. 'Oh! Memories! Memories! Embers of time! The mind's hidden crematories!'

Suiya's face turned dark. 'What do you mean?'

'I wish I knew!'

68

Wrapped in the majesty of the throne, the bubble of glory, Asoka threw himself into administering and rebuilding Kalinga. It helped him forget the images of the dead, the wailing woman, the red river. Now he was reconciled to not conquering all of India. *No glory, no immortality for me! I'll not be a slave to greatness or a slave to Baba. I just want my life back. I miss my happiness. Ah! All philosophies come to grief, life triumphs in the end.*

He prepared to go on a hunt with Anga. She refused. 'Anga, you don't even try. It's been months.' Then looking into her eyes, he coaxed, 'Don't think, just come! In the fresh, fragrant forest air, you'll forget everything.'

Anga looked at him accusingly. 'Piyadassi, hunting is no magic potion. I've come through a storm. I can't go on as if...' She burst into tears.

'A power-crazed King, a religion gone mad!' Asoka said defensively. 'But they are behind us now, Anga. Can't you see?'

Anga looked at him incredulously. 'I can wash the blood of the dead from my hands. But not the tears of the children and widows. There is no eye in Kalinga that is not wet.'

Asoka became impatient. 'Anga, life goes on.'

'So does pain!'

'It's not that I have no regrets.'

'The priest repents today,' she said scornfully, 'and tomorrow fornicates.'

Seeing the hurt on his face, she burst into tears, and held him close. 'Asoka, it is not you I blame. It's me! Me! I'm trying. I just can't help it.'

He forgot his own hurt, and pressed her to him. 'Anga, think of pleasant things. Think of the life we had. Don't be so stubborn! We have to get out of this hole.'

She broke down. 'Asoka, I am so, so unhappy.'

He walked away, frustrated. She does not even try. *I am a King, not a monk!*

He decided to go hunting by himself with the courtiers, hoping she would change her mind. The horses and elephants, the nobles, and the archers stood ready at the palace gate. But at the last minute he changed his mind. *Without her smiling face, without the glint in her eyes, nothing feels the same. Not the day, or the night.* Asoka thought, then tore his hair. *Kalinga is leeching our lifeblood!*

Then he found out she was pregnant. He thought, *it is the best thing that could have happened. Especially to her!*

But Anga was shattered. She anguished, *That day will live in my child's flesh. Every time I hold him, my milk will go dry.*

When Suiya said, 'Now, you'll get well,' Anga shook her head.

'I have a monster in my womb!'

Asoka would take her out for walks and asked her to decorate the Palace, or return to the orphanage, which was suffering from neglect, but she showed no interest. Every day she brought up Kalinga, and Asoka would storm away, thinking *she was wallowing in mud.* Then he had an idea.

He found her sitting by the lotus pond. Seeing him, she hurriedly wiped her eyes and started to chew the lotus petals.

At last Asoka smiled. 'I thought you didn't like lotus flowers?'

She was embarrassed. 'My Lord, I heard it induces amnesia.'

Sitting down beside her, he took out an exquisite necklace from his waistcoat, folded her in his arms and kissed her cheeks. 'For you— the dear mother of our coming prince.'

Sadness came into her eyes. Crestfallen, he asked, 'You don't like it?'

'Oh no. I am thrilled, Piyadassi.' Anga kissed his hand eagerly. Yet, a thought came to her. *I need his love, not necklaces. He is looking for what we have lost along life's trail. He does not understand my pain. Our spirits that once romped together, now wander alone. Much more had died in Kalinga than just men.* She remembered the days she took out his letters from under her pillow, her yearning for him when it rained and thundered at the hermitage, the evenings they played on the Ganges, the day he carried her down from the Palace terrace to the chariot in his arms. All flashed before her eyes. *I can never bring back his happiness. We live by the commandments of our nature, not by pretensions of happiness. Hypocrisy and compromise, to me, are death. If I suffer, I suffer.*

She smiled through her tears and pressed him close to her bosom. Then she changed the subject and told him about the play she had been writing with Bitan. It was called 'The Great Man' and was performed in late spring.

Settling to watch the performance, Anga looked tired as she sat in the front row with Asoka, with Bitan on other side. The councilors and their families sat behind them.

The Great Man— A Play

The play opened with a chorus that addressed the audience.

'Patrons! Do not be surprised by animals in this play. In the Rig-Veda, gods sacrificed the primeval man "Purusha," and created all animals and men from his limbs. That explains why the animal is in us, and we are in the animals. We are not as different as we think. Enough! Enjoy the play!'

Enter Little Boy chasing Pig, then chasing Dog around Deer, Little Boy took bread from his pocket, handfed and stroked Dog affectionately.

Still running around, he sang a rhyme, 'Piggy, Piggy, Little Piggy, pink and brown. Climbed on a branch, the tree fell down.'

Deer said to Dog, pointing to a wound on its thigh, 'A man almost killed me!'

Seeing Man in the distance, Deer and Pig hid behind a tree. Little Boy exited running.

Dog said to Pig, 'Don't be afraid. Man is my friend! You saw Little Boy feed-ing me. Talk to Man, he loves to talk. (Pause) My master went to war. I loved him and he loved me. I sat on his lap. Now he is dead. And I am incomplete. I wish to improve two things about myself. I don't like to raise my hind leg for a leak. And I wish to speak like man. I am working on my barking. (Pause) But I get tired after a few woofs.'

Deer said to Dog, 'We are not fearless like you, O lover of man! Your bark is mightier than our antlers.'

The audience applauds.

Enter Man

Pig bowed to Man. 'We love and fear man. We don't have the words to praise you. We can't th-oink beyond our snout and feet.'

Then Deer spoke. 'What baffles us is why we keep getting killed. We are not at war. A quiet life is all we want.'

Man replied, 'The whole world is our steak. We kill you for sport, we kill you for taste. And we kill you for our God.'

'Did you say dog?' Dog asked sheepishly.

Man was annoyed. 'No, God.'

'Pardon me! God I have not sniffed, as you have, I believe. How does God smell?' Asoka laughed heartily, and turned to Anga who only sighed.

Now Man said, 'Yes, I went to war in the distant land where your master died. No one noticed, no one cried. It was so dignified! I lost only half my arm— he waved his stump— because of God's great plan. How grand!'

Dog asked, 'Tell me more. Is war play?'

Man answered, 'No, you silly creature! No one there sings or dances. It is not a game of nuances. You kill or get killed.'

'Sounds a lot of fun!' said Dog. 'Much better than a dog's life spent wagging its tail. In our animal world, no one is so skilled. Our cup is unfilled!' (droops down)

A donkey descends from above to the sound of chanting

He told Dog, 'Dear Dog! Understand! To fight wars you need a head filled with sand. War is not music, war is not game. Men fight it for fame and other high sounding reasons— all equally lame. We are lucky and wise. So cheer up and rise. Your master would be here, if wars didn't exist.'

Deer turned to Man. 'Do what you please, just spare our lives.'

'Oh Deer! Deer! Understand! If we can kill and maim our own kind, where do you think you and your ilk stand?'

Deer said. 'We feel the same pain, the same joy, as your Little Boy. Is it such a crime that we cannot sing a rhyme? Please develop a gentle touch like ours. Or something close to it.'

Man was contemptuous. 'We care for you? You don't even have a soul!'

'What's soul?' asked Dog

Donkey interrupted. 'Some kind of a hole?'

Man answered indignantly, 'Not a hole, ass! More like a wart between the brain and the heart. It's the stuff of dream. Like the celestial cow, it yields only cream.'

Donkey was puzzled. 'What does the soul do?'

Said Man, 'After life's journey, all the fever and fret, it takes us to heaven on a red carpet.'

Donkey asked, 'What's heaven?'

Man became irritable. 'You know nothing!' Then proceeded. 'In heaven there is no friend or foe. Love is like tickling from head to toe, and not an earthquake. There no hair turns grey. And no one has to pray. In heaven, man can eat, drink, and roam all day free, counting from one to seven, or fall asleep for eternity, dreaming of the life on earth.'

Deer exclaimed, 'Wonderful! And where do we go?'

Man smiled. 'To a deep, dark valley that you know is our belly. God made us so special! We can think, we are vocal. Look at the way we are born, the way we live, and die! Heaven is only for us. Not for the riffraff.'

In an aside, Donkey said, 'Alas! I go nowhere.'

Deer and Pig pleaded, 'O Man Almighty! Take pity! Please cut down your meat in half.'

Man was annoyed. 'You might as well ask us to eat with the nose!'

Donkey suggested, 'Then let's all go to heaven — if you don't object.'

Man answered angrily, 'A very stupid notion that I totally reject.'

A murmur ran through the animals. Resentment rose. Animals sang. 'Hail to your heaven! Hail to your belly!' But "hail" sounded like "hell."

Off to the side, Pig stood weeping, 'There is no heaven for us!'

CURTAIN

When the show ended, Asoka turned pale. *Is she right? Just as I thought on the Dhauli field.* He turned to Anga. 'Do you really believe there is no heaven?'

Anga sighed. 'How can we find out without questioning our assumptions?' Then she left.

'That is Anga!' Asoka told Bitan. 'Always questioning! Always irreverent! And somehow, always right!'

That evening, Anga was happy. She cooked Asoka's favorite peacock curry with nuts and raisins, and surprised him that evening by wearing the blue dress she had worn for the party at the Great Hall. And she put on her new necklace— a plaited and filigreed band of gold rosettes from which hung hollow gold bud-beads and heads of the goddess Athena with one Athena teasing from her cleavage. And that night, she played his favorite melody on the Vina, a stringed instrument. After so many months, she smiled the smile that drove him wild and they made love. 'I wish I were not so imperfect, Piyadassi,' she whispered, wrapping herself around him. 'I love you and always will.' Asoka had not heard those words since the start of the war and he fell asleep in the seventh heaven of bliss.

69

Late into the night he turned about in bed groping for her warmth but his hand fell upon the cold sheet. His hand reached out, circling the dark, empty space and he opened his bleary eyes. He thought she would be back soon and dozed off. A few moments later, the hand rose again as if of its own will, to enclose her roundness, but found no breast.

His eyes opened. From somewhere, a wolf-like ululating sound pierced the night. He was startled. *At this wild, dark hour, what garden perfumes her skin? What lake assuages the fever of her mind?*

He sprang up, threw on a loose robe and went to the ante-chamber, where she often slept at night. The bed was empty. He hurried down the garden path to her favorite lake, passing the lamps along the walkway, their light trembling on the tree leaves. The scent of jasmine wafted by on a wave of wind, then a lamp hissed out, an animal shrieked, and a bird splashed into water.

Then silence. His unspoken thoughts, dark like the night, still whispered. The curse of the woman rang in his head. Near the lake, he was startled by muffled sounds. *Ghosts whispering endearments to the dead?* he wondered. Shadows moved in the distance. Pursued by his own fear, he ran off the path into a bush. Calming himself, he got back on the trail overlooking the lake. Yellow lights flickered on it, the waters shimmered in shades of darkness. A female guard stood knee-deep in the water and others looked on. When they saw the King, they huddled together and waited for him.

The female guard was pulling out a naked body. The night gathered all its darkness and it fell before Asoka's eyes. He ran into the lake and lifted Anga's body, drooping, dangling, dripping. He put her down on the bank and covered her with his robe.

Darkness was all around him. One guard rushed to the royal physician, the others he sent away. Sitting down, Asoka kissed her cold wet lips, and laid his head on her chest. *What was that roar of the sea waves?* He raised her by the shoulders, and drained the water from her nose. Then he lifted her in his arms and started for the Palace whispering along the way, 'Anga, come back, please don't leave me. I'm here, everything will be all right.'

At the foot of the Palace terrace he sat down to regain his breath, then shifted her body in his arms, and her head slumped on his chest; he started up the steps, remembering the day he had carried her down to the chariot.

After crossing the terrace, He stopped at the door and looked up. The sky hung star-less and motionless. Like any other night. In his chamber, where a few hours before he had kissed and embraced her, he put her down on the bed, and fell to the floor, covering his face with his hands. His body shook with sobs. He wished he were dead.

He wrapped her in the floral silk robe she had loved to wear when she was in an amorous mood. Lying beside her, he kissed her eyes, her lips, her cold cheeks. In his mind, he felt the robe rustling. She wore an enigmatic smile, a smile that whispered, 'No sorrows will cross my path again.'

The royal physician arrived at last, looking ghastly and pale. He took her pulse, lifted her eyelids, then hung his head, as if ashamed to be alive when one so beautiful and young lay dead before him. A bird with scattered feathers.

Asoka stood transfixed, gazing at her lily-white face. 'She who loved all creatures is dead!' he lashed out, 'and I, the scourge of men, still breathe! O gods, you just stood by. She should not have died!' Anger rose in his loins. 'O gods! Let loose a conflagration on this earth, turn oceans into flames. Let an inferno roar on this twisted ball of clay. Let no one hide but in oblivion.' He fell limp beside her and heard the walls shout, "You are her executioner! Her hangman!"

He kissed her cheeks, wiped her hair dry, combed it, applied sandalwood paste to her breasts as she had loved him to do, and he whispered, 'Come back Anga. Come back!' A faint jasmine fragrance mixed with the clammy smell of death filled the room. He pressed her cold hands against his cheeks. She was all there. And nowhere. She had become as impalpable as air.

At midnight the following day, he cut a lock of her hair and set fire to her body— the temple of his love— on a sandalwood pyre. With gnashing teeth and flicking tongues, the red flames mercilessly devoured, incinerated her hair and the soft skin of her beautiful body, until the soft white flesh was reduced to just bone fragments and ashes. He stood watching as if he were a slab of stone. She, the goddess Ganga who had come down from heaven to give her bounty to earth, was no more than a few grains of dust! With his own hands he buried her ashes in the garden under the blazing cloud of Amaltas flowers she had so loved. *At last she has found love!* he sobbed.

70

Numb with pain, he returned to Palace. For days, he paced like a wounded tiger in a cage. 'It did not happen. Yesterday she was here!' he'd say one moment, and the next, infernal flames rose in his mind, devouring her soft body, her gentle face

At night his empty bed shocked him. 'Where is she?' he wondered aloud. His eyes searched for her, his hand moved about the space where she slept, caressing the air. 'I killed her! I didn't understand her pain,' he told himself.

He did not leave his chamber for days. The sunsets on the Ganges, the prismatic evening colors on the horizon, the enchanting Ushas, dawn—all suddenly lost color. His appetite for pleasure was gone. Death had burst upon him unannounced, shattering his world. He lay awake in bed. *'Mendicants all, we stand before life with an alms bowl, our scraps taken by thieves. Nothing is like nothing was! Pleasure is a rainbow passing through a cloud. And life? The buzz of a fly!'*

Strange voices mocked him at night, "Powerful King! Great King! You killed one hundred thousand men! And you can't bring her back?" Helpless, powerless, tangled up in the polyp-hands of death and grief, he tossed and turned in bed, terrified to find life so pointless. He yearned for a god to whom he could speak. Yet only the wind whispered to him, and no light streaked down. He envied Anga. Leaning on the Amaltas tree, he broke down one night. 'Anga! You gathered your petals and left!'

He stopped going to the Council. Appeals piled up and frontier tribes harassed his forces. His ministers were sent back, unheard. Radhagupta reminded him, 'Start hearing the appeals! Get your life back!'

Asoka looked at him as at a stranger. 'Why? One day we will all die.'

When Bitan said Puskar had taken sick, he immediately went to see his beloved horse. At the sight of his master the animal snorted and thrashed his tail. Asoka caressed and fed him with his hands. Then he noticed Niguna in the next stall, sadly eating from the trough. Niguna's white coat gleamed. *Unstained like Anga. Niguna had been like her own limb,* Asoka thought. *The head has fallen, the torso straggles.*

He went up to the mare, stroked her withers and whispered in her ears. 'I am told, dear Niguna, that kings and horses have no heart. But when she caressed your mane, I saw the light of paradise in your eyes. I have to break the sad news. Dear Niguna, she is no more! But you and I are. I know you do not live only for sensations. I'll not let grief hurt you anymore, for there is sorrow in the touch of unloved hands.'

That evening he went back to the stable, and tearfully watched the mare die of poisoned oats. Cremating her with his own hands, he buried her ashes next to Anga's.

Anga's words haunted him. 'I can wash the blood from my hands, but not the tears and the pain of Kalinga.' Then one day it dawned on him that war does not stop with the killings on the field. It rages on in the hearts and homes of loved ones. *Fathers, mothers, wives and children, all suffer in Kalinga. As I suffer. And will suffer.*

It was a new awakening. The pain he had inflicted on thousands, became his own. Suddenly the floodgates of remorse burst open the sinews of his heart.

He had read about Hell in scriptures, but now he lived it in his nightmares. The peasant woman's face bent over the ghastly severed head. Deformed, fierce birds cackled, feasting on rotting flesh. He was dragged through a dark forest over mutilated corpses, sharp knives digging into his flesh. Ghosts— visible and palpable— roamed over the ground, drinking blood. The odor was so foul, that he begged for death. But death was denied— hope and death cannot enter hell. Groaning and crying, he was thrown into a boiling river, only to be pulled out moments before death and put through fresh tortures. He woke vomiting and bathed in sweat.

Two Kalinga men had killed five Magadha citizens in a park at
night. Bitan brought them before Asoka on appeal and asked him to
uphold their death sentences. Asoka stared at them, a storm raging
in his heart. Bitan had to remind him several times that the men
must die. He sat still, pale faced, then he pardoned them and left
the Hall.

At the lake, he sat brooding and drinking into the night. Suddenly,
he saw Anga in the water. He jumped in, crying aloud, 'Anga, get out of
Daya.' But each time he approached, she slithered away, splashing water.
He kept going after her, faster and faster in circles. The lake swirling,
his strength sagging, he began to sink. 'I am dying in the Daya!' he cried.
With his right side paralyzed, he crawled back to the shore. He awoke
at dawn. 'I am still alive!'

He was shaken by the dark, dizzying sensation of death, and
thoughts crowded in upon him. *I would have died a traitor to myself!*
Overcome with anger and shame, he smashed his exquisite ram's head
drinking cup. *Only a coward runs from his wrongs. If I'm doomed, I shall pursue
my damnation to the end. Damn despair! Damn death!*

Sometimes wistfulness stole over him but he would admonish
himself. 'Much as my heart yearns for silence, the song must go on
to the end.'

He looked back at his life. *'Once there was no world I could not change. And
now I am a ship wrecked in a squall. Thoughts of the abyss come at me like unceasing
rains. Oh, how it grates me, this incontinence of my mind!*

71

On solitary walks, he heard her footsteps, heard 'Piyadassi', and turned his head, but found only his shadow there. Sometimes when he sat in the garden, she would sneak up from behind and throw her arms around him and cover his eyes with her hands. Sometimes, she would just walk beside him. She came to him at night, hands outstretched. Sometimes, he dozed off in her lap and woke to see her bent over him, smiling lovingly at him with her eyes. If he passed by the Kamarupa Island, she was feeding nuts to the squirrels or chasing butterflies.

In place of the ties that, when she lived, were renewed each day by her touch, her look, her voice, her scent, an intangible connection began to grow between them. Wherever he was, wherever he went, she was by his side, disembodied, nestled in his consciousness. Even on matters they had never talked about, he could hear the echo of her thoughts.

Time passed and one day Bitan asked him to remarry. *Flowers will bloom, the cuckoo will sing again. The seasons will change. But not for me!* After a long silence, Asoka said, wearily, 'I have feasted on life, Bitan. And every feast has to end. Some worlds that I loved have died, some have moved away. Nothing is the same. Then he sighed, 'I have to seek a new world.'

'Those worlds are not for warriors and kings.'

'Are kings deprived of those worlds because they are depraved?'

'It's just that we are what we are,' Bitan said.

'We are also what we become!'

Unknown to him, a new world had awoken within him, resonating with the plaintive music of humanity. His third eye opened like

Siva's. He brooded. *I thought wars were dear to the gods!* He went back to the Vedas and the other scriptures and read that creation arose from a cosmic battle, and that bodies sacrificed on the battlefield go to heaven. In the *Bhagwad-Gita*, Lord Krishna exhorts Arjun to take up arms and kill, free of doubt: "This wavering is not fit for an Aryan; weapons do not cut this soul, fire does not burn it...the soul that dwells in the body is indestructible; therefore you should not mourn for the body."

Not mourn for the body? Does not the spirit suffer along with the flesh? How can one kill men and not think of their suffering? And the suffering of surviving loved ones? He delved deeper, and what he discovered surprised him: that all religions applaud war. *Perhaps, the gods were created to rouse men to kill and conquer.* Nigrodh's face that dark night came before him. *Why is there is no god of peace, no god of reconciliation and compromise? Why is there no mention—let alone condemnation—of bloodshed? Why is there no word of sympathy for the dead? My religion is a warrior religion, written by warring men to inspire men to kill and grab gold and land.* A chilling thought struck him. *How could I be so blind? She died because I lived in the fog of religion.*

He reflected on past wars. *Perhaps there was good reason for the Mahabharata war— the Pandavas had been forced from their land. And for the Ramayana war: a demon had kidnapped Sita, the wife of Rama. Then religion supported virtuous men, and moral indignation led to wars. But now it supports the greedy and the corrupt. Meaningless rituals have replaced conscience. In this jungle, I lost my way. Ever greedy for power and wealth, my priests told me lies. Not one warned me I might be misguided. I thought I would civilize the barbarians with my religion. How easy to chant words! To promise heaven! How easy for ignorant soldiers to believe the priests they completely trust. But who goes to heaven for killing innocent men? I have no one to blame: not the priests, or my religion, or the "karma" of dead soldiers. I was the one who reveled in the lies. I alone am responsible for their suffering. I was dead to the suffering of others; I believed those dying men were bound for heaven, as the Bhagwad-Gita promised. But I always had my doubts. I saw the peasants praying for rains and dying without a single drop of water. Kalinga's soldiers fell on the field like autumn leaves, crying for God's help, and a voice within me said, "Ignorant soldiers, when have you seen gods help the distressed? You are crying in the wilderness!"*

One summer night, Anga came to him in his sleep. 'My Beloved! In your pain, you know the pain of the people of Kalinga. Open your heart to them. Rise above your grief, My Lord. Be their Buddha!'

When he awoke in the morning, the sun was shining in the sky. *"Be their Buddha!"* The words kept ringing in his head. *"Be their Buddha!"*

Now he could not just sit and watch. He must find the key to human happiness. He knew that his world – the world of self-seeking, and seeking glory in war– was dead. *A God who could watch the slaughter of thousands of men without lifting a finger, would not be my God. A God who glorified butchering innocent men could not be my God.*

72

Then a thought flashed: *My God is dead.*

Give up my religion? He could not bear the thought. It was horrifying. Day and night he anguished, brooded, hesitated and debated. *How can I give up my religion? The religion in whose warm bosom I grew to my manhood that gave me power and the throne. Which revealed its secrets to me? The religion of my ancestors! Would I be an apostate, a serpent to my gods?*

But how long can I embrace the dead body of this beautiful woman? He dreaded the days that followed the sleepless nights.

Without faith, he fretted that he would tremble with every gust of wind, without faith, he would drown in the ocean of uncertainty. He decided to seek out Upagupta, the head of the Buddhist Sangha.

In the Palace, his crisis created a tremor. Tissarakka hoped that in his distress, the King would turn to her for solace. She waited for a few days. Then she went to Asoka. Resolved to claim her rightful place in his affections, she reminded him of her loyalty through the years. Asoka listened. 'Are you not a queen?'

'My Lord,' Tissarakka snapped, 'I want to be a real queen as she was.'

Asoka looked baffled. 'But Anga was my woman. And she is gone,' and he turned away.

When Purohit Shivdutt was informed of the King's heretical thinking, his face turned red. 'In any man, much less a king, such thoughts are obscene. I am the royal priest! I decide on spiritual matters for the King,' he said kicking the fat behind of his assistant who had brought him the alarming news. Swinging his silver staff in the air, he rushed to see the King.

'Great King! Conqueror of Kalinga! Inheritor of Earth! You have brought great glory to this empire. You will live a thousand years!' The Purohit said.

Asoka bowed to him. 'Revered One! I am filled with remorse and grief.'

Shivdutt controlled his anger. 'Rejoice O killer of one hundred thousand men! War is the king's glory, his crown, his right; to kill men is his pleasure. When Brahma created the world, men and women were immortal. But the earth could not bear their burden and approached the Creator for relief. Out of the pores of His body, Brahma created a beautiful dark-eyed woman clad in bright red. He ordered her to swoop down and kill men mercilessly. Horrified, she pleaded for mercy. Then Brahma said, "Let the passions of men lead to their destruction! Let diseases and age kill him!" So it is O Great King! Killing is good. Very good! A great king like you comes once in many centuries, to lighten its burden and gladden the earth.'

'It does not lighten my remorse,' responded Asoka.

'I will pray for you, King. A few rituals, a little charity, and slight obeisance to God—that's all you need for God's forgiveness.'

'Revered One,' said Asoka, 'God may forgive me, but I can't forgive myself.'

Shivdutt was undaunted. 'Great King! I have to warn you that the Buddhist dream of brotherhood is just one in the graveyard of religious pipe dreams. You are the greatest of the great. You are the grandson of the great Chandragupta's family of the Sun. I will do a special havan for your peace. And if you still want to live like an ascetic, let your ministers toil.'

Asoka was surprised. 'Gurudev, ascetics live outside the world but I am of this world. And I don't desire any havan.'

Shivdutt's voice rose in consternation. 'Great King, no one should fault his own religion!'

Asoka got up and bowed his head. 'Revered One! The fault is in me.' He left the chamber.

Shivdutt's eyes burned with anger. At that moment he wished he had the legendary power of the great Rishi Durvasa, an ancient sage. When angry, he could turn a man into an animal or a lump of stone. 'I'd turn him into a one-eyed mule,' seethed the Purohit.

73

Upagupta was the Revered Elder, fourth patriarch saint of the Buddhist Sangha. Thirty-five, tall and thin with a pointed nose, he was the son of a Mathura perfume merchant. Clad in a saffron robe, he greeted the King, offered him a tiger skin, and sat cross-legged opposite him on a white cotton rug. Asoka folded his hands. 'Revered One,' he said with sadness, 'I've lost my faith. I've lost my peace.'

Upagupta studied the King's gaunt face. 'Great King,' he said gently, 'power and wealth do not bring peace. Peace comes from within.'

'I don't even know if there is a God,' lamented Asoka,

'In a changing physical universe, an unchanging God cannot exist. Under the laws of our universe, God can make no revelations, and the dead cannot rise from the grave.'

'Can't God exist outside the universe?'

Upagupta smiled. 'God can! But that God would be unknowable. We cannot know if He is cruel, indifferent or kind. Nor can we know about His incarnations, His prophets and sons. No scripture can speak for Him. Authority comes not from speculation but from knowledge and experience. That is why Buddha denounced all religious authority.'

Asoka's eyebrows arched. 'What did Buddha say?'

'When asked about God, Buddha became silent. He himself did not claim to be a prophet, nor the son of a god, nor God's incarnation. He claimed no revelation from God. Buddha said, "You must be lamps unto yourselves. Hold fast to the truth as a lamp, seek salvation in truth alone." He did not ask people to abandon their religious creed, only to watch their thoughts and deeds, and to harmonize their faith with their deeds.'

Asoka flushed. 'And I wasted years reading the scriptures!'

Upagupta said, 'Don't blame yourself. Everyone does it.'

Upagupta's eyes fell upon something. He reached down and picked up a slithering, shiny pink slug. 'If this slug did not exist, can a description of it in a book create it?'

'No.'

'So it is with God. To talk about it, we have to know it.'

'What is your proof that there is no God?'

'Hasn't the universe been working fine for eons without outside help?'

Asoka took a deep breath. 'Can God be worshipped?'

'If you have love and longing in your heart, then by all means worship God. Even sing inspirational hymns. But pray in a quiet place where you can gather your thoughts and feel close to God. God is a spiritual experience, not a pill you can swallow. You need no prophets or priests for the experience. Remember, every doctrine fragments God. Every doctrine distances us from God.'

'What about the soul?'

Upagupta stroked his chin. 'If there is no God, there is no soul. And if God exists outside the universe, the soul still has to live in a mortal body. No immortal substance can live in the body. We are dynamic organisms of sensations, perceptions, impulses, emotions, memories and volitional acts of consciousness, and all these perish with the body. Nothing survives— not consciousness, not God-consciousness. Not soul.'

Upagupta smiled and continued. 'If soul is life force or energy that escapes death, that energy lives on in the universe, but not in the form of "I." Even energy keeps changing under the laws of the universe. But religions have created elaborate belief systems— soul, heaven. Why? To comfort man, to keep their hold on him. These beliefs are nothing but religious hallucinogens.'

Asoka frowned. 'If there is no soul, why does Buddha believe in reincarnation?'

'Good question! Buddha believed that a moral universe parallels the physical universe. The laws of this moral universe, or "karma", determine rebirth. So this moral universe already exists within us. Buddha believed that when we die, energy escapes us and our "karma" attaches to that energy. This birth-death cycle can last for eons. But if we release ourselves from the cravings, desires and attachments that bind us to the narrow "I", we reach "Nirvana". Nirvana is our expanded self — the self that is in harmony with the universe. It can only be experienced, not described.'

Asoka seemed disconcerted. 'It all comes down to beliefs. So what's wrong with soul?'

Upagupta shook his head. 'If heaven is for real, why do we dread death? Intelligent men want real answers, not fairy tales. Man's courage lies in looking his destiny in the face. Doesn't the flower bloom in the desert in the face of its death? Running after illusory happiness— saving soul and visions of heaven— cannot make us happy. Happiness comes from connecting to living beings.'

Asoka stared into the distance. 'No God! No soul! What is real?'

'Nothing in this universe is permanent and independent. Nothing! So this universe can't be real. Keep peeling it away, and you discover a universe that is empty at the core. "Emptiness" is the reality of the universe.'

Asoka touched his arms and shoulders. 'Strange, this emptiness! This body, the oceans, the mountains— all seem so real!'

'Things are not what they seem, King. The word "emptiness" comes from the Sanskrit word "sunya" which means "relating to swollen", or appearing substantial from outside, but hollow inside. You know a swollen head is an empty head.'

Asoka threw his hands in air. 'God is Unknowable. There is no soul. The universe is empty! So life has no purpose.'

'Don't jump to conclusions, Asoka. Can opium, hashish, an imaginary soul, or a hollow heaven give your life purpose? No. Life is life's purpose. But religion encourages irresponsibility. It asks us to put more faith in prayers than in effort. Renounce all doctrines and dogmas, and focus on life. Only life can feel for life, only life can redeem life.'

'But isn't Buddhism a religion?'

'Not in the traditional sense. It is a system of spirituality that is based on moral conduct. It helps us grow through reflection and self-examination. Buddha rejected blind faith. He asked us to investigate all beliefs in the light of our intellect, knowledge and experience. And he went even further. "You need not accept all Buddhist beliefs, only those you agree with."'

'But how can we grow if life is suffering?'

Upagupta's voice rose passionately. 'Suffering is not the opposite of pleasure, King! Some men keep sucking at the honey jar even as they hurtle towards the abyss. Suffering is rooted in the nature of life. We desire permanent youth, love, and good health. And what does life offer? Decay, disease, old age, dejection. disillusionment. And anxiety.

'Buddha asked only that we follow a middle path between sensuality and asceticism, a life of contemplation. To affirm our humanity, our mortality, our common nature, he asked us to practice compassion and generosity. By pitting the narrow "I" against other human beings, we deny our humanity. By expanding this "I", we reach the state of mind called happiness.'

Asoka was bewildered. 'If there is no God, how can morality be there?'

Upagupta shook his head. 'Where did God come from? The idea of God is not God. Look at our gods! They kill, steal pretty women and grant favors for wine and flesh. In other religions, gods seek revenge, brag, even perform miracles to impress us like magicians. But these gods do nothing about oppression, war, hunger, or pestilence. Are these moral gods?'

'And the priests? Many are good men. Others love God but do not love man. Self-righteous, full of moral indignation, they disown all responsibility for human suffering—even that inflicted by them— by attributing it to bad karma or God's will. Every social injustice has been sanctioned, if not incited, by the priests. Various sins have been created by scriptures to vest power in the priests. What mortal can resist such power? Addicted to it, clinging to the past, averse to any change, these priests want to retard our thinking. But the aim of religion is to make man moral, not a moron!'

'The truth is, religion and morality are two different things. Morality cuts across all religions, it is about social justice. A religious man is not necessarily a moral man. If men are moral— and not all are— it is because man has intelligence. Man can think. He has eyes and ears. Most humans are conscious that under the skin, all men are the same, and they all meet the same end. Religious dogmas distort and disdain this truth of common humanity. Should God have preferences?'

Asoka returned home dazed and contemplative. *Suffering has so many faces: the passing away of love, living without love, living with body decay and disease, and so many calamities. We also suffer because others suffer. And we suffer more when we are the cause of it.*

He brooded on his own life. *Anesthetized by religion, I neither saw nor felt others' pain. And yet, to think there may be nothing after death. Am I strong enough to live in a God-less world?*

Emotionally drained, that night he prayed for strength—not to any specific God or image, but to the one Supreme. That is. Or is not. An indescribable sadness gripped him: *I am all alone.*

74

One thought possessed him now: to give his people a little happiness. He was not sure if Buddhism alone could do it. He asked Arhat Yacas, an esteemed Buddhist monk, 'Why the peasants and the poor don't take to it?'

'Merchants and traders practice it. But they do have some intellect.' Arhat admitted.

Asoka's face fell. 'So it can't help the masses.'

Arhat protested. 'Buddha's core message is simple: happiness comes from caring for and helping others.'

Not convinced, Asoka decided to find out.

Incognito, he visited the Pataliputra monastery to see Buddhism in practice. Intrigued by a cheerful monk, he asked him about it. The monk threw his hands in the air.

'The knowledge that life is suffering helps you cultivate happiness.'

It reminded Asoka of what Anga had once told him.

Gingerly, he started out with self-examination and a little meditation. To his surprise, he experienced a sense of liberation. He became less anxious about his future, and free of the false hopes that his previous rituals had raised. He felt stronger and more able to face life without swinging between hope and despair.

He wondered about the laymen. The monks, he suspected, would answer in the affirmative. He travelled to see his brother Tissa. He had not seen him in years, since he had become a monk at Vaishali, and Asoka wanted to make up for his past neglect.

Tissa was in his meditation when Asoka arrived at the monastery so Asoka waited in the Assembly Hall. When Tissa saw his emperor brother sitting there in a plain white robe, he flushed with anger. *Hypocrite! Murderer! He is the brother who banished me*, Tissa thought indignantly, forgetting that after his rejection by Anga in Taxila, he had been contemplating the Buddhist oath. Tissa took a deep breath, as a good monk does when agitated. He realized he was angry at Asoka not for killing Sasima but for taking Anga away. When Asoka married Anga, Tissa had said to himself, *"He takes whatever he wants."* He asked coldly, 'What brings the great emperor here?'

Asoka sensed the contempt and sarcasm in Tissa's voice. Hurt, he implored, 'Brother! I need your help.'

'Brother? A monk has no brother!' Tissa looked away. What he said was correct, but his tone implied, "For me you are dead."

'Tissa, I know you are angry with me. I admit my mistakes, and I want to make recompense. I never intended to hurt you. My affection for you has never wavered. Remember, you left the Palace by choice.'

'Choice? Whatever the great emperor says!' Tissa sneered. 'What do you want from me?'

'Tell me; are lay Buddhists happier after their conversion?'

'What a question!' Tissa flared up. 'Am I happy? Are you happy? Tell me, who is happy?'

Asoka's voice softened. 'Tissa, I am only asking about the laity.'

'Asoka, you never cease to surprise me. You've never stopped to look within and ask, "Who am I? What have I done?" So I'll tell you. You are a thrill seeker, a sexually overcharged wild elephant in musth. Let me recount a few of your great deeds: murdering cannibal, raping Varsha, fratricide, killing Choti-ma, and if I know you a little, Anga's death! Those are your accomplishments! You want to be the greatest, greater than Baba, no matter what! And you didn't annex Kalinga, you razed it to the ground. You've so much blood on your hands, not even the Buddha will forgive you. I beg you Asoka, leave Buddhism alone. It will survive without you. But not if you're aboard.'

Tissa started to storm away, mocking, 'What can a poor monk like me offer to a great emperor!'

Asoka felt dizzy. In his heart he knew every word Tissa said was true. 'Tissa, I'd undo it all if only I could. Yes, I have pursued my desires single-mindedly. With your help, I wish to make amends. Tell me about the laity. If they aren't happier after conversion, Buddhism doesn't work.'

Tissa took a step back. 'Again, you are getting ahead of yourself. There are two kinds of monks. Some wish to change themselves, others wish to change the world. Not one —not even the Buddha – changed the world. If I can change myself, I'll be lucky,' he said impatiently, thinking of his daily recurring fits of lust.

Asoka asked simply, 'Can't one do both?'

Tissa glared. 'Tell me that after you've done it!'

Asoka was disappointed. 'At least, recommend some sermons for me to read.'

Tissa went in, and to get rid of him, tossed a copy of the *Suttas*, discourses of the Buddha, into his hands. 'But these are no good for changing the world!' he said, and left.

Back in the Palace, Asoka carefully read the Suttas. He liked the *Dhammapada*, Buddha's verses, which told him, in easy, human terms how to control the passions and the lust for self-praise.

The simplicity of Buddha's teachings fascinated Asoka. Here, there were no high-sounding discourses on the origins of the universe or the origin of man; no speculation about God's will or God's commands. The sermons talked about day-to-day living and our daily struggles. *If I can follow them, perhaps others can.* But his doubts soon resurfaced, and he returned to Upagupta.

'How can the "self" be unreal? I know I have a self,' Asoka asked.

'The "self" you are talking about is a stream, an uninterrupted flow of consciousness from childhood to death: sensations, experiences, thoughts, feelings, volitional acts, and memories that are unique to each of us. This uniqueness and the continuity of consciousness is the "self" we possess. It creates the illusion of a "self" that we think is permanent. But it is only a stream—never the same. Just as a stream is attached to the land through which it runs, this "self" attaches to those things and people that gratify its desires and goals. And this "self" nurtures indifference or ill-will against those who do not satisfy its goals.

'Is this stream independent of the body? No. But calling it "soul" doesn't turn it into an independent entity that is also permanent.'

Asoka sat dazed.

Upagupta paused. 'King, what does all this mean? That nothing in our body is eternal; that we have no invisible umbilical cord to God. We can die with our eyes closed to what is real. Alternatively, we can free ourselves from the great illusion of self's immortality. Our "nirvana" is not in saving our "self" but in losing our "self" in something bigger than the dot-sized "I". Self-forgetfulness is happiness. To feel part of humanity is happiness. That's what connects us to Creation.'

Asoka struggled to understand.

Upagupta continued. 'Think of the pain this hungry "self" has inflicted on people. How many innocent people have died because zealots wanted to save their "lost souls"? How many have tortured themselves to find their souls? How much time has been wasted preaching about the soul? Time that would have been much better spent on sleep.'

For the next two months, Asoka thought about it. At last, he decided, *'I'll try. I have nothing to lose!'*

75

In his ruminative walks, Asoka wondered if Buddhism could help him in governing the frontier tribes who always made trouble. He invited Arhat Yacas, an esteemed Buddhist monk, to his Council and addressed the meeting.

'Friends, I need your help. And yes, knowing Radhagupta's thinking, I have not invited him today. I want to tell you about an experience I had when I was eleven. I went to Kalinga where I ran into cannibals. They had set fire to a boy of about my age. The tribesmen sang and danced to drums as the boy was being roasted for sacrifice.'

He turned to Narad. 'Would you call the tribe civilized?'

Narad scrunched his nose. 'Cannibals!'

'Are we any different?'

Astonished, Narad said, 'We don't do human sacrifice.'

'We do animal sacrifice!'

'We have the Vedas,' Narad said. 'Our gods are superior. We chant hymns. The tribes are mired in superstitious rituals and false beliefs.'

Asoka probed. 'We too have rituals and beliefs that some might call superstitious. And our gods may be different, but gods are gods! They too have music, dance, and friendships.'

Narad protested, 'It is the way we think and act that makes us civilized.'

Asoka asked, 'So you think we're civilized. How would the tribe resolve their quarrel with another tribe?'

Immediately, Narad said, 'They would wipe out their enemies.'

'Is that not what we did to Kalinga?'

Narad was astonished. The King was condemning himself! 'Well, war is different. All civilized societies have wars!'

Asoka cut Narad short. 'Then we are not all that different!'

He turned to Bitan. 'Bitan, you are a historian. What did the Greeks do if they disagreed with a tribe?'

Bitan thought for a moment. 'The Greeks annexed their land and enslaved the enemy.'

'We are civilized,' Narad interjected, 'because we wouldn't attack as long as the tribe didn't interfere in our affairs. We'd just condemn them as untouchables to keep them out of our lives.'

Asoka turned to Arhat Yacas. 'And how would you settle such disagreements?'

'Our missionaries would go and live with them, preaching by example, not by words. They would see how we treat animals, how animals are just like us, how they too crave happiness and suffer pain. The tribe's sin is ignorance. Once their consciousness about life is raised, they would begin to care for all human life.'

Asoka asked, 'How much time might that take?'

Arhat Yacas paused. 'Three generations.'

'We don't have that much time. What would you do in the meantime?'

'Negotiate,' said Arhat Yacas. 'Compromise, wait. Be patient.'

'If history is our guide,' said Bitan, 'human beings can't wait. Wars won't simply wither away.'

Asoka asked, 'Has anyone tried?'

Bitan considered for a long moment. 'No.'

Asoka rose from his chair. 'It has been very helpful, friends.'

Now the King returned to be initiated as a Buddhist.

Upagupta was pleased, but wary. 'As King, you are used to attaching much importance to yourself. Buddha warned, "Monks, never consider yourselves superior to laymen. It shows contempt, lack of respect and goodwill for other human beings." I will tell you a story, King. A donkey called Pushy fancied he had great musical talent. His friend Jackal warned, "Friend, your voice is not mellifluous." But would Pushy listen? One full moon night, thinking himself a tenor, he belched out his soul. This so inflamed the night watchman he tied a millstone round the donkey's neck. Clueless, Pushy sought his friend's opinion about his singing prowess.

Jackal was gracious. "You did receive a medal for being musical!"

Pushy bowed as if for applause. Jackal told himself, "What a pompous ass!" '

Upagupta walked Asoka to the Assembly Hall. 'As king, you will have unlimited opportunities to do good. Sadly, rulers too often fall prey to that great lure of feeble minds— schemes to glorify the self.'

Asoka stood before the monks in a plain white cotton dress, with Anga by his side, her eyes shining with pride. He recited:

> To the Buddha for refuge I go.
>
> To the Dhamma for refuge I go.
>
> To the Sangha for refuge I go.

Then he took his five vows of moral conduct and Upagupta gave his blessing. 'Great King, we will pray for your success, and your peace.'

Asoka returned to the Palace as the first Buddhist emperor of India.

76

Now that he had become a Buddhist in his eagerness to make people happy, despair engulfed him in the following days and weeks. *I didn't think it through. I have no road map. I can't make people happy by just telling them, "I want you to be happy."*

As the enormity of the task began to sink in, self-doubts rose. *I have only given pain—even to those who loved me. I could not give happiness even to her. And why will people trust me? I have done nothing for them...*

He looked back at his life. *But I always had doubts: surviving the cannibals, winning the horse race, the uprising, the throne that night...even winning Anga's hand. But then I was young and naïve. That I might fail did not stop me.* He lamented he had become so old that he wanted to ensure success before he began.

He started slowly—with half-day fasts, which didn't go well—he yearned for food. Meditation was even more difficult—the difficult questions he faced boomed in his temples and pulsated in his head...*If I gave up wars...the soldiers would rebel. And the Brahmins hate Buddhism. Can the peasants live without rituals? But to think they'd never know happiness if I did nothing! And Kalinga is drowned in pain.*

He closed his eyes, and held his head.

Whichever way he turned, it looked bleak. He would go out horse riding to drive out the dark thoughts. But exhaustion brought no peace. *Where did it go?* It gnawed him that his success depended on others. Each day that went by weighed on his mind. More than three months passed and he still had no idea. No scripture, no counselor could help him. In desperation he vowed: *I know this war is not like the Kalinga war. It will go on until my last breath and ten lives more if I had them. Perhaps, there is no answer. Perhaps, it will come as I go. I would find out on my deathbed. But I can't just sit and wait.*

That evening, he met with Arhat. 'For myself, I will follow Buddha's precepts, but for my people, I will forget all references to sex and alcohol. I will not quarrel with man's little pleasures. My aim is to give them happiness, and to help them notice their behavior that brings them grief. I want them to think for themselves.'

Arhat was perplexed. 'Leave out sex and alcohol? That will encourage immorality.'

'Arhat, for myself I accept the body's few glories and more absurdities. But I want my people to see beyond the body. They have a mind. I want them to see their own injustices to other men, to see how their prejudices cause them and others misery. I want them to live by a few simple rules. Only when they come to value life, they'll see that happiness is possible.'

'That's a tall order, King!'

'Perhaps! But it's time for people to practice tolerance.'

77

Great leaders rule by example, petty men by bluster and speech. Before asking his people to modify their behavior, Asoka set out to follow his own rules: to abstain from killing, speak truth, respect all religions, and be kind to elders, servants and slaves. This was his "Dhamma", the Code of Moral Living. It was the essence of all religions, but without the taint of any specific creed. His conversion to Buddhism greatly surprised the public. He was already forty-one and used to the life of a powerful and imperious ruler.

One day hobbling on a stick, walking alongside Visal, his father, Nakul said, 'Father, the King is impulsive. Who renounces his own religion? A man who loves women, hunting and war can't live like a Buddhist!'

Visal sympathized. 'Son, knowing Asoka, I would not bet my money on it!'

Shivdutt, the former Chief Priest, bitterly told Narad, 'His appetite for pleasure will be his downfall. Self-control in food and sex is difficult even for me.'

Asoka found that changing lifelong habits was not easy. Frequently assailed by doubts, he had to remind himself that Mara, the tempter of mankind, tantalized the Buddha for years before his enlightenment. He confessed his failing in a Rock Inscription:

I have been a Buddhist layman for more than two and a half years, but for a year I did not make much progress...

He started by reducing his consumption of meat. Devi, now a Buddhist and the chief queen, was in charge of the Palace kitchen. She pleaded with him "to live like a king."

Asoka studied Devi– her large sad eyes, darkening skin and graying hair, yet her face aglow. Gently, he said, 'Devi, you make me feel as if being a vegetarian is capital punishment. Yes, I once loved peacock breasts and deer flanks. But believe me, the color, texture and taste of vegetables, curd, beans and fruit, can be just as rewarding. I am touched by your concern though.'

Saddened, Devi remembered the day when Asoka had roasted a deer at her father's house and sat opposite her relishing the meat and casting glances at her. Tearful, she said, 'It's not easy for me to see my King-husband living like a monk.' She grieved for him because it was inconceivable for most people, much less the King, to give up meat. Only the ascetics and the Janis did this and they were few and far between.

For centuries, meat had been a staple food. Thousands of animals were killed daily in the Palace kitchen to feed guests, residents, staff and guards. "Why should we, royalty, eat grass?" the princes complained, repelled.

Even Kunala, Asoka's favorite son, said, 'Father, on the days I don't eat flesh, I feel like a sudra, an untouchable.'

It was not easy for Asoka either, and it took grit and faith. He described the change in an Inscription:

..*Formerly, in the kitchens of the 'Beloved of the Gods', many hundreds of thousands of animals were killed daily for meat. But now only three are killed, two peacocks and a deer, and the deer not invariably.*" The inscription continued "...*even these three animals will not be killed in future.*

Next, he turned to hunting, a royal pastime rooted in royal tradition for centuries. He loved hunting—deer, fox, tiger, lion, even rhinoceros. Of course, he rationalized at first. 'I will kill only one or two a month. And the public loves the spectacle.' Yet, every time he hunted, he shrank inside because of the unfairness inherent in a hunt. It became increasingly difficult for him to release the arrow, to see the animal fall and bleed, and to tear out the flesh. On a hunt, he missed a deer three times and the nobles exchanged glances. But when he discontinued the practice, they were surprised and the public was disappointed. Freed from the anxiety to affirm his manhood by resorting to deceit in order to trap and kill a helpless animal, Asoka felt relieved and elated. For public entertainment, he replaced hunting with spectacle— heavenly chariots, elephant acrobatics, and balls of fire. He explained his new found pleasure in an Inscription:

> *In the past, kings went on pleasure tours which consisted of hunts and similar amusements. The 'Beloved of the Gods', the King Piyadassi, once he had been consecrated for ten years, went to the tree of Enlightenment. From then arose the practice of tours connected with 'Dhamma', during which meetings are held with ascetics and Brahmans, gifts are bestowed, talks are arranged with aged folks, gold is distributed, discussions with people in the country are held, instructions in Dhamma are given and questions on Dhamma are answered. The 'Beloved of the Gods', the King Piyadassi, derives more pleasure from this than from any other enjoyment.*

78

Reflection became natural to him, and his compassion extended beyond humans. He had loved horses and elephants for their usefulness to kings because they literally supported royal splendor and pomp. But he had never regarded animals as worthy of kindness nor thought of them as belonging to the same creation as man. He had believed that animals were made for man's convenience and pleasure, and had no feelings or desires of their own. But when he started paying a little attention, he was surprised by their affinity to human beings: they too cared for their young, and suffered like men when tortured or in captivity. They were even capable of returning affection. Delighted, he started to spend time with them every day, and dedicated a small park in the Palace gardens to the deer. Kamarupa Island was turned over to peacocks, open-billed storks, egrets, cormorants and cranes.

The sorry plight of animals now distressed him. Having grown up watching animal sacrifices in Vedic rituals, he revolted against the cruelty of this practice. *How sad we cannot celebrate ours joys or sorrows without killing animals!* The animals were also tortured and killed for sport and public entertainment on "Samaj" days when people assembled in large numbers on public grounds to watch the fights to death, or the slaying of animals by flamboyantly dressed, chest-puffing "heroic" men, who were much applauded by the crowd and carried on shoulders after the killing.

In the Council, he proposed an immediate stop to all such killings. A violent debate erupted. Arhat Yacas wanted a total ban, while Narad, a staunch Brahmin, vehemently defended animal sacrifices as sacred to the Vedic religion. Bitan wanted the matter left to people's conscience.

Asoka declared adamantly, 'Whether for the gods or for pleasure and sport, all animal killings must be stopped forthwith. No one—certainly not religion–should tear asunder what God has created.'

Narad protested. 'Wise King! This is a sacred Vedic practice going back thousands of years.'

Surprised by Nard's vehemence and his flushed red face, Asoka thought, *when it comes to religion, all thinking vaporizes. We believe what we want to believe, regardless of its consequences. We shut our eyes close, and stick our fingers deep in both ears. As if, traditions were cast in stone.*

'I respect the Vedic religion,' he told Narad, 'but that does not make these killings less repulsive.'

Narad tried to salvage the situation. 'King! We are not talking about human life!'

'Life does not stop at humans!' Asoka retorted. 'Should compassion?'

He issued an Edict:

No animal should here be immolated and offered as a (religious) sacrifice; nor should any 'Samaj' be held, for King Piyadassi sees much evil in social festivals for celebratory and sporting events during which animals are killed.

Festivals that did not involve animal killings were not affected, and the slaughter of horned cattle and other animals for food continued.

79

He had lost his happiness, he knew, because he lacked moral consciousness. No one can ride a horse without reins, or an elephant without a goad. Yet, constantly buffeted by passions and temptations, he saw all around him men passed their lives without any guidelines, drifting into whirlpools of greed and self-destruction. Religion had failed man. The Vedic religion sought only to fulfill man's desires, and its caste system led to social injustice and oppression.

How to spread the awareness that all men are free and equal? The empire was vast. Public announcements were made by beating drums. After much deliberation, Asoka decided on several methods– personal tours, inscriptions on rocks and pillars (an innovation at the time) and the reading of inscriptions to assembled crowds three times a year.

He called on Jaidev, the Chief Engineer, for information about the stone inscriptions.

'Noble King, our craftsmen are skilled in ivory and wood, but not in stone carving. Perhaps we can get artisans from Persia and Greece,' Jaidev told him.

Asoka rejected the idea. 'I want the stonework to reflect the Mauryan, all-embracing spirit of freedom, justice, and equality. And it should last a thousand years. Foreign artisans won't know anything about it. And carvings must be works of art. People do not forget a beautiful thing. And beauty makes an impact.'

It seemed the emperor was asking for the moon. Jaidev collected thousands of artisans, tested their skills on small jobs, and finally selected the best among them. Inscriptions were incised on rocks or sandstone pillars with painstaking accuracy. The interiors of the halls in the caves, such as the Barabar and Nagarjuni hill caves, were polished until they shone like mirrors. Asoka personally inspected the work and was not satisfied until perfection was achieved, and the bulls and lions on the pillars seemed poised to leap. The stonecutters loved their unpretentious King and put their hearts in the work, and their spirit and execution was unsurpassed.

The engineering feat was no less impressive. After they had been carved and polished at a central location, thousands of forty-foot monoliths were transported across the empire to distant locations. The pillars were then carefully erected at selected sites – village centers, near temples, markets, major road crossings and festival grounds—for people to see, read, admire, feel and remember.

Each inscription was published in several scripts and dialects such as Greek, Aramaic, Prakrit, and was appropriate to the region: Kandahar, Kabul, Kashmir, Bihar, Nepal, Kalinga, Bengal, Ujjain, Mysore, and many more, which multiplied the work. Asoka wrote, *Since the empire is vast, much has been engraved and much has yet to be engraved.*

With his facility for language and thought, he personally composed each inscription. In these inscriptions, he addressed himself as "Beloved of the Gods", as was the custom, and also as "Piyadassi", the name which had come to carry tender memories for him. Because of their success, the inscriptions became his diary, his pulpit, and the tool of governance.

A few years after the work had been completed, Nitan Sastri, an art teacher from Taxila, took his students to the Sarnath Stupa near Varanasi to show them the carvings, and told them, 'The history of Indian art begins with King Asoka. No finer workmanship can be found—not even in Athens—than here in the magnificent bell and capital of the pillar with four lions, supporting the wheel of moral law.'

In addition to works of art, Asoka created a special cadre of high officials, "Dhamma Ministers", to read the Edicts aloud to the public, and to answer their questions on the spot. These men toured the cities, visiting local leaders of different religious sects and lower castes. Forbidden from using force, their mission was to gently dissuade the public from performing wasteful religious rituals, and to encourage the organization of charities and charitable endowments for needy and the poor. They were instructed to report their progress to the King whatever the hour, as soon as they returned from a tour.

Every village in the far-flung empire was covered. Thousands of special Rural Officers were appointed, each with jurisdiction over hundreds of villages. Addressing these Rajukas, Asoka said, *Whatever the Beloved of the Gods orders must be carried out in every respect...you will instruct in Dhamma the people of the countryside, assembling them with the sound of the drum, likewise the local chiefs.*

80

He realized that invasion of Kalinga had been a mistake. Though administrative protocol suggested that the matter be left undiscussed, personal integrity required that he admit his error to the public. It did not take him long to decide and he submitted his confession to the Council.

...One hundred and fifty thousand people were enslaved, a hundred thousand were killed and many times that number perished, thus the remorse of the "Beloved of the Gods" on having conquered Kalinga. Verily, the slaughter, death and captivity of the people that occurs when an unconquered country is conquered, is looked upon as extremely painful and regrettable by the "Beloved of the Gods" and weighs on his mind. What is even more deplorable is that those who now dwell in Kalinga all suffered violence, murder, and the banishment of their loved ones. And even if they are settled in their lives now, their friends, acquaintances, companions and relatives went through a calamity which became a kind of personal violence. The suffering of so many men weighs heavily on the mind of the "Beloved of the Gods". Today, if a hundredth or even a thousandth of those slain, died or were captured when Kalinga was annexed were to suffer similarly, it would be a matter of profound sorrow and regret to the "Beloved of the Gods."

Asoka's "Confession" created an uproar in the Council and not a single member supported it. Narad called it an insult to the army.

Radhagupta said, 'Noble King! This empire was created by war. A confession of sorrow over victory is unheard of. It is dishonorable to the King, and to our brave troops. It sends the wrong message of non-violence to our enemies and to the outside world. Even the Buddha did not condemn war. Ahimsa to a king is like virginity to a young woman. No good can come of it.'

Asoka gazed at Radhagupta's silver hair and time-ravaged face. *Age has not mellowed him. He is still living in his youth, as most men tend to do,* he thought. 'Radhagupta,' he said, 'we are giving up wars of aggression, not wars to defend the country.'

Radhagupta's nostrils flared. 'Forgive me Great King! My father and your grandfather fought side by side to build this empire. War is the mother of all that is noblest in man. Our religion praises wars! Our gods are warriors! How can you give up wars?'

As Asoka stared, Radhagupta continued. 'I was not going to speak but now I must. When I supported your bid to be king, it was to further the Magadha glory. And you did it splendidly. You crushed forever Kalinga's ambition to be our equal. To think that these glorious wars will be history hurts me. I see queen Livia squirming in her grave. I see no role for myself in this new empire of yours. So it is time I bid you farewell.'

Asoka was shocked by Radhagupta's vehemence. 'I'd like you to reconsider. Surely a state is not made great by wars and conquests. It is the happiness of its people that makes a country great. Don't our children deserve better than to keep dying in mindless wars?'

Radhagupta was not convinced. 'King! My last advice before I go is that you explain your war policy to the army. Your Buddhism has completely demoralized it.'

'I will,' Asoka said.

In a rare show of his power in the face of the Council's opposition, he went ahead and published his Confession.

81

The King's war policy was on the mind of each army officer that evening as they assembled in the glittering Grand Hall. The capital was rife with rumor that the King was about to cut the army in half. Every soldier looked glum, afraid for his job. Despite the presence of two thousand men, the Hall was tellingly silent. Waiters in green waistcoats and red turbans served hot mixed vegetable curry and steaming boiled rice. Ten thousand fingers began moving rapidly between the plates and the mouths. Only the sight of sweet chickpea balls and liberally sugared saffron rice inspired a gleam of enthusiasm. Then, they put aside their worries about the high expense of mistresses and alcohol, and threw themselves with abandon at the dessert, then toward the end lingered on every morsel, as if in farewell to the departed crumbs. Then, they licked their lips and braced themselves for the news.

Asoka arrived in a white robe and an unadorned gold crown. He did not look grim, but he wore no smile. Waving to some and scanning others with a slow turn of his head, he began to speak.

'Brave officers, the Greeks know it, the Persians know it. And the people of Taxila know it. Today Magadha is the greatest power on earth. It is my pledge to you that we will stay unconquerable. Our ideals, our freedoms, the future of our children, demand it. So I declare to you, there shall be no reduction in the army.'

A deafening roar went up the Hall. Soldiers shouted, clapped and waved their fists. Every soldier was visibly relieved, and wide smiles spread across two thousand faces. Finally the pandemonium subsided. Asoka liked their happy faces.

'Great military power carries great responsibility,' he went on. 'Such power can be dangerous in the hands of an arrogant ruler and an arrogant country. So far, we have used this power to destroy, kill and conquer, but not to improve the lot of man. We must humanize this brute power or it will turn us into savages.'

He paused, and scanned the front rows.

'Today, I declare that Magadha will no longer resort to aggressive wars. If life offers nothing but misery, wars are glorious. Even cannibalism is desirable. But when we look at the faces of our children, and the beauty of this splendid Creation, and think of our short time on earth, we know life is too valuable. We have to change our old ideas. War destroys all human feelings, brutalizes men, women and even children. It destroys past, present and future. It forces man to live in fear and rage. It is a deliberate cruelty against life. We delude ourselves if we call ourselves civilized, and the enemy barbarian. So I say to you, henceforth we shall not use military force to impose our way of life, our beliefs, and our system of government on others.'

Every soldier gasped.

Asoka continued, 'How will we resolve our disagreements then? By diplomacy, negotiations, even sabotage and subversion. But above all by patience.'

Some of the soldiers registered surprise as Asoka went on. 'Conquest! Glory! Honor! Medals! They are good for making great speeches. They resonate in us for a few moments. But after the applause has died down, a deafening silence begins. What glory will bring back the dead? What medal will restore a soldier's severed hands to lift his child in embrace? What speech can clamp together a soldier's broken manhood? Repair the disfigurement of his mind? What gold medal will warm the young widows' lonely nights?

'Truth is brutal and I will not lie. Acting hand in hand, religion and state have glorified wars and made martyrs of the dead. Both the state and religion seek power through wars, and human life does not matter. I should know.'

'The truth is that the rainbow of war's glory has been painted with the blood of our youth, and the tears of our children and widows.'

Then he looked at the faces of soldiers' sitting before him, and said, 'What beauty, soldiers, I ask you, can I show you in non-existence?'

'It is a momentous day for Magadha. Our children must do better. It is only the beginning. It may take time, but it shall happen. It must.'

To a lukewarm ovation, he quietly slipped out by the back door. Most of the soldiers could not shake off the conviction that wars were ordained by God, essential to the country's glory, and that wars were the flower of their manhood. Slowly, the crowd dispersed. On leaving the Hall, an old former army officer lifted his skullcap and mumbled, 'First he becomes an atheist and now he gives up war! I tell you, this empire is going to fall.'

He looked up at the sky. 'God! I don't want to live to see that day!'

82

Asoka found his voice in simple rules for living that were reflected in his domestic policy: *All men are my children. Just as I desire for my children that they should obtain welfare and happiness both in this world and the next, the same I desire for all men.*

Incredulous, the frontier tribes on the north-west borders tested his policy. They attacked garrisons on his borders and killed hundreds of soldiers. The garrison commander repelled the attack but asked the King's permission to teach the tribes a lesson by slaughtering them en masse, as had been the practice in past. Asoka found himself in a bind.

'Great King! This is no time to vacillate.' Visal advised.

'We can't do away with wars,' Bitan said cynically. 'We love them so.'

Asoka persevered. 'If people can give up cannibalism, they can also give up senseless killings. Man should have the freedom to act responsibly. So far they've acted out of fear.'

'Give man freedom and he will destroy himself,' Bitan said sarcastically, 'and others!'

'Perhaps! But so far we have not put our faith in man.'

After dispatching reinforcements, he deliberated, and embarked on an untried path. He sent Narad as his emissary to explain his policy to the tribal leaders and also broadcast it in a border Inscription.

If the unconquered people on my borders ask what is my will with regard to them, tell them the King desires that they should have no fear on his account, should trust him, and should have in their dealings with him only happiness and no sorrow. They should understand that the King will forgive them as far as they can be forgiven.

He added, ...*But the Emperor warns them that the King is mighty even in his remorse. He asks them to repent, lest they be killed. He wishes that all beings should be unharmed, self-controlled, calm in mind and gentle.*

He did not withdraw his reinforcements but achieved the desired result without further bloodshed. Satisfied, he told himself, *It works, But for how long? I'll wait and see.*

83

Gutni, a walled village known only to its inhabitants, was located sixty miles northwest of Prayag, a town on the confluence of the Ganges and Jamuna Rivers. Arhat Yacas had selected this site for the King's first address on Dhamma. Arhat's birthplace, Gutni was lost in the fog of time. As part of a cluster of villages near the dense forests that lined the banks of the Ganges, it was easily accessible from the royal Taxila-Pataliputra highway. Mango and plantain trees surrounded the village hall, and children played on its grounds during the day. The village elders met at the hall to discuss, deliberate and decide village matters.

At the news of the King's visit, excitement ran high. The villagers had seen the ugly faces of tax officials but never the face of their King. Sun baked mud walls were whitewashed, roads were swept, red and green bunting was hung on trees, cow-dung cakes were stacked to one side by the wall, and the shallow pond was cleaned, and filled with white doves. Housewives scattered white and red powder on the thresholds of their homes and strung mango leaves across their doorways and windows.

Around mid-morning on a summer day, a white painted bullock cart drove up to the village. Wearing a white cloak, Asoka got down with big smiling eyes that showed a few wrinkles underneath. There was no royal umbrella overhead, and he carried only a double-knotted white turban to protect him from the blazing sun. The village gate was opened and a drumbeat started, as if a groom had arrived for his bride. Dressed in bright colors, women ran to the oxen cart, to throw fresh flowers and rice at the King. His forehead glinted in the sun, and he walked with the Elders to greet the waiting crowds. The villagers were curious. A King who did not hunt or eat meat: it was like coming to see a blonde gorilla. Hundreds of women, who had never before left their homes, were here to verify if Asoka had a mouth, a nose and two eyes.

On seeing him, after the first shock that all things were in place, the crowds burst into shouts of jubilation. From the raised dais, he smiled back, and waved. Unmindful of the bees buzzing overhead and children shrieking for their mothers, he waited for calm. Then pointing his finger, he asked in a clear, loud voice, 'How many of you are happy?'

A few young men raised their hands.

'You should all be happy,' Asoka said. 'I am happy because I live by a few simple rules. We are unhappy when we have no rule to live by.'

All eyes were fixed on him.

He looked up. 'Do you know what is "Dhamma?"'

Every hand went up this time. Every religious Code of Conduct was called Dhamma.

'My Dhamma has no religion, though it is the essence of all religions,' Asoka said. 'My Dhamma means having few faults and doing many good deeds.'

The villagers exchanged glances. Dhamma without religion?

Asoka paused. 'How many of you have done a good deed in the last month?' Every hand went up.

'And how many of you have done a bad deed in the last six months?'

Not one hand.

Softly, he said, 'We notice only our good deeds and think, "I have done good." We do not notice our evil deeds. Now, to be aware of wicked deeds is something really difficult. Nevertheless, we should notice them and think, cruelty, harshness, anger, pride and envy: these all produce sin. Let them not cause me to fall. Noticing this is important for our happiness.

'So what is Dhamma? A few simple rules for living. When you know them, you will not have to think every time you face a new situation. You will know what to do. Do rules take away or diminish your freedom? Not so. Freedom gives you the choice to do good or bad deeds. When you sow seeds in your field, you want good results. You do not just run out and recklessly start throwing seeds. You follow certain rules. It is the same with my rules. They will give you good results. Take the rule to speak kindly to others. Speak words that bring you good results and avoid those that bring discord and trouble.'

A few villagers nodded at this, and a few raised eyebrows.

'What are these rules? First, do not lie. Call a bull a bull. You will like and respect yourself. What is more, others will like you. You will earn the respect and trust of others. You will not dread getting caught in the web of your lies. Truth will set you free. Truth brings freedom from fear and worry.'

'Second, don't kill. Respect life. Killing creates fear in the victim. This fear will reverberate in your thoughts and deeds and make you hostile to others. Mercy connects you to living things. When you feel this, you will be happy and content.'

'Respect others' religion and they will respect yours. If you have the right to practice your religion, others also have that right. We have many religions, because men have varying desires and passions. But in essence all religions promote self-control through various moral laws. Hating other religions shows a lack of faith— you fear for your religion. You harm your religion by criticizing others. Honor other sects, and you increase the influence of your own; denounce others, and you diminish the influence of your own. Remember the seed!'

'Respect your parents and be generous to your friends and relatives. The more you expand your world, the happier you will be.'

'Treat your servants and slaves with kindness. Do not forget their misfortune; do not forget they are human beings like you. The light you kindle in their eyes will sparkle in your own.'

The baffled villagers sat in pin-drop silence. After a pause, Asoka asked, 'Is it difficult?'

'No,' rose a chorus of voices.

Asoka warned, 'The rules are easy, but their practice is difficult. Take one rule: respect all religions. Why, you will ask, should I do this? Because the message of all religions is the same: self-control and purity of mind. If you inform yourself about other religions, it will open your mind. You will see the similarities and lose the hatred within you. Living in harmony is good for you. This is what I do: I honor all religious sects, ascetics and laymen with reverence. I listen to them. I give them gifts. But I consider that to visit them in person is more important than any gift.'

The villagers sat dazed. Their books, their priests, and their neighbors had never mentioned tolerance. Their priests decried other religions; their neighbors spat on them. An old villager in the crowd, his face wrinkled like a sun-dried prune, turned to his neighbor and whispered, 'Damn it! All these years I've practiced my faith by spitting on other religions. At my age, it's hard to know what my religion is.'

Asoka surveyed the people. 'Too difficult?'

Some kept quiet. Others shouted, 'We can do it!'

Perhaps, because their King himself welcomed all religions.

He tested them harder. 'How many of you perform religious rituals before you sow a crop?'

To his surprise, every villager raised his hand. He knew these rituals impoverished the peasants and kept them from buying seeds or canal water for better crops, even as they put money in the hands of the Brahmins.

So he spoke slowly. 'People perform all kinds of rites: in illness, at the marriage of sons and daughters, at the birth of children, before a journey. Such ceremonies, trivial and useless, bear little fruit. But the one ceremony that has great value is that of Dhamma. Father, son, brother, master, friend, acquaintance and neighbor should all think, "This is good, this is the ceremony of Dhamma I should practice until my object is achieved." '

After the speech, he mixed with the crowds, pressing the flesh and inquiring after their children. Toothless old peasants—sun baked and wrinkled— elbowed through the crowds to touch his cloak or his feet. The young ones stood at a distance, staring in awe, looking lost and confused. Later at the village hall, he met the Brahmins and ascetics to discuss their religious doctrines and bestow gifts upon them.

The masses were spellbound by the simplicity of Dhamma. He knew he had struck at the very heart of Vedic ritual practices, not because he loved Brahmins less, but because he loved the peasants more. The villagers responded enthusiastically. In turn, the public response galvanized Asoka. He began to tour extensively, careless of the sun and wind, cold or rain, and mingling with the villagers, intent on spreading his message of happiness.

On his tours, he saw how lack of water and absence of shady trees alongside the roads brought misery to travelers and animals. Throughout the summer months, beasts of burden– camels, horses, oxen—fell by the roadside panting in the sweltering heat. But their masters flogged them until they staggered to their feet, limped a few yards, and often fell dead.

Comfortable in the knowledge that Magadha was inviolable, he ordered his army divisions to plant trees and dig wells on the roadsides. An Inscriptions described the work:

On the roads I have had banyan trees planted, which will give shade to beasts and men...I have had mango groves planted and...wells dug and rest houses built at every eight kos (nine miles). And I have had many watering places made everywhere for the use of beasts and men...

In Council he declared, "No child, no man or woman should die of sickness for want of medical care in this land." His Army went to work and hospitals for men and for animals sprang up throughout the empire, even beyond his borders, as described in an Inscription:

Everywhere in the empire of the Beloved of the Gods, the King Piyadassi, and even the lands on its frontiers– those of the Colas, Pandyas, Satyaputras, Keralputras and as far as Ceylon; and of the Greek King named Antiochus, and of those kings who are neighbors of that Antiochus; everywhere the two medical services of the Beloved of the Gods, the King Piyadassi, have been provided. These consist of the medical care of man and the care of animals. Medicinal herbs, whether useful to man or to beast, have been brought and planted wherever they did not grow; similarly roots and fruit have been brought and planted...

84

Kalinga was always on Asoka's mind. To bring prosperity there, he deployed special army units to dig irrigation canals, build roads and develop ports. Grain warehouses were built and stocked with corn to avert famine, fisheries improved and trade encouraged within the empire and with other lands by the ocean route. But corruption was rampant among the officials of Kalinga. For them, the opportunity to exploit people who were helpless and down on their knees was too good to pass up. The Administrator Mahabali sent Asoka a letter.

Great King, Thanks to you, Kalinga is on its way to recovery. As can be imagined, the theft of grains and cattle is rampant as the poor have to eat. Unfortunately, I have no control over the judicial officers. The big thieves get away, but the petty offenders, unable to pay bribes, are tortured mercilessly.

Your servant, Mahabali.

Asoka was sickened and demanded that Mahabali send him the names of corrupt officials. When Mahabali skirted the question, Asoka issued an Edict to the officials of Dhauli and Jaugada.

By order of the Beloved of the Gods, the officers and city magistrates at Tosali/Sampa are to be instructed thus:

Whatever I approve of, I desire to achieve by taking action or obtain it by effective means. This is what I consider the chief method in this matter and these are my instructions to you: all men are my children, and just as I desire for my children that they should obtain welfare and happiness both in this world and the next, the same do I desire for all men. You do not realize how far this principle goes. Reflect on it well.

You are in charge of thousands of men; you should win their affection by being impartial to all. You owe a debt to me for granting you power over people. You can discharge this debt by being just and fair to those under you. Injustice is a cause of suffering;

men suffer when they are imprisoned or tortured without good reason; men also suffer when a prisoner is released without reason. You should strive to practice impartiality. Avoid such faults as shortness of temper, harshness, obstinacy, idleness. Be even-tempered and not rash in your work.

This edict is to be proclaimed on the eighth day of the star Tisya, and at intervals between the Tisya days it is to be read aloud, even to a single person. By doing this you may be able to conform to my instructions. This inscription has been engraved here in order that the city magistrates should at all times see to it that men are never imprisoned or tortured without good reason. And for this purpose I shall send out on tour every five years an officer who is not severe or harsh; who having investigated this matter, shall see that they carry out my instructions.

It was Asoka's People's Bill of Rights. When the official Raghunath read the Edict aloud the first time, his face became hot. Sheepishly, he looked at the crowd in front of him to see if they understood. To his chagrin, he saw a man turn to his neighbor, bare his back and display an open wound from a flogging. 'I am going to complain. I know the King listens!'

85

Asoka's sympathy for the disenfranchised led him to realize that human beings suffer as much from social injustice as from illnesses and diseases of the body. The judicial system he had inherited was based on the centuries-old Vedic religion. The Brahmins, the highest class, had created a four-tier caste system that was heavily stacked in favor of the higher castes. It oppressed the lower castes- the sudras–the untouchables. The inequities of the Vedic religion outraged even the enlightened Brahmins. A hymn in the *Rig-Veda* said,

> *You cannot find him (the Creator) who created these creatures; another (priest) has come between you (and God). Those who recite the hymns are glutted with pleasures of life; they wander about wrapped up in mist and stammering nonsense.*

As a pragmatic king, Asoka realized that dismantling the Vedic religion would lead to anarchy, so Buddhism became his great vehicle for social reform. Buddha had proclaimed,

> *As the four streams that flow into the Ganges lose their names as soon as they mingle their waters in the holy river, so all who believe in Buddha cease to be Brahmins, Kshatriyas, Vaisyas and Sudras.*

But Buddhism could not replace the old religion overnight unless there were mass conversions. And for this, force was needed, an idea that repelled him. So he decided to reform the legal system. He issued an Edict to all judicial officers across the empire:

> *Uneven application of law produces much resentment and suffering. Laws will be modified to adopt uniform legal procedures and a uniform penal code. New officers have been appointed to provide relief. They will travel every five years within their jurisdiction and review cases for injustice. These officers will inspect all prisoners; if they are encumbered with a large family, oppressed or old, the officers will make money grants to set them free.*

After the war, thousands of men and women had become slaves which deeply troubled Asoka. Too many of the young women were raped, and masters had fathered many illegitimate children. He decreed that a master who raped a slave woman must pay her compensation. Furthermore, if a female slave had a child by her owner, even with her consent, both mother and child were to be freed.

Asoka went further. He gave slaves the right to own and inherit property that was acquired by money earned outside the services for the master. A slave could buy freedom with such earnings or by taking a loan, and the children of debtor slaves would be freemen.

But he kept a hand on society's pulse to maintain law and order. Faced with a death penalty case, he would anguish for days. In one case, a man had killed the owner of a house and his wife in the course of a burglary, and there were heated discussions in the Council.

'The owner and his wife are dead. Nothing, not even capital punishment, can bring them back,' Arhat Yacas argued.

'What is the governing principle of the judicial system?' countered Bitan. 'Justice. Not compassion. The criminal's right to life cannot exceed that of the victim. If not punished by death, justice suffers.'

Narad agreed but Arhat Yacas protested. 'Should the state stoop to the level of the murderer? A wrong is not righted by another wrong.'

Asoka deliberated, then upheld the capital punishment. He also issued the following Edict:

Men who are sentenced to death are to be given three days respite so their relations may plead for their lives. If there is no one to plead for them, they may make donations or undertake a fast for a better rebirth in the next life.

86

Ghosa, the wiry leader of the Ajivikas sect, lay transfixed in his cave one morning, watching a spider on the ceiling patiently waiting to trap a fly. Finally, the spider ate the fly. 'I too can silence the Buddhist buzz.'

The Ajivikas believed that human beings are "bent this way or that by their fate," that a child's destiny is determined by his temperament and environment at birth. Like the Buddhists and several other sects, the Ajivikas had revolted against the caste system and the unceasing parade of Brahmanic rituals. But after Asoka' conversion, Buddhism caught fire which caused much heartburn among all other sects.

The former enemies— Ajivikas and Brahmins— now banded together to attack and kill Buddhist monks. The Ajivikas infiltrated the monasteries, where they slept late, skipped confessionals, and fought with householders for fresher food. In the Assembly they distorted Buddha's teachings with materialistic interpretations.

The news unnerved Arhat Yacas. 'Buddhism will perish if this does not stop,' he told the King, who was now also the head of the Buddhist sect. Without wavering in his policy of tolerance, in the same year Asoka gave the Banyan cave and a cave on Khalatika Mountain to the Ajivikas, and donated gold to Brahmins as he searched for a way to save Buddhism.

Under Buddhism, heresy was the violation of the rules of conduct. Asoka expelled the heretics, and then called a meeting of the Dhamma Ministers for the appropriate regions. His address to them was commemorated in the Schism Edict:

No one is to cause dissension in the Order. The Order of monks and nuns has been united. Whoever creates a schism in the Order, whether monk or nun, is to be dressed in white garments and to be put in a place not inhabited by monks or nuns. For it is my wish that the Order should remain united and endure for long. This is to be made known to the Order of monks and the Order of nuns. You must keep one copy of this document and place it in the assembly hall and give one copy to the laity. Throughout your district you must circulate it exactly according to this text.

A furious Tissa called on Asoka at the Palace. 'The white-robed Brahmins have been playing fast and loose with our lives for a thousand years,' he said. 'They even guard their knowledge from their wives, whom they consider profane. Now they've joined forces with the Ajivikas to destroy the Buddhist faith.'

Baffled, Asoka asked, 'What do you want me to do?'

'Use state force to convert the Brahmins and Ajivikas to Buddhism.'

Asoka turned pale. He had seen religion murderously exploited in Kalinga. 'Brother Tissa,' he said apologetically, 'that thought has crossed my mind. But think about it! Force degrades people. People don't want the state to tell them what to believe in, which god to worship. Religion is a personal relationship, like love. Where is the room for force in this relationship? Do you really want to be part of a monk police force, ramming Buddha down people's throat? The very idea is ridiculous.'

Tissa was adamant. 'Are you blind? These people are out to destroy Buddhism!'

'Tissa, one is virtuous by choice, not by force. State intrusion will turn officials into tyrants, and private citizens into spies. It will make everyone's life miserable, and weaken the social structure. Is that what you want?'

Tissa was indignant. 'Can't you see what's happening?'

'Tissa, it has nothing to do with you. The answer to bigotry is religious tolerance and freedom, not state oppression. Remember, happiness is the destination of human beings. Aren't wars, tyranny, and intolerance barriers on that road?'

'I thought you cared for Buddhism!' and Tissa stormed out.

87

Pleased with the spread of Dhamma, Arhat Yacas congratulated the King, 'The whole empire is undergoing moral regeneration. Your glory will last forever.'

Asoka smiled. 'King Piyadassi sets no great store by fame or glory unless it helps people to follow Dhamma. We all have evil inclinations and they are hard to resist, particularly for the highly placed.'

To him only Buddhism encouraged the moral life. As the masses, if not their religious leaders, began to follow his messages of non-violence and religious tolerance, this increased his own faith. He made pilgrimages with Upagupta to the Bodhi Tree where the Buddha had achieved Enlightenment and to Lumbini where the Buddha was born. He built pillars there to commemorate his visits.

Once burnt, twice shy, he did not even accept Buddhism as he found it. To infuse it with feeling, he included physical representations of the body of the Buddha in the Stupas, and had the details of the bustling, cheerful life of Buddha's time carved and painted on stone. These small gestures helped to create an emotional bond between the Buddha and his devotees. The result was far-reaching, and helped to transform what had been a dry, intellectual set of beliefs into a colorful, emotionally satisfying religion for the masses.

Large numbers were now flocking to Buddhism and were becoming vegetarians, and he sensed that his people were ready for the next step. He issued another Edict, which contained many prohibitions:

The killing of the following species of animals: parrots, mynahs, certain geese, swans, pigeons, flying foxes, female tortoises, boneless fish, skate, porcupines, hare-like squirrels, deer, twelve-antler stags, domesticated animals, rhinoceroses, and all quadrupeds which are of no utility and are not eaten. Also she-goats, ewes and sows which are with young or in milk, and their young up to six months of age. Cocks shall not be caponed. Chaff which contains living things must not be set on fire. Forests must not be burned in order to kill living things or without any reason. An animal must not be fed to another animal.

The catching, killing, selling and eating of fish was also banned on certain weekdays. To respect the sentiments of people in the northwest regions, oxen, cows and bulls– except stud bull– could still be killed.

88

Asoka was not one to rest on his laurels. He confessed in an Edict,

I find no satisfaction simply in hard work or the dispatch of (royal) business...For I consider that I must promote the welfare of the whole world...Whatever may be my great deeds, I have done them in order to discharge my debt to all living beings...May this (inscription of Dhamma) endure long. May my sons, grandsons and great-grandsons strive for the welfare of the whole world. But this is difficult without great effort.

He knew that every success carries the seeds of its own destruction. The quick spread of Buddhism alarmed him. Afraid that the monks might become complacent, even arrogant, he donned his orange robe and addressed the Pataliputra monastery as head of the Buddhist Sangha. In his speech, he recommended seven passages in the Buddhist Canon, emphasizing, among others, Discipline, Silence, and speaking Truth. His preferred sermons told the monks that self-control and spiritual growth was the essence of Buddhism—not its ritualistic and metaphysical aspects.

He encouraged Upagupta to convene the Third Buddhist Council at Pataliputra to consolidate Buddha's teachings. For a year, the Council deliberated, then organized the treatise called *Kathavatthu* which established the *Theravada* school of Buddhism. A famous Stupa was built in honor of Upagupta at Mathura city.

After the Council, he helped Upagupta to send Buddhist missions to various parts of the empire including Kashmir and Kandahar in the north west, the Tamil kingdoms, the Malabar coast and Madura, near the Western Ghats. A successful mission was also sent to Burma.

His fame had now spread beyond the empire and the neighboring King of Lanka watched Asoka's progress with particular interest. His own people were still lost in tribal wars, superstition and animism. He sent Arritha, his tall, dark nephew to Pataliputra, with gifts of jewels for Asoka.

Asoka welcomed Arritha and invited him to visit the Pataliputra monastery to see Buddhism in action. Impressed by the enthusiasm of laity and the monks, and the way they resolved their differences through discussion, not fist fights, Arritha asked, 'How have the people been won over by Dhamma?'

'They know it is hard to find happiness in this world and the next. It takes much vigilance, much obedience, much fear of sin, and extreme energy. But their love for Dhamma has grown day by day and will continue to grow. My subordinates too practice it to win over the doubters.'

'What do the officials do?' Arritha asked.

Asoka replied, 'Some concern themselves with the Buddhists, some with the Brahmins, the Ajivikas, the Jains and various other sects. Some are busy with the distribution of charity, or assist in the recognition of virtuous deeds. They work with all religious sects to raise interest in Dhamma among the Greeks and other people of the west. Among servants and nobles, among the poor and the aged, they promote the welfare of prisoners, releasing the aged or afflicted, or those with children.'

Arritha hesitated for a moment. 'And the villages?'

'Just as a person feels confident entrusting his children to the care of a good nurse, I've appointed the Rajukas for the welfare and happiness of the country people. They have independent authority to fulfill their roles calmly and fearlessly. They are models for the villagers as to what makes for happiness and unhappiness.'

'How have you spread Dhamma?' Arritha explored.

'Through legislation and persuasion. But of these two, persuasion has been more effective. What gives me satisfaction is that I have never used any force in promoting Dhamma. I have proclaimed through legislation, for instance, that certain species of animals are not to be killed. But men have been persuaded by Dhamma not to injure living beings and not to take life.'

Asoka glowed as he added, 'The sound of the war drum has now been replaced by the sound of Dhamma.'

He sent his son Mahinda to Lanka with Arritha. Mahinda converted the Lanka King, who then wanted his queen and the other noble-women at his court to convert. So Asoka sent Sanghamitta, his daughter, who had become a Buddhist in the year of his own conversion. She took with her a branch of the Bodhi-tree and planted it in Lanka—a tree that is still growing there.

Mahinda found his work so fulfilling that he stayed on. The Ceylon King and his successors built several splendid Buddhist buildings, and later founded the great city of Anuradhapura, where large hill-like dagobas were built on huge tracts of land.

Asoka had maintained friendly relations with the Greeks and had earned their goodwill by establishing hospitals in their lands for animals and men. Now he sent Buddhist missions to Hellenistic kingdoms in Asia and Africa, and in the Middle East: to Antiochus Theos of Syria, the grandson of Seleucus Nikator; to Ptolemy Philadephus of Egypt; to Magas, the ruler of Cyrene west of Egypt, and to Alexander, the King of Epirus in north west Greece.

89

Time and toil had taken their toll. Asoka was now sixty-nine. His eyelids had grown heavy but his face was always serene. He continued to tour the countryside and visit the villagers whom he had come to love. His audience swelled and country people now came on bullock carts, some travelling for twenty days. They loved to listen to their beloved King Piyadassi, who walked among them like the Buddha's own son.

He caught fever after a tour of Vaishali, but not one to pamper his body, he prepared for a long trip to Kashi. Kunala pleaded with him to wait until the fever abated. Asoka looked at him with loving eyes, 'Son, a few more converts to Dhamma before this life flows out in the cesspool of time.' Unshaken, he left. On the second day, his physician brought him back to Pataliputra. He was very ill.

By throwing themselves into a frenzy of work, by distracting and amusing themselves, by driving away all thoughts of death, some secretly hope that death too, will somehow forget them. But death does not suffer from amnesia. It sneaks up and springs a surprise, like a deft, mean player of the game of life.

Asoka knew his time had come. He called Tissarakka to his side and she caressed his hand with tears in her eyes. 'Perhaps I was unjust to you,' he said. 'The time has come to say goodbye.' Feebly he touched her hand, then asked for Kunala. As Kunala entered the room, Asoka smiled. *He has her big eyes!*

Kunala sat down by his side. 'Kunala, I was not a good father to you!'

Misty eyed, Kunala kissed his cheek. 'Father, you gave me more by your example than any father could. You changed my thinking about war, animals, religion, and life.'

Asoka held his face, kissed his forehead and whispered, 'A father is good only if he is followed after death. Worship God by caring for life, not by building monuments and temples.' Reaching under his pillow, he took out a little silver box. 'Empty it in your hand.' Kunala took out a hair, a few torn brown lotus petals, and a pinch of ash. Asoka looked at the contents. 'Keep the Buddha hair as a memento, mix the ash and the petals with my ashes, and bury me next to her under the Amaltas tree.'

After Kunala left, Asoka lay thinking. *Life, like lightning, cuts the vast skies of time in two. Is it darkness to darkness? Silence to silence? A water-bubble? Will my flash make a difference? Perhaps I will flicker when the word Dhamma is whispered on earth. One thing I know, life is consciousness. It was real. My joy was real, and so was the pain of existence. God may or may not be in heaven, but life is here!*

Like sparks from fire, memories flooded his mind. *Anga, I killed you. You killed the beast but saved the man. But I was reborn from the womb of your spirit. You showed me a happiness that burns with a steady flame. If only I could have held you in my arms!*

He turned to his side. *This world, this sky, the moon and the stars that sprang to life with my first breath, will vanish when my eyes close. This sun-filled universe will go dark and cold. And a new world will begin. New flowers will bloom. Another lover will see his beloved in the Ushas.*

He felt the world closing in on him. His skin cooled, taste soured, and colors grayed before his eyes. Sounds faded like ripples in a lake. He lay still, but the sensory world was moving away. Once the temple of the enchanting senses, his body was emptying out sensations, feelings and thoughts—his energy—and dispersing it into the void.

He heard a faint murmuring but knew not where it came from. His sons stood before him, yet he saw only shadows. He did not feel Kunala's hand on his hand. He did not see his misty eyes. A new cold, dark world was tightening its arms round him. Pallor set on skin, and his cheeks sank. He opened his eyes. No light came in, none went out. His eyelids fluttered. His throat burned, his lips stirred, and the tongue failed to utter "water." He became quiet. Kunala read his lips. Raising his head on his arm, Kunala trickled a few drops into his mouth. A thin stream ran down onto his chest.

He turned over on his right side. His legs stretched out, one knee slightly bent, his left hand on his thigh and the right under his chin. Unconsciously, he assumed the posture in which the Buddha is said to have died.

A palpable darkness began to descend before his eyes. Breathing became difficult, and a fire burned inside. Shadows of death, gobs of darkness tumbled around, like goblins gamboling at night. Memories of Anga pulsated in his mind. Warmth surged, like the last burst of heat of a dying star in the deep folds of the sky. *Did she orbit the sky? In the immensity of the constellations, it was a marvel she and I had come together.* He feebly stretched out his arms— she came, and faded into the dark.

Then a mountain pressed down on his chest, the centre imploded and collapsed, and his head fell to one side.

It was November 19, 232 BC, a little before noon, and the sun went into eclipse. When the news of his death spread, stillness settled over the city like the terrifying beauty of a dark night over wilderness.

90

His body, covered in white linen, lay in the Grand Hall. His face was white, and his open eyes still glowed with love. Every man and every woman in the city—councilors, rich, poor, Brahmin, the low sudra caste—touched and bid farewell to their beloved 'Piyadassi.' The women cried bitterly, men struggled to hide their eyes.

Bitan spoke before the nobles and the army officers. 'To the end he ruled with strength. In his lifetime, he transformed a morally degenerate people into a moral society. In his compassion for animals, he climbed a peak that many civilizations will never glimpse.'

Arhat Yacas spoke. 'He is the only conqueror in history who heard the cries of the vanquished. He was the second coming of the Buddha. A seeker, he found truth in love. He showed us that both Hell and Paradise exist on earth. By his tireless energy, he transformed Buddhism into a world faith.'

Narad said. 'Compassion is the essence of enlightenment. That's the message of his life.'

As he left the Hall, an officer said to his friend, 'Thanks to his vegetarianism, his obsession with people's happiness, and his love of non-violence, he weakened the empire.'

His companion looked astonished. 'To me, the wonder is such a King lived!'

Main Characters

Anga—grand-daughter of Pushyagupta, Bitan's younger sister, favourite wife of Asoka

Ansuiya—a nun, later Anga's companion

Arhat Yakas—a monk high in Buddhist hierarchy

Atossa—Pushyagupta's wife

Bhairavi—slave girl, Dasrath's sweetheart

Bhrigu—Asoka's religion teacher at Taxila University

Bindusar—2nd Maurya emperor. Asoka's father

Bitan—Pushyagupta's grandson, Radhagupta's nephew and Asoka's friend

Chandragupta—the first Maurya King who set up the empire. Asoka's grandfather

Chanakya—Chandragupta's minister, author of *Arthasastra*—a treatise on statecraft

Charu—Dasrath's sister, wife of Sisupal

Dasrath—Bindusar's 2nd son

Devi—Asoka's first wife (from Vidisha)

Dhanur—a soldier loyal to Asoka

Drona—a soldier

Gajadhar—Bindusar's Senapati, supporter of Sasima

Jaidev—Asoka's chief engineer

Jaya—Bitan's wife

Kalanos—Administrator of Taxila who conspires secession of Taxila

Kalyan—a soldier

Kamal—Pushyagupta's 3rd son, father of Bitan and Anga

Kunala—Asoka's son by Anga

Karuvaki—Asoka's wife before Anga

Kausal—an actor, Asoka's friend

Livia—daughter of Persian emperor Seleucus, trophy wife of Chandragupta

Madhatter—a soldier

Mahabali—Kalinga army commander-in-chief

Mahinda—Asoka's son from Devi who converted to Buddhism

Marut– Bindusar's 3rd son, (also called Hot)

Nakul—a soldier, son of Visal

Narad—Asoka's statecraft teacher at Taxila University, later Asoka's minister

Pavan– Bindusar's 4th son, (also called Tot)

Priyambada—a nun at monastery where Anga lived

Purandas—Asoka's commander-in-chief

Pushyagupta–ex-Governor of Taxila; father of Radhagupta, Viswa and Kamal

Radhagupta—eldest son of Pushyagupta, Prime Minister of Bindusar

Risa–Greek courtesan in Taxila

Roxanne—Livia's Greek maid and confidante

Sasima—Crown prince, Bindusar's eldest son, Asoka's step brother

Sewak—an orphan and a soldier who adores Anga

Shivdutt—Asoka's royal priest

Sidhnath—Brahmin priest and Varsha's grandfather

Sisupal–Kalinga's Prime Minister 'son, later King of Kalinga

Sonara—Kamal's wife, Bitan and Anga's mother

Suba— youngest wife of Bindusar, 2nd Maurya King

Tissa—Bindusar's 6th son, Asoka's younger brother

Upasila—the head of monastery where Anga lived

Varsha—flower girl in Pataliputra who charges Asoka with rape

Visal—Asoka's boyhood friend who joins military

Viswa– Pushyagupta's 2nd son settled in Alexandria, Egypt

Glossary

Aarti—a devotional ritual of worship

Amaltas– *Cassia fistula*, known as the Golden Shower Tree

Atharva-veda– one of the four Vedas, it has spells of black and white magic

Ayurveda—a treatise on traditional Indian medicine

Bhagwad-Gita—the most revered Hindu scripture; part of Mahabharata

Bhikkhus—Buddhist monks or mendicants

Brahmeshwara–the Lord of Creation, also Brahma

Caravaka—a philosopher who rejected all the Vedas and believed in materialism

Chapati—Indian flat bread looks like tortilla

Chimta, Dhap, and Damru—god Shiva's musical instruments.

Choli–blouse

Choti-ma—younger mother

Danda—the stick used for punishment

Dasyus– aboriginal people in India so named by the invading Aryans

Devanampiya–dear to the gods; a form of addressing the king

Dhammapada– versified Buddhist scripture of Theravad Buddhism

Dhamma—the code of right conduct or path

Du-pata—a piece of cloth that covers breasts, worn in India

Ganesha—a Hindu god with elephant head

Ghats—steps leading down to a water body for bathing or washing

Guruji, Gurudev—revered teacher, scholar

Hanuman—the monkey god of Lord Rama who could enlarge or reduce his body

Hauda—the seat on elephant's back, made of wood or brass

Havan—a ritualistic fire ceremony performed by priest to wish or celebrate success; a symbol of sacrifice. Originally, animals were sacrificed.

Indra—god of rain and lightning—hence the 'thunderbolt'

Kachnar—a tree with white and purple flower

Kali–goddess of the dark feminine power

Kasaya–an intoxicating drink made from rice meal and flowers

Kathavatthu– a Buddhist scripture

Krishna—a dark colored Hindu god associated with dancing, & playing flute to female admirers

Lakshmi—goddess of wealth and prosperity

Madhuparka—a wine made with honey and curds

Mahabharata—an Indian epic (9th century BC) about war between two clans

Mahout—the driver of elephant

Mimosa—aka Silk tree

Munia—a very small bird

Musth—a period when a young elephant's hormones are raging

Mynah– a dark brown slightly crested bird

Neem—a big tree known for its medicinal properties

Pana—a silver coin in currency during Maurya times

Palas—a measure of weight

Parvati—consort of god Siva

Pipal— sacred fig (Bo)is a large <u>dry season</u> semi-<u>deciduous</u> tree–to 90 feet tall

Prakrit—the language spoken by common people in Asoka's time

Purusha—the cosmic male in Rig-veda who is the source of all men

Raj-Mata– Mother Queen

Raj Purohit—the head priest of King

Ramayana—an epic about god Rama

Ramlila– story of god Rama's deeds

Ravana—the demon king of Lanka (Ceylon) who kidnapped Rama's wife Sita

Rig-Veda–the main Hindu scripture having over 1000 hymns

Rishi– Seer; sage

Sastra—a treatise

Satisar–lake of the Goddess Sati

Savitri– the story of *Savitri and Satyavan* in "The Book of the Forest" of *Mahabharata*. She brings back her dead husband by devotion; the ultimate good wife

Sati–Siva's consort,

Shakti—the female energy

Soma– an intoxicant juice from a plant, also a Vedic minor god

Sramana–ascetics

Srinagari—Srinagar (Kashmir)

Surya—Sun god

Swaha—end of mantra chant–please take this offering—when grains etc are tossed into fire

Tilak—a vermilion red mark painted on the forehead by mother, wife, sister or a priest as a symbol of good wishes.

Rakshasa–demon

Sangha—Buddhist Church

Senapati– Commander-in-Chief,

Sita—wife of god Rama

Soma—an intoxicant believed to confer immortality

Suttas– discourses of the Buddha

Thali—a flat plate for serving food

Uposatha—Buddhist assembly

Theravada—the first (original) school of Buddhism

Ushas—the goddess of dawn

Vedas—the four holy Hindu scriptures written around 1500 BC

Vihara—Buddhist Church

Vishnu—preserver of the Universe

About the Author

After his M.A. in English literature from Allahabad University, Harish Singhal briefly taught there before joining the Indian Revenue Service. Soon he left to get a J.D from UC Berkeley. Invited by Harvard, he spent a year there, published in Harvard Int'l Law Journal and then worked as an int'l tax lawyer for Fortune 500 corporations. After recovering from a death-threatening illness, he had his own transformation and decided to dedicate himself to his passion—English literature. *Asoka* is his first novel. He lives in the San Francisco Bay Area with his wife. He has two married daughters.

CPSIA information can be obtained
at www.ICGtesting.com
Printed in the USA
LVHW111619100719
623686LV00006B/889/P